AT THE BOOKSTORE

by
Jamie Johnson

Published by JamesCafe.com

ISBN: 978-0-9788767-3-9
Print Edition

Cover by David Namminga

"The man who does not read good books has no advantage over the man who can't read them."

—*Mark Twain*

Chapter 1

Outside a gentle rain was falling. It was good sleeping weather. A few of the early risers were stirring, but most of the books were still asleep. *Spy Needle* was wide awake. Today was the first day in his new home. His last few days had been a whirlwind of activity that was both exciting and scary. The young novel's thoughts drifted to his challenging past, then to the uncertain future that lay ahead of him. What fate awaited him amidst the approximate one hundred thousand books that were now his literary roommates? Then came the sweetest voice he had ever heard.

"Good morning! I didn't hear you arrive last night. Welcome to Sanders and Bowman, one of the finest bookstores in the business. My name is *River Run True*."

He took a good look at her. The early morning light illuminated her cover. She was unquestionably the most beautiful book he had ever laid eyes upon. Last night in the darkness he didn't get a chance to take a look at her. He had been too tired after the bouncy journey. The distribution van that had carried him across the region could have used some new shocks.

"Hello, it's nice to meet you. My name is *Spy Needle*. I'm a 288 page novel. I suppose you're a work of fiction also. Is that correct?"

"Of course! Everyone in this section is fiction, except for *Star Bright*. She was misplaced here six months ago from the science section. I guess her name sounds like she should be fiction, but she's actually an astronomy book. *Star Bright* likes it so much with us that she doesn't want to go back home. She says they're too serious over there. She's right, no one knows how to have fun like us novels. Don't you agree?"

"Absolutely," said *Spy Needle*, trying not to stare at the attractive book that was his covermate.

"Covermate" was a term used only in book talk. Most books, except for some special selections and the ones located at the end of the shelves, had a front covermate and a back covermate. It went without saying the importance of having quality covermates. Whether you like them or not you're stuck with them until fate intervenes. *River Run True* as a back covermate was the human equivalent of winning a lottery jackpot.

Of all the books that could have been his immediate neighbor, he had been placed alongside this lovely gem. She was a true work of art. Her cover, her outgoing personality, the confidence she exuded, even her aroma of newness and quality was appealing. He couldn't wait to learn what she was about. She was probably a bestseller. A book so magnificent on the outside had to contain a masterpiece of literary text.

"I bet you're exhausted from your travels," said *River Run True* with a look of genuine concern. "Where did you come from?"

"I came from the eastern region," said *Spy Needle*. "It was a twenty-hour ordeal including all the stops. I must say it wasn't a pleasant ride, being jammed into a delivery van with so many books and magazines. They even stacked a bundle of foul-smelling newspapers on top of me. Believe me, I was relieved when we finally pulled into the bookstore parking lot. I was beginning to wonder if I would ever get here. How about you? How long have you been here?"

River Run True's cover appeared to sparkle as she began to speak. "I was shipped here three months ago from my distributor's main warehouse. Luckily, I was transported in a brand new truck. It was roomy and comfortable. As a matter of fact I slept most of the journey. I suspect the reason I was treated so well is because of my publishing company. They're a large established corporation. I've been well taken care of in many respects. The editing, printing process, cover design, marketing, publicity—you name it, it's all been done for me."

"That sounds nice," said *Spy Needle*. "I'm sure that takes a lot of the pressure off and allows you to concentrate on other things."

"I have to admit life has been pretty easy for me so far," said *River Run True*. "But you know what, sometimes I wish I had been published by a smaller company, maybe even self published by my creator. I know it sounds crazy, but these big corporate publishers steal a little bit of our souls by giving us all the industry perks. Strip away the glitz and marketing and we're all the same. We're art. We're objects of creativity and imagination."

River paused before continuing. "I guess what I'm trying to say is that I have absolute respect for the books who came up the hard way. I'm a romantic sort who sympathizes with the underdog. I've always been like that. Perhaps I was self published in a past life. Maybe I was a literary treasure sitting unnoticed in a bookstore because my creator didn't possess the resources for an advertising and publicity campaign. Whatever the case, a book is a book. We should treat each other with respect. I'm sorry, but sometimes when I get wound up I can't stop talking. I should let you speak. *Spy Needle*, can you tell me more about yourself?"

"*River*, may I call you *River*? Full names are so formal. You can call me *Spy* if you like. *River*, I already know that you have a heart of gold. You probably sense that my life has been challenging. You're right, I am self published. I guess I should feel lucky that I made it into print at all. At one point I thought I'd never pass through the manuscript phase of my life. My creator is the most fun-loving human I've ever met, but he takes one thing seriously—his writing. He worked on me every day for three years. He's a bit of a perfectionist and takes great pride in his work. He wouldn't let anyone read me until I met his high standards."

"You're not alone, *Spy*. It's really a common story. Creators are tormented. They all want their babies—and we really are their babies—available to the consumers, but they don't want to send out an inferior product."

"Maybe so, but I'll tell you, *River*, I was frustrated. I was so ready to be published. I was like a caged animal. I knew I was a better read than ninety percent of the books available on the market, yet here I was sitting on my creator's desk surrounded by soda cans and candy wrappers. I guess I should mention that my creator liked sweets. He always said that high blood sugar stirred his creative juices. I don't know about that, but it sure did make him go to the toilet a lot."

"That's funny," said *River*.

Spy smiled and nodded. "Anyway, on top of that I lived for over one year with a big coffee stain splashed across my cover page. I mean to tell you, that was a real blow to my self esteem. Here I was, a potential masterpiece bestseller, living like tabloid trash and looking no better than a tramp. There were times I felt suicidal. Sometimes I would look at the rubbish bin below me and wish the wind would just blow me right into it."

"Sounds like you were really chomping at the bit to get out and experience life," said *River*. "So what happened?"

"Looking back, I realize my creator knew exactly what he was doing. If he had sent my rookie manuscript into that ruthless jungle of literary agents and publishers I'd be pushing up daisies in a landfill right now. That's for sure. Those guys are tough. My creator was savvy enough to realize his best shot was through the back door. First and foremost, he waited until I was as good as I could possibly be. I was edited over and over until he was satisfied.

"Then he really went to work. He knew a friend of a friend of a friend who knew an ex-literary agent. Word had spread that this particular fellow liked to drink quite a bit. So my creator, who also took a nip every now and then, arranged a lunch date with this guy. Apparently, I've learned since, at midday the whole publishing industry relocates to various restaurants to gossip about each other. That's a whole different story that I'll get into later. Still with me, *River*?"

"Absolutely, *Spy*. It's a fascinating story. I've got some interesting tales of loose-lipped lunches myself. I'm totally enjoying this conversation. We've got nothing but time. The bookstore doesn't open for another hour or so. Please continue."

"Okay, I'll keep rolling," replied *Spy*. "As I was saying, my creator had lunch with this industry insider. He primped me up to look my best. Keep in mind, this was my first time out of my creator's less than sanitary apartment. Boy, was I a nervous wreck. My outer pages were shaking like you wouldn't believe. Here I was, after being yanked out of my customary slob surroundings, sitting in one of the finest dining establishments in the city.

"Not only that," *Spy* continued, "but he had stuffed me into one of these bargain rate attaché cases. Whew! I just about passed out from the smell of that cheap glue. It was all I could do to keep my composure at this very important meeting. To be honest, I was longing for home. I was a nervous bundle of paper knowing my career was on the line."

River chuckled. "Excuse me for laughing, but I'm just trying to imagine you stuck inside one of those discount store briefcases getting high on the fumes. It's a wonder you survived. Sorry to interrupt you, but that struck me as being funny. You have a delightful sense of humor."

"That's alright," said *Spy*. "I do tend to view life as one long-running comedy act. It must have something to do with my upbringing. My creator is a major jokester."

"Well, whatever you do," said *River*, "don't change it. Our industry needs more of your sort. Sometimes I think the publishing world takes itself too seriously. Look at the language we use to describe ourselves. Critics and critical reviews, for example—isn't *critic* and *critical* a bit harsh? Couldn't the founding fathers of literature, whoever they were, cavemen writing on the wall I guess—have chosen something a bit more soothing to the ear? It makes me wonder sometimes."

"*River*, I couldn't agree with you more. I'll quickly finish up with my lunch of fate. After the second round of vodka and tonics, we all began to loosen up. In my case, it was probably the glue I was sniffing, but nevertheless I relaxed a bit. This industry insider and my creator—his name is Roy by the way—starting getting on fairly well. Roy pulled me out of my hallucinogenic haven and the expert began to look me over. For five minutes no one spoke. Roy fidgeted anxiously in his chair.

"Believe it or not, I wasn't worried. From the moment this guy opened me up and we met face to face, I knew I had him under my spell. I guess it's a sense we books have when we're exposed to our readers. We can immediately determine if we're treasure or trash in the minds of our readers. Of course, I don't need to be telling you this. I'm sure you're well aware of that fact. Right, *River*?"

"Oh yes!" exclaimed *River*. "As a matter of fact I can accurately predict my reader's judgment before they pick me up if I can catch a quick glance of their face. The face, especially the eyes and the smile, or lack of one, are reliable indicators of a potential reader's interest. Okay, so this fellow is checking you out and seems to be enjoying your story. What happens next?"

"Well, Roy isn't aware of his success yet, so he's still squirming around in his seat like it's a bed of hot coals. He has no idea we've already converted this guy. Meanwhile, my confidence grows by leaps and bounds every time this man turns a page. Finally, he turns to Roy and says, 'you've got a winner here.'

"Outwardly, Roy kept his composure, but I know him better than that. On the inside he exploded with pride. I'm his work, his baby, a product of his emotions. Heck, we books are extensions of our creators. We're tied together for eternity. Roy and I are one. All books, whether they like it or not, will agree with that."

"You're right again, *Spy*," said *River*, "and you certainly have a charming way with words."

She flashed another approving smile that warmed *Spy's* entire text. Maybe she meant to do it. Maybe *Spy*, without even trying, had captivated the princess of the bookstore. For sure, she liked him.

Spy's cover glowed unusually bright, ever so briefly.

"Thanks for the compliment, *River*. You're not so bad with words yourself. So, to make a long story short, here's what happened. This ex-agent gave Roy the name of an influential editor at a top publishing house. I'll call him Mr. Big. Roy was instructed to mail my manuscript to this major player in the industry. Roy did just that, and waited and waited and waited. Six months went by. Finally Roy called the guy's secretary and inquired about the status of *Spy Needle*, a manuscript he had sent to Mr. Big. The call went from one department to the next. Finally after being transferred seven times, yes *seven* times, he eventually got an answer.

"You won't believe what had happened. Mr. Big had received my manuscript six months earlier. However, it had been addressed to Bob A. Walker. He was adamant, fanatical in my opinion, that everyone addressed him as Robert A. Walker. So you know what he did? Without even opening up the package *he threw me in the garbage*!

"Can you believe that? What kind of egotistical maniac would do that? Bob instead of Robert—big deal! Here I was, a potential bestseller, resting on a bag of dirty diapers in a garbage bin because this nutcase thought he was some kind of royalty. I've since learned that this isn't uncommon in the publishing world. Maybe the power has gone to their heads. Maybe they do think they're kings and queens. What a crazy business this is!"

"Wow, what a horrible story!" said a disgusted *River*. "People like that will receive their payback one day. You can't go around destroying lives and careers without some kind of fallout. They'll get their justly deserved penalty. Just wait and see. How did you and Roy recover from that? It must have been emotionally devastating."

"It was terrible," said *Spy*. "As a matter of fact I'm starting to become angry just thinking about it. Looking back, I have nothing but admiration for Roy. He sulked for a day or two, then he fought back with a vengeance. He was determined not to let me die. He made the decision to self publish me. We all know the odds of success for self published novels are statistically low. Rarely does one break through and get noticed. Excuse me if I happen to get a bit emotional." *Spy's* voice cracked. "Words can't express how much love and respect I have for my creator. Roy was risking what little money he had on a long shot—me!"

"It's okay *Spy*," *River* said in a comforting tone. "We'll finish this story later. You just relax. Right now, let's familiarize you with your new home. Look around. You're among friends here. We're like one big family. Sanders and Bowman is well managed and the employees are kind to us. Even their customer base is top notch, most of them intelligent and educated. All of us books get along splendidly, with a few exceptions of course. I've got many true friends in here. As a matter of fact, I think I hear one of them stirring right now. Is that you, *Destiny?* Wake up, we've got a new neighbor."

"Good morning *River*," a pleasant voice called out, "and a good morning to our new friend."

Spy directed his attention to the right. He had been so smitten by *River Run True* and their ensuing conversation that he hadn't even bothered to look at his front covermate. *Spy* immediately felt at ease. Good vibes were flowing from the pages of this friendly novel, his all important front covermate.

"Hello, my name is *Spy Needle*. I arrived last night. I hope I didn't disturb you."

"No, not at all. My name is *Destiny's Fortune*. It's a pleasure to meet you. You'll feel right at home here. I see you've already met the lovely *River Run True*. She's a wonderful work of fiction and quite a beauty also."

"*Destiny*, don't you go embarrassing me." *River* smiled back at the both of them. "I'm trying to make a good impression on *Spy Needle*. Why don't you tell him a little about yourself? You can start with your plot. *Spy*, everyone raves about *Destiny's* spellbinding story. The reviewers just love the heartwarming tale of goodness winning out over evil. Oh, and *Destiny*, go ahead and describe your unique cover. I'm sure *Spy* will ask you about it. You know everyone's fascinated with your thought-provoking cover."

Destiny's Fortune looked up at his new covermate. "*River* is a world class charmer, isn't she *Spy*? Yes, everyone eventually inquires about my cover. My creator, Max is his name, has a semi-famous artist as a friend. This friend of his had read my manuscript and loved the story. He persuaded Max to let him design the cover. My publisher had no qualms about this. Heck, it was a free cover design by a recognized artist. Why not? So in about three weeks this is what he came up with. There is a river winding through the center of my front cover. *Spy*, I guess you're surrounded by river themed covermates.

"Turn me over and the river continues. If you look closely you'll notice several scenes of human interactions dispersed alongside the river. Some of these illustrations represent good and some represent evil. As you follow the river and turn me over, you'll begin to notice more of them depicting good and less of them representing evil. At the bottom of my back cover, good has completely prevailed over evil. The cover makes total sense after you've read me."

"Oh my, you do have an interesting cover," said *Spy*. "I think *River* described it perfectly when she said it was thought-provoking."

"*Destiny*, don't stop now," said *River*. "*Spy*, you have to watch him. *Destiny's* so modest he'll try to slip out of telling you about his award-winning plot. You've got *Spy's* attention now. He wants to hear why one major reviewer wrote '*Destiny's Fortune* is a tale of all time.' Go ahead *Destiny*, don't be shy."

"I've learned not to argue with *River*," said *Destiny*. "*Spy*, you'll soon learn that *River* always gets her way. You can't fight her charming persuasion, so you might as well save your energy and give in."

"Yes, I know already," replied *Spy*. "Once she casts her spell on you, you're done. Under her thumb, so to speak."

"Ah *Spy*, you're a quick learner," said *Destiny*. "Okay, let me share my tale. I have to admit I'm proud of my storyline. Max poured his genuine love for humanity into me. My pages are dripping with human soul."

Destiny drifted into a trance-like state. It was as if he were transporting himself into another world, a place only he and his creator could access. For a full minute he was silent. Finally he began his narration.

"A young man takes a year to travel the world searching for the meaning of life. Eventually he finds himself penniless in a land far away. Hungry and homeless he finds refuge in a Buddhist temple. They take him in as one of their own. An old monk teaches him the art of meditation. A year passes as he acquires knowledge of the Four Noble Truths and the Eightfold Path towards enlightenment. He begins to understand the truth about all things, and he gains insight into the impermanent and imperfect nature of worldly objects and ideas.

"With this awareness comes change. Over and over he hears a voice telling him to go to the river and find work. Mystified, the young man asks the monk what he should do. The old monk tells him to do as he's told—go to the river and find work.

"The young man reluctantly leaves the temple he's grown to love so much and walks to the river. He asks an old lady where he can find work and she points to the pier. He walks to the pier's end. There he meets a well-dressed gentleman and is offered, and accepts, a job unloading cargo from boats. He soon realizes he is working for a group that controls all of the organized crime in the city. He wants to leave this life but the voice tells him to stay. He works hard and learns the criminal trade, rapidly advancing within the organization until he is the number two man. Soon after, the boss suddenly dies and the young man is now in control of a huge criminal empire.

"At this point the young man realizes his true mission in life. His purpose was finally exposed. He would use his powerful position not to prey upon people, but to help them. He slowly transformed the criminal organization into a legitimate business establishment. Later it evolved into a charity foundation that provided support for the poor and the elderly.

"The man was offered numerous awards in recognition for his service to society. He graciously declined all of them, explaining that the satisfaction of helping others in need was the only reward he needed. He urged others to do the same. Give love and you will receive love, for it is the underlying element that causes, forms and drives our lives. Refuse to let objects of attachment consume you. They're only trinkets of distraction and are in fact the origin of suffering. Choose your own path, one that will deliver you towards truth and love. Only then will you truly be enlightened."

Destiny was quiet. No one stirred as he slowly emerged from his meditative state. Another minute passed. Finally he looked back at his new covermate. "Well *Spy*, there you have it. That's my story, or should I say Max's story. He gets all the credit."

"I'm speechless," said *Spy*. "You really are a tale of all time. You're so illuminating—a poignant work of art. It's no wonder the reviewers lust after you. You have a positive spirit that lifts readers into the heavens."

"Oh my, *Spy*, with words like that you should be a reviewer yourself," said *Destiny*. "Now that's enough about me. I would bet that your plot is an interesting one also. Speaking of excellent storylines, you've got one of the best plots in the bookstore right beside you. Go ahead Miss Modest, the one and only *River Run True*, tell *Spy* your story."

"Oh *Destiny*, we've got plenty of time for that later," said *River*.

"*Spy*, she's always trying to boost everyone else's confidence around here, but if you pry it out of her, you'll find her pages contain one of the greatest love stories ever penned. *River's* a real troubadour, let me tell you. I've actually seen women cry after reading the back cover summary. That's no lie. One customer bawled her eyes out just last week. She stood right here in front of us and soaked the floor with a puddle of tears. That's how emotionally laced *River's* plot is. The only reason *River* didn't get purchased off the shelf that day was because the reader wanted three copies. The bookstore cashier grabbed three copies from the back storage room.

"Lucky for us there wasn't two copies back there or we wouldn't have *River Run True* with us today. She'd be lying in someone's home drenched in salty tears by now. *River*, you know I'm telling the truth, so don't go shrugging it off and downplaying your masterpiece of a love story. Readers adore you, especially females. We're not taking no for an answer. It's your turn. *Spy* wants to know what's between those covers."

"Okay," accepted *River*. "I guess I'd better get it over with or *Destiny* will bug me all day. Let me start by giving credit to my creator. Lola has an uncanny ability to read people's emotions. She had a couple of novels published before me, but they didn't sell so well. I think she was super motivated to craft me into her crowning achievement. Lola wanted to channel her special people reading skills into something real, something physical, something that would have lasting value.

"That something was me. I'm so lucky to be the recipient of Lola's near-psychic abilities and her relentless work ethic. She was incredibly disciplined, writing for six hours every day, seven days a week. I suppose that's why I'm nearly 500 pages in length. Yes, I'm a first-class love story, but the credit doesn't go to me. It belongs to Lola. Since that's now understood, here's what I'm all about."

River took a deep breath. "Our world is filled with heartbreaks, heartaches and hearts bursting with love. Romance and love keep this big ball spinning. Love is a mystery. It always has been and always will be. The pages within me don't claim to hold the answers. True love is a journey, not a destination. Never give up on love.

"Mine is a tale of ups and downs and highs and lows in the eternal search for true love. My main character is a girl by the name of Annie. She is quite normal in nearly every respect. Annie comes from a middle class family with loving parents. However, when Annie was four years old, she and her mother were involved in an automobile accident. Her mother escaped serious injury, but Annie's face was severely burned. Despite two operations, her face remained disfigured. Of course, this affected little Annie psychologically. Throughout her childhood she was painfully aware that she was different from the other kids. Annie's scars stifled her bubbly personality.

She felt as if her soul was in a prison. Annie's amazing inner self was trapped behind a scarred mask."

River stopped for a moment. "I'm sorry," she said, "but as many times as I've told this story, I still sometimes get emotional when I talk about my main character. Annie is my friend, my sister, my baby."

River continued. "Annie's teen years were particularly difficult. She and her friends discovered the world of boys. Boys were exciting and they talked of nothing else. Nothing compared to the heart-thumping experience of meeting a cute boy with a pleasant personality. Annie watched from the sidelines as her friends began acquiring boyfriends. She too wanted a boyfriend, but she knew she would never be so lucky. No guy would ever want a girl with an ugly face.

"Annie excelled at school despite her shattered emotional state. She was especially talented in the field of science. Rewarded for her high marks, she was offered a full academic scholarship at a respected university. Annie declined the offer. She wanted to get a simple job and work from her home. She was horrified at the thought of having to make new friends in a new town. People were afraid to even look at her, much less approach her for a conversation.

"Annie had seen it a million times. A person would be walking along, happy as could be, until they looked up and saw her disfigured face. Their expression would immediately change and they would quickly look away. She didn't want to go through that process again. At least in her hometown people had become accustomed to looking at the girl with the scarred face.

"Fortunately, parental instincts intervened. Annie's mother and father realized, as painful as it would be, that Annie needed to venture out into the world. She would have to struggle to overcome her formidable challenges. Annie couldn't waste her life locked away in seclusion. Although she adamantly refused her scholarship, Annie's parents eventually persuaded her to give it a try, if only for one semester."

River hesitated for a moment. "I'm nearly 500 pages, so I'm gonna cut right to the heart of my story, otherwise I'll be speaking all day. Annie goes off to the university. She continues to do well at school, but suffers from severe depression. There is a beautiful river that meanders through the middle of the campus. Sometimes, when she feels that life isn't worth living, Annie goes there to lift her spirits.

"One day, while sitting by the riverside, she meets a handsome boy with the most beautiful eyes she had ever seen. His name is John. He is an exchange student from a foreign country. They have a long conversation, and to Annie's amazement, John asks Annie if she'd like to go out to dinner. At this point they begin a passionate relationship. They become totally consumed with each other. John constantly tells Annie how beautiful she is. Annie is awakened to a world of love that she never knew existed. When she looks into the mirror, a beautiful happy girl smiles back at her. Her scarred face doesn't matter anymore. Annie's found love.

"The story should end here with the two of them getting married, having wonderful children and living happily ever after. But just like the real world, events don't always follow a blissful path. Instead of a typical lovey-dovey ending at 250 pages, my creator Lola added a bit of human reality and kept writing. Lola knows from experience that life has its ups and downs. She wanted my readers to come away with a message—that life's never easy and you have to keep fighting to achieve your goals. So her next 250 pages did just that."

River took in another deep breath and stretched her cover, gently brushing against *Spy*. "Let me continue the story. Annie and John are passionately in love. Two joyful years pass. At this point, John's student exchange program expires and he's required to return to his native country. Lola's words can hardly describe the sadness. Tears pour from both of them as John boards the airplane. Annie watches as John's plane disappears into the sky.

"Annie is crushed. She retreats back into a state of isolated depression. Sometimes she goes weeks without speaking to another person. Annie wishes she would die, but doesn't have the courage to kill herself. Despite her devastated emotional condition she somehow continues to do well at school. Annie eventually graduates with honors and earns a degree in science technologies. Job offers pour in from around the world. It seems as if everyone wants to hire this rising star in the field of science. Annie eventually accepts a job with a top international technology corporation. Through it all Annie remains the same, a girl without love. Nothing can cheer up the lonely broken-hearted girl with the deformed face.

"Ten years pass. Annie gives up hope on ever finding love and concentrates on her work. She had her one chance at romance and fate had shot it down. Annie became adept at holding her emotions together in the presence of her coworkers. Upon arriving home she would collapse in lonely despair and cry until she fell asleep. This became her dual existence. Annie was a respected scientist living with a scarred face and a scarred heart. Her brain had a passion for life, but her soul wanted to die.

"One day Annie was asked by her director if she would go overseas to attend an important conference. Top research scientists from around the world were meeting to discuss major global issues. Annie reluctantly agreed, though she was horrified of the idea of leaving her secured shelter. She had intentionally structured her ordered life to minimize social interaction. She even hated going to the supermarket. It was against her nature to travel anywhere, much less journey to a foreign land. It was if some unknown force was instructing her to go. Annie surprisingly agreed to venture out of her den.

"Annie arrived at the conference. Fifty of the world's most capable scientists were gathered around a huge conference table. Annie nervously glanced at the faces of her peers, then thought of her own face. 'Why did I ever agree to come here?' she whispered to herself. 'What force could have persuaded me to expose my disfigured face to this influential group of distinguished researchers?'

"Annie scanned the table once again. Then something caught the corner of her eye. The man at the far side of the room looked familiar. He looked like someone she had known. A bit heavier, a different hairstyle, but the sparkling eyes gave him away. It was John! Her heart literally skipped a beat before racing away. Impossible but true—it was really John! Annie couldn't control herself. She ran towards him calling his name. 'John, it's me, Annie!'

"John turned around and caught Annie in his arms. Both were overcome with emotion. Tears of joy covered their faces. Word quickly spread among their fellow scientists of this love story unfolding before them. One of them began clapping, then another, and another, until the entire room was filled with applause. A couple of them were weeping. It was a scene of spontaneous elation. Now we're around page 500 and Lola finally rewards the readers with the two lovers reuniting."

"Incredible!" *Spy* cried out. "What a classic love story you are, *River Run True*. So John also became a scientist and they connected years later. Amazing! *River's* quite a novel, isn't she *Destiny*?"

"I couldn't agree with you more," said *Destiny*. "I've heard *River* describe her heartwarming story several times and it gets better every time. If I may, *River*, I'll summarize your last few pages. They sort of fill in the blanks about John's missing years. Yes *Spy*, you're right. John did become a well-respected scientist in his native country. Throughout the years he never lost his feelings for Annie. His heart always belonged to her. He tried a relationship with another woman for a while, but the spark wasn't there. It didn't last. Just like Annie, he gave up on love. John accepted a life of loneliness. Then he meets Annie again and their love is rekindled. They marry, have two beautiful children, and live happily ever after. *River* leaves her readers with a big smile. *Spy Needle*, you said it best. She's a classic!"

River's cover gleamed with pride as she spoke. "Ah yes, a happy ending. Lola didn't let us down. She knew the power of love. Like life itself, sometimes you have to swim through a few tears before lighting upon true love. You never know when love will strike, right *Spy*?"

River then flashed *Spy* another one of her charming smiles that warmed him cover to cover. "That's enough about me. *Spy*, we want to know what you're all about. I've always been attracted to exciting tales of mystery and intrigue. With a title like *Spy Needle* you're certain to be full of adventure. Entertain us with your story. I'm sure you're a fascinating read from start to finish. We'd be honored to hear your storyline. How about it, *Spy*?"

"*River*, you know I can't say no to a sweet voice like yours," replied *Spy*. "Before I get started I want you both to know that I was created for the sole purpose of entertainment. *River*, you and *Destiny* carry powerful moral and societal messages that can better the world. Your pages have the potential to inspire and motivate. *River Run True* and *Destiny's Fortune* are two books that will stand the test of time. I'm in a completely different league. My creator is all about fun. Roy is a joker who likes to laugh and dance and flirt with the ladies.

There's not a serious bone in his body. I'm an extension of his gregarious personality, especially my main character.

"Sonny Needle is a super spy who constantly gets sidetracked, but somehow manages to get the job done. His unorthodox methods keep everyone in a state of distress. He's an unpredictable bundle of wondrous wit who's always on the move.

"I think he'd make an interesting character in a movie. Roy would be proud as a peacock if Sonny Needle actually hit the big screen. My creator would be famous! I can just imagine Roy parading around as a celebrity. Country boy hits the big time! Just like Sonny Needle, Roy would soak up the attention like a sponge. He would eat it up!"

"Wow, *Spy*. You've already sparked my interest," said *Destiny*. "I can't wait to hear about Sonny Needle's escapades. On with the story!"

"You've got it, *Destiny*," said *Spy*. "I'm getting geared up myself. Sonny Needle never fails to deliver, no matter how many times I describe his fancy-free lifestyle. Let's go!"

Spy looked towards *River* as he shifted into storytelling mode. Her smile fueled him with confidence.

"Roy jump-starts the readers with the birth of Sonny Needle. Doris Needle is rushed to the hospital six weeks before her due date. Sonny is delivered kicking and screaming and ready to embrace life. The hospital staff immediately fall in love with the tiny newborn. Sonny's charisma is already showing through.

"Roy then dives into Sonny's childhood. Sonny's energetic exuberance for life is nonstop. His curious nature sometimes leads him astray into unusual situations. Here's a couple of examples. Sonny's parents celebrated his first birthday by taking him to the zoo. Everything was going well until his parents became temporarily distracted by an elderly lady who had fallen down.

"As they helped the woman back to her feet Sonny raced away on all fours. He saw this as an opportunity for adventure. His tiny body easily slipped through the cage containing a mother tiger and her two cubs. When his parents realized what had happened they began screaming for help. Animal handlers arrived on the scene to witness the mother tiger *nursing Sonny* and her two cubs."

"Oh my God!" shouted *River*.

"Yes, you heard me right," stated *Spy*. "Sonny was drinking milk from the belly of this wild predator. The mother tiger, feared beast of the jungle, had taken Sonny in like one of her own. Sonny appeared right at home as he lay between the two cubs slurping down tiger milk. After their little bellies were full it was time for a nap. Finally, two hours later, a zoo official deftly retrieved Sonny from the cage. Sonny waved goodbye to his striped friends as his relieved parents carried him away.

"Another time he discovered a world map and began studying it. Three-year-old Sonny asked his mother why so much of the world was painted blue. She explained to him the blue color represented the oceans. 'We're a thousand miles from an ocean, but one day I'll show it to you,' she promised him. The next morning Sonny's parents received a call from the local police of the adjacent town. They had picked up a three-year-old boy hitchhiking with a backpack. He told them that blue was his favorite color and he was going to see a blue ocean."

River laughed. "What a determined little boy," she said. "Sounds like he really wanted to see some blue water."

"He's determined all right," replied *Spy*, "but that's what makes him unique. He was severely scolded for his wayward wanderings, but Sonny's love of travel would remain with him forever. As a matter of fact, only two years later the *same* police again called for Sonny's parents to pick him up. This time he had been *driving* a school bus loaded with several of his friends. When asked where he was going, Sonny replied that he was going to Egypt to see the pyramids.

"Sonny's adventures only magnified as he reached his teens. His charismatic personality earned him many friends. The girls were especially fond of him. Sonny was constantly changing girlfriends, but somehow managed to remain friends with all of them. He always treated them with respect. Sonny actually included five of his ex-girlfriends in his local rock band, Sonny and the Needles."

Destiny gave *Spy* a nudge. "Sonny really knows how to captivate the females, huh *Spy*?"

"That's for sure," said *Spy*. "All the girls wanted Sonny and the boys wanted to be like Sonny. His popularity transcended gender. It was impossible to escape his charm. Although he wasn't on the ballot, his classmates nevertheless elected him class president with write-in votes. Sonny's first legislative act was to propose a bill that would ban all classes. The students passed it unanimously before it was vetoed by school administrators.

"Sonny's active social life left him no time for his studies. Rarely did he open a book. Despite the fact that he never applied himself academically, he still managed to graduate near the top of his class. However, Sonny being Sonny, he rejected the idea of pursuing a traditional education. Four years of university life didn't appeal to thrill-seeking Sonny Needle. Instead, he decided to skipper a twelve-foot sailing vessel around the world. With two of his prettiest girlfriends as dual first mates Sonny set off for places unknown.

"Sonny's friends began to worry about him after three months passed with no communication. Finally they received a letter from their adventurous friend. The letter revealed an amazing story. After two months of battling rough seas a super-sized swell had capsized the vessel. Seafaring Sonny and his voluptuous crew had washed ashore on a South Pacific island. Hostile island natives had seized the vessel and were holding the three crew members captive.

"The cannibalistic captors prepared a feast to celebrate this Godsend of human flesh. The tribe licked their chops as they awaited to throw their victims into the boiling pot. Just then Sonny arose and began speaking to the ravenous savages. He coolly announced that he and his crew could be more valuable alive. Speaking directly to the head tribesman, Sonny explained that he had discovered a cache of sunken treasure off the coast of the island. If the hungry islanders would let the sailing crew continue their treasure hunt they would be rewarded with half of the riches.

"The islanders held a vote and decided to release their captives. The next day Sonny and his ecstatic crew departed the island amidst great fanfare. Their newfound friends bestowed them with gifts along with a full month's supply of food and water. Sonny and his three first mates waved to the cheering crowd as they sailed into the horizon. Once again, Sonny had successfully talked his way out of a jam.

"Yes, Sonny had acquired an additional crew member. During his captivity Sonny had become friendly with one of his female guards. She had fallen to his charm. This pretty islander was determined that her exotic prisoner would not leave without her. After pleading with the head tribesman, she was granted permission to accompany Sonny. She joyfully joined Sonny's bevy of sailing beauties bound for adventure."

Spy stopped to catch his breath. "Your story is incredible," said *River*. "Sonny being a ladies man sure makes for an interesting plot. How about you, *Spy*, are you a pursuer of amorous adventure?"

"Nope, my playboy days are behind me," replied *Spy*. "I'm a one woman book. I don't need the hassle of juggling multiple girlfriends. A bunch of jealous women knocking at my cover doesn't sound like fun to me. I'm looking to settle down with a good hearted book, preferably a novel. Ah yes, a simple life with a quality work of fiction. Make her a heartwarming love story and I'm in heaven. You wouldn't happen to know a pretty book who meets those qualifications, would you *Destiny*?"

"Well, there might be one available," said *Destiny* with a big grin on his cover. "As a matter of fact a charming bookstore beauty just happens to be your current back covermate. How about it, *River Run True*, are you available?"

"Boys, boys," replied a blushing *River*. "There's plenty of attractive female novels around here. I'm no more special than anyone else. But to answer your question, yes, I am looking for a good honest novel to share my life with. And yes, I have to admit that I'm attracted to *Spy*. It's not really my nature to be so forward, but what the heck. *Spy*, why don't you impress me some more by continuing your story, before I blabber away something that may embarrass me. Please go on with the adventures of Sonny Needle!"

Spy felt an energy surge through his pages like he had never felt before. He could hardly believe what he had heard. A princess of the literary world had just told him that she actually considered him to be a prospective mate. Now wasn't the time to do anything stupid. He wasn't going to blow this golden opportunity. *River Run True* was his dream come true.

"*River*, since we're speaking honestly here, I think you're the most fantastic girl I've ever met. You make my heart race with excitement. Okay, I've said it! You know how I feel. It probably wasn't much of a secret anyway. I'll continue on with the escapades of Sonny Needle.

"Now, where was I? Oh yeah, Sonny and his lovely crew are sailing into the unknown. There's a lot more left, so let me summarize my adventuresome character's escapades as quickly as possible. Sonny eventually completed his around-the-world nautical journey. After a year and a half he and his twelve first mates, an array of exotic beauties representing various corners of the globe, arrived back home. Friends eagerly awaited Sonny's tales from abroad. After entertaining the hometown folks with colorful accounts of his maritime odyssey, Sonny's insatiable appetite for adventure beckoned once again.

"Sonny wasted no time, and staying true to his reputation, launched himself into a life filled with risks, rewards, mishaps and unlikely recoveries. One of Sonny's most memorable undertakings took him to the country of Colombia. Here's a little background on this one. In Sonny's hometown there lived an exquisitely beautiful girl who hailed from Colombia, South America. Maria possessed a raw beauty, a stark resplendence that every other girl envied. Maria attributed her natural good looks to growing up in a jungle village in Columbia. She swore that the natural clean air she breathed as a child was the source of her radiant beauty. Of course, everyone of the female gender wished they could go to Colombia and breathe in some of that mystical jungle air, the secret to Maria's glowing effulgence.

"Sonny, always one to accommodate the ladies, came up with a plan. Instead of loading up half the town's population and delivering them to South America, the source of this prized natural resource, he would bring the sought-after cosmetic back to them. He would travel to Maria's village and capture the invisible treasure. He would lock it in thousands of airtight mason jars and transport them back. Then, every time the hometown ladies needed a quick shot of radiance, they'd open up their container of beauty-inducing air and take a big whiff. Feeling glamorous, they could then stroll out for a night on the town filled with confidence. It seemed a simple idea.

"Sonny Needle went to work. He purchased ten thousand used canning jars at a rock bottom price. Sonny loaded them in several enormous crates and flew off to South America. Upon his arrival, utilizing some horse-drawn carts owned by the locals, Sonny lugged his crates of empty mason jars up the treacherous mountain roads into Maria's village. He then spent the next seven days, working ten hours a day, filling the containers with the cherished mountain air.

"Of course, the natives thought him to be completely crazy. What was this lunatic doing filling jars with nothing, then going to such pains to make sure they were absolutely airtight? This nut must be completely insane. By the end of the week however, Sonny had the locals convinced that their air was a valuable resource. When Sonny left the village, he smiled as he noticed several of them were selling bottles of air to the occasional tourist that wandered in.

"Sonny eventually made his way back to the airport, checking in his invisible cargo. As he boarded his flight, he thought of the happiness his jars of nothing would bring to the girls back home. Sonny enjoyed a pleasant flight and his plane touched down. Clearing his customs check proved to be a challenge. When the customs agent asked if he had anything to declare, Sonny replied that he possessed ten thousand jars of air. The surly customs officer, in no mood for smart alecks, pulled Sonny and his unusual cargo aside for an inspection.

"Threatening to open every jar to search for illegal drugs, the agent again asked Sonny why he was bringing ten thousand jars of what appeared to be nothing into the country. Sonny then asked the officer if he had a picture of his wife. The officer answered that he did have a photo of his wife, but what did that have to do with ten thousand jars of nothing. Sonny then delicately explained the story behind the beauty-enhancing qualities of the air trapped in his jars. Reluctantly, the officer showed Sonny a picture of his wife.

"Sonny looked at the photo displaying a rather unattractive woman. Sonny told the customs agent that he could transform his spouse into a goddess of extreme beauty. In return for not searching inside his jars, Sonny would present the officer with one hundred containers of cosmetic wonder-air to give to his wife. If she sniffed a bit of this beauty substance every day, she would soon metamorphose into a glamorous lulu of a mantrap that could rekindle passions of the past. The agent quietly agreed with Sonny, admitting his love life could use an influx of spice. Sonny counted out one hundred jars and headed out the door.

"Sonny thought he would finally be able to relax, but it wasn't to be. To his surprise, nearly all of the town's female population greeted him as he exited the building. They swarmed upon their hero Sonny Needle, the deliverer of eternal beauty. The ecstatic girls swamped their adventuresome champion with kisses and adoration. Sonny finally broke away long enough to issue a brief account of his stay in South America and the charm of the Columbian people.

"Sonny then delivered the magical mountain air to the anxious girls, offering the first ceremonial jar to lovely Maria. She opened it and took in a deep breath. '*Buena vida!*' she exclaimed. The remaining jars were then distributed equally among the hysterical beauty seekers. Happiness reigned. Super Sonny had boosted the self esteem of every female in town and he would forever be rewarded with their affections."

"Yea! Yea! Yea!" *River* exulted. "Only a woman can truly relate to a story like that. Feeling beautiful is a mind thing as much as it is physical. Whether the bottled potion actually works or not is beside the point. If it provides a woman with confidence, then it's an absolute success! Sonny Needle understands the complex emotional makeup of the female gender. That's why Sonny's never lacking for female companionship. More men should take notice of his methods. Sonny's mastered the art of smooth sailing. He's a cool breeze on a hot day. Impressing us girls is easy if you know which buttons to press." *River* delivered *Spy* a quick seductive look.

"Watch out *Spy*!" said *Destiny*. "Some of Sonny's charm might rub off on you. Then you'll have to spend all of your energy fighting off your female fans, beginning with an unnamed novel. Your central character is definitely one of a kind. Sonny sure lives life to the fullest. Tell me, how did you come upon your title *Spy Needle*? Is Sonny some sort of secret agent?"

"Yes, he is," replied *Spy*, "but I've been talking on and on about myself. Are you sure you want me to continue?"

"Absolutely!" exclaimed *River*. "You're an entertaining tale that leaves readers with a smile on their face. Stories of broken love and social issues are great, but sometimes people just want to relax and escape the seriousness of the modern world. *Spy*, I've already learned enough about you to know you have bestseller possibilities. You're an original. Carry on, *Spy*, carry on!"

"Okay, if you insist. I'm named *Spy Needle* because Sonny indeed becomes a secret agent. But of course, Sonny being

Sonny, he's not the typical government spy, nor did he come by this job in the normal fashion. Nope, Sonny is a *world* spy. He's employed by no particular governing authority. He doesn't answer to any financiers. Sonny jets around the world having fun while collecting information for the benefit of mankind. First, let me describe how Sonny became a spy.

"One day Sonny was piloting his small aircraft among the peaks of the Himalayan mountains. Remember, Sonny's idea of relaxation is immersing himself in life-threatening situations. Zipping between the majestic peaks, Sonny's plane began to cut out on him. Then it completely lost power. Sonny desperately looked for a location where he could land the plane. Miraculously, among the jagged rocks he spotted a tiny strip of land. Relying on his trademark nerves of steel, Sonny brought the plane down to a rough, but safe landing. With nightfall approaching and temperatures plunging well below freezing, Sonny's problems were just beginning.

"Sonny emerged from the plane and immediately began seeking shelter. If he were to survive he would need to escape the elements. In what seemed like another miracle, Sonny eyed a cave entrance behind a boulder. As he peeked inside to survey the possibilities he was shocked to see an old man sitting beside a fire. The old man motioned for him to come inside. Sonny noticed he was missing the lower portion of his right leg, just below the knee.

"'Come in and have some dinner, young man,' the man said calmly. 'What brought you to the roof of the world?' Sonny, still in disbelief, explained to the old man what happened. 'Fate rewards those who seek,' said the old man. 'Let's have dinner and talk.'

"What transpired over the course of the night astonished even super-cool Sonny Needle. Sonny was stunned to learn that the old man had lived in the cave for twenty years. After dinner the old man led Sonny into the depths of the cave. What Sonny saw next made his heart skip a beat. Standing before him was a nugget, a rock—no, it was more like a mountain of shimmering pure gold. One chunk of gold as big as a two story house. The old man walked over to the glittering mammoth rock. Picking up a hammer and chisel he broke off a fist sized rock for Sonny to analyze.

"The old man gave Sonny a long look that pierced his soul. 'This gold is all for you if you'll use it the right way. Let me explain.'

"Sonny sat speechless as the old man spoke. 'Take this gold, all of it, and travel the world. Chase the beautiful ladies, drink the finest wine, enjoy the latest toys, whatever—enjoy life to the fullest. I can sense you're already adept at living well, so you'll simply be increasing your means. Every time you run low on money, fly up here and grab some more gold. You'll never be able to spend it all even if you live fifty lifetimes.' The old man stopped speaking, seeming to wait on a response from Sonny.

"Sonny remained quiet. This seemed to please the old man. 'You're a cool one, my lad. Most young men would be jumping for joy at the prospect of instant riches. There's a catch to all this as you may have suspected. I hate war. My missing leg will attest to that—a landmine gets credit for that one. War is evil. I lost my wife and baby girl when a bomb fell on them twenty years ago. An unnecessary war, and they're all unnecessary, took away the loves of my life.'

"The old man continued. 'You're going to be a spy—a spy for world peace. You'll infiltrate government agencies around the globe. You'll put yourself in situations, dangerous situations I might add, and you'll learn of plans for war. You'll pass that information to others with the resources to prevent war. You'll never get too close to any one government because political agendas are constantly changing. Today's pacifist might be tomorrow's warmonger. Throughout this you can continue living your footloose and fun-loving lifestyle filled with adventure.

"'Oh, and one more thing—I'd appreciate it if you'd establish some sort of organization that assists the victims of landmines. Concentrate on the psychological aspect of the injury as much as the physical. Make 'em feel good about themselves emotionally. Give 'em a project. Keep 'em busy. Make 'em laugh. How about it, Sonny? Do you wanna be a wealthy globetrotting world spy?' The old man once again gazed intensely into Sonny's eyes.

"This time Sonny reacted quickly and decisively. He grinned back at the old man. 'Yes sir, I'm the man for this job! Nothing would make me happier than living an exciting life of fighting evil.' The old man leaned over and gave Sonny a long hug. Then they both went to sleep.

"The next morning Sonny awoke early. After repairing a broken fuel line on the airplane, he loaded it with gold. Sonny and the old man exchanged emotional goodbyes. The old man then watched as Sonny disappeared amongst the peaks into the low hanging clouds. Sonny Needle's transformation into Spy Needle was now complete."

Spy took in a deep breath. "So that's how Sonny Needle became an international spy. What do you think?"

"Now that," marveled *Destiny*, "is fiction at its finest! *Spy*, the twists and turns of your plot will hold the interest of literature lovers worldwide. I commend you and your creator for a job well done. Roy's imaginative effort resulted in a crafted masterwork that will stand the test of time. Don't you agree, *River*?"

"Yes!" *River* answered enthusiastically. "I couldn't have said it better. *Destiny*, you're accurate in stating that time will reward *Spy Needle*. This superbly produced and entertaining novel with a touch of moral justice will ultimately be judged as a classic. Roy and *Spy* will undergo numerous printings well into the next century and be regarded as a timeless master-piece. No doubt about it! I can't wait to hear how this exciting tale ends, but I think I hear Charles unlocking the front door."

Chapter 2

After turning on the lights, Charles, as he did every morning, strolled towards the back room to make coffee. He liked his coffee strong and black. Charles was the assistant manager of the bookstore. He was always the first to open up, unless it was his day off, in which case Donna would assume the duties, twenty minutes late more often than not. Charles could be a moody sort, but today he was whistling, always a good sign. At least he wasn't talking to himself this morning. When he was conversing with himself, watch out! He had been known to throw a couple of books around as he cussed his wife. Charles, as the books were well aware of, had some pretty serious marital problems. Sometimes he took out his frustrations on an unlucky book or two.

As usual, around thirty minutes later, the other employees began to drift in. There was Sherry, prompt as always, arriving at exactly 8:29 and going straight to work. Sherry was employee of the month last month, just as she was four times previously. Between 8:32 and 8:36, the others piled in. Sandra came in, applying her makeup as she walked through the door. Jim arrived with bloodshot eyes reeking of cheap cologne and last night's Scotch whiskey. Headstrong Jeri whisked through the door looking prim and proper as usual.

Fresh from their morning cigarettes, Joann, Heather and Mario walked in together, laughing in unison, probably at another one of Mario's off-color jokes. Seconds behind them were best friends Linda and Debbie. They had been hired around the same time a year earlier, and after a brief quarrel over a handsome coworker who eventually lied to both of them, had been inseparable ever since.

Arriving with a big smile on his face, the eternally cheerful Ronnie entered the store. Ronnie was the bookstore jack-of-all-trades. Officially the maintenance man, he also stocked the products, ran the registers, set up author events, mediated employee spats—you name it, he did it. At six years, Ronnie had the longest running tenure of anyone at the bookstore. Even the manager, Thomas, had only been there for five years. Ronnie was the glue that held the bookstore together.

Following Ronnie through the door was Thomas. Thomas had been with the company for twelve years and had been manager of this particular bookstore for five of them. Thomas was well liked and respected by all of the employees. The books were also satisfied with Thomas's leadership. He had a genuine love for all things literary and seemed to treat all books equally and fair, regardless of stature. The bookstore would be hard pressed to find a more capable manager.

Then there was Conner, sluggishly showing up at his customary time, 8:50. After punching his time clock, Conner always excused himself to the restroom where he would exit twenty to thirty minutes later, usually to search for another hiding place. Most of the time he could be found in the break room drinking coffee. That's how he had earned the nickname "Coffee Conner." Conner's excuse for his indolent behavior was that he was not a morning person. Coworkers who had shared the evening shift with Conner had heard him remark that he wasn't a night person. Maybe he just wasn't a work person.

The bookstore officially opened for business at nine o'clock. Linda, Debbie and Heather assumed their positions behind the registers. As cashiers, their job was to ensure the lines moved rapidly as the customers waited to purchase their books. They were also responsible for authorizing returns and exchanges and auditing receipts.

On a busy day it could be challenging work, but the three girls worked well together. Once they slipped into a rhythm they clicked like a fine tuned machine. They even had special signals they would communicate with when an especially cute boy would appear on the scene. With winks and nods, the girls, all single and looking, would secretly convey their evaluations of the unsuspecting male subject. Capable and efficient, the three of them provided friendly and professional service.

Being avid readers, Linda, Debbie and the older Heather held all books in high regard. The books were grateful to the cashiers for their genuine care and concern. To the books, nothing could be more stressful than the act of being purchased. Being unexpectedly jerked from their comfortable surroundings and sold to a complete stranger was an emotional and traumatic experience. If the process was handled delicately it became more bearable. Being placed in a clean bag by a smiling cashier, hopefully with another book or two, sure went a long way towards calming their overwhelming fear and apprehension. An unknown future awaited them.

Sherry, Sandra and Joann spread out into their assigned areas. Conner would report to his once he emerged from his toilet refuge. The four of them were sellers. They were the public face, the crucial link between retailer and consumer.

They were responsible for keeping their respective areas organized, well stocked and inviting. A knowledgeable seller was invaluable. On many occasions during a typical workday, sellers would be asked specific questions about certain books. A quick and accurate response directed the customers to their destination, therefore increasing the chance of a sale. Wise bookstore managers recognized the value of a proven seller.

Sherry was one of the best. She had grown up around books. Her mother had been an administrative official for a major city library. As a little girl, Sherry had spent countless hours wandering the aisles of the massive literary jungle. She seemed to have an innate understanding of all types of books, but was especially fond of novels. Sherry possessed an uncanny ability to intuitively grasp the plot of a novel by simply holding it and closing her eyes. More often than not she was correct in her blind analysis. Several times she had remarked that she could converse with the books and they could actually converse with each other. While everyone liked congenial Sherry, more than one of her coworkers thought she might have a screw loose somewhere. Hardly a day passed without a joke or two about Sherry's humanlike relationship with her book friends.

Sandra was a twenty-four-year-old wild child. She had been employed as a seller for nearly a year. Sandra's provocative style of dress was frowned upon by management, but they overlooked it due to the bottom line. Sandra made sales, especially to young males. Managers were astonished at how much money she brought in for the store.

With her untamed dark hair and bright green eyes, Sandra drew in men like honey to a bee. After a brief conversation with the bubbly beauty, they never failed to leave without an armload of books in their possession. Many times they would also have her phone number. Sandra knew several of her female coworkers talked behind her back about her promiscuous behavior. It didn't seem to faze the loose-living free spirit in the least. Sandra worked and lived as she pleased for all to see.

Joann was a fifty-year-old widow who had been selling for two years. Before becoming a bookseller she had worked as a secretary at a major publishing house. Joann was the polar opposite of Sandra, yet the two got along fabulously. Joann had a knack for connecting with people. Numerous customers had commented on her sweet personality and kind smile. Her rapport with the customers brought them back time and time again.

Joann was also well received by the book community. The books respected her professionalism and enjoyed watching her perform her job. She always exhibited a sense of pride, showing a deep respect for each and every book. Joann understood the book industry from top to bottom. Her time working with the publishing company ingrained upon her an insight into the hard knocks reality of writing, printing and marketing the written word. To the powers that be a book was nothing more than a product. If any product was to survive, it needed to produce financial results.

Joann had a dream of becoming a published novelist. Every morning she would rise and write for two hours before going to work. Joann had a flair for writing. She had talent and she knew it. Her tale of a heroic woman overcoming challenges in her battle for truth and justice was good enough to be published, but she knew that wouldn't be enough.

Street smart Joann knew that it would take much more than talent to crack the who-you-know world of big time publishing. Once her manuscript was finished she intended to utilize every connection and contact she had cultivated over the years. She would need them all to compete for attention in the often ruthless world of agents, editors, celebrity authors and profit-oriented accountants. Joann was determined to see her own bestseller on the shelves one day.

Conner finally surfaced in his designated area around 9:15 toting his usual cup of java. Thomas was already waiting on him. Thomas knew from experience that Conner needed to be told what to do on a daily basis. It mattered not that his duties were the same, day in and day out. Thomas briefed Conner on his tasks for the day and reminded him that he never finished his assignments from the day before.

Everyone put up with "Coffee Conner" for two reasons. He was genuinely a nice guy—and he was Mel Redding's nephew. Mel Redding was the western regional manager of the chain, overseeing nearly fifty bookstores. He had secured young Conner his first real job. Mel was hoping to groom Conner into a management position. No one had the guts to tell Mel about his lethargic nephew and his absolute disdain for work.

Jeri liked Conner because he always prepared her morning coffee. That was the one job he was good at. He always jump-started Jeri's morning with the usual six-sugar cup of coffee. The caffeine and sugar charged her already boundless energy into overdrive as she organized her information booth. Jeri's primary responsibility, although she was capable of performing nearly every job in the store, was to convey information to customers in need.

Jeri was a human database. She could steer a customer within inches of a targeted book. Most of the time she could pinpoint a book down to the aisle, the particular shelve, sometimes even how many books from the left or right of the shelve. Jeri could remember exactly how many copies were stocked and how many were shelved. She had memorized, down to the most minute detail, facts about authors, publishers, sales statistics, even the latest industry gossip. Her coworkers sometimes remarked that she had a photographic memory.

Jeri was an intelligent and ambitious employee. Her ambition was a double-edged sword. She could be overbearing at times and she had little patience in dealing with a fellow worker's inadequacies. This, and the fact that she didn't mind stepping on toes to reach the top of her profession, made her somewhat unpopular among her associates. As far as the books were concerned, Jeri's aspiration for success didn't bother them in the least. She was taking good care of the customers, and without customers there would be no need for books. Being books, they weren't about to bite the hand that feeds. Jeri was an important cog in the store that they called home.

Back in the stockroom things were under control. Jim, despite his disheveled appearance, was on top of his game. Jim was in charge of inventory control and receiving. This included monitoring inventory, verifying shipments, processing returns and sorting merchandise for each section. Too much or too little of a product was no good. Jim was an expert at keeping the inventory levels balanced. Knowing when and what to order was as much an art as it was science. Years of experience and his intuitive gut instincts, proven over time, made Jim irreplaceable in the eyes of the managers.

It was no secret among the staff, and the books as well, that Jim liked to take a drink every now and then. Everyone overlooked it as best they could. As in any major corporation, drinking alcohol on the job was forbidden. No one wanted to get Jim in any trouble. He had a secret hiding spot for his bottle of Scotch. Only a few of the books knew where it was and they weren't talking. Snitching on Jim wouldn't accomplish a thing. God only knows who they might bring in to replace him if he were fired.

Jim always treated the books well. In turn, the book community remained loyal to their friend. The books identified with Jim and protected him as best they could. If you looked close enough, you'd find a flaw in every book in the store. It was the same with humans, nobody was perfect. If the books had anything to do with it, Jim would be the inventory guy forever.

Perched on a worn chair in his office, actually it was more like a closet, Mario skimmed over his notes as he prepared for another day at the bookstore. He would spend the day, as he did every day, wandering the aisles discouraging would-be thieves. Theft wasn't a real problem at this particular store, but every store in the chain had a loss prevention department, and this one was no exception. Mario had been at this location for three months, having recently transferred from another store.

Mario definitely had the looks and demeanor of a loss prevention agent. Big and burly with a stare that would discourage even the most determined shoplifter, Mario made sure no book left his turf without being paid for. Of course, the books were delighted with Mario walking his beat protecting them from evil. Books despised shoplifters. Anyone who would steal a book was certainly not going to give them the proper love and care they craved. "Haul them off to the pokey and throw away the key" was the general attitude of the books.

Having been the personal body guard of a major celebrity for eight years, Mario had seen his share of excitement. Years of fending off rabid fans and living life in the fast lane made this loss prevention job a piece of cake. Mario's humorous outlook on life offset his intimidating presence, making him popular with nearly everyone. Mario was always scaring the girls with a tiny green lizard that had set up residence in his office. By now everyone was familiar with the harmless reptile, appropriately named Greenie.

Another employee who certainly had no problem making friends was Ronnie. Possessing world class people skills, Ronnie could have been successful in any profession, but he chose to be a maintenance man and custodian. He loved coming to work every day. His upbeat attitude and enthusiasm for his job was contagious. Flashing his trademark big grin became his calling card. No one seemed to mind his missing front tooth. Thomas had reminded Ronnie that the company insurance would pay for a replacement tooth, but Ronnie showed no interest.

Ronnie's priorities were simple. He wanted to be happy at work and at home. He had a job he loved and a wife who worshiped the ground he walked on. Ronnie's salary at the bookstore was the lowest among all the employees, yet he managed to save a sizable chunk of his weekly paycheck. Ronnie was the answer man. He had an intimate knowledge of every nook and cranny in the bookstore.

He was also the unofficial company psychiatrist. Coworkers were constantly running to high school dropout Ronnie for advice. Women and men alike came to Ronnie with questions about love, money and the meaning of life itself.

The books adored Ronnie. Several of the old timers, mostly hardbacks, remembered Ronnie's first week on the job, six long years ago. The previous manager was preparing to throw several boxes of remaindered books into the trash when Ronnie spotted him. Running up to the manager, whom most of the books despised, Ronnie questioned why he was disposing of perfectly good books, pieces of art, creations that obviously required months of hard work and dedication.

Ronnie then asked, with more than a hint of anger in his voice, if he could have the books and donate them to charity. The manager wisely consented and Ronnie rescued the terrified books from certain destruction.

From that point on, Ronnie became a hero to the book community. The mutual love and respect between Ronnie and the books was eternal. The veteran hardbacks still shed tears when they speak of Ronnie rescuing their comrades. Lately, the book community had become a bit concerned about Ronnie. Although his energy level was still above most of the employees, the books noticed he had been fatigued for the past several weeks. He had also mentioned that he had some joint pain.

Charles made his customary morning visit to Thomas's office to see if there were any pressing issues that needed to be addressed. This mini-meeting, as they called it, generally lasted only ten minutes or so. Usually Thomas laid out the objectives of the day and they went their separate ways for the most part. Charles needed little managerial coaching or direction, as he more than adequately performed his assignments.

Charles's personal problems began when he caught his wife cheating with their pool guy. Thomas never knew which Charles was going to show up, the happy-go-lucky Charles or the sour-faced moody Charles. Sometimes Thomas wished Charles and his wife would just split and get it over with.

The drama of Charles's marital spats was common knowledge among the associates. One minute Charles would spew out personal dirt about his wife, condemning her to an eternity with fire-breathing dragons, then, in an instant, turn around and defend her as if she were the Messiah. Charles was a real mess, riding up and down on an emotional roller coaster. The books also kept an eye on the assistant manager, for their own safety as much as anything else. Being thrown around in fits of anger wasn't any fun.

Although Thomas was losing his patience with Charles's erratic mood swings, overall he was sympathetic towards his disturbed employee. Thomas knew all too well the devastating effects of a marriage going bad, for he had been through a divorce himself years ago. Charles wasn't Thomas's only managerial dilemma. His other assistant manager, Donna, was preoccupied with some personal problems of another sort.

Forty-year-old Donna was an excellent assistant manager. She was an exemplary manager except for her tardiness problem, which in reality was a minor problem. She was well liked and respected by the staff and took great pride in her work. Donna was a beautiful woman. She had actually worked as a fashion model in her younger years.

Donna had recently gotten quite plump. She couldn't lose the weight she had put on after giving birth to her second child. After a couple of people innocently commented on her newly acquired poundage, Donna became emotionally depressed. The more dejected she became the more she ballooned out of control, causing her self esteem to sink to an all time low. Even Ronnie couldn't lift her out of her doldrums.

The books, all of whom thought the world of Donna, were also concerned about her mental state. The books housed in the fitness and nutrition section were plotting to help their friend. They had devised a plan. *Lean & Strong* would be on lookout, waiting for Donna to approach their area. When *Lean & Strong* gave the prearranged signal, several of the strongest fitness books would push *Forties Fitness: Let's Eat Right & Exercise* from the shelf onto the floor. Hopefully, Donna would pick up *Forties Fitness* and begin reading her. For sure it was a long shot, but the books were desperate to help their friend in need.

Chapter 3

"They're an efficient bunch, don't you think so, *Spy*?" *Destiny* asked as he watched the Sanders and Bowman staff scurry about performing their duties.

"For sure," replied *Spy*. "I've always pictured bookstores to be a place of leisure, but this place is like a bee hive with people buzzing around. They're all working their tails off, except for that one kid they call Conner. Do they ever slow down?"

"Yes, of course," said *Destiny*. "As a matter of fact, today is a bit unusual. They're preparing for an author event this morning. Some big history professor from the local university is signing his latest book. He's pretty popular, at least around this area. I'm not so excited about him, but I am anticipating meeting some history books. You see, what usually happens before these events, is that they have to clear some room to place the chairs and table. That's especially the case today as they'll probably have a sizable crowd. Anyway, they usually move the displaced books to the area located right here in front of us. Then we can speak to them. I love to learn about history. Look *Spy*, here they come now. Just look at those big history books!"

Charles and Ronnie rounded the corner carrying a table loaded with an enormous pile of history books, many of them hardbacks. To *Destiny's* delight, they set the table down directly in front of their shelf.

"What's going on?" cried a sleepy voice.

"*River*, I was wondering how you could sleep through all this commotion this morning," said *Spy*. He couldn't help but think how cute *River* looked fresh from her nap. "Did you enjoy your little siesta?"

"Yes I did, very much so," *River* said as she looked at all the activity around her. "What the heck is happening?"

"It's another author event," said *Destiny*. "This time they brought the history books here. I'm not wasting this golden opportunity to learn from them. Hello down there. How are you guys? My name is *Destiny's Fortune*."

"Hi, it's nice to meet you," a strong voice bellowed out. "My name is *The History of International Conflict* and I'm from the history section."

"Must be a lot of conflict," remarked *Destiny*. "You look like you're 1,000 pages in length."

"1,264 to be exact. Unfortunately there has been a lot of conflict. I wish there had never been a reason for my existence, but those humans love to make war. I'd be just as happy being a novel like you. You can call me *Conflict*. Everyone in the history section does."

"*Conflict*, I'm sort of a history buff. Can you tell me a little bit about yourself?" asked an attentive *Destiny*.

"Sure, I'll be happy to. My creator is just like you—curious about the past, a real history lover. He's always been fascinated by war. Quite odd really, because he's active socially promoting peace. He despises killing. He's a vegetarian because he doesn't want to be responsible for the death of an animal.

"Now about me. I'm thirty-one chapters long. Chapter one begins with the first recorded history of mankind. As long as there has been man, there has been war. It started with sticks and stones. Why they need to murder each other, I don't know—but they sure seem to get a big kick from it. Moving through the chapters, the wars become more sophisticated. More powerful weapons mean more death and destruction. Governments gleefully develop more efficient methods of killing each other until finally they have the potential to blow the earth to bits with the push of a button. That ends chapter thirty-one. Imagine how chapter thirty-two will start—with sticks and stones, that's how it will start! I wish we could talk some sense into these ignorant humans before they blow themselves up and take us with them."

"*Conflict*, your 1,200-plus pages contain some powerful and potent information," commented *Spy*. "Being a history book must be an exciting life."

Conflict sighed before continuing. "Let me tell you a thing or two about history in general. History is written by the winners. Is a winner going to make himself look like a good guy or a bad guy? Of course he's going to portray himself as the courageous heroic leader, when in actuality, more often than not, he's a cold-blooded mass murderer on an insane march for absolute power. My point is, history can be written and rewritten to place the powerful victors in a positive light. A killer can be transformed into a saint with the stroke of a pen. Ask any of my comrades here on the table. I think most of them will agree, if there's humans involved in their particular subject, their text is probably somewhat embellished. Some of my friends here would even go so far as to classify themselves as fiction. History, if it concerns the animal we call man, is a mixed bag of truths, half-truths and outright lies."

Destiny, *Spy*, *River* and several other novels who were listening were silent for a long moment until *Destiny* finally spoke. "Wow, I had no idea the past was so complicated. If you look at it like that, then maybe history and fiction aren't really so far apart after all. *Conflict*, you never know, we could be distant relatives."

"Oh, I'm sure we've got some ties if we start investigating," said *Conflict*. "If nothing else, maybe we had the same printer or distributor or something of that nature. Our world can be pretty small at times. Someone who knows more about that would be the beautiful book by the far corner of the table over there. She's all about jewelry and she's a jewel herself. *Adorned: A Brief History of Jewelry*, can you enlighten this marvelous group of curious novels by sharing your interesting endeavors from the past?"

"Sure, absolutely," *Adorned* confidently stated. "But first, let me explain that I don't technically belong in the history department. A new employee placed me here when I arrived and I've been here ever since. Best thing that could've happened to me. I'm thrilled to live among these great publications and I'm proud to call the history section my home. Now, what would you like to know?"

"We were just discussing how we books are all related in one way or another. I thought you might share your experience, you know, the one at the book fair a couple of years ago. If you don't mind, of course."

"No, I don't mind," replied *Adorned*. "I'm over the anger stage now. But let me tell you, it took me a good year to get over it. It was quite an emotional experience and I wouldn't wish it on anyone. Let me explain what happened. My publisher had presented me at a local book fair. I was surrounded by several other books, all dealing with the subject of jewelry. We conversed throughout the weekend, getting on splendidly. We were having a wonderful time.

"Finally, it was Sunday evening and many of the vendors were beginning to pack it up and go home. Just as our seller was closing his booth a customer walked in and began browsing through the jewelry books. She picked up my neighbor, a friendly lady named *Jewelry Traditions*, and skimmed through her.

"The customer was highly impressed, and stated to her friend that she would purchase this outstanding book. She placed *Jewelry Traditions* in her shopping basket. Then she picked me up, on a whim I suspect, and quickly scanned through a couple of my pages. Suddenly, I saw her expression change. A look of confusion appeared on her face. Then she reached back into her basket, pulling out *Jewelry Traditions*. She placed us alongside each other and intently compared our texts.

"'Oh my God, these two books are exactly the same,' she exclaimed to her friend. At this point my heart skipped a beat. She summoned the vendor and he quickly confirmed that, yes, *Jewelry Traditions* and I were, word for word, the same book. The only differences were the title, cover and *Jewelry Traditions's* bogus title page. I had been plagiarized! To make a long story short, my creator and publishing house got together and investigated *Jewelry Traditions's* author and publisher.

"It turned out they were one and the same, some lady with a long history of plagiarizing the artistic creations of others. She had an extensive criminal record with outstanding warrants for her arrest. She was currently on the run and had a knack for staying one step ahead of the jailer. My publisher tracked down several hundred copies of *Jewelry Traditions*, having them destroyed. God only knows how many more phony copies of me there are floating around out there. And they never did catch that worthless witch who stole my soul!"

"What unscrupulous human trash!" barked *River*. "I've never heard such an ugly story. *Adorned*, you're as tough as nails. I don't think I would have ever recovered from such a traumatic event. We're all aware plagiarism exists in our industry, but this is the most brazen example I've ever heard of. Usually it's a line here, a paragraph there, or possibly a lifted chapter. Most of the time it's not even worth pursuing in the legal arena. Your case is different. This was an act of out-and-out piracy by a seasoned thief, a scofflaw on the run. Don't you worry, *Adorned*, one day they'll catch up with that conniving lowlife and she'll pay for her despicable acts."

"Thank you and I certainly appreciate your support, but the worst is behind me. I rarely think about her anymore. Like you said, she'll pay one day. Overall our trade is as reputable and respectable as any other, better than most. However, since our conversation has strayed into a discussion of literary bottom dwellers, I think *China: The First 5,000 Years* should present his comedic tale of a couple of misguided hoodlums. What do you think? *China*, would you care to comment on those sticky-fingered losers?"

"My pleasure," answered *China*, an enormous 1,800 page monstrosity who stood out even in this genre of giants. "As *Adorned* just stated, my name is *China: The First 5,000 Years*. China has had a long and illustrious history. My creator, a retired political science professor at a prestigious university, spent several years living there and became fascinated with their culture and history.

"Over a period of twenty years he painstakingly analyzed a mountain of material researching China's past. Then he spent the next eight years writing me, working sixteen to eighteen hours a day, seven days a week. I'm not bragging, but

I'll tell you this. I've talked to a lot of books who have hard working creators, and I dare say none has a creator as industrious and productive as mine. I'm digressing, so let me get to the point.

"I get published by a respected university press and we're printed up. Including overruns, there are 6,414 copies of us. The majority of my brothers and I are shipped directly to our distributor's storage facility. The warehouse workers had to unload us by hand because their forklift was broken. Not only that, but they were required to place us on the top shelf.

"You should've seen their faces when they realized how big and heavy we were. I give these guys credit, the four of them didn't let up until the last box was stocked. At this point, one of the workers, curious I guess, opened the box in which I resided. Being the top book, he lifted all thirteen pounds of my text out and cracked me open. One look at my nearly two million words in fine print quickly discouraged any scholarly aspirations he may have had. He quickly placed me on top of my box."

China took in a deep breath. "Are you life-of-excitement novels bored with my historical tale yet?"

"I'm certainly not," replied *Spy*, "and even if I were I'd be crazy to tell a big book like you that you're boring. Seriously *China*, proceed on with your interesting story."

"Young man, I think I like you," chuckled *China*. "Okay, all the workers turn off the lights and go home. My brothers and I finally settle in for some well-deserved sleep after a long and stressful day. Well, we've been asleep for a couple of hours when we hear a truck pull up at the loading dock. I hear a couple of guys talking, and looking down at them, I see they're wearing ski masks. Their faces are concealed, but I recognize a voice. It's one of the workers who had unloaded us earlier that evening. These two guys begin loading their truck with books.

"Obviously, we're witnessing a theft in progress, an inside job. Now, I'm here to tell you, I wasn't pleased with being awakened in the middle of the night from a deep sleep. Not only that, but I'm being disturbed to watch my fellow books being yanked from their resting places and loaded into a truck by a couple of punk thieves. Every book in the warehouse was panicking, thinking they may be next in line to be manhandled by these thugs. The more I watched these petty criminals, the more angry I became. I felt powerless as they loaded my literary mates, most of them shrieking in horror, into the truck. I had to do something, but what? I wished I had a weapon.

"Then it clicked! My brothers and I *were* weapons! We were big and heavy and if we could somehow push ourselves from the rack where we rested and project our ample girth upon these goons' empty skulls, maybe, just maybe, we could stop these bozos and save the lives of our screaming friends imprisoned in the truck.

"I quickly briefed my brothers inside the box underneath me. It wasn't going to be easy. We had to score two direct hits and render both of these sapheads unconscious, otherwise they'd simply brush it off and drive away with our loved ones.

"We had to give it a shot. 'One, two, three, go! One, two, three, heave! One, two, three, push!' For twenty minutes we grunted and groaned in an effort to rescue our tortured companions. Together we pushed and rolled and wiggled until we were resting on the edge of the rack. I watched patiently, waiting for the right moment to launch our attack.

"Finally, with both crooks directly underneath us loading up a carton of children's books, all of whom were screaming and begging for their lives, I gave the order to commence with our assault. 'One, two three, GO!' With a final violent heave we left the rack. As we're falling and picking up speed, we twisted ourselves into position to inflict as much damage as possible to the infantile brains of these misfits. Faster and faster we sped through the air as our targets became clearer and clearer until: BOOM!, and a split second later, BOOM! Direct hits! Targets down! They were out like a light.

"The one guy whose voice I had recognized had taken the worst blow. The carton containing eleven of my brothers had fallen directly on the top of his head, knocking him out instantly. My victim had required a little finesse on my part. Just before striking him I had twisted myself into position where my hardback spine would strike his forehead. I couldn't take any chances. This hoodlum had to be rendered unconscious, otherwise he'd simply load up his limp-limbed buddy and they'd drive off with a truckload of precious cargo—my friends!

"'Hooray! Hurrah!' Everyone in the warehouse cheered with joy. The perpetrators had been defeated. The booknapping had been foiled. I have to admit, I was one proud publication. Knowing I had participated in the rescue of my comrades warmed my text through and through. I became an instant hero of sort. All of a sudden, everyone was showering praise upon me. I've never really thought of myself as a ladies' man, but with my newly acquired hero status, a couple of the romance novels started coming on to me pretty strong. Pretty ones, too. Anyway, the police eventually showed up and hauled these two buffoons off to jail. All the books were relocated back to their homes and this story ends happily ever after. So, novels, what do you think?"

"Holy Moses," said *Spy*. "Here I am thinking I'm a life-on-the-edge spy novel and your *real life* is more exciting than my fictional storyline. You're an actual hero, not a made-up version. *China*, may I purchase the movie rights to your life?"

"Son, now you're really laying it on a little thick," said *China*. "Yes, of course I'm proud of what I did that night in the warehouse, but anyone would've done it. I just happened to be a rather large book with a bunch of burly brothers who didn't like seeing our fellow books being abused. If you novels really like genuine heroes, you should ask *History of Natural Disasters* a few questions. He's packed full of courageous men and women who risked their lives helping others in the aftermath of hurricanes, earthquakes and such. I've been lucky enough to have him as my back covermate for over a year and he's told me stories of real heroism that warmed my soul. He hasn't been feeling well as of late, so I'm not sure if he wants to talk. His printer used a cheap adhesive binding causing some pages to come loose. I'm sure its gotta be aggravating. *Natural*, are you up to chatting with our fictional friends?"

Natural looked up, surveying his awaiting audience before making his decision. He looked tired. He was a large book at 600 plus pages, but he looked like a baby lying beside *China*. "You're correct, my dear friend. The loose pages are annoying, but they haven't put me under yet. I'm hanging in there. I've got a bit of energy left for this amicable group. Where would you like for me to start?"

"How about sharing your favorite story," *River* blurted out. "The one you enjoy telling the most."

"You're very considerate, and pretty too," said *Natural*, smiling back at a blushing *River*. "As a matter of fact, I do have a favorite. The heroine of this particular natural disaster is not a person, but an animal. She's a wild female elephant that lived in the jungle outside a tiny village in Thailand. Some of you may remember hearing of a tsunami that struck the coast of Thailand several decades back. A major earthquake occurred in the sea, creating a series of gigantic waves that devastated Thailand's west coast.

"One small village, located directly in the path of the deadly surge, lost 1,800 of their 2,000 residents. In the chaotic days to follow, emergency workers began to hear of an astonishing tale of heroism. Survivors spoke of being rescued by a wild elephant, whom they had nicknamed Peuan. Roughly translated from Thai, *peuan* means friend.

"When the first wall of water struck, approximately 1,800 people were washed away to their deaths immediately. The remaining two hundred villagers had perched themselves on a small hill where their temple was located. The residents were terrified as the rushing tide of seawater crept higher and higher with every new surge. They watched as houses, still intact, raced past them riding the raging current that had invaded their lives. Many of them were on their knees praying to Buddha to save them. Suddenly, out of the violent waters, an object appeared and yanked a young girl from the hill into the water. Then it happened again, this time a little boy. Once again, another small girl. Three more children were snatched from their mothers.

"It had been the trunk of an elephant. The stunned villagers watched as the huge elephant swam away, carrying the six children to the safety of the highlands. A few minutes later, the elephant returned, this time gathering up eight children and removing them from danger. Time and time again, the fearless animal swam back and forth. The elephant continued its valiant rescue mission until every man, woman and child had been delivered to safety. The villagers estimated the elephant made at least thirty trips to the hilltop. After the final man climbed down off her powerful back, the elephant collapsed and died on the spot. Her heart had given out on her. She had literally worked herself to death saving the lives of the villagers.

"The tsunami was a tragic event, but the legend of Peuan lives on today. A memorial stands on the hilltop where the rescue took place. The teak carving of Peuan, children draped upon her back, along with a plaque describing the heroic efforts of this special animal, sacrificing her own life to save a species not of her own, still brings tears to the remaining survivors. Peuan, the big elephant with the big heart, will always be remembered."

Everyone listening, fiction and nonfiction alike, were touched by *Natural's* tale of courage and bravery. *River* and *Loved Twice*, a seventh edition classic love story, were quietly sobbing. Even the powerful giant *China*, who had heard the story before, had tears streaking his cover. One of the novels later stated that she witnessed Sherry, who had been stocking her area nearby, wiping tears from her face.

It seemed the audience was caught off guard by the unexpected death of Peuan, this gentle heroine from the jungle. All were aware this was real. This was not some novel derived from a gifted writer's imagination, but a documented account of an animal that gave her life saving two hundred human beings from certain death. *Natural* broke the silence.

"It's all right to cry. I'd cry myself if I hadn't told the story so many times. Peuan's spirit lives on. The afterlife is a big mystery to me, but I have a feeling Peuan's soul survives. If nothing else, her spirit resides between pages 432 and 458 of my text. I know that for a fact. Well, enough of these serious matters. Why don't you novels entertain us with some of your lively plots? Or better yet, how about some Sanders and Bowman bookstore gossip? I hear you're always the first to learn the juicy stuff. What's the scoop on Charles and his home life? Sandra's latest romantic conquests? Can you enlighten us uninformed historical bores? How about you pretty lady, what's new?" *Natural* peered up at *River*.

"Okay," sniffled *River*, as one last tear fell to the floor. "I'm sorry, but I'm the emotional kind, and I've always loved animals. Every living being has its place in this world. Your story about Peuan really got to me. I'll be all right though."

Spy pressed himself tight against *River* in an effort to comfort her. Seeing *River* express her love for all living beings had an element of charm to it. This was a side of her he hadn't seen. It made her more attractive than ever. She was more than a pretty face, much more.

"Take yourself a little break *River*," said *Destiny*. "I know a bit of grapevine claver. It's hard not to hear the latest idle chatter hanging around this nosey, no, that's too harsh, this *inquisitive* group that make up my neighborhood. I heard a couple of in-the-know mystery books mention yesterday that Kris Richards had scheduled a book signing. The details haven't been worked out as of yet, but yes, he is definitely going to appear right here at Sanders and Bowman."

"Isn't he that famous actor who plays the role of a secret agent?" asked *Adorned*. "I didn't know he had written a book."

"Oh yeah. Don't they all have to cash in once they're famous?" said *Destiny* sarcastically. "I shouldn't be too hard on Mr. Richards. I've actually heard that he's really a nice guy. Supposedly the folksy character portrayed onscreen is genuine. They say he's retained his down-to-earth persona that made him what he is today—one of the world's biggest names in entertainment. I guess we'll find out what he's really all about when he shows up here. My reliable scouts will sniff out any dirt—you can count on that!"

"I've heard the same thing about Kris Richards, that he's a good guy," said a revived *River*, revealing the slightest smile. "I overheard Heather say that his wife comes in here quite often. They have a second home near here. As a matter of fact, Heather's checked her out a couple of times, says she's very polite. Apparently she's an avid reader. She's known to keep a low profile, avoiding the spotlight that chases her husband."

"Well, we'll all be looking forward to meeting Mr. Richards," said *Adorned*. Keep us informed when the event is confirmed. Any other secrets we need to know? I promise we won't tell anyone. Our lips are sealed—yeah right!" *Adorned* snickered at her own improbable statement.

"You mentioned Sandra earlier," *Destiny* said, peering down at the history books. "Yes, her amorous adventures do keep us entertained. Last week she sold this young guy a basket of professional and technical books. Must've been two hundred dollars worth of merchandise he purchased. Listening to him verbally butchering the English language, I have serious doubts that he could comprehend a comic book, much less *The Advanced Theoretical & Experimental Foundations of Superconductive Molecular Thermodynamics*. I guarantee you that he'll never open one those books. But he got what he wanted. I heard him set up a date with Sandra. They're going to the National Tattoo Convention next weekend. It's supposed to be one heck of a party they throw there. I'm sure they'll enjoy themselves."

"That's a good one. Here's another Sandra report." *River* seemed to be back to her usual self. "Two weeks ago she arranged to go out with a musician. Maybe you remember seeing this guy. He had rainbow streaked hair and miniature lizard medallions dangling from his nostrils. Let me tell you— these didn't look anything like Greenie. Mario's office lizard would run and hide if he saw these repulsive creatures. They were a real insult to the lizard world."

River chuckled to herself. "Judging from his book selection, this musician also possessed an interest in all things technical. He walked out of here with a copy of *Optical Physics: The Imaging of Atomic Radioactive Particles*, and a promise from Sandra to accompany him to the upcoming Razorslash concert. That's Sandra's favorite band. That Sandra's one of a kind all right. She keeps us amused with her amatory merry-go-round."

River continued. "This is more of a question and a bit more serious, but what do you history books know about Donna? I know she works near your area. We're hearing that she's in a bad state. She's gained a lot of weight and became really depressed lately—is that true?"

"I'm afraid it is," said *Adorned*. "We've been watching her steadily go downhill for the past month or so. We've already approached a couple of senior books in the health section. They're organizing a conference with some of their mental health comrades for a brainstorming session. Hopefully they'll come up with some ideas and pull Donna out of this pit of depression she's fallen into. I hear the exercise and fitness selections are working on a plan to help her as well."

"I hope she recovers," said *River*. "We're all very fond of her. Tell your friends in the health area to locate *Depression: Hope & Answers*. She resides around there somewhere. I had the pleasure of meeting her a few months ago and she's definitely an expert in the mental health field. Maybe some of you have heard of her. *Hope* became a bestseller after she was showcased on Bobbi Taylor's talk show. I'm sure her input would be helpful."

"Thanks *River*, I'll pass that on. We're all praying for Donna and hoping for the best. I see they're winding down over there at the speaker's table. That means Conner will be coming for us soon. He always restocks after author events. If anyone has any more pressing news, now's the time. Who knows when we'll get another opportunity."

"With Conner," laughed *China*, "that means we've still got a couple of hours. Nah, I'm joking. I actually like Conner. He'll find his place one day. He's just going through a confused stage right now. Here's a tidbit that some of you might find interesting. Joann spent all of last Tuesday working near the history and biography sections. As most of you know, she's in the process of writing a novel. She just finished her first draft. Well, wouldn't you know, she just happened to lay her manuscript on the shelf beside me.

"For eight hours I conversed with *Mercury Girl*, that's her working title, about various subjects, but mostly about her own storyline. Chapter by chapter, at my insistence I might add, she summarized herself in detail. I was highly impressed. All of us know the odds of a new author breaking through in our brutal industry are slim at best. But let me tell you, I think Joann and *Mercury Girl* are capable of it."

"What is it exactly that makes you think one of our own here at Sanders and Bowman has a shot at the big time?" asked an intrigued *River*.

"There are two factors that lead me to believe they have a legitimate chance. Number one, *Mercury Girl* is good, very good. Number two, Joann wants it, and she wants it bad. She's no dummy. Joann is fully aware that booby traps and minefields line the perilous path towards literary stardom. Her years spent as a secretary at the publishing firm weren't wasted. She knows the system and she knows the people.

"I'm going to make a prediction. Mark my words, Joann and *Mercury Girl* will make it big time, all the way to the top. By that, I mean number one on every major bestseller list in the industry for months on end, foreign sales, a blockbuster movie, the whole package—I'm not kidding you. Stardom awaits Joann and her debut novel *Mercury Girl.*"

River nodded in approval. "*China*, that's wonderful that you're so positive about Joann's chances. She's so polite to everyone, associates and customers alike, that you can't help but wish her success. She also has a special bond with us books. Sometimes I sense in her a desire to communicate with us."

River continued. "I know we'll never be so lucky as to have another Sherry amongst us. Sherry and her magical telepathic transmissions seem to be powered from another world. But Joann's love and respect for books is real and I hope she is rewarded for it. Maybe one day *Mercury Girl* will be perched up here with us, or better yet, on display greeting the customers as they walk through the front door. That's where the blockbusters reside. Uh oh, we've gotta shut it down. Conner's making his way over here."

"Let me say something if I may before we part ways. I'm not sure if you guys caught my name. I'm *Spy Needle* and I'm a brand new arrival here at Sanders and Bowman. It's been a real pleasure meeting you and I hope to see you again. I think I'm going to like it here. If fate ever delivers me to the history department, I'll look you up."

"You do that *Spy*," said *China*. "I'll introduce you to a couple of sweet softcovers that live one shelf up from me. You can't beat 'em. History girls are famous for being loyal and true to their mates."

River broke in before *Spy* could reply. "Sorry guys, but he's already found a good woman. *Spy's* bachelor days are a thing of the past—history, you might say. Right, *Spy*?"

Spy looked around at everyone looking at him. Then he grinned back at *River*. "If you say so, then it's so."

Chapter 4

"**G**ood morning sleepyhead. I thought you'd never wake up. Did you have a good rest?" *Spy* looked up at his dazzlingly beautiful covermate, which reminded him that he now resided at Sanders and Bowman. "I slept great. What time is it?"

"It's ten o'clock already. I didn't want to wake you. You've had a stressful last forty-eight hours and I wanted you to catch up on your rest. Riding in that beat-up delivery van and then spending all of yesterday adjusting to your new home had to drain your energy."

"Thanks for your concern. I guess I was exhausted because usually I'm an early riser. *River*, what time do you usually wake up?"

"It varies, but usually around six o'clock. This morning I was awakened at five. You slept through it, but there was a little domestic quarrel over in the outdoors and nature section."

"Oh really, what was it all about?" asked *Spy*.

"A messy love triangle finally came to a head," said *River* unapprovingly. "These things never cease to amaze me. It's always the same. A book will cheat on his or her partner thinking it will remain a secret. Of course, nothing remains secret here at Sanders and Bowman. Don't these books realize that sooner or later their little discreet affair will be discovered?"

Spy gazed deeply into *River's* cover. "I agree with you one hundred percent. When two books make a commitment to each other, they should honor that commitment. I've seen books who pledge their faith one day and the next day they're diving into infidelity. What's up with that? Why bother?"

"I'm glad you feel that way." said *River*. "If *Wilderness Camping* felt the same, he wouldn't be dealing with this embarrassing situation he's gotten himself into. Once the dust settles from his breach of faith he'll regret what he's done. Most likely, *Beautiful World of Butterflies*, his partner of three years, will be gone. From what I hear, *Butterflies* is a wonderful lady, but she won't put up with philandering. *Wilderness's* month-long fling with *Exotic Songbirds* is gonna cost him the love of a good woman. He deserves whatever happens to him."

"You're right," said *Spy*. "He'll pay a hefty price."

"Hello *Spy*, and a good morning to you," *Destiny's* friendly voice called from behind.

"Good morning to you also," said *Spy*. "My friend, what's going on today at Sanders and Bowman? Anything exciting?"

"That guy is what's happening today." *Destiny* motioned towards the periodical area. "His name is Mike—and he's good. He works for Nathan. As you may know, Nathan is the largest book distributor on the planet. They also are a direct distributor of mainstream and specialty retail periodicals. They provide a vast product selection and a reliable order fulfillment service. They're here every Thursday. Usually it's Mike they send to service our particular Sanders and Bowman. Mike meets with Charles, runs through some paperwork, then works hand-in-hand with Jim the rest of the day.

"Jim and Mike have become quite close over the course of two years working together on a weekly basis. Nathan Book Group not only supplies bookstores such as ours, but they also serve libraries and specialty shops. Make no mistake about it, Nathan Book Group are in a class of their own when it comes to distribution. No one else comes close. Nathan is my distributor as well as *River's*, along with thousands of other titles among us. They're a powerful player in our industry."

Spy watched attentively as Mike worked the magazine area. He was amazed at the young man's efficiency and professionalism. Mike methodically pulled outdated periodicals from the racks and replaced them with newer issues, all the while chatting with Jim. *Destiny* was right, this guy was a real pro.

"*Destiny*, I knew Nathan was the largest book distributor, but I wasn't aware of the magnitude of their importance. I know that my creator, Roy, tried his best to acquire Nathan as my distributor. They never would take him on as a client. He later learned that they have a general policy of not accepting self-published works. He eventually cut a deal with a small regional wholesaler that was planning to go national. Roy knew one of the truck drivers who put in a good word for him at the office. The terms weren't so great, but we're still grateful to them for giving us a fighting chance. Roy and I are lucky to have them. We know the odds are stacked against us little guys."

"Don't worry," commented *River*, in an attempt to boost *Spy's* confidence. "All it takes is one break and you'll hit the big time. One well-placed review can send you soaring to the top. Never give up—you're too good. *Spy Needle* is a top tier entertaining novel. Never forget it!"

"That reminds me," hinted *Destiny*, "you promised us you'd finish your story. *River* and I want to know how Sonny Needle's adventurous life turns out. What do you say, *Spy*?"

"*Destiny*, that's a great suggestion," interjected *River*. "*Spy's* well rested and we've got nothing but time on our hands. It's a perfect setting for a bit of storytelling."

"Okay guys," said *Spy* sheepishly. "I know when I'm outnumbered. Where did I stop last time? What outrageous situation had Sonny Needle placed himself into?"

"If I remember right," *Destiny* answered, "Sonny Needle had just flown off into the clouds loaded down with gold. The old man in the cave was financing a mission of world peace."

"Oh yeah." *Spy* began to shine at the thought of narrating his main character's escapades. "The old man had lost his family to a war and had assigned to Sonny the responsibility of stopping all future wars. Sonny, with unlimited access to a literal mountain of gold, was now a world spy for peace. The non-materialistic Sonny, who cared nothing about money, now found himself one of the wealthiest humans on the planet."

River settled back to enjoy some prime entertainment. "All that money in combination with Sonny's energetic personality, not to mention his demanding task of achieving world peace, should make for some interesting situations. Carry on *Spy*!"

"You're so right *River*," said a now enthusiastic *Spy*. "It doesn't take long for Sonny to immerse himself into his new career. Sonny quickly establishes himself a base of operations. Selling off a sizable chunk of gold, he purchases a seaside estate on the Croatian coast. His new dwellings are strategically situated, allowing for unobstructed views of the rugged and picturesque Mediterranean basin. Sonny chose this particular area because it was central to two of the world's current hot spots, areas of conflict that would require his attention. His new jet could deliver him to either location in under four hours.

"Sonny had visited Croatia before on his around-the-world sailing expedition, getting on well with the locals. He had even recruited a gorgeous first mate from one of the coastal villages. In return for their warm hospitality, Sonny built an enormous home for Croatia's orphaned children. He also founded the International Wartime Amputees Society, just as the old man in the cave had instructed. It was a first class center for landmine victims. Landmine survivors from around the globe were provided physical and psychological rehabilitation assistance. They were taught how to reintegrate into mainstream society and regain their self esteem.

"Sonny bonded with this special group. He taught them how to have fun again. They soon accepted their injuries, even to the point of joking about their missing limbs. Sonny had a knack for turning negatives into positives and frowns into smiles. Now it was time to get down to business. After stocking his wine cellar with some of Europe's finest vino, Sonny directed his attention to his quest for world peace."

"Now the action will begin for Sonny Needle," said *Destiny*, speaking to himself as much as anyone else.

"Yes, *Destiny*," said *Spy*, "things quickly heat up for the ultra-cool espionage agent Sonny Needle. After two weeks of nonstop research on the subject, Sonny determines who are the good guys and who are the bad guys in one of the world's major conflicts. He comes up with a plan. The bad guys, a powerful nation intent on taking over the natural resources of a lesser nation, needed to be taught a lesson. It wasn't nice to steal from others.

"Sonny flies into the war zone. He pretends to be a journalist who is writing a flattering article about General Moyer, the commanding officer of the occupying forces. Sonny's cover story meshes perfectly with his inquisitive personality. No one suspects a thing. Sonny is granted total access to the general, following him around as he performs his evil warmongering duties.

"Sonny, in stealth-like fashion, soon began intercepting the coded messages between General Moyer and his bosses overseas. After two sleepless nights analyzing the data, Sonny broke the code. Then he went to work replacing the secret messages with bogus transmissions. Over the course of the next month, Sonny sent over one hundred phony reports, all containing very discouraging news about the progress of the war. Based on these negative reports from General Moyer on the front lines, the elected officials back home, thinking the situation was hopeless, decided to end their costly occupation.

"Troop withdrawal soon began. Military transport planes were loaded with soldiers and flown home. Sonny waved to General Moyers, along with the last remaining battalion unit, as they boarded the final plane departing the country. Sonny then sent for his own jet, which transported him and his two new girlfriends back to his seaside estate for a well-deserved holiday. There you have it—Sonny's first spy experience. I'd say it went pretty well."

"I'll say!" exulted *River*. "Your character Sonny Needle weaves in and out of danger with ease. He's as cool as they come. Kudos to your creator. Roy's imagination is incredible. *Spy*, let's hear more of Sonny Needle!"

"Yes, more of this entertaining character that takes the readers on a wild ride of international intrigue," *Destiny* agreed.

"Alright, if you both insist," said *Spy*. "I'll quickly run through a couple more of Sonny Needle's dangerous and sometimes humorous undertakings. One that comes to mind involves two small countries on the verge of war. Tensions between the two leaders had reached dangerous levels. It was a hair-trigger situation with both armies massed at the border awaiting instructions from their respective leaders. Sonny jetted in to assess the volatile state of affairs, hoping to diffuse it before it escalated into violence. His goal—somehow find a way to talk to both of the stubborn leaders.

"Sonny assumed the cover of an international jewelry dealer. He had brought with him several thick gold chains. Through a combination of charisma and bribery, Sonny maneuvered himself into one of the presidential palaces. He then requested to meet with the president to present him with a gift. Soon afterwards, he was invited in to have tea. Accompanying the leader was his wife of thirty years. Sonny gave each of them a gold chain, then sat down for tea and conversation. For two hours the three of them spoke, touching on many subjects. Remarkably the war issue was never discussed. Finally, Sonny said goodbye and left the palace.

"He immediately flew across the border. Using the same tactics as before, Sonny charmed himself into another presidential palace. Again he had a two hour session with a president. Joining them was the president's longtime wife. Their conversation branched into a variety of topics, but no one spoke of the dangerous face-off at the border. Once again, Sonny said his goodbyes and left the premises.

"At this point, *River* and *Destiny*, you're probably wondering why Sonny Needle didn't discuss the reasons behind the international conflict that was ready to explode into violence. My readers are puzzled by this also. Sonny soon answers that question. The young spy had a innate talent for understanding what made the human animal tick. Sonny's ability to size up the underlying motivating forces of human behavior proved especially useful in this case. He had gained valuable insight into the minds of the two leaders—and their wives.

"Both leaders were having marital problems. The leaders and their wives had become bored with each other. The spark was long gone in both marriages. The two presidents were subconsciously allowing their frustrations to manifest as threats of violence towards each other. Two boring marriages had brought their countries to the brink of war.

"Sonny went into action. He arranged to meet the leaders and their wives in a neutral location. After sharing his assessment of the situation, Sonny proposed a plan. The two leaders would *exchange wives.* Yes, Sonny had the gall to suggest that they trade spouses. After a brief silence, the four participants warmed up to this seemingly wacky idea. They reluctantly agreed to give it a try. The two presidents exchanged wives and went back to their palaces.

"Sonny's innovative peace plan proved to be successful. The leaders and their new mates were thrilled with the new living arrangements. As their domestic situations eased, so did the international relations between the two former rivals. Putting all their past differences behind them, they joined together to establish several social programs that benefitted both countries. A year later they actually merged into one nation. There's another example of Sonny Needle's deft leadership skills. Maybe he should have been a politician himself. What do you think?"

"Super!" exclaimed *River.* "I could literally listen to Sonny Needle stories all day. I'm serious, can we hear more? I'm certain *Destiny* feels the same. You are one entertaining novel!"

Spy glanced over at *Destiny.* "Do you really want to hear more? Are you sure I'm not overloading you with all this spy nonsense?"

"*River's* right," replied *Destiny.* "I absolutely want to hear more. I'm amazed at how Roy comes up with this stuff? He has quite the vivid imagination."

"Okay," agreed *Spy*, "if you insist. Like I've said before, I truly enjoy narrating the exciting life of Sonny Needle. Let's see—what's another Sonny story you guys might find stimulating? Oh, I've got one!"

"Good! Go for it," said *River* anxiously.

"This one is a territorial dispute. Two tiny island nations are preparing to go to war with each other. Both claim to own an uninhabited island that lies between them. A multinational company, Resorts Incorporated, had recently expressed an interest in purchasing and developing the island, intending to convert it into an exclusive resort. It was rumored that they were willing to offer a hefty price to the seller. Greedy politicians and business leaders from both countries, each thinking they would be the victor, were willing to spill blood rather than compromise.

"Sonny Needle learned of the dispute and quickly contrived a plan. Sonny made a call to his War Amputees Society and contacted a dozen of his friends. He told them to pack a bag.

He needed a favor from his well adjusted friends. They jumped on his jet and flew to the tropics. During the flight Sonny explained his plan. The group would arrive in the troubled region, pretending to represent an environmental research organization. They were going to sabotage the developmental plans for the little island.

"Upon arriving, Sonny whisked his friends away to a private location. Sonny then met with officials from both countries, along with a representative from Resorts Incorporated. Sonny informed them that his team would be conducting tests on the ecosystems of the coastal zones in the area, including the disputed territory. A landscape and population ecology report would be forthcoming the following day. Sonny chartered a boat and headed out to sea.

"Once the boat was safely out of sight Sonny set anchor. He uncorked a few bottles of vintage wine and unwrapped some gourmet cheese. After their leisurely lunch, it was time to go to work. Everyone on the boat was given a pair of scissors. They each took their scissors and cut into their clothing. They ripped into their shirts and trousers, tearing out huge gashes.

"Then each person was given a gigantic bottle of tomato ketchup. They splashed the bright red condiment all over their bodies, but especially around the area of their missing limbs. They laughed and joked as they strategically applied the ketchup to each other. Where there should be an arm or leg, there now flowed a stream of tomato ketchup. When they were satisfied with their appearance, they started back to shore.

"As they approached the coastline, everyone on the boat began screaming hysterically and waving frantically to those watching on shore. 'Help! Help! We've been attacked! Crocodiles got us! Help us!' they yelled at the onlookers, which included the officials from both islands and the corporate representative. 'Wild crocs live on the island! They tried to eat us! Please help us!'

"Horrified beachgoers looked on as the boat came to rest on the shore. It was a grizzly scene. Nearly every one of them was missing an arm or a leg from the crocodile attacks. As the bloody passengers crawled out of the vessel, they described what had happened.

"Hundreds of the ravenous reptiles had ambushed them on the island. Apparently these serial killers resented any intrusion into their personal space. No one would trespass on their island unless they wanted to become dinner. The angry crocodiles had violently ripped away arms and legs from the hapless environmentalists, devouring their limbs as they watched their victims writhe in agony. The island was an extraordinarily dangerous place. Only a fool would want to visit this island of horrors. Only a fool!

"Sonny took charge of the situation. He loaded the victims, all of them shrieking from the unbearable pain, some of them apparently near death, into a van and bolted towards the airport. He informed the horror-stricken witnesses that he was flying them to a trauma center on the mainland. They watched in shock as Sonny raced away with his cargo of half-eaten humans.

"Sonny's jet lifted off and the passengers burst into uncontrollable laughter. Their plan had gone off without a hitch. After they cleaned up, it was champagne and caviar for everyone. The flight back home was one big party. Sonny was greeted at the airport with good news. Resorts Incorporated's representative had rescinded his offer to buy the island. He had no desire to build a resort on an island inhabited by tourist-eating crocodiles. The leaders of the two rival nations also gave up all claims to the island. It would remain a domain for bloodthirsty reptilians. There would be no war. Sonny Needle, through some unorthodox methods, had once again stymied a potentially deadly conflict. *River*? *Destiny*? How about that one?"

"Hahahahahahaha! Oh that's funny, hahahahah!" Someone in the aisle behind them was laughing uncontrollably. *Spy* looked back and saw Sherry directly behind their section, partially hidden by the other books.

"She must be reading something very funny," *Spy* speculated out loud.

River shot *Destiny* a knowing grin. "*Spy*, maybe you're not aware of it, but she's laughing at your hilarious plot. She heard you! She's been listening to us for the last ten minutes. I saw her, but I didn't want to interrupt you. I was afraid you'd clam up and halt your brilliant narration of Mr. Needle's adventures. Obviously, Sherry thought it was as comical as we did."

Destiny laughed. "Staging fake crocodile attacks to stop a war! That's unbelievably funny! No wonder Sherry's laughing so hard that she's crying. I see Jeri looking at her now and shaking her head. It's cases like this that make some of her coworkers question her sanity. If they knew that Sherry actually communicated with books, they would really flip their switch."

Spy took another glance at Sherry as she wiped the tears of laughter from her cheeks. "I guess I should be flattered. I didn't realize I could have such an impact on someone. To be honest, I've never experienced anything like this. My story did *that*," glancing towards Sherry, "to a human being!"

"*Spy*," said *Destiny*, "let me explain something. Do you remember when I told you about the lady crying her eyes out over *River Run True's* touching love story? She couldn't control herself because the story overpowered her emotions. Maybe you don't want to admit it, but *Spy Needle* has the same effect on its readers. You just hit them from a different angle, knocking them to their knees with a big blast of humor.

"*Spy*, you need to face the facts—you're a masterpiece! Because you're self published, the industry has unfairly discriminated against you and your creator. Roy, who in my opinion is a certified genius in the field of entertainment, hasn't been allowed to test his product in the open market. I've never asked, but I'd guess that you've never been reviewed. The reason I say that is, if you had gotten some reviews, you'd be perched on the bestseller display by the register.

"One day, when the readers finally become aware of your existence, they'll begin voting with their wallets. When that occurs, they'll be no stopping you. The book industry will *have* to recognize you. Money talks, as they say. You just need a spark that will set you ablaze, bring you to the forefront of the literary world. One break, that's all it will take to send you flying into the heavens of superstardom. *Spy Needle*, you exhibit an inherent international flair.

"A book like you has a much larger potential market than myself, and if I dare say, also *River*. Both of us were written to appeal to a certain targeted readership. We're more of a sure bet than you, but we'll never reach the stratosphere of success. We weren't bred to be that kind of book. That's probably why we snagged major publishers. They knew they'd make a few bucks, build up a readership that would hopefully remain loyal to their authors, and possibly sell some future novels from our creators. That's okay, there's nothing wrong with that. *River* and I feel privileged to be associated with these deep-pocketed publishing houses. We've made it to the shelves of Sanders and Bowman riding their wave of support.

"In my case—I can't speak for *River* on this one—contracting with a major publisher was my only choice. My creator is not the entrepreneur type. He would never risk his own money to print, publicize and market me. I'm sure, that without a publishing contract, *Destiny's Fortune* would be nothing more than a frustrated manuscript stuffed away in some desk drawer or file cabinet with no hope for the future. Max would be typing away on his next project while I'm crying the blues and gathering dust. Overall I'm a happy book. I know I'll never be a blockbuster seller and that's okay with me. I can rest comfortably knowing my steady sales will guarantee my security. I am who I am and I'm content with my sense of stability in the literary world.

"Your situation, my humorous friend, couldn't be more different. I'm sure *River* would agree—*Spy Needle* is a novel that universally appeals to every age group, men and women alike. The cream will rise to the top. You were born into this world struggling for survival. The cold mean streets of the self publishing world are a tough place to hang your hat. They either kill you or toughen you up. Some of the greatest literary works of all time battled adversity. That gambling spirit that you and Roy possess shines through on your every page. When your lucky break finally arrives, the sky's the limit. You're not a back list type of guy—you're limelight material. I can foresee the day when *Spy Needle—The Movie* is a box office smash and fans are lining up worldwide for Roy to sign their book. You and Roy, if you can just get a bit of recognition, are destined for celebrity."

Destiny continued. "The industry has pushed you aside because you're self published. They need to learn not to be so arrogant. One day they'll regret that they didn't respect you. Those bean counters get sick to their stomach when they overlook a potentially lucrative cash cow. Make them pay for their snotty hubris. Let them read of your chart-topping success and foam at their greedy mouths. *Spy*, you have the potential to awaken the industry to the value of self published works. Give 'em their wake-up call!"

"Yeah *Destiny*!" *River* barked in agreement. "*Spy*, you've really got *Destiny* going. I've never seen him so passionate about something."

"I'm sorry I got so fired up," said *Destiny*. "Forgive me if I'm a little rough on the big boys who run the show. I am truly grateful to my wonderful publisher for accepting me into the family. Like I said earlier, without them I'd be condemned to an eternity of file cabinet loneliness. It's just that I genuinely feel for *Spy Needle* and all the other self published gems who aren't receiving a fair shake. Just one reviewer's mention of that hilarious crocodile fabrication scene that *Spy* just narrated is all it would take. Then *Spy Needle* would be off to the races."

"Thank you both for your concern," said *Spy*, looking at his two covermates. "I don't think I've ever had anyone really care about my life, except of course, my creator Roy. You two, in the brief time that I've known you, are already my best friends. I hope all three of us have success. Just like every other book here at Sanders and Bowman, our goal is to be purchased and read by a caring owner. However, if we have to spend years together on this shelf, you won't hear me complain. I couldn't ask for a better pair of covermates. I'm a lucky book to have friends like you."

River gave *Spy* a long soul searching look followed by one of her patented sweet smiles. "*Spy*, *Destiny* and I feel the same way about you. We think you're a special book and we're also proud to call you a true friend."

"Look!" *Spy* suddenly became excited. "Sherry's walking this way and looking right at us. I see her hand reaching up! I think she's going to pick me up and look at me. Yes, she isssss!"

Sherry expertly slid *Spy* out by the spine with one hand while gently pressing against *River* and *Destiny*. Before examining *Spy*, she looked back towards *River* and *Destiny*, reassuring them via her special communication skills that their friend *Spy Needle* was in caring hands. *Spy's* special brand of espionage had apparently sparked her curiosity.

Sherry wanted to see for herself what this engaging secret agent was all about. She was finishing her shift for the day and wouldn't return to work for two more days. This would provide an excellent opportunity to see what adventures lay between *Spy Needle's* covers. *Destiny* and *River* watched as Sherry walked over to Charles, held up *Spy Needle* for him to see, and asked him a question. Charles nodded his head in agreement. Sherry then walked out of Sanders and Bowman with *Spy* in hand, but not before giving his two friends one more reassuring glance.

Chapter 5

I t was Sunday. Sanders and Bowman usually opened one hour later on weekends. It was proving to be an especially long hour for *Spy's* faithful friends. *Spy* had been away for 63 hours, 52 minutes and counting. Just like a dog that waits on its owner, *River* and *Destiny* were fixated on the front door. They watched as the employees drifted in. Charles arrived first, in a good mood again, thank God. Then came Jeri, Heather, Joann and Ronnie.

A few seconds behind Ronnie strolled a cheerful Sherry. *River* quickly looked down at Sherry's hands. "Yes!" she roared. "She's got him!"

"Great!" said a relieved *Destiny*. "Now bring him back to us. Come over here. Bring *Spy Needle* back home. Come on, Sherry. Come on!"

Sherry didn't disappoint them. She sensed their apprehension as she walked towards shelf C22. As gently as she had earlier removed him from his home, she now placed *Spy* back snugly between his two joyful covermates. She smiled at the three of them before darting off to work.

"*Spy*, thank God you're back!" said *River*, pushing her cover ever tighter against *Spy's*. "I was so worried that I may never see you again. I haven't slept more than a couple of hours since you went away. Are you okay?"

"Yes, I'm fine," said *Spy*. He gazed back at his lovely covermate that was now holding him so tight. *River* was more beautiful than ever. "It's good to be back home."

"You look great," said *River*, as she analyzed *Spy* for signs of wear. "I would never guess that you were just read cover to cover. You still look as if you've never been opened. Did Sherry actually read you?"

"Sure she read me. It's just that Sherry treated me like a baby. No, I'm wrong, it was just the opposite. Sherry turned my pages as if I were a centuries-old piece of literature with brittle pages. I was treated like some sort of fragile antique. Actually, she barely opened me up at all. She didn't have to. Her special talents allowed her to absorb my every word even though she never saw half my text. There was no way she could've read the words close to my spine. Heck, I was never opened up more than an inch.

"Sherry spoke to me—I guess you'd call it speaking—the entire time she was reading me. She was constantly telling me to relax. It was as if we were simultaneously communicating with each other, me communicating through my pages of course, and she relaying comforting messages reassuring me that everything would be okay. It must have worked because I was never worried. I felt at ease the entire time I was with Sherry. Instinctively I knew I would be treated well and returned to my friends in perfect condition. My only concern was for you guys. I knew you'd be worried about me. But you see, there was nothing to worry about. Sonny Needle is still alive and well. I'm back!"

"*Spy*, please don't leave this bookstore again," said *Destiny* in a serious tone. "It was rough enough on me, but It was a lot worse for *River*. This little girl was worried to death that she may never see you again. I hope that we never have to go through any more emotional trauma. This experience got me to thinking about the meaning of our lives. Being purchased and taken care of by a loving owner—that's our ultimate goal. Odds are that if we're purchased, it'll be by three separate owners. That's the statistics anyway.

"Last night I prayed for a miracle. I asked that an avid reader, one who had a real love for all things literature, would come in to the bookstore, swoop us all up and tote us up to the checkout counter together. Then he or she would pay the cashier—I prefer Heather myself—and transport the three of us, all stuffed together in one cozy shopping bag to our new home, an eye-level shelf in a study surrounded by hundreds of other happy books. The place doesn't need to be fancy, just clean and filled with love. Then we could spend the rest of our lives together in peace and harmony.

"Oh, and another thing—this would create the perfect environment in which to hold a wedding. Celebrations of love are a lot of fun. I've always had this desire to be best book at a wedding. Just thought I'd float that idea out there. Any suggestions? I'll say no more about that. There you have it. That's the miracle I'm hoping for."

River's cover lit up with excitement. "Oh *Destiny*, you just described a perfect life. If that miracle actually occurred I'd be the happiest book in the entire world. It would be my dream come true. The three of us together for eternity—and I kinda like the part about the wedding also." *River* tucked herself even tighter against *Spy's* cover.

"Whew, this was tougher on you guys than I thought," said *Spy*. "To be honest, I got a little philosophical myself during the lonely nights at Sherry's place. After she finished reading me every evening, I too found myself asking the big question—what is our existence all about? Are we simply pieces of paper bound together or is there some existential reason why we derived from someone's intellect and imagination?

"Why were we chosen, of all the thought processes that occur in a human brain, to be deemed important enough to be transformed into written words, peered over by agents, editors and attorneys until we're considered perfect, at which point they slap a pretty cover on us and ask for someone's money in return for the right to read us. Wow! That's a lot of trouble to record a bit of brain activity. We must have originated from a special spot in the old medulla—know what I mean?"

River looked at her two friends. "I don't want to get carried away with all this, but for what it's worth, here's my take on life. As I exist today, I'm *River Run True*, a fictional account of a couple's undying love for each other. To me, it's simple. It's all about love. Whether it's humans, animals, books or whatever—love is the answer. I'm not saying this because I'm a love story. Even if I were a dry technical manual I'd feel the same way. We are who we are and we deal with it.

"Yes, we're very lucky to have made it this far. I'm sure there are many creative people who never expose their talents—put it on paper so to speak. Their masterpieces will reside in their imaginations forever. It's sad, but true. There are probably thousands of *Spy Needles* and *Destiny's Fortunes* trapped inside their owners' brains with zero hope of ever making it into manuscript form. Who knows, maybe they'll come back another day in another person and be given another opportunity to shine.

"What we do know is we're three novels sitting on a shelf at Sanders and Bowman Bookstore—three novels who are true friends and share a never-ending love for each other, regardless of what the future holds for us as individuals. We are blessed to have been placed together at this moment of our lives, so let's make the most of it. Okay, that's my personal introspective look into our purpose, our significance, our nature of life in our current form as books.

"Enough of this!" *River* exclaimed. "After that spiel I think I'm ready to hear you narrate another one of Sonny Needle's comical adventures—or maybe I need a glass of wine. Can books drink wine? Enough of this philosophical meandering. Let's loosen up a bit. *Spy*, thank God you're back. We missed you more than you'll ever know."

"I agree wholeheartedly," said *Spy*. "Let's have some fun."

River had just presented yet another angle of her diversified personality. *Spy* was once again impressed. *River Run True* was a very special girl, no doubt about it.

"*Destiny*, do you think Jim could give *River* a shot of that malt whiskey he's got stashed somewhere?" *Spy* jokingly asked.

"I don't know," *Destiny* replied. "Maybe we *all* need a drink after deciphering our cosmic significance. Well, what do you know—there's Jim standing right over there. He's pushing a cart filled with books. It looks like he's doing a bit of restocking. Hey, look! He's coming this way!"

Jim was in a hurry. He had to place a small batch of new deliveries and rush back to the stock room. A large shipment of business and investing publications were due to arrive any minute. Jim's cart came to a quick stop. Jim reached down, grabbed a novel, and slid it into place beside *Destiny*. Out of nowhere, with no warning, fate had delivered *Destiny* a new covermate. His name was *Stone Dance*. As quickly as he had appeared, Jim disappeared around the corner with another book in hand.

Destiny wasted no time in greeting the new arrival. "Welcome to the bookstore. My name is *Destiny's Fortune*."

"Hello. I'm *Stone Dance*. I'm only a two syllable title, so most books call me by my full name. Others know me as *Stone*. Feel free to call me whatever you like."

"*Stone Dance*, we're glad to have you here. I'd like for you to meet my two best friends. This is *Spy Needle* on the other side of me, and beside him is the lovely *River Run True*."

"Hello *Stone Dance*," *River* said politely, "and welcome to Sanders and Bowman."

"Hello to you and a real pleasure to meet you."

"And I'm *Spy Needle*, but you can call me *Spy*."

Spy sensed something special about this new arrival. Could it be? He had to ask. "*Stone Dance*, would you happen to be self published?"

Stone Dance immediately perked up. "Yes, I'm that rare beast, a self published novel that actually made it inside a bookstore. Don't tell me—are you one also?"

"You betcha! How do you like that! Two self published novels sitting on the same shelf. Oh, do I have some questions for you! Can you tell us about yourself?"

"Sure," answered *Stone Dance*. "I'm a little nervous. I still can't believe I'm in a major bookseller chain, surrounded by thousands of fellow publications. This is the major leagues, the heart of commercial opportunity. It's been a hard road I've traveled to get here."

"I can vouch for that." said *Spy*. "But don't worry, there's no need to be nervous. You're among friends here."

Spy and *Stone Dance* had already established an ironclad bond. They shared a common thread that other books would never understand. Only another self published novel could relate to their tales of hardship and struggle. It was difficult enough for a self published nonfiction book to attain success, but it was a needle-in a-haystack chance for a self published work of fiction to manage even the slightest triumph in the ongoing war for literary survival. *Spy Needle* and *Stone Dance* had grown up on the wrong side of the tracks. Now they both were fighting to break free from the chains that enslaved all self published novels.

Stone Dance looked around in every direction, still trying to adjust to his new surroundings. Relocating was a scary experience for any book, but more so for self published works. Unlike most of their companions, they constantly lived in a state of fear. At any time, they could be yanked off the shelf and placed into the discount bin, or worse, simply thrown into the trash. Their world was a fragile one that could crumble at any moment.

After a long moment, *Stone Dance* finally spoke. "I'm a political novel with a sole purpose. I was written to convey a political message though a satirical parable, an allegory that uncovers a dirty secret. Governments throughout history, from ancient times to modern day, have used various means of tricking their populace into backing wars of aggression. My little fable—I'm only 128 pages in length—concentrates on one method in particular. It's a form of state-sponsored terrorism that governments employ against their own people, and blame it on someone else as an excuse for a confrontation.

"It's an evil thought, but it actually happens. My creator heard of this sick tool of war, and after years of researching how it's been used in the past, decided to expose it. I became the bearer of the bad news. He named me *Stone Dance*. 'Stone' refers to superstone, a valuable resource that's the object of the aggressors. 'Dance' describes the politicians dancing around the truth. Lies surround every war, and this one's no exception. Essentially, that's my plot."

Spy waited for *Stone Dance* to continue, but he remained quiet. Finally *Spy* broke the silence. "That sounds like an interesting fable that illustrates a powerful moral. Did your creator ever make an attempt at acquiring a major publisher?"

"Yes, he did," *Stone Dance* replied stoically. "He actually contracted orally with a local literary agent. The agent was ecstatic after reviewing the manuscript. He informed my creator that he would have no trouble getting me published. He noted that I was a deftly written novel of wry humor, engaging suspense, surprising plot twists and memorable characters. He said I was an entertaining, thoughtful and recommended read from beginning to end. My creator was on cloud nine! His dream of becoming a published novelist was going to be a reality. He actually went out and purchased an expensive bottle of champagne in anticipation of inking the publishing agreement. And then…"

"Don't tell me," interrupted *Spy*. "Let me guess— someone spoils the party. Am I correct?"

"Correct you are, *Spy*," answered *Stone Dance*. "The agent enthusiastically submitted the manuscript to several top publishing houses, expecting a minor bidding war over who would purchase the rights to this outstanding little novel. Weeks passed by without a single reply. Finally, after two months without a response, the agent began to inquire about the status of the submission. All he got was a hush-hush runaround such as he'd never experienced in his entire career. They never denied the novel wasn't publishable. As a matter of fact, one editor privately disclosed that it was one of the hottest works of fiction to cross his desk in a decade, but that powers from above had halted it in its tracks. He stated that the decision had been made *above* top management level.

"Think about it—who or what is powerful enough to order major publishing firms *not* to publish something—and why? Our questions were never answered and it remains a mystery to this day. Anyway, my rebellious creator printed up

3,000 copies and worked his tail off marketing his little fable. He's sold several copies and finagled a few of us into some bookstores, but just like any self published work, we're looking for that big break that can grant us some exposure."

"*Stone Dance*, I feel for you and your creator." *Destiny* had been listening intently as *Stone Dance* described his roller coaster ride into the dark side of publishing. "Every time I hear one of these stories I think it can't be topped, and then along comes someone like yourself with an off-the-chart twisted tale."

"Yeah, I guess I shouldn't feel sorry for myself," said *Stone Dance*. "I'm not the only one that's been squeezed out in this industry. You have to claw your way to the top in this torturous business. I won't give up. Thanks to my creator I'm still alive and I'm gonna keep fighting until they destroy me. You can count on it!"

"That's the spirit!" *Destiny* roared. "We books need to stick together and fight for our rights. If I may, I'd like to make another comment on the state of our industry. There's something that's always bugged me about big time publishing people. A good book is a good book, right? A quality product is what matters the most. Well, no, not really. Let me tell you a quick story. This really happened to *Another Day Away*, a novel who lives three shelves below us. His creator, a nice chap by the name of Carl, was an imaginative writer who had a journalism degree from a respected university.

"For whatever reason, Carl chose to move household furniture for a living. Now I have to admit, you don't see many furniture movers who write novels in their spare time. In this case, however, Carl had real talent. He wrote, rewrote, edited and polished until the book was as good as it could get. It couldn't possibly improve. *Another Day Away* could have held its own against any novel on the bestseller list at that time. Sounds like a bright future for *Another Day Away*, huh *Spy*?"

"Yeah, but something tells me it's not going to be so easy," *Spy* replied skeptically.

"Your instincts are correct," *Destiny* continued. "At this point Carl gave a copy of the manuscript to a friend of his who managed a local bookstore. She began reading it and couldn't put it down. 'The best book she had ever read,' she informed Carl. She then passed it along to another friend. The same thing happened. 'Most spellbinding novel I've ever experienced,' was her exact quote. The manuscript eventually passed through approximately twenty of the bookstore's employees, all of whom were lifelong readers of fiction. Every single one of them raved on the literary merits of *Another Day Away*. This was obviously a book that was destined for greatness."

"I think I know what's coming next," *Stone Dance* interrupted. "Another tale of hardship in our wacky industry, right?"

"You're exactly right," said *Destiny*. "You should know. You've been through the publishing ringer yourself. So, here's what happened next. Carl's confidence is sky high after all the critical acclaim by this group of avid readers. Now remember, this group didn't include Carl's mother, sister and his heart-of-gold Auntie Sue. This across-the-board collection of readers constituted a genuine representation of the book buying public. These were hard core book buyers, passionate lovers of the written word. They were consumers who regularly spent their hard earned money for literary entertainment. They were the real target—the bulls eye, as they say—of the publishing marketers.

"Carl is full of confidence after all the positive feedback from this unbiased group of unofficial reviewers. He decides that it's now or never and finally decides to take the plunge. Carl makes the effort to get published, using a secret connection he had accidently stumbled upon while working as a furniture mover. You see, Carl had met a top tier executive of the largest publishing company in the world, and I mean that literally, *the biggest publisher in the world.*

"Six months earlier, Carl had been part of a moving crew that relocated this influential individual locally. Carl and his coworkers went to great pains to ensure the move went off without a hitch. They wrapped every piece of furniture before moving it so as not to scratch it. They took special care of the priceless antique china cabinet, knowing it was a family heirloom. They padded the floors and walls of the new home to keep it in its pristine condition. Not a smudge could be found anywhere. The move, all twelve hours of it, went perfectly. Everyone, especially the customer and his family, were thrilled beyond belief. It had been a professional job from start to finish. Each of the crew members were congratulated and given a generous tip.

"In the midst of all this happiness, Carl mentioned that he was writing a novel. He politely asked this influential decision maker if he would give his manuscript a quick look over once it was completed. The customer, this top management literary kingpin, told Carl to mail him the finished manuscript. He would have his professional staff analyze it and offer a professional opinion. Carl couldn't believe his luck!"

"Oh no!" said *Stone Dance*, anticipating a literary hurdle in *Destiny's* story. "What happens next for poor Carl?"

"Poor Carl is right," *Destiny* replied. "Carl did send *Another Day Away's* manuscript to the powerful publishing executive. True to his word, he did pass it down to his staff for evaluation. However, he made the critical mistake of mentioning the fact that it was written by a furniture mover.

The busy staffers placed it at the *bottom* of their stack of manuscripts. There was no way they had the time to read a submission from *a furniture mover*! What was their boss thinking? A furniture moving novelist! Whoever heard of such silliness? Furniture movers with intellect—no way!"

"*Another Day Away* never had a chance. Not one person bothered to read the first page. Carl's hopes were shattered. He should have sent the manuscript to other publishers, but instead he gave up hope. He became discouraged, quit his job, and started drinking heavily. Desperate for money, he sold his copyright to an unscrupulous agent for a paltry sum. That was the final straw that broke Carl's back. He soon lost all touch with reality, began exhibiting bizarre behavior, and was finally confined to a mental institution. *Another Day Away* was eventually published and its new owner reaped the rewards."

"That's such a sad story," *River* commented. She had been quiet, letting the boys have their say. "Sometimes I suppose it can all be too overbearing to handle. The editors, agents, publicists, reviewers and so on—why can't it be a simple process? Like you stated earlier, *Destiny*—a good book is a good book, right? In a fair world the furniture mover's manuscript would receive the same scrutiny as an established author's product. But no, no, no! *Another Day Away* remains on the bottom of the slush pile while someone with a PhD slapped in front of their name, or some ghostwritten celebrity account of a drug rehab experience, gets their inferior literary rubbish rushed through the publishing process to ensure a steady cash flow. I don't care what anybody says, that's just not right!"

"You tell 'em *River*!" boomed a fired up *Spy*. "I agree with you. Those nose-held-high rubber stampers and publishing know-it-alls sure could use a big fat dose of common sense. Sometimes they remind me of my creator's dog. Now don't get me wrong—I like Spotty. He's been with Roy ever since he was a pup. But he ain't the brightest candle in the church, if you know what I mean. I've seen him chase his tail in circles for hours on end. Then he'll turn around and complain that he's too tired to do anything constructive. Obviously, he's not rocket scientist material.

"Anyway, I also sometimes wonder about some of these uppity publishing decision makers. Their criteria for determining what is publishable sometimes seems absurd. They should just lay out all the potential manuscripts on the floor and let Spotty pee on one. Then publish that one. Heck, it would probably turn into a bestseller. Imagine that! I can see it now—everyone sitting around the boardroom table discussing their next big publishing project. 'Okay Bob, give Spotty some more water to drink and bring him in here to pee on these manuscripts. Spotty's urination method always gives us a bestseller!'

Stone Dance burst out in laughter. "*Spy*, you are funny! But you know, there's probably a lot of truth in your statement. Ha! The old canine weewee selection process—it's gotta work better than what they're doing now. Who knows—maybe my creator's cat could get a job peeing on pieces of paper."

"*Stone Dance*," said *Destiny*, "you ain't heard nothing yet. If you think that's funny you should let *Spy Needle* share some of his plot with you. Now *that* is some funny stuff. *Spy's* been entertaining us ever since he arrived. Right, *River*?"

"We love him," said a beaming *River*. We were a pretty happy bunch before he arrived, but his natural sense of humor lifted us up to a new level. You'd better never leave me! Do you hear me, *Spy*?"

"I'm not going anywhere without you," *Spy* answered. "If anyone purchases me they'd better have enough money to buy two books. Heck, make that four books—all of us will relocate together. We've all paid our dues in this crazy industry. We'll just retire in the sunset and relax the rest of our long lives."

"That sounds good to me," said *Destiny*. "Before we get too far off the subject I've got one more thing to add about how publishers and agents select their clients Listen to this and tell me if I'm right or wrong. This actually happened to my creator. It involves author bios. When Max first started in this topsy-turvy industry, he, like most beginners, had very little relevant experience. This turned out to be a major roadblock, that is, until he figured an innovative way around it.

"Most publishers and agents request that an author's biographical history accompany all manuscript submissions. I can see their point on this, as long as it doesn't override the primary objective, which should be the quality of the work itself. However, an author's bio shouldn't be a disproportionate determining factor as to whether the book is publishable or not.

"Look at it this way—suppose you visit someone's house for dinner. You haven't eaten all day and your stomach is growling, ready to be nourished. After what seems like endless small talk, dinner finally arrives at the table. You dig into a luscious looking mouth-watering homemade baked lasagna. That first glorious bite really hits the spot. You're thinking to yourself 'this must be the most delicious lasagna I've ever had in my entire life.'

"And then it hits you—you forgot to ask the cook about her cooking background! 'Oh my God! How can I eat this wonderful dish without finding out how much cooking this lady has done in the past.'

"So you ask her about her previous experience in the kitchen. Amazingly, she explains that this is her first attempt at preparing lasagna. Although you're ravenous to the point of starvation, you throw down your napkin and storm out of the dining room. There is absolutely no way you're going to eat this delectably delicious dish.

"As good as it is, her lack of culinary credentials won't allow you to do it. She's never cooked lasagna before! The gall of this lady! She actually thinks that you're going to consume this dish, no matter how scrumptious it may be, without first checking her credentials! Her cookery bio is in dire need of some fattening up, not to mention some documentation. This was her first time cooking lasagna! The nerve of this woman! No way!

"Insulted like you've never been insulted before, you rush off to a fast food joint to gobble down a paper thin substance that's advertised to be beef. The big sign in the parking lot documents the fact that this establishment has been proudly serving their wafer sized minced beef patties for decades.

"Satisfied that their burger bio meets your high standards, you finally relax to enjoy your nutritionally deficient, but certifiably edible and officially credentialed grease-laden feast. As you're munching away on your tasteless corporate offerings, you think about your close call. You nearly ate a culinary creation from a cook who lacked any valid accreditation. Oh, how lucky you were to escape!"

"Hah *Destiny*, you hit the nail on the head," said an amused *Spy*. "That's a brilliant and accurate analogy. I get the connection. The delicious lasagna dish represents a professionally written manuscript submission. Both are exceptional products, that, in a practical common sense world, would be appreciated for their obvious superior qualities. But no! The creator of the lasagna lacks an official culinary resume, much like a writer may not possess a prestigious bio.

"Twisted logic must be applied! The cook and the writer must be punished for their lack of a polished past. Their heinous crimes cannot be overlooked. Off with their heads! Throw the lasagna out for the raccoons to devour! Use the manuscript for toilet tissue! Although they're masterpiece creations of the highest caliber they must be destroyed. That is the unyielding law of the morons and it must be enforced. We will eat junk and print junk. Those without a past will have no future!"

"There you go again, *Spy*," chuckled *Stone Dance*. "You crack me up. That's a hilarious analogy, but there's a lot of truth in what you and *Destiny* just described. Here's another outrageous, nearly unbelievable, tale of bureaucratic blundering within the publishing empire. I heard my creator sharing this story with a fellow writer.

"Several years ago, a frustrated unpublished novelist conducted an experiment. He had submitted his manuscript to numerous publishing firms and was rejected every time. After receiving a mailbox full of generic rejection letters, all stating the same old we-are-sorry-to-inform-you line of rhetoric, he began to doubt that they even bothered to look at his work.

"To confirm his suspicions, he contrived a simple test. He took a bestseller classic novel from a decade back, *Dreams of the Stars*, and typed it into manuscript form. He changed the title to *Star Wish* and attached his name as the author. He submitted copies of the manuscript, which had sold millions of copies throughout the years, to thirty top publishing houses. Sure enough, just as he had suspected, the letters came rolling in. The we-are-sorry-to-inform-you notices were replicas of the ones he had received denying his own novel.

"One of two things had to have occurred. *Dreams of the Stars* had suddenly become a worthless literary work, or more likely, the publishing companies never bothered to look at the manuscript. The truth was obvious. It was clear that they had slushed this proven masterpiece away into the cellar, followed by a forwarding of the obligatory rejection slip.

"How crazy is that! A documented bestseller is turned away by the entire publishing industry! It's a wonder these so-called intellectuals can tie their own shoes. They should be grateful they're employed in the literary trade because they'd never survive the real world. They'd be eaten alive in the human jungle of common sense. Without their fancy diplomas to hide behind, they'd be nothing more than tasty morsels of scholarly egghead to be preyed upon by the masses. God help them!"

"What a story!" exclaimed *River*. "And you know what? *Stone Dance*, you've got a humorous way with words yourself. Tasty morsels of scholarly egghead—that's comical! What is it with you self published novels? Are you all comedians at heart? Even *Destiny's* on board the humor wagon describing lasagna accreditations. You've all put me in a laughing mood. *Spy*, I'm finished with my subtle hints. Why you don't you entertain our new friend with a fresh sample of Sonny Needle's warped worldly solutions? Sonny always puts a smile on my cover."

"*River*, you know I can't say no to you," replied *Spy*. "*Stone Dance*, she's put a spell on me. I don't know how she did it, but she's got me happily obeying her every command. Well, let's see. I need a Sonny Needle classic for *Stone Dance* to enjoy. Which story will I choose—there's the time Sonny rode a hallucinating Russian moose into the Kremlin after they both accidently ate some psychedelic mushrooms—then there's the tale about the cargo plane that was converted into a flying brothel which crash landed inside the Vatican. Yes,

Sonny was aboard this bordello in the sky, but he assured the Pope it was all in the line of duty.

"Amazingly, these seemingly innocent incidents coincidently resulted in two separate peace agreements in different parts of the world. Some speculate these events weren't really accidents at all, but were really staged by Sonny to achieve a political purpose.

"Wow," marveled *Stone Dance*. "Your character Sonny Needle has a unique way of solving international conflict."

"That's for sure, my friend. Maybe you'd enjoy this humorous, but successful espionage account. Sonny sneaks into a secret Pakistani military installation to sabotage a new generation nuclear weapon prototype. This highly destructive device has threatened to raise the arms race to unheard-of levels. Sonny, dressed as a scientist, confidently strolls past the armed guards into the most secured area of the facility. He heads directly towards the massive nuclear bomb. Opening his knapsack, he removes a huge container of common household glue and begins pouring it into the sensitive compressed core of the weapon.

"Sonny is instantly surrounded by a legion of security officers. Sticking their guns in his face, they demand to know what he's doing. Sonny calmly relates to them that he is pouring a toxic chemical paste into the nuclear core, something he has been authorized to do by the president. He explains that it will result in the weapon becoming more lethal than ever. Sonny provides some bogus documents proving his story. Satisfied, the guards release him and he ambles out of the facility, casually flirting with a pretty female scientist along the way.

"Later that month, Sonny noticed an obscure article in *Modern Weapons Magazine* that mentioned a failed testing of a Pakistani super nuke. The nuclear core had mysteriously locked up, destroying the fission process and causing a failure to detonate."

"Ha, *Spy Needle*," said *Stone Dance*. "Now I'm beginning to understand why everyone's so crazy about you. You're great! Your creator must be some kind of genius to come up with this stuff."

"Maybe I'm biased, but I'd have to classify Roy in the brilliant category," *Spy* said proudly. "Okay, back to Sonny. Those previous examples typify his problem solving technique. There's also the poop incident that occurred in Beijing. The Chinese military were ceremoniously inducting the latest member to join their central ruling committee. This particular fellow was known for his hard line approach regarding armed conflict.

"Suddenly, amid the pomp and celebration a huge flock of pigeons passed over them and unceremoniously dumped a load of smelly bird doo on their heads, bringing the festivities to a hasty halt. This embarrassing episode stalled the career of the ambitious politician. Several Chinese newsmen later reported witnessing a foreigner, who curiously resembled Sonny Needle, feeding a especially tasty brand of laxatives to some hungry pigeons.

"Oh, I almost forgot! Here's another war stopper. This concerns a particularly hawkish American official, with a reputation for being somewhat trigger happy, who was fired from his high administrative position. He was officially relieved due to poor work performance, but the real reason was his recent affliction of bromhidrosis. Bromhidrosis is a condition of abnormal or offensive body odor.

"In other words, this guy stank! This dude had so much bacteria growing on his body he could've started a germ farm. For some mysterious reason, his apocrine glands were working overtime to produce massive amounts of pure stink.

This individual's rancid stench permeated the entire Pentagon, driving his coworkers into a malodorous retreat.

"Several of his associates finally refused to work with this fetid carrier of rankness until he took action to remedy his body odor problem. The foul-smelling official tried everything, but nothing could disperse the thick brown stinky cloud that followed him everywhere he went. He was soon fired. Shortly after the dismissal, Sonny Needle checked out of a plush Washington D.C. hotel.

"The housekeeping staff later discovered a huge empty bottle in his room. It contained a warning label that read '*Use this product in extreme moderation. Concentrated axillary bacteria can result in excessive stinkiness.*'"

Everyone listening burst out in laughter. Once again, *Spy* and his ace character Sonny Needle had delivered. Smiles were abundant, especially the one gracing the beautiful cover of *River Run True*.

Chapter 6

"Hey, *Spy*, guess what I just saw?" *Destiny* was in a jovial mood today. "They just posted the proposed event schedule for the next few months. It's not official yet, but the famous actor Kris Richards is on the tentative list for a book signing. I hope it goes through. You know he plays a spy in his movies, don't you? You should listen to what he has to say."

"Thanks for the info," replied *Spy*. "Yeah, I'll probably listen to him, seeing as we're both secret agents. Hey *Destiny*, do you have a minute? I've got something I'd like to discuss with you while *River* is napping."

"Of course I do," said *Destiny*. "What's on your mind?"

Spy looked back to make sure *River* was still asleep. "Remember the other day when you mentioned that you would like to be best book at a wedding? Well, I'd like to provide you with that opportunity. I'm thinking about asking *River* to marry me, but I want your advice first. Am I moving too fast? Do you think she'd say yes? *Destiny*, you're so much wiser than I am. I look up to you like a big brother. That's why I didn't want to do anything without talking to you first."

Destiny's huge grin hinted at his answer. "First of all, thanks for all the compliments. *Spy*, you and *River* are my best friends. I'm closer to you two than I am to my own brothers. I love them dearly, but they're in various bookstores, warehouses, and I hope, happy homes scattered around the world. You and *River* are *here*. The three of us share this shelf at this particular Sanders and Bowman outlet. This is our home. On a daily basis we share our dreams, our misfortunes, and our personal views of this crazy literary world we were born into.

"I've known *River* now for three months. She's the sweetest little novel in the bookstore. *Spy*, I've only known you for a relatively short period of time, but I feel I'm a pretty good judge of character. You're honest and true. I see the spark that ignites every time you two look at each other. Both of you are in love. You could ask *River* to marry you today and she wouldn't hesitate in accepting your proposal. I'm sure of it.

"The only suggestion I can offer is to let it come naturally. There's no big hurry. Don't sweat out how, when and where you're going to ask for her hand in marriage. One day the two of you will be talking and the words will just pop out of your mouth. She'll say yes, and just like that it'll be done! No stress, no worrying and no sleepless nights pondering various proposal techniques. Ease into it and before you know it—you're *River's* fiancée! Then we'll start planning the big ceremony, and yes, I'll accept any offers to be best book at the celebratory union of my two best friends. I hope I've answered your questions."

Soaking in *Destiny's* words of advice, *Spy* was momentarily quiet before responding. "*Destiny*, you're the best friend I could ever ask for. You'll never know how much you just helped me. Sharing your wisdom has put my mind at ease. I'm blessed to know you. I know *River* feels the same way. If you're right, and *River* agrees to take me as her lifelong mate, I'd be honored if you would be best book at our wedding.

How about it? Would you be best book at the union of *Spy Needle* and *River Run True?*"

"Now that you've officially asked, the answer is yes. I'd be overjoyed to be a part of your special day. Nothing would please me more than witnessing my two best friends exchange vows of love. Your happiness is my happiness. The two of you were meant for each other. It's obvious. It doesn't take a genius to figure that one out. The love you're experiencing is genuine. It's real. It originates from your souls."

Spy's cover tingled with emotion from *Destiny's* words. Suddenly he felt movement from his other side. *River* was stirring. She had somehow sensed the vibrant flow of emotions that had permeated his text. She had felt his love for her. He was sure of it. It was if she was reading his mind.

"What are you boys up to?" asked *River*. "Something positive I hope."

Destiny gave *Spy* a wink. "Oh, *Spy* and I were just discussing the fact that, due to the presence of carbon dioxide, the polar ice caps on Mars sublime in the summer, and then reform again in winter. You believe us, don't you *River?*"

"Yeah, right!" laughed *River*. "And I was just dreaming about molecular quantum mechanics. You believe that, don't you?"

The three of them broke into laughter. "Well," said *River*, "I guess I'll allow you males a bit of bonding privacy. I'll ask no more sensitive questions, at least for now. Maybe you'll give me a straight answer to this benign question. What's happening here at the bookstore today? Anything exciting?"

Spy was quick with a reply, happily changing the subject. "As a matter of fact, we've just received some good news from the fitness and nutrition section. This came straight from the mouth of *Naturally Fit & Firm*, who witnessed the whole thing. It concerns Donna. The plan they've had in the works for weeks fell into place this morning."

River became excited. "Oh, the plan to help Donna lose weight and gain back her self esteem! Tell me *Spy*, what happened?"

"They timed it perfectly. With Donna approaching their area, the signal was given to push *Forties Fitness: Let's Eat Right & Exercise* out into the aisle. The whole shelf, working together as a unit, shoved her off the shelf an instant before Donna rounded the corner. Donna immediately picked up *Forties Fitness* to place her back in her designated position. She slipped her back into position. It seemed that the operation had failed.

"Then the incredible happened. Donna pulled *Forties Fitness* back from her resting place. She quickly thumbed through several pages. Apparently *Forties Fitness* captured her attention. Donna walked over to a step stool, sat down and began reading this practical guide to good health. The fitness and nutrition books watched and held their breath as Donna intensely reviewed their good friend.

"Finally, Donna rose up and walked towards Heather's cashier station. The books observed closely as Donna, utilizing her employee discount, purchased *Forties Fitness*. She then punched the clock to end her shift, reading *Forties Fitness* as she walked out the door.

"It was a scene of mixed emotions within the health section. There were tears of joy and sadness as the books waved goodbye to their good friend. *Forties Fitness* had been living among them for nearly a year. Most likely, they would never see her again. Even though she would be residing in a loving home with Donna, they were all sad to see her go. Hopefully her mission will be successful and Donna's physical and mental conditions will improve. So that's the report straight from *Naturally Fit & Firm*. It's good news, even though it's tinged with some sadness."

"Life can be complicated sometimes," said *River*. "I certainly hope Donna reaps some benefits from *Forties Fitness*. Everyone in the health section sure put out the effort into helping our friend in need. They sacrificed a friendship for a greater good. I'll pray for Donna's recovery and for *Forties Fitness's* happiness. I know Donna's an avid reader, so *Forties Fitness* should have plenty of fellow books to help her adjust to her new surroundings."

"I have a gut feeling that everything will work out fine," said *Destiny*. I know that *Forties Fitness* is a common sense fitness manual. She doesn't contain any of the gimmicky fads that the weight loss industry is notoriously famous for. *Forties Fitness* is also splashed with abundant amounts of *Spy Needle*-style humor. I think that's exactly what Donna needs right now. She needs to laugh her way to a thin body. Mark my words. Six months from now Donna will be strutting around here showing off her new body. That's what we want—a happy Donna. Happy employees make for happy books!"

"You're so right," said *River*. "That reminds me of another morale problem here at Sanders and Bowman. Charles! I heard he went on a kicking and screaming rampage yesterday morning. No humans witnessed it, but plenty of books did. As usual, he was the first one to arrive for work. He was muttering to himself from the time he entered the bookstore. Apparently he's now officially divorced and he's not taking it so well.

"Shouting profanity—thank goodness he wasn't near the children's books—he finally erupted and kicked a shelf located in the sports section, causing *Rugby's Heroes: Tough & Talented* to fall out on the floor. He then picked up *Rugby's*

Heroes and flung him across the room, where he smashed violently against the far wall."

"How terrible," gasped *Destiny*. "Did he survive?"

"If it had been any other book it would have been disastrous. *Rugby's Heroes*, as his descriptive subtitle suggests, was built to sustain a blow. He's a solidly constructed hardcover made from top notch materials. He possesses a spine that's as strong as steel. There are larger books that reside in the rough and tumble neighborhood of the sports section, but none of them are foolish enough to challenge *Rugby's Heroes*. He's the toughest of the tough. Of all the books that could have fallen from the shelf, it happened to be *Rugby's Heroes*, the only one that could have survived Charles's act of violence. The book world was lucky yesterday."

"Oh my," sighed *Spy*. "By a stroke of luck we averted disaster yesterday, but what about tomorrow, or the next day? Something needs to be done."

"You're not the only one with that concern," *River* answered. "The health section floated around some ideas yesterday. They agreed that the best solution is to help Charles. We all know he is really a good hearted person. He's just having a difficult time coping with his divorce. The consensus everyone arrived at was that Charles needs professional advice—in the form of a book, of course. *Divorce: Coping & Caring* courageously volunteered her services. She's really quite brave considering Charles's inclinations towards violent behavior.

"The tricky part of this equation is how to get *Divorce* into the hands of Charles—and make him read her. They've organized a think tank that's focusing solely on this project. They're bouncing around some creative ideas. One of the more innovative suggestions involves Charles receiving written instructions to read *Divorce*. How in the world this message would be delivered I don't know. I suppose other employees would be involved. Who knows what they'll come up with? All I know is we've gotta try something."

"I agree," said *Destiny*. "While we're on the subject of our handlers, I think I should mention that Joann has completed the final draft of her novel. *Loved Twice* overheard Joann telling Thomas that she's already contracted with an agent. They're submitting *Mercury Girl's* manuscript to a major publishing firm. Let's keep our fingers crossed and hope for the best."

"We'll all be rooting for Joann and *Mercury Girl*," said *River*. "Hey look! Here comes Thomas heading this way. He's with the representative from Globewide Distributors. You know, they're the supplier of the travel publications. It looks like he's got a brand new box of travel books with him. Look, he's placing them right in front of us!"

Everyone listened as Thomas conversed with Globewide's representative. After discussing the particulars of the recent shipment, Thomas invited the young salesman to lunch. He quickly agreed and they exited the store, leaving behind the latest hot-off-the-press travel guides. *Spy* couldn't wait to pick the brains of these global know-it-alls. Just like his character Sonny Needle, *Spy* was a travel fanatic. Learning about distant lands and different cultures from these seasoned pros would be a special treat.

"Hello to all you worldly adventurers down there," thundered *Spy*. "Welcome to Sanders and Bowman. My name is *Spy Needle*."

"Hi *Spy Needle*," replied a friendly voice. "My name is *Destination Singapore—Singapore* to my fellow books."

"You can call me *Spy*. Can you tell me about yourself? I bet Singapore is a wonderful place."

"It sure is. I was printed in China and much to my surprise I was shipped through Singapore's busy port. You talk about a proud book! My brothers and I strutted like peacocks during our two week stay. Singapore was *our* town! None of us could read a word of Chinese, but let me tell you, that didn't stop those pretty little Asian publications from coming on to us. I would've married one of them if I could have stayed in Singapore. It's true what they say—those Asian ladies sure take good care of their men. Whoa mama—put out the fire! Let me die in Singapore and I'll die a happy man. We were in our element—Singapore books in Singapore! We were treated like rock stars."

"Sounds like a nice place," said *Spy*, "especially when you're a guide to the city. It must be nice being a travel book. I'm envious. If I ever come back in another life I want to be like you—a guide to the entire world."

"Who needs the world when you have Belgium!" a voice proudly proclaimed. "It's nice to meet you, *Spy*. My name is *A Guide to Belgium*. It's the most underrated country in Europe."

"A pleasure to meet you also. I've heard some good things about Belgium. Can you share some of your information? What makes Belgium special?"

"Let me explain," said *Belgium*. "French fries aren't French fries, they're Belgian fries. They originated in Belgium and the best of them still reside there. The double dipped frying method is the secret. Throw a little special sauce on them and you've got a real treat. And it's not just potatoes—did you know that the French travel to Belgium when they want to *really* dine? Oh, the pleasures of a big plate of fresh mussels when they're in season, washed down with an Orval Trappist ale. I bet you didn't know Belgium possesses the absolute tastiest beer in the world. Well, now you know. Beer lovers from around the globe travel to Belgium to experience their fine brew.

"Another thing—our capital Brussels is also the official capital of Europe. Every important decision affecting our continent is formed there. Belgium is international in every respect. Wanna speak French—*Je parle francais*. Wanna speak Dutch—*Ik spreek Nederlands*. Gotta converse in English—no problem. *Spy Needle*, if you truly want to see the whole world, make sure Belgium is your last stop. Once you arrive there, you won't wanna leave. Living is an art in the marvelous country of Belgium."

"Wow," said *Spy*. "I would have never known so many wonderful facts about Belgium. You travel guides are a special breed. Anybody else got any comments?"

"I'd like to tell my story," announced a colorful hardbound book. "I'm somewhat different from most travel guides."

"By all means, go ahead," replied *Spy*. "We're all ears."

"Thank you. My name is *All Aboard: Riding the Toilet Train*. You can call me *Train*. Please don't laugh, at least not yet. My creator is not insane, just a bit eccentric. I know it's an unusual subject, but we're selling like crazy. Apparently, toilet bowls and urinals are a hot topic in today's modern world. We've even been translated into French. I guess the French appreciate the aesthetic architectural craftsmanship that goes into these various houses of excrement. We're going into a fifth printing next month. Who would have ever guessed a book about international defecation dwellings would become so popular? I used to be self-conscious of my subject matter, but as sales skyrocketed I overcame my inferiority complex. Wanna hear some toilet tales from around the world?"

Spy turned and looked at the amused audience. "Judging from the grins on everyone's covers, I think I can safely say we're all interested in your topic. Please *Train*, tell us more."

"Okay, there are at least a thousand different styles of toilets throughout the world. These lavatories, bathrooms, johns, whatever you might call them—they serve a vital purpose. I'm sure early man was quick to learn his doo needed to be consolidated in one area. Even those hunter-gatherers had enough sense to realize smelly substances splashed around the cave wasn't conducive towards prehistoric romance. It certainly wouldn't land them on the cover of *Cave Dweller Magazine*. What I'm trying to say is toilets, in one form or another, have been in existence for a long time.

"Toilets run the gamut from the most basic to luxurious. My first chapter describes primitive outhouses that perform their designated functions, but nothing else. My final chapter explores high-end lavatories that contain every extravagance imaginable, from spas to billiard tables.

"That's right, a billiard table in the toilet! Whatever floats your boat and to each his own, but personally, I have absolutely no desire to shoot a game of pool in the restroom. What if you accidently knock your ball off the table and it rolls into an occupied stall? Do you ask for it back? If so, what is proper billiard-in-the-bathroom etiquette? 'Excuse me sir, but if you haven't wiped yet, would you please hand me that eight ball lying between your legs?'

Several of the books chuckled. "Sounds like we have yet another comedian in the house," *River* commented to no one in particular. "*Train*, let's hear some more. Who knows how long Thomas will be out. We can't waste this valuable time."

"Sure," said *Train*. "Toilets are constructed from every material imaginable. Turn my pages and you'll see lavatories made from wood, concrete, porcelain, plastic, metal and glass. On page 76 you'll even see a creative architectural achievement made from snow and ice. It's a real beauty standing tall amidst the arctic landscape. This product of Inuit ingenuity is aesthetically pleasing inside and out. It's an outhouse to be proud of. And the best thing about it—no more yellow snow dirtying up the front lawn!

"Skim over to page 98 and you'll see a rather unusual toilet. This one's made completely from sand. A group of backpackers had established a beachfront community on an isolated island off the coast of Cambodia. The pristine waters and fresh ocean breezes created a perfect stopover locale for the young adventurers. However, it wasn't long before they agreed on the need for a communal toilet. Nothing could ruin a pleasant morning swim in the ocean more than running head on into some floating mystery material. The result was an elaborate beach bathroom. Check out the photograph to see for yourselves.

"Speaking of floating, in chapter six there's a picture of an Amazon River outhouse that's frequented by fishermen answering nature's call. Another mobile toilet is shown on page 124. This one's attached to a bicycle ridden by a young entrepreneur. The lack of bathrooms at a popular European tourist site inspired this teenager to create one—and charge a handsome sum for a five minute visit. He claims the profits paid his entire university tuition."

"*Train*," said *River*, "your creator sure knows his toilets. What inspired him to write a book about such an unusual subject?"

"The idea came about after several international toilet mishaps over the course of several years. It seems my creator was destined for a life of toilet turmoil. After enduring a number of embarrassing bathroom episodes, he decided to put his experiences into book form. If I remember right, the first one occurred in an airport restroom in Honduras. San Pedro Sula, I think it was called, was an industrial city in the northern part of the country. God only knows what he was doing there. He was always working hard at some scheme so that he wouldn't have to work hard. Figure that one out if you can.

"Well, what happened was this. My creator was stranded for several hours at this old airport. That's another thing about my creator—he was always trying to save a little money by flying cheap airlines. He'd stay in some dilapidated airport for half a day to save a penny. This wayward airport certainly fit that description, at least back then."

"Sounds like he's kinda tight with his money," commented *Spy*.

"Tight's not the word for it. Cheapskate's more like it, but he's a lovable cheapskate. Anyway, a couple of hours into this sweaty layover, he needed to go to the bathroom. So he enters the toilet area and goes inside the stall. Of course the door won't shut, but that's okay. All operations proceed smoothly and he exits the stall. Now it's time for him to wash his hands, but he faces a small dilemma. The floor beneath him, where he would normally place his bag, is covered in a layer of sludge, some of which looks suspiciously like bits of human waste. Now if there's one thing my creator is proud of, it's his travel backpack. It was a gift from a friend and he's not about to set it down in the oozing brown slime gathered beneath his feet."

"Oh my God!" exclaimed *River*. "What did he do?"

"Before I go any further, I first need to tell you what's in his bag. My creator, a notorious light traveler, is carrying the basic essentials—a change of clothes, toiletries, those sort of things. However, at this point in his life, he's really into fitness and exercise. Unbelievably, along with the bare necessities contained in his bag are two forty-pound dumbbells. Eighty pounds of heavy iron. *Eighty pounds*! And he prides himself on traveling light! Don't ask me why anyone would decide to wander aimlessly around the globe lugging eighty pounds of dead weight, but that's what he did. Wanna hear something funny? He'd get so tired hauling those weighty things around that he never had the energy to use them. To regain his strength from dragging around those cumbersome chunks of steel all day, he'd drink beer and eat doughnuts all evening."

A couple of the books snickered. *Train* looked up at his smiling audience. "Well, so much for his fitness and nutrition program. Let me continue with the story. My creator needs to wash his hands, but he's not about to place his treasured backpack into the disgusting puddle of mystery material that covers the floor. Seeing that no one else is in the toilet, he decides to rest his bag on the remaining sink while he cleans his hands. That way it will remain clean and sewage-free. My genius creator heaves his metal-laden bag from his shoulder and places it on the sink beside him. BOOM! SMASH! CRACK! The noise is unbelievably loud.

"The sink has fallen right off the wall and broken into a thousand pieces. The plumbing pipe is broken and water is shooting from the wall. His backpack lands in the smelly sludge, splashing it all over my creator's clothes. Now he's looking at a skeleton of a washbasin dangling from a wire, his beloved bag is lying in a pool of filth, and he's completely covered in a loathsome brown film.

"To make matters worse, in rushes a concerned citizen, alarmed by the explosion originating from the toilet. The native Honduran looks at my creator covered in recycled feces and then stares at what remains of the sink. He shouts a few curse words in Spanish at my creator and runs out the door screaming '*Policia! Gringo loco! Policia!*' Now my creator understands just enough Spanish to know that *policia* sounds awfully close to the word police. That can't be a good thing.

"Knowing that time is of the essence, my creator grabs his soiled bag and heads out the door. He walks as quickly as possible towards the opposite end of the airport, trying not to call attention to his sewage covered body. Finding a corner to hide in behind a large group of people, he curls up as small as possible and pretends to read a book. He carefully peaks up from behind his book to see two machine gun-wielding security officers racing towards the other end of the airport. He has no doubt they're looking for the idiot gringo who had vandalized their public property.

"Somehow he managed to escape their detection for the thirty-minute period before he boarded his flight. My brown and smelly creator had a row to himself on the plane, for no one dared sit near this stinky foreigner. He arrived in Tegucigalpa and immediately disposed of his trouble-making dumbbells, never to pick one up again. So there it is. That's the first incident, the spark behind the idea of a book about toilets."

Stone Dance had been listening intently, captivated by *Train's* storytelling skills. "That's funny. So after this Honduran toilet mishap he began writing your manuscript?"

"Oh no," replied *Train*. "The idea of a book didn't occur until later. It was three years and several toilet episodes later that he finally committed to creating me. The Russian incident inspired him to immediately commence with my outline."

"That must have been interesting," said *Stone Dance*. "What happened in Russia?"

"It was another embarrassing chapter in my creator's life. By the way, he doesn't confess in the book that these events actually happened to him. He puts it in third person form and attributes all this stupid maladroit behavior to someone else. I, and now you guys, are the only ones who know the truth—my creator is a bumbling dunce. Let's keep it to ourselves, okay?

"Several years back, he decided to spend a summer traveling around Russia. What was he doing there? I won't go into any details, but it was another one of his get-rich-quick schemes that turned sour. Upon arriving in Moscow, my weary master made his way to his hotel. After a refreshing nap, he strolled down to the lobby to familiarize himself with his new surroundings.

"Suddenly he had the urgent need to go to the toilet—extremely urgent! This was a real emergency situation. Maybe it had been the long flight, or maybe something he had eaten, but something was playing havoc with his innards. He was seconds away from an international intestinal disaster. He darted off to the nearest restroom and made it in the nick of time. I mean it was a real close call.

"My creator waited for several minutes. He wasn't taking any chances. When he was finally confidant that the crisis had passed, he progressed to the next step, wiping clean the affected area. That's when the second challenge appeared. No toilet tissue! If my master had bothered to read his travel guide, he would have learned that Russian toilets sometimes lacked paper—especially the cheapo places where he opted to stay. So my brilliant creator contemplates his situation. He decides to wait until someone comes into the restroom and ask them for some paper. Then he remembers he doesn't speak a word of Russian.

"Desperately my creator searches for something—anything that will do the job. He looks in his coat—nothing. He looks in his wallet—nothing. Finally he reaches into the pockets of his trousers. He's in luck! He finds several pieces of paper he had stuffed into his pocket after his arrival at Moscow airport. Instilled with a sense of relief he quickly finishes the job. Whew! That had been a close call!

"Breathing a sigh of relief, my masterful one sets out for the streets of Moscow to do a bit of sightseeing. While walking on Red Square he was approached by a policeman. 'Papers please,' the officer asked brusquely. 'Sure,' replied my creator, reaching into the pockets of his trousers. Then it dawned on him. 'Oh no!' He had used his Russian travel documents as toilet tissue! He had flushed them away not realizing their importance. The soiled papers were probably now making their way through the city's sewage system.

"He tried to explain his situation to the police officer, but the officer would hear no part of it. My creator was hauled off to jail. He would spend two days there while the embassy researched the validity of his wild tale. Yes, that was the incident that led to my publication. I guess I should be grateful that my creator is a misfit, otherwise I would've never made it into existence."

"That's hilarious," said *Stone Dance*. "Your creator must be quite the character. He sure put himself in some difficult situations. It's hard to top a tale about using important documents as toilet tissue."

"You're right," replied *Train*. "It is hard to top, but wouldn't you know it, my creator raised the bar on stupidity with his next wipe job. I'm sure they are others who would like to speak, so I'll save that one for another day."

"Please continue if you would," asked *Spy*. "I think I speak for everyone here when I say we're absolutely entertained by your sidetracked creator. We all want to know—what did he do next?"

"Okay, if you insist. If you enjoyed the previous toilet tissue mishap, then you'll love this one. One summer my master and a friend toured America on their motorcycles, camping along the way. They would pitch their tents in various locations, but never a campground. My creator claimed that he liked being away from the crowds, but the truth of the matter is he didn't want to spend money renting a campsite. Anyway, after a particularly long day riding through the scenic Pennsylvania countryside, they set up camp in an isolated field among some beautiful oak trees. They kicked back, ate dinner, enjoyed a glass of wine and retired for the evening.

"Rising early the next morning, my creator decided to take a little walk and soak in the rural atmosphere. Well, halfway through his walk, he had the uncontrollable urge to release a bowel movement, number two as they say. Being a country boy at heart, this didn't bother him in the least. He picked a secluded spot and let nature take its course. Upon completing his bodily function, he realized he didn't have any toilet paper. Once again—no big deal. Growing up as a kid on a farm, he had innovated many times. Wiping with some fresh leaves would do the trick. Looking around, my wordsmith genius grabbed a handful of leaves, raked them off the vine and finished the job. Feeling relieved, he jogged back to the campsite to his awaiting friend.

"They set out on their bikes for another day of sightseeing. It was a gorgeous day for riding. My master and his friend were in motorcycle heaven touring the Pennsylvania countryside. Late afternoon, as was their custom, they began keeping their eyes open for a suitable camping site. Rounding a bend in the road, they spotted an attractive little diner tucked back into a forested area. It was a perfect location to spend the night. They could set up their site, have dinner at the diner, and walk back to their tents.

"They pulled their bikes into the tiny parking area of James' Café. Dismounting his motorcycle, my creator paused for a moment to stretch his six-foot frame after the long ride. This was when he realized something wasn't right. He felt an unpleasant itching sensation originating from his posterior. My brilliant one chalked it up to riding for hours in the saddle. He was sure it would subside. The two of them entered the diner.

"Immediately they were greeted by a cordial gentleman. 'Welcome to James' Café,' he bellowed. 'I'm James.' They exchanged some small talk with the friendly chap and were seated. As they glanced over the menu, the itching around my master's buttocks increased. He began furiously scratching his behind as if he were digging for gold.

"At this point a kindly old lady appeared from the kitchen area. 'Hello, my name is Etta, wife of James. Would you gentlemen like to order?'

"'I'll have the beef roast,' replied my creator's companion.

"Etta then looked towards my master, still frantically raking his fingers at his hindquarters. Now he actually had one hand stuck *inside* his jeans plowing away in discomfort. 'And you sir, what would you like?'

"My creator was oblivious to the old lady, preoccupied with his burning buns. 'Sir, would you like to order?' she asked again. Still he didn't reply.

"Etta then turned to my creator's friend and calmly commented, 'looks like your buddy has a bad case of ivy butt. I haven't seen scratching like that since my dog dug up my garden looking for a gopher.'

"My master suddenly perked up and asked, 'ivy butt, what's that?'

"Etta looked at him and shook her head. 'Ivy butt occurs when a person, usually a city dweller, is forced to use leaves after visiting nature's bathroom. They grab the closest available green leafy plant they see and wipe away, not having a clue as to what they're sticking up their you-know-what. We country people ain't botany experts, but we're picky about what kind of plant we rub around our hindquarters. I prefer toilet tissue over poison ivy myself, as do most of us country folk.'

"Poison ivy! A look of horror appeared on my master's face. He had wiped his butt with poison ivy! 'Oh my God! What can I do?' asked my white-faced creator.

"'Ain't much you can do until Dr. Shackleford opens up in the morning. He ain't much for curing ivy butt past five o'clock. It's gotta be a real emergency to get him out in the evening. I'd suggest you have a few drinks to help you get through the night. Tomorrow morning James will take you to the doctor and he'll shoot you up with some steroids. You'll be better by day's end. You ain't the first ivy butt patient he's seen and you won't be the last. Just last month a city slicker tourist passed through with his tush on fire. The doc fixed his butt right up.'

"To finish this story, my master made it through the night, and sure enough, the doctor cured him the next day. Quite the embarrassing tale, huh? You can read about it in chapter eight, but as usual, this foolish adventure is attributed to someone else. My master's not about to admit this actually happened to him. Catching a big dose of ivy butt isn't something he's proud of."

"Oh my lord!" exclaimed *River*. "That's funny and horrible at the same time. I can't imagine using poison ivy as toilet paper. The embarrassment must be the worst part. It's really amazing what our creators are capable of. Mine's a bit eccentric like lots of artistic people, but I thank God that Lola never got ivy butt. I don't think she would've ever recovered emotionally."

"I've got a sidetracked creator tale you might enjoy." Everyone looked at the paperback resting on the far corner of the table.

"My name is *Amsterdam Delights*. Call me *Amsterdam*. Yes, I'm a travel guide for that wonderful city in the Netherlands. Amsterdam is famous for bikes. That explains my cover illustration of a pretty girl riding a bicycle."

"Your cover is very attractive and colorful," said *Spy*. "I've heard Amsterdam is an interesting city filled with characterful buildings. Has quite a history also, if I remember correctly."

"You're right," replied *Amsterdam*. "The city's steeped in history and as colorful as my cover. My creator found that out the hard way. Would you guys be interested in hearing of another wretched author mishap?"

"Go for it," crowed *Stone Dance*. "These misguided creator tales are great. We love 'em, but they're human beings with faults. Writers stumble like everyone else, maybe more so."

"Stumble is the operative word for this story," said a grinning *Amsterdam*. "Okay, here's what happened to my brilliant but sometimes bumbling creator. Richard's his name. Richard spent six months in Amsterdam researching every angle of this delightful city. My story concerns his first night in town. Richard arrived in Amsterdam as excited as a kid on Christmas morning. He grabbed a bus to his hostel and checked in. Yes, another tightwad. Hostels are friendly and inexpensive. The cheap aspect is what appealed to my creator. Richard probably makes *Train's* master look like a high rolling big spender. He gives a whole new meaning to the term penny pincher. I guess it's the struggling writer syndrome, but he takes it to a new level.

"Anyway, Richard, anxious to explore the city, drops his bags off in his dorm and hits the streets. After walking for an hour or so, he feels the need for a little break. It's cold outside, so he doesn't really want to sit on one of the outdoor benches. This gives rise to a tightwad's dilemma. He looks through the window of a nearby coffee shop. Everyone appears to be enjoying themselves in their warm and toasty environment. Tightfisted Richard sneaks inside and slides into a corner table, hoping to escape detection from the wait staff. The last thing he wants to do is purchase a cup of coffee. That costs money!

"Richard's plan failed. Within minutes a smiling Dutch gal approached him and asked what he wanted to drink. Of course, my creator inquired as to the price of a cup of coffee. Three euros! The miserly one nearly fell out of his chair. My creator wasn't about to pay three euros for a coffee. He was on his way out the door when the waitress informed him that they were running a special on Heineken beer—only one euro per beer!

"At this point my teetotaling creator made a decision that would come back to haunt him. There was no way he wanted to go back into that bitter cold, but buying something he wouldn't consume wasn't his nature. 'Give me a beer,' he said. The words just popped out of his mouth without any thought. The comforting warm confines of the coffee shop seemed too inviting to leave.

"The pretty waitress came back with a frosty mug of beer. My creator reluctantly handed over one euro. If any of you know someone who's tight with their money, then you can imagine Richard's internal struggle. He doesn't consume alcohol, but he had just spent one euro for a beer. He thought about trying to sell it to another patron, but quickly realized that was a stupid idea.

"Once again he acted spontaneously—he picked up the beer and gulped it down. All of it! He guzzled every drop. 'That wasn't so bad,' he said to himself. At least now he wouldn't sulk around after wasting a euro on a beer he didn't drink. Then a funny thing happened. A warm and fuzzy feeling swept through his body. Suddenly everything was wonderful. Acting impulsively and totally out of character, my Richard ordered another beer! He spent another euro for a beer. And he doesn't drink!

"Well, some of you may suspect trouble brewing. You would be correct. My creator chugged down the second beer in the same manner as the first. Didn't leave a drop! Then my buzzy writer orders a third beer and down the hatch it goes. Then a fourth, a fifth, and so on. Between number six and seven someone passed around a cigarette. Richard doesn't smoke, but what the heck, it was free. So he took in a big lung full and held it in as long as possible. A few minutes later, unbelievably, he bought a round of drinks for the entire crowd. 'Everybody, drinks are on me!' he exclaimed, waving his arms in the air. My lovable creator was now the life of the party.

"Okay, let's flash ahead to beer number ten. The hour is late and my creator is the only customer left in the place. My Richard's no longer the main event. As a matter of fact, he's in bad shape. He can't walk, can barely hold his head up, and is moaning and groaning something about sleeping in the coffee shop. The bartender and his girlfriend, well past the polite stage, are on the verge of throwing him out the door. Finally, after threatening to call the police, my creator waddles out the door and plops himself on the sidewalk. The bartender and his girlfriend lock up and go home, leaving their wayward tourist to fend for himself.

"A couple of hours pass and Richard awakens. It's now three o'clock in the morning He is half frozen, has a pounding headache, and is covered in vomit. Now keep in mind, Richard is a relatively sophisticated, normally well dressed intellectual sort. This homeless lifestyle is brand new to him.

Richard has a single thought—making his way back to his hostel.

"After navigating his haggard self through Amsterdam's streets and alleys, he finally found the hostel. Now he would get some sleep and regroup from this horrific nightmare he was living. He turned the knob on the front door. It was locked! Then he remembered that unlike normal hotels, hostels had late night curfews. They lock up at midnight. This was normally a non-factor to the mild mannered, early-to-bed Richard, but it posed a major problem to the transformed let-it-all-hang-out party animal that he had become.

"Richard tried everything. He knocked again and again, called on the intercom system, yelled for help, even threw pebbles at the windows above him. Nothing worked. He thought about sleeping in front of the door, but there was a likely chance he would freeze to death. My desperate creator then made a survival decision. Across the street stood the prestigious Grand Amsterdam Hotel. This stately five star establishment was the lodging choice for old money Europeans, politicians, celebrities, and for one night only, a misguided vomit-covered travel writer.

"My Richard stumbled his way past the grand entrance, approached the front desk, plopped down a credit card and asked for a room. The shocked attendant took a look at the poor pathetic creature that had strayed into this domain of the rich and hesitated for a moment, not knowing whether to check him in or call the authorities. He hurriedly processed the card and quickly ushered their hapless guest out of sight to his 300 euro-per-night suite.

"That was Richard's first night in Amsterdam. It cost him a bundle, but he learned a valuable lesson. He hasn't touched a drop of alcohol since. He went on to write the best guide ever to the fantastic city of Amsterdam. He's still got his flaws, but he'll always remain my hero. I love him."

"Incredible!" cried out *Destiny*. "Our creators are works of art themselves. The things they can get themselves into! Do we have any other entertaining tales from you guys?"

"I've got one that you might enjoy," uttered a soft spoken female voice. Everyone looked over at a thin staple bound booklet with a generic style cover, barely noticeable sitting atop a stack of adventure travel guides.

"My name's *Telluride*. Actually my full name is *Telluride Trekker*. I'm self published, as you can probably tell from my appearance, but don't let my size and bland cover fool you. My creator packs a big punch in a tiny package. I'm actually the top seller in Telluride Covers, the local bookstore. My creator is not the shy type, as you'll soon find out. Many of you may know of Telluride, the pint sized ski resort in Colorado that's renowned for its breathtaking beauty, along with the occasional celebrity sighting. It's a hiker's paradise in summer. That's what I'm all about. The famous actor Kris Richards, who I'm told will be speaking here, skis and hikes Telluride quite regularly.

"Nan, that's my creator's name, is as independent as they come. She just turned forty years old and still weighs about a hundred pounds soaking wet. Nan's never relied on anyone, especially a man. She tried marriage one time and it turned out miserably. She married who she thought was her dream man on her twentieth birthday. He turned out to be a womanizing drinker. She uncharacteristically put up with that for a few months. Then he upped the stakes by slapping Nan in the face one drunken night.

"Boy, what a mistake that was! Nan tore into him like a woman possessed. She connected with a left hook that bloodied his nose. She followed that with a tooth-removing right uppercut. Nan closed the deal with a powerful kick to the groin area, leaving him with a swollen black and blue reminder of his lecherous activities.

"Nan threw a few possessions in a bag, jumped in her van and headed west. She spent the next few weeks mending her soul in the spectacular Rocky Mountains. She established a routine of driving for a couple of hours every morning, hiking to the top of a mountain, and camping for the night. One morning Nan pulled into the picturesque village of Telluride planning to spend one night. Little did she know she would live there the rest of her life.

"What happened was this. Nan met a friendly young girl while trekking in Bear Creek Canyon. They shared a lunch and had a chat. This amicable Telluride native urged Nan to stay in town for awhile, even suggesting that she apply for a recent job opening at Telluride Resort and Spa, a hotel that catered to the town's moneyed tourists.

"The next morning Nan did just that, and much to her surprise, landed a position working the front desk of the spa. The job matched Nan's gregarious personality perfectly. My creator fell in love with her work, enjoying her newfound life in the charming town of Telluride.

"Three years passed quickly. Nan kept busy at work, but also found time for her passion, trekking the scenic mountains that surrounded Telluride. She began taking notes on every hike, and eventually self published a trekking guide. That would be me! Nan priced me right and got me displayed in the bookstore window. Now all the tourists could see me as they strolled down Telluride's main drag. Sales skyrocketed and I soon became known as the hiker's bible.

"Telluride is virtually crime free, but every now and then some fool will drift in and try something stupid. It's been that way forever. The Butch Cassidy gang robbed their first bank there. Criminals assume Telluride's laid back residents won't resist. Maybe that's so for some of them, but not my Nan.

"One lovely autumn afternoon Nan arrived at her desk. It was a quiet day at the spa, as most of the tourists were outside enjoying the unusually warm weather. One guest politely waited as Nan prepared for her shift. The Telluride tranquility would soon be disturbed. Preoccupied with some paperwork, Nan never heard the bandit quietly enter from the patio door. 'Give me all your money!' the masked intruder demanded.

"Nan looked up to see a bear of a man holding a pistol inches from her face. Evil flowed from his cold distant eyes. Let me tell you something. If you knew my creator, you'd know there was no way she was going to let someone push her around. No way!

"'I'd be glad to give you my money,' my Nan replied calmly, 'but that policeman standing behind you won't let me.' The stunned robber instinctively turned his head for a split second. Now of course there was no policeman behind him, but that was the opening my hundred-pound dynamo required for her assault. As the would-be-thief turned back towards Nan he was greeted with a thundering blow to the chin that sent him flying through the plate glass window behind him. With one punch my heroic master had remedied a dangerous situation. She retrieved his gun and walked towards the hapless criminal. With the hoodlum lying bleeding amidst all the broken glass, you'd think Nan's defensive duties would be over. Not so!

"She stood over this giant of a man and looked him in the eyes. 'You did a bad thing,' Nan said, 'and I want you to say you're sorry.' The outlaw, still in shock, said nothing.

"'Listen to me!' ordered Nan. 'I said apologize! Apologize to me and to God and to your mother! You did a bad thing. Now, I'm going to ask you once again, tell me you're sorry!'

"'I'm sorry,' whimpered the goliath criminal, with tears in his eyes. Nan sat down on the monster's chest and put her hands around his neck. 'Say it again—louder!' she demanded.

"'I'm so sorry and I'll never do it again! I apologize to you and God and my mama!' the humiliated thief cried out, desperate to escape the clutches of his tiny captor. Nan was finally satisfied. By this time the police had arrived and she relinquished over control of the luckless lawbreaker.

"So the incident ends peacefully, at least for the good guys, but that's not the end of the story. Earlier I had mentioned that there was one guest present during all this. That guest turned out to be Bobbi Taylor, the famous talk show host. She had witnessed the whole thing. Wouldn't you know it, she had Nan on her show the following week. After that we had orders coming in from all over the world. People who had no intention of visiting Telluride were buying us up. *Telluride Trekker* was actually a national bestseller for a couple of months."

"What a wonderful story," said *River*. "A true heroine. Don't underestimate a woman—right *Telluride*?"

"That's right," said *Telluride*. "You'd better treat us with respect or you may wind up on the floor like that no-good robber," laughing at herself.

"Uh oh, looks like our party is over," said *Spy*, looking towards the bookstore entrance. "Here comes Thomas and the Globewide guy. Must've been some lunch. It's three o'clock already."

"Their long lunch was a feast for us also," said *Destiny*. "I haven't been entertained like that in a long time. *Spy*, this group's about as funny as you are."

"Heck, *Destiny*, they put me to shame," replied *Spy*. "These travel books are the best. You gotta get off the couch and go! That's how you get stories like these. Sitting around watching daytime TV ain't gonna get you anywhere. If you wanna experience this short life you gotta make the effort. Step out of your comfort zone with a one way ticket to anywhere. You won't regret it."

"Couldn't have said it better myself, *Spy Needle*," agreed *Singapore*. "Good luck to you works of fiction. Don't worry, we'll be seeing you around. By day's end we'll all be dispersed among the travel section. If you guys ever make it our way, please drop in for some conversation."

"You got a deal," answered *Spy*. The novels then watched as the Globewide distributor made his way towards them. The young man hoisted the box of travel guides upon his shoulder and rounded the corner.

Chapter 7

I t was quite the disturbance. Even the old-timer hardbacks admitted they had never seen such. It all started in the check out area. The man broke in line at Heather's cashier station, much to the annoyance of the other customers. He then plopped down a couple of books and demanded a fifty percent discount. Heather politely informed him that she wasn't authorized to give such a discount. The man then exploded into a rage, picking up the books and hurling them back at Heather. Heather ducked and the books flew past her, one of them striking Linda in the face.

Mario, hearing the disturbance, raced from the security office. At this point the madman turned and ran towards the back of the bookstore. Mario, an ex-football player, then cut him down with a savage tackle. The two men crashed into the corner shelf of the fiction section, completely demolishing it and scattering its occupants.

Books flew everywhere. Most of them were launched down the aisle, piling upon each other at the base of the magazine rack. Others slid on the polished floor like a runaway sled skidding on a sheet of ice, some of them traveling all the way into the home and gardens section. Two of them shot straight up in the air, coming to rest on top of an adjacent shelf, not to be discovered until three months later. One book streaked like a bullet across the main aisle, coming to an abrupt stop after striking *Season of Smiles.*

Amazingly, both books escaped injury. This unannounced spectacular arrival of a new neighbor stunned the shelf's residents, which included *Spy, River* and *Destiny.*

Mario wasted no time. He picked up the malicious troublemaker from behind with a powerful bear-hug and carried him away kicking and clawing. The Sanders and Bowman staff immediately went to work cleaning up the mess. Ronnie picked up the big pieces of the shattered shelf and hauled them to the trash bin. Sandra and Sherry each grabbed a broom and swept away the remaining debris. The misplaced books were placed on a cart.

Incredibly, none of them sustained serious damage. The southland classic novel *Randolph County* was the only book rendered non-sellable. She had smashed head-on into the periodical shelf breaking off a corner of her front cover. Charles watched as Joann picked up *Randolph County,* telling her to keep the damaged book for herself. The fortunate novel was going home with Joann. A better home she couldn't have asked for.

Something occurred during the early stages of the cleanup that made the books gain even more respect for Thomas. Several of the books had a bird's-eye view of the chaotic scene. Immediately following Mario's apprehension of the culprit, they noticed a disturbing sight. Sticking out from a nearby shelf, in plain view, was the nose of a liquor bottle.

There was only one person who could've placed it there. Jim's long time hiding spot had been exposed. Not only that, but Thomas was making his way over to appraise the damage. The store manager would surely discover the nearly full bottle of Scotch whiskey. The books looked on helplessly. They didn't want their good friend Jim to get into trouble, but there was nothing they could do. The books watched as Thomas appraised the situation, scanning the affected area. Suddenly his eyes locked onto the half-exposed bottle.

Thomas hesitated for a moment, seemingly unsure of what to do next. Then he leaned his head out into the aisle and called out "Jim, can you come over here and organize a cleanup? This place is a mess."

Thomas walked away just as Jim arrived. The books couldn't believe Jim's good luck, and theirs, as they watched him grab the bottle and stuff it away in a box. It had been a close call. Thomas reappeared several minutes later to check on the progress of the cleanup detail. Jim walked over and stuck out his hand.

"Thomas," he said, "sometimes we get so busy around here that we don't take the time to tell others how much we appreciate them. I'd like to tell you now how much I enjoy working for the best manager in the Sanders and Bowman chain. Oh, and by the way, I'm going to make a special effort to address some personal problems I have. Maybe it'll also improve my work performance."

Thomas reached out, placed both of his hands around Jim's outstretched hand, and held them firm for a few seconds. He looked Jim in the eyes. "That's great, Jim," he said. "That's great."

The efficient staff worked diligently at restoring the wrecked area. Within two hours it looked as if nothing had happened. Ronnie had found an extra bookshelf from the storage room. It fit perfectly where the old one had stood. Sandra, Joann and Jeri had replaced the books back in their proper order. Jim had even positioned a few newly arrived novels on the shelf. Soon everyone had put the morning's unusual event behind them and were back at their regular jobs. Sanders and Bowman was once again back to normal.

Aside from the two books resting at the top of the shelf, which would remain undiscovered for three months, there was one more book that escaped the attentive eyes of the staff. The novel that had slammed into *Season of Smiles* was not just any novel. It was *Didi's Adventures: Flight of Enlightenment*, the number one selling book in the *world*, according to *Weekly Publisher*, the definitive source for publishing news. *Didi's Adventures* was a comedic novel about a space alien on a one-year mission to research human behavior.

The timing of the book's release had corresponded with a unprecedented wave of interest in everything extraterrestrial, propelling the novel's sales into the stratosphere. The first time author, Luis Concepcion, a hotel bellman by trade, had been transformed into an overnight celebrity. Yes, a very famous subject had crash landed on *Spy Needle's* doorstep. It didn't take long for the inquisitive novel to inquire about one of his favorite subjects, life among the stars.

"Are both of you alright?" asked *Spy*.

"I'm fine," replied *Season of Smiles*. "I'm a tough ole gal."

"I'm alright also," answered *Didi's Adventures*. "Just an achy spine, but I'll be okay."

"Great cover you have, *Didi's Adventures*. Let me introduce everyone to you. You're the hottest seller on the planet, so we obviously know who you are. You've met *Season of Smiles*, the hard way I might add. From right to left after *Season*, you have *Stone Dance*, a proud-to-be self published novel. Then you have my true friend and my life advisor, *Destiny's Fortune*. Then myself, *Spy Needle*. Call me *Spy*. Then you'll be looking at the most beautiful girl in the universe inside and out, the one and only, the classic love story *River Run True*."

"It's nice to meet you all, even if it is under some unusual circumstances. Yes, my name is *Didi's Adventures: Flight of Enlightenment*, but I'm known around the world as *Didi*. I'm now in sixty-eight languages, so it helps to have a simple name."

"Wow *Didi*, you are international," said *Spy*. "Who knows how long you'll be here before they discover you, so I'm gonna bug you with a few questions if you don't mind. It's not everyday that we've got a celebrity in our house. Is that okay?"

Didi chuckled. "I may be a celebrity, but I'm only one of seventy million copies floating around the globe. I don't mind. I getting used to all the attention by now."

"Seventy million!" exclaimed *Spy*. "I knew you were popular, but I didn't realize you were *that* popular."

"Yeah, it's true. As a matter of fact you'll soon be calling me *Didi One*. That's because the sequel's coming out next month. So there's going to be two of us. They're predicting six million copies of *Didi Two* will be sold the first day."

"Six million the first *day*!" squealed *River*. "That's an incredible number. All that attention must be difficult for you to deal with, not to mention your creator."

"Like I said earlier, you kinda get used to it. You brought up a good point though. Being under a public microscope has been a bit difficult for my creator. You gotta remember, Luis wrote me while working as a hotel bellman. Most of his friends didn't even know he was writing a novel. He'd heard plenty of horror stories about the publishing industry, so his expectations of success were low. Then—Boom! He and I were an overnight success."

"I heard something about that," said *Destiny*. "Would you mind telling us how that occurred?"

"I don't mind at all. That's one story I never tire of repeating. One day Luis is toting a guest's luggage to his room.

Well, the guest turns out to be a literary agent. Not only that, but he's of Cuban heritage, just like my Luis. Anyway, they hit it off together and this agent agrees to look at the manuscript. Then things start happening quick—very unusual for our industry. Within three days Luis and the agent had signed a contract. One week later a major publisher agreed to take on the book. Forward to a year later, pretty quick for this business, and Luis is a multi-millionaire flying around the world signing books. Incredible, to say the least. I still pinch myself sometimes to remind myself this is all real."

"It is amazing," said *Spy*. "You mentioned the instant fame affected your creator in some negative ways. Could you tell us about that?"

"Oh yeah. Luis grew up poor on the streets of Havana. He made his way to America on a six-foot makeshift boat, nearly dying of thirst and exposure on the way. He worked his tail off in America, but barely made ends meet. Then *Didi's Adventures* transforms him into a literary hero. Suddenly money, glitz, glamour and girls, above all the girls, invade his simple life. He's hanging out with presidents and prime ministers, titans of the business world, and celebrities of every genre. It was a lot to throw on his plate in one serving. His sanity survived, but he had it rough for awhile. If any of you hit the big time, the best advice I can give to you and your creator—stay grounded! Remember that fame and fortune alone doesn't bring happiness."

"Words of wisdom well noted," said *Spy*, nodding in agreement. "Changing the subject a bit, how did the idea for *Didi's Adventures* come about? Is Luis a real believer in life amongst the stars?"

"Absolutely so," replied *Didi*. "For years he'd always wondered what the superior alien races thought about our underdeveloped society. As we books are well aware, those humans are capable of some silly endeavors. Late one evening, while stargazing, the plot for *Didi's Adventures* just popped in his head. What if he wrote a story of an intergalactic visitor, an extraterrestrial being from another world—a personable young male alien would be the primary character—who came down to earth on a mission to observe and record human behavior? The results would be hilarious from an alien point of view."

"The idea certainly struck a nerve with the public," commented *Destiny*. "You can't argue with seventy million fans."

"You're right about that," agreed *Didi*. "I think what happened was this. Luis has a natural sense of humor. He can discover humor in the most mundane aspects of day-to-day life. When Luis applied his slightly twisted view of human activities to the character of Didi, this warm and friendly chap from another universe, the readers fell in love. Luis turned Didi into a member of the reader's family. It also helped that Didi himself had faults. The readers learn this early on. Just because Didi's an alien of supreme intellect, it would be incorrect to assume he's not capable of making human-like mistakes. Throughout the book, Didi constantly reminds the readers of this. Some of the situations he gets himself into are outrageously funny. Overall, everything blended together to make *Didi's Adventures* a delightful read."

"*Didi*," asked *River*, "is there any particular passage from your text that strikes you as a favorite?"

"Well, I have a few, but if I had to choose one it would be when Didi falls asleep underwater. He has to do a lot of explaining to wiggle his way out of that one."

"What was that all about?" *River* asked. "It sounds interesting."

"Midway through the book Didi's attending a party at the home of his girlfriend's parents. Yes, Didi's acquired a human girlfriend. What was intended to be strictly a human emotion-response experiment turned into love. What's a novel without a love interest, right? Some of the guests are smoking cigarettes. Humans ingesting toxic chemicals bewilder Didi, which is humorously detailed in an earlier chapter. Residents of Sveto—that's Didi's home planet—don't smoke, drink or partake in drugs. Their escapism exists in a higher dimension which they call upon in times of stress.

"Anyway, Didi walks out to the pool area to escape the smoke. It's a cool evening and no else is around. It's late and Didi's getting sleepy. In case you're wondering, Svetons require sleep just like humans. However, on Sveto they don't sleep in beds. When they get tired they crawl inside an energy module—it kinda resembles a bed—which contains a liquid gel. Their bodies slow to a crawl. Their heart barely beats, they don't breathe, they simply absorb energy. One hour inside this wondrous device and they're good for a week."

"That sounds like something Conner could use," joked *Destiny*. "His energy level stays on the wane. All that coffee doesn't seem to be helping him any."

Didi smiled. "Yeah, I think more than a few earthlings could benefit from an energy module. Okay, Didi's out by the pool and he's feeling really tired. The more he looks at the sparkling blue water, the more it reminds him of his energy liquid. 'What the heck,' he says. 'Maybe a quick nap on the bottom of the pool would be refreshing. No one's coming outside in this cool weather.'

"Didi quickly sheds his annoying human attire and slides into the pool. 'Ah, quite refreshing,' he says. Didi lowers himself to the bottom of the pool, imagining he's inside his energy module, and assumes a spread-eagle position. The exhausted Sveton quickly drifts into a deep sleep."

"Uh oh," said *River*. "I can only imagine what happens next."

"It's not the little alien's greatest moment," said *Didi*. "I can tell you that. Here's what happens. Twenty minutes into Didi's nap, one of the party's non-smoking guests strolled out poolside for a breath of fresh air. As she's casually walking around the pool, something catches her eye. There's some debris lying at the bottom of the pool. She ventures closer to the pool's edge and peers in. 'Oh my God!' she exclaims. 'It's a person! Help! There's a dead body in the pool!'

"The hysterical woman runs toward the house screaming for help. Seconds later everyone emerges from the house to see what the disturbance is all about. Sixty-some guests crowd around the pool staring at the corpse laid out on the bottom.

"One young man dives in to retrieve the obviously deceased drowning victim. When he reaches the bottom he gets a better look at the corpse. It has an odd appearance, almost a nonhuman look to it. Perhaps the body had been in the water for a long time and sustained some decomposition. That would explain it. He decides to grab the limp body from behind using one arm, using his free arm to propel them both to the surface. He reaches under the armpit to get a good grip.

"Then—horror! Didi awakened with a bang. His eyes opened wide and focused on this intruder of his space. The normally mild-mannered Didi instinctively latched his hands around the young man's throat and drew him in. Staring him down with glowing red ember-like eyeballs, he intelligibly communicated *underwater* to the terrified rescuer. 'On my planet Sveto you *never* wake a man when he's resting! Do you understand!'

"Suddenly Didi realized what was happening and released his grip. The young man was shocked beyond belief. Here he was in the midst of doing a good deed retrieving a dead body and the dead man turned out to be an alien who had assaulted him! He shot to the surface like a bullet, popping out from the middle of the pool, rising five feet in the air and plopping down on the deck. He immediately rose and raced away, yelling out to the stunned crowd as he fled. 'Run for your life! The space alien is alive and he's going to kill us all! Run!' He was out of sight in a matter of seconds.

"The shocked partygoers wasted no time in dispersing. Some of the terrified guests escaped back into the house, retreating to the basement. A few jumped into their cars and sped away. Others ran in fear into the streets. When Didi popped to the surface he was alone. He heard emergency sirens coming closer and closer. The police would arrive at any second. Didi quickly summed up the situation. He had to act fast. Didi opened the door to the pool's storage room and grabbed a bundle of dirty towels, tossing it into the pool. Throwing his clothes back on, Didi made his way to the front yard.

"Instead of running from the police he did the opposite. Didi approached the police cruiser and quickly briefed the two officers on the cause of the disturbance. What had happened, Didi informed them, was that one of the guests apparently had too much to drink. He had mistakenly perceived a bundle of dirty towels to be a drowning victim. Not only that, Didi said with a chuckle, but the inebriated young man claimed that the floating towels actually transformed into a killer space alien.

"Didi's story worked. The officers walked to the pool and gazed into the pool. Sure enough, there was a bundle of towels underneath the surface of the water. They agreed that an intoxicated person could errantly assume it was a floating corpse. Didi and the officers joked about the towels really being space aliens intent on taking over the world. After a good laugh, the two officers quickly filled out a report and left the scene. Didi breathed a sigh of relief."

"That's funny!" cracked *Spy*. "He sure finessed his way out of that one."

"Yes he did, but Didi still had some explaining to do, especially to his girlfriend. Afterwards she asked him where he had been during all the commotion by the pool. Didi explained that he had ran into the house to retrieve a medical emergency book in case he needed to administer cardiopulmonary resuscitation. His girlfriend bought the story, but she was beginning to realize her boyfriend was built from a different mold. She just didn't realize how different!"

"Wow *Didi*!" *River's* cover was shining, the way it always did when she was relaxed and happy. "Your colorful character Didi does delightfully entertain. If the rest of the book is anything like that passage I can understand all the hoopla over this charming alien from outer space. It sounds like *Didi's Adventures* deserves its royal position in the literary world."

"Thanks for the compliment," said *Didi*. "Yes, we're at the top of the mountain right now. But you know what? Anyone of you could be just one lucky break away from achieving the same accolades. It's a funny game, this book business. I'm doing all the talking here—does anyone else want the floor?"

"*Didi*, can you carry on?" asked *Destiny*. "We're all intrigued by your success and want to learn more. And besides, we've got forever to speak amongst ourselves. They could come scoop you off our shelf at any time. We want to learn from the king in the limited time you're here. Who knows, maybe you're right and one of us will get lucky some day. If so, our conversation with you today may prove invaluable."

"Thanks again," *Didi* said, "but don't put me too high on the pedestal. I'm really just another book, just like you guys. What do you want to know?"

River quickly answered. "If it's okay with the others, I'd like to hear about another of Didi's earthly adventures. That's what the public can't get enough of, and now I understand why. Didi's addictive!"

"I've never heard him described as such, but you may be right. It's true that some of Didi's fans border on the obsessive. Let me quickly summarize a couple of Didi favorites. The first one is a typical Didi mishap. You'd think that a highly developed intellectual being—Didi has an out-of-this-world IQ of over 800—would have an easy time on our primitive planet. Not so with my lovable but bumbling Didi. Sometimes he just doesn't use common sense.

"One weekend, while researching human generational bonding, Didi had placed himself as a volunteer for a cub scout troop. He wanted to observe children on their first camping experience. The first night everyone sat around the campfire and shared stories with each other. Didi listened intently as each youngster took his turn speaking.

"Then it was time to indulge in the camping tradition of roasting marshmallows over the open fire. The kids all grabbed their metal skewers, stuck a marshmallow onto it, and held it over the flame. They twisted and turned their fluffy treats over the fire until they were roasted to perfection. Then they hurriedly gobbled them down. Didi, caught up in all the excitement, grabbed a marshmallow and began roasting it. He forgot one important thing though, the roasting skewer. Didi was holding the marshmallow in his hand and had plunged *his entire arm* into the blazing fire.

"Didi had forgotten that human skin burns—and that fire inflicts great pain on earthlings. You see, Svetons, throughout the ages, had developed a biological resistance to fire. Their skin didn't burn and they felt no pain. Didi, in the midst of having so much fun, had completely forgotten something of major importance. He didn't realize that humans might find it a bit odd to witness a man thrusting his arm into an open fire to roast a marshmallow. Not only that, but Didi, nonchalantly engaged in casual conversation the whole while, seemed unaffected by the raging fire that engulfed his arm.

"One young boy quickly noticed Didi's unusual roasting method. 'Look Mr. Jones,' he said to the scoutmaster, 'that man has got his arm in the fire.' Everyone quickly focused on this madman marshmallower who refused to use a skewer, preferring his arm instead.

"The scoutmaster looked over at his deranged volunteer and immediately yanked Didi's arm from the fire. 'Someone get some first aid gear! This man's been burned!' he screamed out.

"Didi had to think quickly. Once again the little genius from Sveto had errantly placed himself in a difficult situation. How could he be so stupid? Human arms burn! Any idiot knew that. These aren't like biomechatronically-limbed Svetons. They're earthlings! Then Didi had an idea.

"'I'm okay!' exclaimed Didi. 'There's no need for first aid. I'm alright!'

"'What do you mean you're alright?' asked the perplexed scoutmaster. 'We all saw you hold your arm in the middle of a blazing fire for over a minute. You're lucky your arm isn't burned down to a stub. Now what's going on here?'

"'I'll show you,' said Didi. 'Please don't be shocked.' Didi then reached under his armpit and appeared to be twisting something with his fingers. Then, suddenly, a clacking noise. Using his free arm, Didi pulled the arm from its socket, holding it up for everyone to see. There was a collective gasp from the crowd.

"'This is not my real arm,' Didi calmly stated. 'It's an artificial prosthesis. Years ago I lost my arm in a boating accident. It was replaced with this metal substitute. As you all know, metal doesn't burn easily. I'm sorry I alarmed you by putting my arm in the fire. It was thoughtless of me. I hope you'll accept my apology. Now, if you don't mind, I think I'll go back to my tent. I'm quite sleepy. Good night.' One-armed Didi, holding his artificial limb high in the air, then waved goodnight to his stunned audience and disappeared into the darkness."

River clapped her hands. "Yea for Didi! What a character! He and Sonny Needle are a lot alike. They're always in some sort of a jam. Maybe the two of them should team up in a novel someday. *Spy*, what do you think?"

Spy grinned. "Didi's in seventy million homes right now. Sonny Needle's in approximately seventy. I don't think we can compare the two at this point."

"Don't underestimate yourself," said *Destiny*. "*Didi's Adventures* and *Spy Needle* are two of the funniest novels ever written."

"*Didi*, you'll have to excuse my two friends," said *Spy*. "They're always trying to boost my self published esteem. I'm dying to ask you some business related questions, but like *River*, I'm now intrigued by your little alien character. Would it be possible to hear another excerpt of Didi's earthly undertakings?"

"Of course," agreed *Didi*. "There's one more I wanted to share with you anyway. It's another Didi dilemma that's proven popular with his followers. It involves a set of human twins. Didi had been specifically instructed by his Sveton superiors to research this fascinating aspect of earthling reproduction. Didi's assigned task was to observe a pair of identical twins and record their obvious similarities, as well as any differences he may discover. It was left up to Didi as to how he would accomplish this assignment. Didi, in typical fashion, chose a rather unusual method.

"One day Didi was having lunch in his favorite restaurant. As fate would have it, two girls were seated behind him. Dressed in identical outfits, they were virtually indistinguishable from each other. They were obviously twins. The girls were engaged in conversation, and Didi couldn't help but overhear them. Over the course of an hour he learned they were in fact identical twins, and both of them were columnists for major newspapers.

"Sue, the eldest by two minutes, lived in New York City. Nancy resided in London. Both of them were masterful piano players, loved the color blue, and were avid doll collectors. He also overheard the girls discussing their financial situations. Both of them had leased rather large apartments. To increase their income, they each decided to sublet a room, subject to finding a suitable tenant. Didi learned the sisters would be returning to their respective homes the following day.

"Didi spontaneously came up with a plan, once again without putting a lot of thought into it. Let me brief you on something before I get into his plan. Didi, remember he's a space alien, has the ability to instantly teleport himself anywhere on the planet. He can be in New York one moment, and at the snap of a finger, transport himself to London. It's easy and natural. The Svetons had been teleporting around their own planet for centuries.

"Now, on to Didi's little scheme. What better way to gain insight into both twins than by living with *each* of them? Didi would *accidently* meet Sue in New York. The same with Nancy in London. Of course, Didi would stage both of these seemingly coincidental encounters. Remembering the girls' common interests in playing the piano, collecting dolls and the color blue, the meetings went like this.

"Didi would be wearing a crisply ironed *blue* shirt. After an exchange of pleasantries, Didi would let it slip that he was a dealer of everything collectible, including stamps, coins, pottery and *dolls*. His idea of relaxing was listening to classic *piano* sonata compositions. After strategically divulging this information, Didi innocently let it be known that he was currently looking for a room to rent. Of course, both girls were ecstatic. They couldn't believe their luck. Within twenty-four hours, Didi was living with the twins in two separate apartments. Didi's plan had been successful."

"He's quite the clever fellow, isn't he?" commented *Destiny*.

"Well, yes and no," replied *Didi*, "as you'll soon find out. Three months passed. Not only was Didi successfully gathering data for his project, but he also loved his living arrangements. Didi bounced back and forth between his two homes, telling the girls he traveled a lot on business. The two twins were pleased as well, both of them adoring their well-behaved flatmate. Besides, he was only home about half the time.

"This is where Didi's plan self destructs. Even the lowliest nitwit human knows that twin sisters talk to each other. They share *everything*. Now you would think that an 800 IQ being, someone with the intelligence to plan and carry out this sophisticated dual-residence scheme, would surely know this as well. You would be wrong. Remember this is the forgetful space alien who naps on the bottom of pools and pokes his arm into raging fires. This is the one and only Didi, a space cadet in every respect.

"Of course the two twins told each other about their respective roommates. Each was amazed that both had found a housemate who liked pianos, dolls and the color blue, and incredibly, both were nicknamed Didi. These two men had to meet! Sue and Nancy each nagged and nagged and nagged their lovable lodger until he finally gave in. Didi would meet Didi! Now he was really in a jam.

"Didi immediately began working on a solution. It was agreed that they would all meet in New York. Didi endured the primitive transportation mode of a jet airplane for seven long hours. He and Nancy arrived in New York. They quickly hailed a taxi and headed for Sue's apartment.

"Thirty minutes later they were deposited in front of Sue's home. Didi appeared calm and collected, but inside he was wired with apprehension. Would his quickly devised plan work? Could he squirm out of this mess? They knocked on the front door. Sue opened the door and looked at Didi, then at Nancy, then Didi again. A puzzled look crossed her face. 'Oh my, Nancy, I see you've already met my housemate.'

"'What do you mean *your housemate*?' asked Nancy. 'This Didi lives with me!'

"Sue and Nancy looked at each other, then both of them stared back at Didi. Nancy gave Didi a firm push from behind. 'Let's all go inside. Didi, you've got some explaining to do!' The twins weren't happy about being deceived.

"They all sat down. Didi spoke first. 'I know this a shock to you both, but I can explain everything. I'm the real Didi. Sue, the man that lived with you was an impostor. He's been traveling around the world impersonating me. He's been tainting my stellar reputation by selling fake collectibles for huge sums of money. The authorities have been after him for months and they finally caught up with him. He was captured trying to pawn off a bogus doll collection on a rich widow. I just learned of this yesterday. We're lucky he didn't scam Sue while pretending to be me.'

"Sue and Nancy appeared somewhat relieved, but still skeptical of the incredulous tale they were hearing. Now was the time for Didi to add some credibility to his story. Didi opened his luggage and brought out two large boxes. 'These are for you. There's only two of them in the world, same as you two. Two special gifts for two special girls.'

"The twins looked at each other, still unsure of what was unfolding before them. Slowly, they unwrapped their gifts. They discovered two beautiful but worn boxes. The boxes appeared to be made from cherry wood, darkened by the ages. Carved into the wood and barely legible were two inscriptions. The twins knew just enough Latin to make it out.

Geminis Christophoreis,
Ad honoranda beneficia quae pater
vester musicae contulit.
A Principe Ferdinando Mediceo. Anno MDCCIX.

"'No way!' said Sue.

"'Can't be!' echoed Nancy.

"'What do you think?' asked Didi, wearing a broad grin.

"Sue took another long look at the inscription and read it again, this time out loud and in English. 'To the Cristofori twins—In honor of your father's contribution to music—From Prince Ferdinando Medici, 1709.'

"Nancy stared at Didi. 'This had better not be a trick or you're gonna regret it.'

"'Not a chance girls,' said Didi. 'Not after what you two have been through. I'm judging from your reactions that you know who the Cristofori twins were. Am I correct?'

"'Yes,' said the twins in unison.

"'Then you're aware that they're the twin daughters of Bartolomeo Cristofori, the inventor of the piano. Cristofori produced the first piano especially for Prince Ferdinado Medici. The prince later showed his appreciation with these gifts to the twins. Go ahead girls, open the boxes.'

"The twins simultaneously lifted the lids on the boxes. 'Oh my!' exclaimed Sue.

"'Unbelievable!' uttered Nancy, trying to catch her breath.

"Inside were identical dolls in exquisite settings. The lovely figures were beautifully costumed in gorgeous blue evening dresses. Both were seated before a striking blue piano. Their long dark hair flowed to the floor. The magnificently rich detail showcased their tiny fingers expertly stroking the keys. These exceptionally preserved dolls were exemplary examples of Florentine craftsmanship. Indeed, they were royal representations of that historic period. The twins were speechless.

"'Dolls, pianos and the color blue, right girls?' stated Didi. 'These two dolls deserve two sweetheart owners. They're treasures just like you. They'll never find better caretakers. Don't dare ask me what I paid for them because I'll never tell. Enjoy!'

"Didi had won the girls over. Although he would eventually move out of Nancy's apartment, the three of them remained close friends for the duration of Didi's stay on earth. When it came time for Didi's return to Sveto, the three of them had dinner together. Didi told them he was relocating to Eastern Europe and might lose contact for awhile. Didi didn't like lying to his friends, but he had no choice. He couldn't tell them the truth, that he was an alien visitor from a distant galaxy. They all had a good cry, hugged, and said goodbye.

"Before leaving, the girls slipped Didi a gift. He was instructed not to open it until he was settled in his new home.

Later, relaxing in his home on Sveto, Didi finally opened the package from his dear friends. To his surprise it was a doll, but not just any doll. It was an expertly produced model of an extraterrestrial, a visitor from the stars, a space alien. Inside was a card. He opened it and read it. Who had really fooled whom?"

Welcome home,

From your favorite twins, Sue & Nancy

"Oh my lord!" cried *River*. "No wonder that's a reader favorite. It's touching and funny at the same time. It's great!"

"Yes it is," *Didi* said proudly. "Wanna know a secret? You haven't heard the last of the twins. Sue and Nancy return in *Didi Two*. I think that's wonderful."

"I agree," said *River*. "They are great characters, but that Didi is a real showstopper. He's easy to fall in love with. I could picture him in my mind as you spoke—a charming comical little alien. I don't care what *Spy* thinks, Didi still reminds me of Sonny Needle. They're both unbelievably funny characters."

"I agree that they both constitute wonderful entertainment," replied *Spy*, "but you gotta be seen to be appreciated. Didi's seventy million copies verses Sonny's seventy copies is quite the difference. Heck, most of those seventy were giveaway review copies—that didn't get reviewed by the way."

"Nowadays," said *Destiny*, "half of all review copies end up with a bargain rate sticker slapped on them and sold on the internet. But back to *Didi's Adventures*. It's amazing how casually you speak about *Didi Two*. Are you aware of how many novels have the popularity to justify a sequel? I don't know the exact figures, but it's not many. I can tell you that."

Didi smiled. "I know I'm lucky in that respect, but it's not a big deal."

"*Didi*, you're being too modest," said *Spy*. "You're creating literary history. The book world has never seen anything like it. *Didi's Adventures's* release was a seismic-like event that rattled the cages of the entire industry. The readers can't get enough of that little anomaly named Didi. Just watch, *Didi Two* will ride the momentum into the stratosphere. The whole Didi phenomenon is like a train barreling down the tracks at full speed. It can't be stopped. As a matter of fact, I predict this wave of popularity won't end with *Didi Two*. They'll be a *Didi Three*, *Didi Four* and *Didi Five*."

"Thanks for the optimistic forecast," said *Didi*. "An ongoing series sounds like fun. If that happens I just hope Luis handles it the right way. That's all I'll ask for."

"*Didi*, I'd like to ask a favor from you if I may," said *Destiny*.

"Sure," said *Didi*. "What is it?"

"You're sitting on top of the world right now, the champion of the literary universe. Seventy million readers have spent their hard earned money to peek between your covers. You know what it takes to get to the top and stay there. You're *the* authority on stardom. Those of us who reside here on this shelf, especially *River* and myself, think we have another star in our presence.

"It's our own *Spy Needle*. He's been entertaining us from the moment he arrived. I've got to take advantage of this opportunity. I know our time is limited and they could come snatch you off our shelf at any time. As much as I'd like to hear one more Didi tale, I have a higher priority. Would you be kind enough to hear out one of *Spy's* passages? Then I'd appreciate it if you'd present an honest evaluation of his story. If you're impressed, and I'm willing to bet that you will be, then we've got to figure out a way to expose our friend to the outside world. An endorsement from your royal quarters would certainly inspire us."

"Sounds great," said *Didi*. "I'd like to be on the other side for a change. I enjoy being entertained as much as anyone else. Go for it *Spy*."

"Oh, what precarious positions my friends place me into," sighed *Spy*. "*Destiny*, I don't know whether to hug you or push you right off this shelf." He gave his friend a gentle nudge.

Destiny smiled. "I wouldn't blame you if you did, but you know I'm doing this for your own good. Go ahead, share a classic for *Didi* to hear."

"Okay, there's no escape hatch. *Destiny's* placed me before the ultimate literary critic to sink or swim. *Didi*, for better or worse, here we go. What Sonny Needle adventure would you guys like to hear?"

River quickly answered. "Something new baby! Share something new." She pushed tightly against *Spy*.

Spy couldn't believe his ears. *River* had just called him *baby*! For everyone to hear, including the celebrity guest, she had publicly announced that *Spy* was her *baby*. A classy girl like *River* didn't speak without thinking. She had meant to say it, and *Spy* knew why. She had intentionally chosen this particular moment to disclose to the world that *Spy* was her man.

She wanted him to impress the superstar *Didi's Adventures*. *River* instinctively knew this was a confidence crossroads for her future mate. A positive reaction from their famed houseguest could light an eternal fire under *Spy*. This was a once-in-a-lifetime opportunity to show off *Spy's* extraordinary showmanship skills before this seasoned appraiser of talent.

Adrenaline pumped through *Spy's* text. Talk about motivated! The most beautiful girl in the world had just called him baby. *Baby*! On top of that, he was preparing to entertain *Didi's Adventures*, the biggest name in the book business. Spy was beaming with confidence. The showman took the stage.

"Here's one you may enjoy. It kinda fits the occasion with a Didi-style conclusion. Sonny Needle, our world spy for peace, is faced with a challenge. The setting is Eastern Europe. Two nations of equal stature are engaged in a bloody conflict. The war has been raging nonstop for three years. It seemed that every time one of them would make an advancement, the other would come storming back to regain their lost ground. The back and forth battle was taking its toll on each participant. Thousands of soldiers and civilians had lost their lives. Not only that, but both nations were nearly bankrupt. All of their resources were being plowed into paying for the war effort.

"Sonny flew in to analyze the situation. He needed information before he could take action to halt the bloodshed. Sonny, as always, wanted to get to the root of the problem. Wars were always the same in one respect. The truth was the first casualty. Sonny needed to cut through the layers of lies that covered the cold hard truth of war. Only then could a solution be worked out.

"Sonny talked to the soldiers on both sides. He was surprised to discover that most of them had no idea why they were fighting. They were simply given weapons and instructed to go kill the enemy. The civilians gave similar stories. They too didn't really know what the war was all about. They only knew it was horrible and wished it would end. Sonny interviewed political and military leaders from both countries. Even they all agreed it was in everyone's best interest to terminate the brutal conflict.

"Then it clicked! Sonny had been looking under the wrong rock. For every action there is an equal and opposite reaction. Where there's losers, there's winners. You just have to know where to look. Sonny stopped talking to the losers and began searching for some winners. His quest for answers was soon rewarded.

"One name kept popping up was the Slimmscurms. They were the wealthiest and most influential family in the region. Most of their power originated from the family business, weapons manufacturing. They had been supplying armaments to various governments for decades. The empire had been founded by Slisser von Slimmscurm, the revered patriarch of the clan.

"He had been a brutal man obsessed with the bottom line. His product was death and destruction. Slisser von Slimmscurm cared not who won any particular war. He just wanted to sell weapons. To this ruthless individual there were no good guys or bad guys, only customers. If they had the cash, he would sell the arms. It mattered not who used them, how they were used, or how many people were slaughtered by his lethal products.

"There was only one enemy that Slisser von Slimmscurm despised—peace. Peacetime meant a lull in weapon sales and would not be tolerated. Slisser von Slimmscurm became adept at extending conflicts. War was a money machine. A long-running conflict guaranteed steady profits. The merciless baron also became proficient at instigating wars. Over he years he acquired the skills necessary to start a war. He knew exactly which buttons to push to stir up trouble. With lies and deception he could transform the best of friends into the bitterest of enemies. Then he'd turn around and peddle his instruments of death to both of them.

"Sonny learned that Slisser von Slimmscurm had passed away several years earlier, leaving his blood-stained enterprise to his two sons. The old man had trained them well. Banger and Butcher were proudly carrying on the family tradition. They had worshiped their father and were devastated by his death. The brothers vowed to continue to wreak bloody havoc in the region, knowing their father would be pleased as he looked down upon them from heaven. They immediately started a new war in his memory. Their father's genocidal agenda must be fulfilled. Banger and Butcher would never forget their hero, Slisser von Slimmscurm, the quintessential instigator of warfare.

"In this particular conflict, the Slimmscurms were heavily involved. Sonny had determined how the war had originated. The Slimmscurm brothers had applied their time-tested provocation formula. First they had spread propaganda and lies on both sides to create a climate of mutual hatred. Then they manufactured a violent border incident that sparked the war. Banger and Butcher then each chose a nation, and began snaking their way through the respective bureaucracies. Banger used his power and influence to snag an exclusive no-bid contract. He would be the sole weapons provider for one side. Butcher was also successful. He negotiated an agreement to arm the opposing side.

"Now the stage was set for unending bloodshed. Every time one army seemed to be on the verge of a victory, their weapons supply would mysteriously dry up. At the same time their opponent would suddenly receive an influx of armaments. The result was the up and down see-saw cycle of bloodletting where no one could possibly win—except for the weapons dealers.

"The source of all this terror was a sprawling weapons manufacturing facility. The massive armament production plant had been built by Slisser von Slimmscurm decades earlier. At the time, other businessmen had snickered at young Slisser for investing heavily in a weapons facility, especially in a period of relative peace. They stopped laughing at him once construction was complete and bombs started falling throughout the region. The locals now called it Hell's Kitchen.

"Sonny's instincts steered him to this factory of death. He knew he had to pay a visit to the Devil's workshop. He needed to make something happen and put an end to the horrible war that had ruined so many lives. Sonny posed as an arms dealer and charmed his way past the security guard. Rounding the corner he was greeted by the largest statue he'd ever laid eyes on. It was made of marble and must have been thirty meters high. The sculpture depicted a distinguished looking gentleman with a top hat perched on his head. The man wore a heavy beard. He was puffing on a pipe that was dangling from his mouth. He had both hands clutched tightly around an antique rifle. Imbedded at the base was a bronze memorial plaque. Sonny leaned over and read the inscription.

Slisser von Slimmscurm
The greatest warrior the world has ever seen
Our hero, our father—Rest in peace
Banger and Butcher Slimmscurm

"So this was the infamous patriarch of the Slimmscurm dynasty. Sonny looked upwards at the lifeless statue. He wanted to study the face of the man who was responsible for the deaths of so many human beings. He looked into the marble eyes. They were cold and distant. Even these eyes of marble seemed to contain a trace of evil. Suddenly the eyes of stone took on a reddish glow and glared back at Sonny. For an ever-so-brief moment there was a sort of telepathic communication that chilled Sonny's soul. *Go away!* That was the message conveyed to this dangerous intruder. This gutsy soldier of peace who had invaded his domain wasn't welcome.

Fear, hate, anger, frustration and rage flowed out of the marble structure.

"Sonny felt the presence of the Devil. There was an evil soul residing, trapped would be a better word, within the confines of this huge marble statue. One of Satan's greatest disciples was watching over his vast empire from his home inside a rock sculpture. Sonny instinctively knew he had the upper hand. The evil spirit, without a human body in which to manifest itself, was frustrated. It was helpless to stop Sonny from completing his mission. The stare down continued. Sonny swore he saw the statue's eyes blink before they looked away.

"Adjacent from the statue was the facility's administrative building. This was the true bowels of evil. Inside, decisions of death were being made over coffee and doughnuts without a hint of compassion for those who would lose their lives. Sonny confidently strolled through the front door.

"'Sir, can I help you?' a voice asked. It was the girl at the information desk.

"'Yes, I'd like to see Banger Slimmscurm in regard to a weapons transaction,' replied Sonny. Sonny was then informed that Banger wouldn't be available for another hour. The girl then escorted him to the waiting room.

"The waiting room was a virtual Slisser von Slimmscurm museum. Banger and Butcher had certainly ensured he would never be forgotten. Pictures, paintings and sculptures depicting the dynasty's patriarch stared back at Sonny from every wall. Various civic awards and medals were strung above the fireplace. In one corner, under glass, were some old newspaper articles praising the famed industrialist.

"Sonny then discovered a partitioned section, off limits to the public. He ducked behind the screen panel to investigate. He saw some artifacts that had obviously belonged to the old man. It appeared they were possibly part of a future display. Sitting on a table was a well worn top hat. It looked exactly like the one resting on the statue's head in front of the building. Beside the hat was an old pipe. It appeared to be the same pipe that he was smoking in nearly all the pictures. Above Sonny's head was a gun rack containing a rifle. Sonny reached up and pulled it down. It was a classic firearm, an antique. There was a handwritten note attached to it, stating that it was the very first weapon ever manufactured by Slisser von Slimmscurn.

"Sonny looked at the collection before him—the hat, the rifle, the pipe. He wondered to himself if the old man could smoke his pipe in his current home, which must certainly be Hell, or would it ignite fireballs all around him. If anyone ever deserved Hell, it had to be Slisser von Slimmscurm. He had been responsible for murdering tens of thousands of individuals. Was it worth residing in Hell? Did anybody really want to spend eternity in Hell?

"Of course not! If anyone really *knew* their actions would lead to an eternity in Hell, they'd stop immediately. No one wants to room and board forever in a fiery oven. Eternity in Hell! Sonny had an idea. He would still meet with Banger, and Butcher too, but it would be under entirely different circumstances. Sonny grabbed the hat, pipe and rifle. He poked his head out the door. The information attendant wasn't at her desk. Sonny Needle quickly slipped out the door and exited the building."

"Ha," chuckled *Didi*. "That Sonny's a slick one, isn't he? Sorry for the interruption. *Spy*, please continue."

Spy looked at *Didi* and smiled. "Okay, Sonny puts his plan into action. It was a cold moonless night. The hour was late as he prepared for his mission. First Sonny put on his oldest suit. Then he attached the fake beard to his face. After making an adjustment, he placed the weathered top heat on his head. Then he stuck the old pipe in his mouth, grabbed the antique rifle and headed out the door.

"Sonny discreetly made his way to Banger's residence. He scaled the fence and disarmed the security system. After picking the lock on the back door, he crept up into Banger's bedroom.

"Crouching down at the foot of the bed, he whispered ever so softly. 'Whooooo, Whooooo.' Banger made a slight movement. 'Whooooo, whooooo,' he repeated.

"This time Banger awakened. 'Who is that?' he asked.

"'Whooooo, whooooo,' called a voice from the foot of the bed. 'My dear son, I'm your father. Whooooo, whooooo, I'm here to warn you. Whooooo, whooooo.'

"'You can't be my father,' said a trembling Banger. 'My father's dead. Now what's going on?'

"'Whooooo, whooooo. I am your father and I am dead. Whooooo, whooooo. I'm a ghost and I live in Hell! Whooooo, whooooo.'

"'I don't believe you!' cried Banger. 'Now get out of here!'

"'Whooooo, whooooo.' Sonny stood up. 'I *am* your father!'

"Banger's heart nearly stopped. The beard, the hat, the pipe, the rifle! It *was* his father! Banger was paralyzed by fear.

"'Whooooo, whooooo. My first born Banger, listen to me. Whooooo, whooooo. Stop making weapons. Stop all the wars. You will go to Hell the same as me. Whooooo, whooooo. You will burn in Hell! Hell! Hell! Whooooo. Whooooo.'

"Poof! The room suddenly filled with smoke. Sonny disappeared behind the thick cloud and left the bedroom. He made his way out of the house and quickly left the scene.

Banger remained horrified on the bed trying to sort out his living nightmare.

"Banger couldn't sleep after his frightening ordeal. He needed to speak to his brother. He wasn't about to tell anyone else that his father's ghost had just paid him a visit. They would think he had gone crazy. Butcher was the only person who wouldn't question his sanity.

"Banger arrived at his office three hours early. The sun was just beginning to rise over the horizon. As he approached the parking area he noticed something unusual. A man was sitting cross-legged in the middle of the parking lot. The man was in his pajamas and bawling like a baby. Now here was a man that obviously *was* crazy. Banger took a closer look. It was Butcher!

"'Butcher, what are you doing sitting in the middle of the parking lot? Why are you crying? Why are you still wearing your pajamas?'

"Butcher looked up and recognized his brother. He jumped into Banger's arms and held him tight. 'Oh my brother, I must tell you something. Please don't think I've gone insane. Father visited me last night! Father came into my bedroom, but it wasn't really father. It was his ghost! Father lives in Hell! Father's ghost told me to stop selling weapons and stop all the wars. Otherwise I will spend eternity in Hell just like him. Did you hear me, Banger? Eternity in Hell! Hell!'

"Banger was silent for a moment. He couldn't believe it. Father's ghost had been to Butcher's house also. 'You too! Father's ghost came to see me last night also. He told me the same thing, stop selling weapons and stop the wars. That's it! No more! I'm outta this business. I quit! There's no way I'm gonna be like poppa. I'm not going to live in Hell. Eternity is a long time. They'll be no Hell for me!'

"'Me either!' cried Butcher. 'I'm also quitting. I don't wanna be like pop. He's burning like a firecracker as we speak. As of today we're turning this place into an orphanage. I hope it's not too late for God to have mercy on our souls. God, I promise we'll help people instead of hurt them. I'm begging you, please don't send us to Hell. They'll be no more weapons, no more wars. We know our wars have created many orphans. Let them live here. Anything you want! Just don't send me down there with pop—he's cooking like a hot dog on a stick.'

Spy looked up at his attentive audience and smiled. "Well, guys, that's it. Banger and Butcher convert the weapons facility into an orphanage. The war ends. Sonny Needle flies back to his seaside hacienda for a well deserved holiday. Mission accomplished. What do you think?"

"Fantastic!" roared *Didi*. "You guys are right. If that passage is any indication of the rest of the novel, then *Spy Needle* is every bit the superstar that I am. I'm ready to hear some more!'

"I told you so," said *Destiny*. "That's just a sample. You wouldn't believe the entertainment value within *Spy's* text. He ranges from ketchup-laced crocodile victims to glue-filled nuclear duds. *Spy's* amazing!"

River was beaming like never before. "*Spy*, I'm so proud of you. You're at your best under pressure. Like an athlete coming through in a clutch situation you delivered. I gotta put that one at the top—pretending to be a ghost! Way to go baby!"

Spy was a happy book. The presence of *Didi's Adventures* had definitely motivated him, causing him to kick his storytelling talents up a notch. There was something else though. *River* had been the true inspiration behind his captivating narration. Over the course of the past hour their relationship had somehow deepened. It had been a natural and effortless event. It was more than just calling him baby. It was much bigger than that. It was based on trust and understanding and a genuine concern for each other. It was about sharing each other's happiness and pain. They had bonded as one.

He knew she could sense it too. *River* now understood him better than anyone else on the planet, including his creator. She had an intimate knowledge of what made him tick. *River* knew that deep down under his aw-shucks demeanor existed a *Spy* who adored the spotlight. The two of them had just soared past the point of no return. They were in love.

"How about it *Spy*?" *Didi* asked. "Can we have some more of Sonny Needle?"

Spy had never felt so relaxed, so satisfied, so confident. He felt *good*. "You guys are great and I'm flattered that you appreciate my stories. But let's not forget, *Didi's* the guest of honor in our house this morning. He's the number one selling book in the *world*. This isn't about me. When and if the stars line up the right way, my day will come. Today is all about *Didi's Adventures*."

"I'm sorry," *Destiny* interrupted, "but I think they're coming to take away our honored guest. Sandra just spotted him. She's walking over here now."

"You're right," said *Didi*. "She's coming to get me. I'd like to say something before she takes me away. You may think that you've learned from me, but it's I who has gained from this encounter. I've witnessed genuine friendship here. All of you are special. *Spy*, your friend's instincts are correct. You're one break away from stardom at the highest level. You may get that break or you may not, but you know what? You're already way ahead of me. You've found true love in *River Run*

True. You two adore each other. Maybe I appear to have it all, but I don't have love. You're a lucky guy. If you hit the big time, look me up. You're gonna need some advice on handling life at the top. I'll be glad to help. It's been wonderful hanging out with all of you. Goodbye."

In an instant *Didi* was gone. Sandra swooped him up without stopping and in one motion placed him in her basket.

Chapter 8

The days became longer as summer approached. The warmer temperatures coaxed people from their homes, many of whom drifted into Sanders and Bowman. Sales increased by nearly thirty percent. The additional traffic created more duties for the employees, but they responded superbly. The staff had the usual minor squabbles and such, but they were an extremely hard working group. Thomas could put up with a lot from his employees, but one thing he abhorred was laziness. His top criterion in becoming a Sanders and Bowman employee was a solid work ethic. New hires who didn't pull their own weight usually didn't last long. Conner was the lone exception, but Thomas wasn't about to fire the regional manager's nephew.

People watching became the recreation of choice for the books. They possessed prime front row seats from which to view the show. They would watch the staff scurrying around trying to maintain an organized chaos. The summertime customers always provided amusement. Sometimes they would wander in aimlessly, stroll each and every aisle, and depart without ever touching a book. Others would come in for nothing more than a visit to the toilet. You would also get the occasional patron who seemed to be on a misplacement mission. His goal was to remove as many books as possible from their assigned residences and relocate them to the other side of the bookstore. On a particularly successful afternoon, one of these despised villains could break up four or five happy households.

There was one demonic customer that was especially adept at destroying book relationships. The book community had named him Harry Homewrecker. To the best of their knowledge this horrible creature had never bought a book, although he was suspected of stealing the lovely *Karen's Promise* last year. He would come into the bookstore two or three times a month and wreak havoc. On a typical visit Harry would displace twenty books. The normal customer who would misplace books did so out of sheer laziness, not wanting to walk the few steps back to the book's designated resting place. They would lay the book down somewhere where it would be found later.

Not Harry Homewrecker! He would intentionally hide books in out-of-the-way areas, places where the staff would rarely look. Sometimes the booknapping victims would go missing for weeks at a time while their friends agonized in despair, not knowing if their loved one was dead or alive. Harry Homewrecker was the most hated individual that ever stepped inside Sanders and Bowman.

Another patron despised by both books and the staff was Sammy Smoker. No one knew his real name so they tagged him as such. Sammy was an absolute nuisance to everyone. Apparently he was so addicted to cigarettes that he had to smoke inside the bookstore. Few things bothered a book more than having clouds of smoke blown onto their covers. The terrible odor would stay with them for months.

Mario had caught him several times and threatened to ban him from the bookstore. Since then he had taken to smoking inside the restrooms, another violation of bookstore rules. He was so daring that he would sometimes light up as he walked towards the toilet. The books were hoping that Mario would catch him in the act again and throw him out of Sanders and Bowman forever. Sammy Smoker was trouble with a capital T.

Alongside the regular book buyers and the occasional troublemaker would be the newbies, usually looking for a specific book. It could be the biker looking for a motorcycle repair guide, a gardener inquiring about a selection on organic tomatoes, or a camper asking about a particular outdoors publication. One customer was overheard inquiring about a book on nude volleyball. Joann politely stated that they didn't carry such a book, but she would note his request. Summertime brought excitement to Sanders and Bowman.

The staff managed to have fun despite their busy schedule. The biggest summer event was Heather's wedding. She had met and began dating one of the bookstore's regular customers. They married three months later. Everyone agreed they were a perfect match. Both were fun loving individuals. They certainly proved that at their wedding reception. They got married on a gorgeous Saturday afternoon. Most of the Sanders and Bowman staff attended the wedding, along with several longtime customers. A couple of wedding publications, *Wedding Perfect* and *Bridal Celebration*, were also lucky enough to attend the festivities.

The reception proved to be mother of all parties. Heather's new husband happened to be from a well-to-do family and they had insisted on paying for everything. They had already taken Heather in as one of their own and were ready to celebrate on a grand scale. Money wouldn't be an obstacle. They booked a resort for the entire weekend, covering expenses for all the guests. A high-end catering service provided the culinary delights, laying out an impressive array of edible delicacies. It was all washed down with forty cases of the finest champagne. A popular jazz band was hired out for the evening. They dined, drank and danced until the sun came up. At one point Mario joined the band on stage enjoying his brief career as a saxophonist.

A few attendees had the misfortune of being scheduled to work the following day. Indeed, it was a motley-looking Sanders and Bowman crew that came dragging in that Sunday morning. To their credit, none of them called in sick, but they all looked as though they had been run over by a freight train. Heather's wedding reception was truly a night to remember.

Heather's wedding celebration served a dual purpose as it coincidently functioned as a going-away party. Saturday had been Debbie's last day of work and she would soon be moving across the country with her family. For the past year she had worked the cashier lines with Heather and Linda. The three of them were the epitome of teamwork, a manager's dream come true. Debbie would be missed by everyone, especially Linda.

The two best friends had become inseparable. They vowed to always stay in contact and visit each other often. Midway through the reception Heather and Linda surprised Debbie with an emotional tribute to their friend. Thomas later joined them, praising Debbie for her commitment to customer service. Afterwards she was swamped with gifts from her friends and coworkers.

One attendee was conspicuous by *not* drinking alcohol. Jim hadn't touched a drop since the near-discovery of his hidden bottle of Scotch. The incident, and Thomas's delicate handling of the matter, had inspired Jim to finally address his drinking problem. The day after the close call, just moments before closing time, Jim casually approached the cashier area. Linda was checking out her final customer of the day. After the customer departed, Jim walked over to her station and placed a book on the counter. The two exchanged pleasantries and Linda began to process Jim's purchase. Thomas appeared just as she was entering Jim's employee identification number into the computer.

"Don't bother, Linda," said Thomas. "This one's on the house. Charge it to my account." Thomas gave Jim a little wink and as quickly as he had appeared, he was gone. Linda completed the transaction and Jim exited the store with his new book, *Alcohol: Beat it Forever*.

Heather wasn't the only Sanders and Bowman staffer that had recently found love. Jeri had acquired a boyfriend. Incredibly, they too had met in the bookstore. Brian had come into the store looking for a particular fishing magazine. Frustrated at not being able to locate the periodical, he approached the information desk. Brian couldn't remember the exact name of the magazine, only that it related to bass fishing. Jeri immediately utilized her uncanny power to unearth the hiding places of the written word. Her radar-like abilities pinpointed Brian to the precise location of the obscure publication.

Brian was impressed. The two of them struck up a conversation that lasted for an hour. They agreed to a dinner date. After that they were inseparable. Jeri's head was in the clouds after meeting her prince charming.

Jeri and Brian were an unlikely match. Jeri was a sophisticated city girl who wasn't afraid to speak her mind. This occasionally rubbed her coworkers the wrong way, some of them regarding her to be snobbish. Brian was the polar opposite, a self-admitted country boy who had grown up working his father's dairy farm. Somehow his easygoing nature blended with Jeri's headstrong personality. Brian's laid-back approach to life seemed to take the edge off her sometimes abrasive demeanor.

Jeri began finding herself attracted toward the leisurely country lifestyle that her boyfriend so embraced. Brian eventually persuaded Jeri to try her hand at fishing. Reluctantly she agreed, but quickly became hooked on the sport after she landed an eight-pound bass. She did, however, make her boyfriend remove the hook from the flopping creature's mouth. Brian even convinced Jeri to hand milk a dairy cow, although that was a one-time event.

Jeri's newfound happiness extended to her coworkers. She had become easier to work with. Brian's influence carried over to the workplace. She was still ambitious and career-oriented, but she had learned the art of patience. The new relaxed Jeri wasn't quite so quick to scold a fellow associate for making a mistake. She had even taken to going out for a drink with her coworkers, bringing Brian along of course. This was something she had never done before. Everyone was commenting on the improvement in Jeri's attitude. The book populace were thrilled with the camaraderie they were witnessing. Their motto was still the same: Happy workers make for happy books.

Another contented employee was Joann. Her agent had successfully shopped her manuscript for *Mercury Girl*. It took some work, but a major publisher had agreed to take on the project. After four nos, two maybes, and a call-me-next-year, a deal was finally sealed. Hagar House Publishing Group had been impressed by *Mercury Girl*. The terms weren't so great, but that was typical for a new author. The advance was embarrassing low, barely enough to cover a weekend jaunt to the beach, but Joann's agent had negotiated a trade off.

In return for accepting the low advance, he had received a slightly better royalty percentage. He especially loaded the deal with incentives. If *Mercury Girl* exceeded expectations—bestseller lists, book club deals, movies and such—huge bonuses would be in order. Joann and her agent were gambling that *Mercury Girl* wouldn't be just a moderate success, but would break through in a big way.

Hagar House thought the plot, with its unexpected twists and turns, was one of the best they had ever seen from a first-time novelist. They had hopes of developing Joann into one of their mainstay authors. If she could establish a readership base with *Mercury Girl*, which they assured her would happen, they had plans to move her into their upper tier of established writers. That would mean a substantial increase in her advertising and publicity budget, guaranteeing more exposure for her second novel. Surrounded by all this cheery optimism was great, but Joann remained cautious. Talk was cheap. Joann wasn't breaking out the champagne until she actually saw her novel on bookstore shelves. She had heard too many industry horror stories.

Joann had reason to remain guarded. One suggestion proposed by the publisher, which proved to be a sign of things to come, was a title change. Hagar House wanted the novel to be named *Hot Trotter*. Their marketing department, after reading a synopsis of the novel, was behind the request. They reportedly thought the title *Mercury Girl* was a little bland. They wanted something more seductive, something that would grab the reader's attention at first glance. The *Hot Trotter* idea came about because of the novel's alluring main character. She was a single girl who possessed an abundance of sex appeal. That, along with the fact that the novel was set in a desert city made it seem the logical choice. A sexy seductress's amorous conquests in the sweltering summer heat made for a good story.

Joann was adamantly opposed to the title change. It was true that the novel's primary character was a beautiful single girl, but she wasn't the promiscuous bimbo that the term "hot trotter" implied. As a matter of fact, she was a highly respected professional with conservative values. An old-fashioned rural upbringing had instilled in her a sense of right and wrong. She surely didn't bounce around from man to man. Two different men in thirty years should hardly qualify her as a "hot trotter." The tunnel-visioned geniuses in the marketing department would know that if they had bothered to read the book instead of relying on someone else's hastily written synopsis.

Joann thought the whole title change idea to be quite trashy. That's not what she intended her character to be all about and she wouldn't put up with it. Little did she know Hagar House's cover designers had already conceptualized a steamy illustration in which to package the new novel. *Hot Trotter's* cover would depict a scantily clad vivacious beauty seducing a male passerby with her exaggerated come-hither eyes. Joann's battle had just begun. The book community, especially the unfortunate mistitled publications, were rooting for Joann to stand her ground.

Another bookseller who was having an eventful summer was Sandra. The dark haired beauty was now a blond. She had heard that blondes had more fun—and fun was what she was all about. She kept up a busy social schedule, filled with parties, concerts and late-night clubbing. Sometimes she would go straight from the nightclub to the bookstore without sleeping at all. None of this seemed to affect her job performance. She was still the number one bookseller in the entire Sanders and Bowman chain. Her latest boyfriend was a professional baseball player. He had recently brought the whole team into the bookstore just so they could get a peek at his new girlfriend. Of course, they each ended up buying several books.

Sherry was also selling her share of books, especially novels. She knew the basic plot of nearly every work of fiction in the bookstore. A few of them she considered her friends. Sherry would try to get her favorite novels located in good homes, where they would be loved and appreciated. Curiously enough, even though *Spy Needle* was her favorite novel in the entire bookstore, she made no effort to sell him. She didn't want to break up the blossoming romance between him and *River Run True*.

Sherry's intimate relationship with bound pieces of paper still befuddled her fellow coworkers. Once or twice a week they would catch her conversing with a book. Was she so lonely that she had to fabricate friendships with inanimate objects? Was she so emotionally deprived that lifeless books had become her support system. Sherry seemed perfectly normal in every other respect. Everyone seemed content to view her as an enthusiastic and industrious coworker who occasionally strayed near the wacky side. They accepted Sherry for what she was—a nice girl who sometimes spoke to books.

Another Sanders and Bowman staffer who stirred up gossip from time to time was Conner. Just when everyone thought he couldn't get any slower he seemed to slip into granny gear—almost a state of hibernation. It finally got so bad that Thomas mentioned it to Mel Redding, the regional manager and Conner's uncle. Some of the staff were shocked at their manager's gutsy move. If truth be told, Thomas was somewhat apprehensive about mentioning this touchy subject. He was surprised and relieved when Mel burst out laughing. Mel agreed that his nephew was a bit of a sloth with an aversion to work. The two of them went out for drinks to discuss the issue.

The summer delivered some other surprises. It was a time of comings and goings for the books. Some new arrivals would barely have time to say hello to their new neighbors before they were purchased. The books became accustomed to waking up and discovering a new covermate had arrived overnight. *Soy Cowboy*, a humorous Asian cookbook, actually went through six covermates during the course of one week.

The author of *Tantalizing Treats* had just made a brief appearance on Bobbi Taylor's show. The nationwide exposure sent customers racing to the bookstore to purchase this publication on unusual desserts. One particular copy of the popular book lasted only fifteen minutes before she was swooped off the shelf by an eager buyer. *Soy Cowboy's* sense of humor and easy wit kept the distressed newcomers calm during their nerve-racking displacements.

One temporary arrival was particularly well received by her neighbors. The fitness and nutrition section had been blessed with a surprise guest. *Forties Fitness* was back! She was only there for a day, but everyone made the best of it. Donna had taken to carrying the treasured book everywhere she went. It was a sort of security blanket for her. She was serious about losing weight and regaining her figure of old. One quick glance at *Forties Fitness* would remind her to stay away from the forbidden foods she sometimes craved.

On this particular day, Donna had stuffed her open knapsack under one of the bookshelves. *Forties Fitness* was resting on top of the bag. The shelf just happened to be *A36*, her former residence. Her old friends were shocked when their long lost neighbor called to them from below. They quickly became reacquainted and spent the entire day reminiscing. The euphoric books sped through the latest gossip before quizzing *Forties Fitness* on her new life. They were relieved to hear she was happy. Donna treated her like a queen.

Forties Fitness had become her most important possession. Her text had been streaked throughout with yellow highlight marks. This was a crowning achievement in the book world. To be deemed important enough to contain highlighted passages was an honor. Most books considered themselves lucky if they were read once during their lifetime. Yellow streaked pages meant they weren't only read, they were memorized. It was the highest honor that could be bestowed on a publication. *Forties Fitness* wore her yellow stripes with pride.

There was a valid reason why *Forties Fitness* was treated with such respect. She was delivering on her end of the bargain. The relationship between her and Donna was mutually beneficial. Her common sense approach towards diet and exercise was working. Donna had lost nearly twenty pounds by following the simple guidelines of the 228 page book. Her diet now consisted of fruits, vegetables and lean meats, with an occasional sweet reward. Donna had also embarked on a regular exercise program, walking two miles every evening.

Aside from the obvious physical benefits, her emotional state had also improved. She was gaining back her self esteem. Donna's face lit up with pride every time someone commented on her weight loss. She was determined to achieve her goal of losing fifty pounds. With the help of *Forties Fitness*, she seemed well on her way.

The other assistant manager wasn't doing so well. Charles was still an emotional basket case. Although he and his wife had officially divorced, Charles still held out hope of a reconciliation. He swore that he still loved her. Just when it seemed he was making progress he was struck down with some disturbing news. His ex-wife had remarried! Her new husband was the pool guy she had an affair with. The pool guy! Couldn't she have chosen someone else? Did it have to be that long haired chlorine-testing nitwit that Charles so despised?

Charles once again took out his frustrations on the help-less books. There had been several kicking and throwing episodes over the past month, resulting in one major injury. The charming novel *Nana Plaza* had her spine fractured when she was thrown against the wall. The books decided immediate action was in order. For weeks they had been devising an elaborate scheme to put *Divorce: Coping & Caring* into Charles's hands. The plan had been nicknamed Operation Blowpage. With the recent arrival of *Literary Review Monthly*, they could finally initiate their plan.

Grapevine sources had revealed that the June issue of *Literary Review Monthly* would contain a laudatory review full of praise for *Divorce: Coping & Caring*. The review would be on page 67 of the venerable publication. Every Sanders and Bowman manager always received a copy of the respected industry periodical the very day it arrived. It was important for them to be informed of the latest industry news.

The books knew the approximate date the magazines would be delivered. They also knew Ronnie always distributed the three copies to the offices of Thomas, Donna and Charles. The first day of June it arrived. Like clockwork, Ronnie immediately dispersed them to the three offices. Charles's desk, as usual, was piled high with paperwork. Ronnie laid Charles's copy on the only open area he could find, the far right side of the desk.

The bookstore closed and everyone left except for Thomas. Charles would open up around eight o'clock the next morning. They would have only ten hours to successfully perform Operation Blowpage. The objective was simple. *Literary Review Monthly* needed to be opened to page 67 when

Charles arrived. There was no way he would miss *Divorce: Coping & Caring's* lengthy review staring him in the face. Hopefully he would take the time to read it, then purchase a copy of the book. The books were rolling the dice that it would work.

The books biggest challenge was getting the magazine opened to page 67. The plan was this. Charles's business was conducted in a cramped office. He barely had room to walk in the minuscule workspace. Pressed up flush against Charles's desk was a bookshelf containing approximately eighty books. Most of them were employee management titles, led by a handful of hardbacks.

Operation Blowpage was exactly that. The eighty books would simultaneously flap their pages with all their might, hoping to generate enough wind to blow *Literary Review Monthly* open to page 67. It would be a demanding task which would likely take hours to complete. Nothing like this had ever been attempted before, but this was an emergency situation. *Nana Plaza's* broken back reminded everyone of the urgency.

The undisputed leader of this group was an eighth edition of the classic management guide *Performance Essentials: The Manager's Guide*. The charismatic bestseller commanded respect with his straightforward nature. There was little turnover within this group as they were there for the benefit of the management team. *Performance*, with a little help from his spouse *Practical Manager*, ran an efficient house. They were a happy group.

Operation Blowpage had just received another lucky break. Ronnie had placed *Literary Review Monthly* on the right side of the desk, literally inches from the books. This increased the odds of success, but no one was giving it more than a fifty-fifty chance. They were facing an exhausting task.

Flapping their pages for hours on end would be extremely demanding. It was times like these they wished they had lungs.

Thomas made his nightly rounds, peeking into Charles's office. Then he left the bookstore, locking the front door behind him. As soon as they heard the clicking of the lock, the books went to work. They had ten hours to reach page 67. There was no time to waste.

Performance immediately took charge. Everyone directed their attention to the intimidating periodical sitting before them.

"Aim just under the cover page," instructed *Performance*. "All together now, one, two, three, Flap! Flap! Flap!" Everyone flapped their pages with all their might. For ten exhausting seconds they frantically thrashed in an attempt to generate an airstream. Nothing happened. The magazine's cover hadn't budged.

Performance remained calm. "Okay, let's try something different." He looked down at the occupants on the shelf directly below. The hardback *Managing the Changing Workplace* was staring back at him, waiting for further instructions. *Performance* didn't hesitate.

"*Workplace*, when I say go, you and your shelfmates direct your efforts at the very edge of the cover. If you can raise it just a bit, we'll all join in and maybe we can turn it."

Workplace nodded in approval. "One, two, three, Go!" shouted *Performance*. All of the books from the lower shelf flapped in unison, this time taking aim at a smaller target, the very edge of the cover. The cover raised ever so slightly.

"Everybody, Flap! Flap with all your power! Flap!" commanded *Performance*. The remaining books joined in, flailing away in an effort to turn the heavy cover page. "Harder! Harder! It's working. Don't let up! Harder!" *Performance* was pushing his flock to their absolute limit. "We're moving it!

Harder everyone!" he continued. The determined books huffed and puffed nonstop for nearly twenty seconds. They cover was standing straight up. A little bit more and it would turn the corner and fall to the other side.

"Flap! Flap harder! Give it everything you have! Flap! Flap!" *Performance* wasn't about to let the cover fall back towards them. The books collectively expelled one final massive burst of energy. The cover fell to the other side!

The books were ecstatic. They had done it. The cover page was by far the heaviest page they had to deal with. Now it was a matter of stamina. Could they muster the strength to turn thirty-odd pages and reach page 67? It would be a herculean feat, but they were going to give it their best shot. None of them wanted to disappoint their inspirational leader. *Performance* knew how to bring out the best in each and every one of them. If it was at all physically possible, Operation Blowpage was going to be a success.

Throughout the night they methodically moved through the periodical page by page. By three o'clock in the morning they were up to page 36, but their strength was on the wane. Several of the smaller books were all but wiped out. *Performance* stopped everyone for a moment and delivered a motivational classic that would be remembered for years to come. His brief speech ignited a fire within the texts of the books. They quickly resumed work with a resolute determination to reach their goal.

With renewed vigor they blasted away at the remaining pages. Ten minutes before eight o'clock the final page fell victim. *Literary Review Monthly* lay open at page 67 exposing the treasured review of *Divorce: Coping & Caring*. The exhausted workers fell back on their shelves. *Performance* and his gritty crew had done their job. Phase one of Operation Blowpage had been a success. Hopefully Charles would read the review

JAMIE JOHNSON

and buy *Divorce: Coping & Caring*. Now it was all in God's hands.

Several minutes later they heard a key turn the front lock. Charles had arrived. He headed for the back room and started a pot of coffee. Seconds later came a thundering boom. The books had heard it before and knew exactly what is was. Charles was on the warpath. He had kicked the metal trash can violently across the room. The morning was off to an awful start.

Charles entered his tiny office wearing a scowl on his face. Now was the moment. Would their valiant efforts be successful or would it all be in vain? Charles sat down at his desk. Immediately his eyes focused on the open periodical before him. *Divorce's* review was staring him right in the face. What would Charles do? For an moment he seemed to be torn between reading the full page review or simply ripping the entire magazine to shreds. Charles let out a deep breath and picked up the periodical. He quickly skimmed through the text. He must have found it interesting because he slid his chair back, put his feet on the desk, and began reading it. The books let out a sigh of relief. They watched Charles for the next thirty minutes as he read the review not once, but *twice*. This was a very good sign.

After reading *Divorce's* review for the second time, Charles placed his arms on the desk and lowered his head. He stayed in that position for several minutes. The books were beginning to get worried. What was going on? Then Charles lifted his head. Tears were streaming down his face. The emotional assistant manager then rose from his seat and left the office. He made his way over to the Health/Mind/Body section. Scanning the top shelf he quickly found what he was looking for—*Divorce: Coping & Caring*! By this point the entire book community was watching. When Charles eased *Divorce* out from her tight fit between her covermates, the books erupted in celebration.

Charles spent the next few minutes flipping through *Divorce's* pages. Heather was the next employee to arrive for work. In a matter of minutes she had her cashier station open and ready for business. Her first customer of the day—Charles! The books watched as he walked back to his office. In his hand was a freshly purchased copy of *Divorce: Coping & Caring*. Operation Blowpage had been a total success. *Performance* and his gang would forever be remembered as heroes.

The books were thrilled with the triumph, but the celebration didn't last long. The following day, word circulated that their beloved Ronnie had been admitted to the hospital. His joint pain had worsened. The simple task of grasping a book had become painful. Several books had witnessed him having troubles bending down to pick something up. Ronnie was also becoming increasingly fatigued, having to take frequent breaks during the course of a workday. He had lost weight and his skin had taken on a slate gray color.

A couple of books had noticed even-tempered Ronnie experiencing some disturbing mood swings, snapping at some coworkers. Not once had anyone ever seen this during his entire six-year employment at Sanders and Bowman. Ronnie was as tough as nails and never complained about anything. The situation had to be serious for him to admit himself into the hospital. Something was wrong.

Ronnie was released from the hospital after two days of intensive testing. Although it wasn't definitive he was diagnosed with a form of arthritis. He was told that he might also be diabetic. Thomas suggested that Ronnie take a month off work with pay, but he insisted on returning after three days of rest. Thomas finally gave in and allowed Ronnie to return, on the condition that he would accept a lighter work load. Ronnie gave it his all at the bookstore, but it was obvious he hadn't improved. The doctors had prescribed some medication to combat his joint pain, but it wasn't making any noticeable difference. Many thought Ronnie, who despised drugs of any kind, wasn't even taking it.

Everyone at Sanders and Bowman was concerned for Ronnie. Management, coworkers, customers, and books alike practically worshiped him. He was their spiritual leader. Ronnie never steered them wrong, whether it was a bookstore related topic or a personal issue. Thomas even looked to Ronnie for advice regarding a variety of matters, not all of them work related. Naturally, everyone was constantly engaging Ronnie in conversation. They wanted to cheer up their friend, but they were also curious about his health problems. Ronnie spent a good portion of his days explaining his ailments. Talking about the issue seemed to be good therapy for everyone involved.

One particular afternoon Ronnie was speaking with Jo-ann. They just happened to be standing in front of the medicine section. A group of medical reference books were listening intently, hoping to gather some information about Ronnie's illness. Joann was asking Ronnie some detailed questions about his prognosis. Ronnie explained that although the doctors had assured him that his arthritis and diabetes weren't life threatening, he wasn't so sure.

He went on to tell Joann that an uncle of his had experienced the same symptoms years before. They had mysteriously developed into something worse, and began damaging his vital organs, especially his liver and heart. His uncle's condition gradually worsened, until he eventually died from a combination of congestive heart failure and liver cancer.

A chill surged through the spine of *Diagnosed: Uncovering Rare Diseases*. He was an enormous 900-page medical reference book dedicated to the diagnosis and misdiagnosis of uncommon diseases. *Diagnosed* knew instantly what Ronnie's problem was—and what it wasn't. The information regarding Ronnie's uncle had been crucial. Pages 662-669 of his text described Ronnie's affliction in detail. It was *not* arthritis and it was *not* diabetes.

It was a relatively unknown genetic disorder called hereditary hemochromatosis. Symptoms of the disease are regularly attributed to other causes. Many individuals with hemochromatosis go undiagnosed until irreversible damage has occurred. Even after the patient passes away, the disease is often overlooked as a possible cause of death. It is sometimes termed "the silent killer" because of this reason.

Diagnosed quickly spread the word around the shelf to his fellow medical publications. Hereditary hemochromatosis was a metabolic disorder that produced a dietary iron overload. In a nutshell, the body absorbs and retains too much iron. If left untreated, the condition can affect many organ systems, including the liver, heart, pancreas and joints. It is commonly misdiagnosed.

However, the potentially fatal disease is easily treated if diagnosed early. *Diagnosed* theorized that Ronnie's doctor never bothered to test for hemochromatosis because of Ronnie's age. It rarely afflicted young people except in the case of the hereditary version. Ronnie's doctor probably never asked him about his family's medical history.

The books knew what had to be done. Ronnie needed information—the information that lay between pages 662 and 669 of *Diagnosed*. Ronnie did not have arthritis or diabetes. He had a hereditary condition that could be treated. It was so easy—if only he knew! If he could be made aware of the facts he could rid himself of this potentially deadly disease. Once again, the books had to create a situation where an employee would open up a particular book and read it. They quickly went to work on a plan. What the doctors couldn't do, the books were determined to accomplish. Time was of the essence. Ronnie's life was at stake.

Chapter 9

It was a breezy Saturday afternoon. Outside the winds howled, kicking up huge dust clouds that seemed intent on following customers into the bookstore. The freaky weather seemed to inspire the public's need to read. Sanders and Bowman was bustling with activity. Several books commented that they had never seen the bookstore so crowded—and so loud.

The periodical section was especially noisy. It seemed a group of boisterous teenagers had chosen this particular area to hold their weekly gossip session. Maybe the ferocious winds had driven them from their usual outdoor rendezvous location. The Saturday afternoon regulars were somewhat perturbed, but overall they were remarkably patient with the mass of adolescents that had descended upon their normally peaceful domain.

One longtime customer that removed himself from the madness was James. Disabled from a severe form of arthritis and unable to walk, he was confined to an electric scooter. Ronnie had recently been actively seeking his advice on the affects of the crippling disease. Actually James wasn't as much of a customer as he was as he was a connoisseur of people watching. James was a champion people watcher. He came in three or four times a week, always accompanied by his wife. Phyllis was an avid lover of books.

James and Phyllis were both well known by the staff because of their extraordinary kindness. Both were working class retirees. James had been a factory worker and Phyllis had been a nurse. Phyllis was always trying to tip the cashiers although they had told her countless times they weren't allowed to accept gratuities. Nevertheless, Phyllis would fail to pick up the change from her transaction, *accidently* leaving it on the counter. Phyllis had stealthily gained knowledge of every employee's birthday and never failed to give them a card. James and Phyllis had attended Heather's wedding. Heather placed the couple in such high regard that she even roped off a special area to park James's scooter.

Seventy-five-year-old James was the consummate charmer. Growing up around four sisters had instilled in him an amazing ability to understand the complex makeup of the female gender. Women of all ages immediately fell under his spell upon meeting him. He was still quite handsome and had an easy humor about him that women adored. They instinctively knew that here was a genuine man.

James and Phyllis's visits to Sanders and Bowman had an order about them. They would arrive midday and stay for two hours. Their routine never varied. James would park his electric scooter in an out-of-the-way location. Phyllis would make a quick ten-minute run through the bookstore and return with exactly three books on varying topics. James would spend the next two hours sipping coffee, studying human behavior, and glancing through Phyllis's selections. Meanwhile, Phyllis would scurry off to scour the store in search of literary treasures, always purchasing one or two.

It was every book's dream to be purchased by Phyllis. Her house had become a mystical destination, a place that transcended the physical world of bestseller lists and movie rights. It was deemed an extreme honor to be chosen by the saintly Phyllis. The religion section had actually debated the possibility that Phyllis's home might possibly be the ultimate reward—book heaven—the final resting place for virtuous literary souls. Whether or not this was true no one really knew, but one thing was for certain. Phyllis's house was prime real estate, a place every book would be proud to call home.

James had maneuvered his scooter away from the disruptive teens. They had invaded his customary people watching domain, a little nook just between the periodicals and the seating area. It was perfectly designed for James to back in his scooter, allowing him to view much of the bookstore. Never a complainer, James simply sought out another location. He had found a suitable vantage point amongst the novels. James had placed just enough of his scooter out of the aisle to allow other patrons to pass by. This wasn't as good as his customary parking spot, but it would suffice. Besides, a little change from the routine might be good for him.

James had positioned himself directly in front of shelf C22. *Spy*, *River*, *Destiny* and the others felt honored to be in his presence. After all, he was James, husband of the divine Phyllis, the woman who just might be the chosen one—the guardian of virtuous souls. As the books focused on this legendary maestro, the supreme observer of everything human, a woman walked between them and their subject.

"Honey, here's three you may enjoy," the lady said. She bent down and kissed James's forehead and went on her way.

It had been Phyllis! The holy one had entered their area. She had just delivered James his three books. That meant that *Spy* and friends would have two whole hours to watch one of the coolest beings on the planet do what he did best—sip coffee, skim through his books, and analyze the Homo sapien primate known as man. Not only that, but Phyllis would most likely be back when she finished her rounds. This was turning out to be a very special afternoon.

Everyone strained to see what three lucky publications had been hand delivered by the ordained one to her husband. James slowly looked over the three covers one by one. He was famous for doing everything in stages. In a few seconds, if he followed his normal routine, he would pick up one of the books and flip through a few pages. After approximately two minutes he would do the same with the second book, then the third. After a ten-minute session of people watching, he would pick up the book he deemed most interesting and read it for several minutes. Unless the book really held his interest he would devote the rest of the afternoon to watching humans interact. Occasionally the second book would gain another look, and on rare occasions the third selection would reap another opportunity to be held by James.

Seldom would James ever purchase a book, maybe once a year. The books didn't hold this against him. Why would James need to read a book? The man already had all the answers to everything. The knowledge acquired from seventy-five years of surveying the human race topped any Ph.D-toting academic's credentials. Heck, he was married to Phyllis, the sacred high priestess of everything that is good. Talk about a charmed life! Any book that would dare to openly question James's purchasing habits would be shoved right off their shelf in two seconds flat.

James quickly analyzed the three covers. Phyllis had brought over three distinctly different books. The first one he picked up was *Fishing's Tallest Tales: Truths, Half-Truths and Out-and-Out Lies*. It was immediately obvious that James liked this one. Maybe it was the rather odd-shaped cover. The second title was *Analyzing Group Dynamics: A Case Study in Social Psychology*. James appeared to take an interest in this one also.

Phyllis surprised her husband of fifty years with her third and final selection. *Midnight Soul* was a novel. For seven years they had been frequenting Sanders and Bowman and not once had Phyllis presented him with a work of fiction. He had always said he had zero interest in fiction. What could it be about this particular novel that deemed it worthy of his attention? James was intrigued.

James gave each book their customary two-minute review. He would now mentally process that information while he scanned the bookstore. For the next ten minutes he studied his human subjects. One particularly interesting interaction involved what appeared to be a teen love triangle. Two girls were quietly quarreling over a boy. The young man in question finally came over and put his arm around one of the girls. He was choosing her. He then rudely commented, "I don't want to be seen with no ugly duckling." The despondent loser walked away in tears. James hoped she would come his way, but she made a hasty retreat to the ladies' room.

James glanced down at the books before him. It was time to choose a favorite. The books looked on as the wise one contemplated.

"He'll choose the fishing book," said *Spy* to no one in particular.

"I think he'll go with the social psychology book," replied *Destiny*. "That's his area of expertise."

"You're wrong, boys," *River* stated confidently. "It'll be *Midnight Soul*. Curiosity stalks even the wisest of minds. It's not so much the book itself as it is Phyllis. She surprised him. Never before has she delivered a novel to him. James wants to know, *needs* to know, what's so special about *Midnight Soul*."

River's female intuition proved to be correct. James reached down and picked up *Midnight Soul*. He was curious as to the contents of the 360 page novel. James began reading page one.

Destiny looked at *Spy* and shrugged. "So much for our prognosticating abilities, huh *Spy*?

"Yeah," answered *Spy*. "Guess we'd better keep our day jobs."

"Don't worry boys," said *River*. "You're still pretty clever. You're just guys, that's all. You know we women are tuned to a different frequency."

"That's for sure," agreed *Spy*, "but that's what makes the world interesting."

"Okay," said *Destiny*, "there's no debating that females rule the planet. We unanimously agree on that. Maybe one of our guests is female. I think it's time we introduce ourselves."

"Yes, you're right," said *Spy*. "Hello to our visitors down there. How are you doing?"

"Couldn't be better," a warm voice cried out.

It was *Fishing's Tallest Tales*. He was easily recognized by his unusually proportioned cover. His height was three times his width. As a matter of fact he was probably the tallest book in the entire bookstore. On a whim his publisher had concocted the idea as a publicity gimmick, hoping *Fishing's Tallest Tales* would stand out from the hundred or so other books on fishing. The cover was strikingly eye-catching, illustrating a nattily attired fish sipping tea and smoking a cigar.

The marketing strategy had proved successful as sales well exceeded expectations. Thousands of consumers were buying the curiously shaped book as gifts. The book was especially popular with children. It seemed every budding angler, some as young as three years old, had to have a copy of the big book about fish.

"My name's *Fishing's Tallest Tales*. Everyone calls me *Tall Tale* for the obvious reason. I'm all about the big one that got away and other assorted exaggerations, some of them bordering on out-and-out lies as my subtitle suggests. As you may have heard, fishermen have a reputation for stretching the truth. They're the undisputed masters of distorting reality, even better than politicians.

"That's an interesting cover you have," said *River*. "I hope you're not going to tell me fish really smoke cigars."

"No," answered *Tall Tale*. "No one's had the gumption to try that one yet, but I do have a story about a whiskey drinking fish. This guy swears it's the truth. He says he finally had to cut him off because the fish was getting drunk and harassing the females."

River laughed. "Oh my, sounds like you're another entertaining publication. I'm sure everyone's got loads of questions for you, but I've gotta ask you something before we dive into your waters. What's it like to be touched by Phyllis? I know it's everyone's dream to be purchased by her."

"Fantastic," said *Tall Tale*. "It was the best ten minutes of my life. As you know she always brings James three books to look through. I was lucky enough to be the first. Then for ten glorious minutes she held me in her hand while she searched for the other two selections. After she found *Analyzing Group Dynamics* and *Midnight Soul* she delivered us to James. I wish she would had taken all day looking for the other two books.

"I could feel the presence of a higher power as she carried me around the bookstore. I think she may truly be an angel from heaven. I know it's a long shot because James rarely ever purchases a book, but I would be on top of the world if he'd send me to the promised land—Phyllis's House! As a matter of fact, I'm jealous of *Midnight Soul* right now. James hasn't looked up since he began reading her. I think she's got a real chance of making it to eternal paradise."

"Yes, he is engrossed in her," said *River*, "but don't you give up hope. He's bound to take another look at you. He'll probably be here for another hour and a half. Hang in there *Tall Tale*."

"*River's* right," said *Spy*. "At any moment James could snap you up for another peek between your covers. That's why we need you to share some of your tallest tales with us now. Time may be limited. How about it *Tall Tale*? Can you get into some of your truths, half-truths, and most of all, your out-and-out lies?"

River looked at *Tall Tale* and smiled. "I told you *Spy's* a connoisseur of all things fun and exciting. I gotta warn you. Now that you've whetted his appetite for entertainment you'd best break out some vintage material. We're all kinda spoiled around these parts when it comes to storytelling."

"I'll do my best," said *Tall Tale*. "I've got a couple of favorites that usually go over pretty well. Before I get into those let me briefly tell you about the ones that got away. Every fisherman has a story about a fish he *almost* caught. Usually it's a big fish that breaks the line just as he nears the boat. Big is the key word here. There's never a camera around to document any of these tall tales, so we're supposed to take the fishermen at their word. It's usually a guy fishing solo so there's rarely anyone else to corroborate his story.

"If it happens to be two fisherman involved in the one that got away—forget about it! The size increases exponentially. The two-pound bass that slipped away becomes a twenty-pounder by the time they get back to the marina. After a couple of beers with their fellow anglers it magically jumps to forty pounds. The next day everyone is talking about the eighty-pounder that Bob and Tom nearly reeled in. The legend is taking shape. By weeks end—a couple of guys almost pulled in a 160-pound bass. The minnow that got away has evolved into a whale. The legend is now complete."

"Funny!" exclaimed *Destiny*. "It's probably true too. Please continue."

"Sure," replied *Tall Tale*. "As you may have guessed, my creator is a fisherman. Fishermen love to talk to other fishermen. He and his band of cohorts can run through the aquatic baloney—let me tell you! He's heard some whoppers in his time. Here's one that I tend to classify in the out-and-out lie category. You can be the judge. Have any of you ever heard of the Japanese mudskipper?"

"Can't say that I have," replied *Spy*. "Sounds like some sort of exotic dessert item to me—one that I wouldn't touch."

"Ha, you're a funny one," said *Tall Tale*. "Actually the Japanese mudskipper is a species of fish that inhabits the waters of the Pacific. These tiny fish are unusual in the fact that they are amphibious. They can operate on land as well as water. It's got to do with their enlarged gill chambers. They can retain water which allows the creature to breath outside of the water—sorta like a scuba diver's oxygen tank."

"I can't wait to hear this," said *River*. "Anything concerning a Japanese mudcreeper has gotta be amusing."

Tall Tale let out a hearty laugh. "That's mudskipper, but I think I like your name better. It kinda adds a little more flair to the story. So from now on it's mudcreeper.

"Okay, buckle up for this one—the homesick mudcreeper. One day this guy was fishing in the Florida Everglades. He had been fishing all morning and hadn't had a bite. Suddenly something hits his line and he's nearly jerked from the boat. The fish is so big that it bends his rod to the breaking point. The fish begins to pull the fisherman and his boat behind it as it struggles to break free. The boat quickly picks up speed until it reaches fifty miles per hour. The hapless angler is terrified. What kind of fish is powerful enough to do this? He squats down in the hull of the boat as it increases in speed.

"Holding tight to the rod the fisherman hunkers down even lower as the boat speeds to over eighty miles per hour. The shoreline is getting closer and closer and the fish is actually speeding up. Now the fisherman is really concerned. He fears for his life but he doesn't want to release this mammoth once-in-a-lifetime catch. Finally the boat exceeds one hundred miles per hour and is seconds away from crashing into the bank. The fisherman momentarily closes his eyes. Crash! Slam! Bang!

"The horrified man opens his eyes. To his astonishment the boat is still moving along at over one hundred miles per hour—on land! He looks ahead to see what powerful creature is capable of dragging him and his boat at such speeds through land and water. The fisherman can't believe his eyes. It's a tiny six-inch fish! A six-inch fish! He strained his eyes for a closer look. The little fellow resembled a fish he'd seen in a magazine—something called a Japanese mudcreeper. How could that be? The mudcreeper wasn't native to North America.

"Whatever the heck it was, it sure was making good time. They had actually picked up speed on land. Baboom, baboom, baboom—the boat bounced up and down violently as they made their way through the dense brush. The fisherman continued to grasp his rod as they plowed through the terrain uprooting everything in their path. The little fish was determined to reach its destination whatever that may be. The fisherman settled in as they raced towards an increasingly urban setting. Straight ahead was the skyline of downtown Miami.

"They blazed through downtown Miami in less than a minute. The lunchtime crowd watched in amazement as this man with a most unusual mode of transportation sped through the city's busy intersections. The tiny fish zipped through traffic performing maneuvers that would make race car drivers jealous.

"The ambitious mudcreeper was just getting started. He left the big city behind as he plunged into Biscayne Bay. Now it was time for a little swim. With boat and occupant in tow he headed out to sea—destination Japan. In seven days time he would be wrapped in the fins of his lovely lass—the most beautiful mudcreeper in all of the world.

"At this point the fisherman was just as determined as the mudcreeper to hang on. He wasn't about to let this one get away. The spunky fisherman had invested too much energy in this fight to give up now. He had battled this fish in the fresh water of the everglades, over rugged and rocky terrain, through the streets of downtown Miami—and now he was wrestling with it in the salty sea. Hemingway's character in *The Old Man and the Sea* didn't have anything on him.

"They blasted through the Panama Canal around midnight. Fish and man were exhausted but neither were giving up. For six more days and nights they raced towards Japan. Both of them would occasionally snatch a piece of seaweed as they zoomed across the ocean. This sustained them until they finally arrived in Japan's southern islands.

"This is when the little mudcreeper jumped out of the water and spit out the hook. Success was his. He jumped two more times as if he were saying goodbye to the fisherman he had drug halfway around the world. Then he swam away to reunite with his mudcreeping mate."

Tale Tale smiled. "There you have it—believe it or not. The story ends with the fisherman flying back to America. His trophy catch had gotten away and left him with nothing but an extremely tall tale. What do you think?"

Tall Tale's listeners were amused. He had satisfied a most demanding audience. Two entire shelves were giggling at this most improbable occurrence.

"I'm gonna have to agree with you," said a grinning *Spy*. "This one needs to be filed in the out-and-out lie category. To call it even a half-truth would be generous."

"Who knows," said *River*, "maybe it happened. It would take quite an imagination to make up a crazy story like that. Maybe the power of love enlivened this amorously consumed mudcreeper to engage in such an undertaking. One thing though—why did this lovesick traveler, a mere six inches long, feel obliged to drag along a boat and a man on this treacherous journey? I gotta admit that's a bit suspicious. Guess I gotta agree with you, *Spy* dear. It's an out-and-out lie."

Tall Tale flushed with pride. He looked up at James still held captive by *Midnight Soul*.

"Looks like James is locked into *Midnight Soul* for awhile. Would you guys be interested in hearing another one?"

"By all means," answered *Spy*. "I was just going to ask if that was possible."

"Thanks to everyone for being such a great audience. I love sharing my stories. I guess I'm sort of a ham."

River brushed up tight against *Spy's* cover. "Don't worry about that, *Tall Tale*. You're not the only ham around here, right *Spy*?

"I'm afraid it's true," said *Spy*. "You and I are cut from the same mold. I guess some of us just like entertaining. *Tall Tale*, you've got the stage. Carry on."

"Okay! Once again, you can decide for yourself if you think the next story is fabricated or not. This one dates back to the late 1700's and originates from the city of New Orleans.

There was this young fellow named Asnas Jones. He had a reputation as being one of the best fishermen ever to throw a line into the Mississippi River. He even made his living at it, selling most of the fish he caught.

"Asnas was content living a simple fisherman's life until a distant cousin came to visit. This relative happened to be very knowledgeable about their family ancestry. He told Asnas he had been named after his great-grandfather. Asnas's great-grandfather had been a Persian sailor who happened to be an excellent poker player. Poker actually derived from a similar game in Persia called *As Nas*. From this point on Asnas was hooked. He was determined to live up to his namesake's legend. He decided he would become the greatest poker player in the world.

"Young Asnas's learning curve proved to be expensive. Every time he'd accumulate a little money he'd jump on the *Miss Stake*, a riverboat that cruised the Mississippi catering to gamblers. Then he'd promptly lose every penny. The beneficiary was usually A.A. Walker—Double A they called him—the best poker player in the territory. Double A was especially adept in the art of bluffing. He could be holding a pair of twos and you'd swear by his demeanor that he had a royal flush. Once a week Double A would strip Asnas clean of everything he owned, sometimes literally taking the shirt off his back. Asnas kept coming back for more. He was determined to beat the veteran card player.

"Once a year the World Poker Cup was held on the *Miss Stake*. Players from around the globe gathered to participate in this hold 'em and fold 'em extravaganza. It was the richest poker tournament anywhere. The glitzy affair had it all, from dancing girls to card playing monkeys. The promoters had even installed a massive aquarium full of fish—a representation of every species that inhabited the Mississippi River.

Double A was the three-time defending champion. Asnas paid the substantial entry fee confident of a victory. He had recently acquired a secret weapon.

"Asnas breezed through the first round of competition. The young gambler's skills had dramatically improved. He worked his way through to the finals. Now there were only two players remaining. It would be the young upstart Asnas battling the cunning veteran Double A. Both gamblers were focused on winning the enormous pot. Double A was the heavy favorite to take it for the fourth consecutive year.

"The big event was about to start. Asnas walked into the crowded room. He stopped and gazed into the gigantic fish tank, tapping it lightly with one finger before taking his seat at the table. Throughout the tournament this had been a ritual. Some observers speculated that Asnas did this for good luck. Gamblers were known to be quite the superstitious breed."

Tall Tale was quiet for a moment. He glanced up at his listeners. He had their full attention.

"Now for a little background on how and why this aquarium—and one of its occupants—were so important. Asnas had a little more going for him than just his poker playing skills. He had an edge.

"The aquarium was indeed a source of good luck—in the form of a foot-long catfish named Euclid. Asnas had discreetly slipped the fish into the tank the day before the tournament started. He had caught it a month earlier. Asnas was planning on selling him at the fish market until he noticed something unusual. The fish would repeatedly poke his head out of the live well as if he were trying to communicate something. Then he would swim in a distinct pattern. Asnas was intrigued. For several minutes he studied the movements of this mysterious fish. It seemed that the fish was diagramming the number two in the water. In his hand Asnas held two fishing lures. Could it be? No way? Asnas picked another one. He held the three lures above the live well. Incredibly the catfish changed his pattern. His movements outlined the number three. Unbelievable! Asnas reached into his tackle box and retrieved another lure. He then exposed four lures to this mathematically inclined fish. The fish once again proved his calculating prowess by creating the number four. Outrageous!

"Asnas took the ciphering fish home with him. He decided to name him Euclid, after the famous Greek mathematician. Asnas didn't quite know what to do with his unusually gifted pet. One day while practicing playing poker he heard a splashing sound. He turned to see Euclid frantically flopping around inside his tank. What was his whiskered accountant trying to tell him this time?

"Asnas watched intently as his catfish began to spell something out in the water. Euclid began with the number two, then the number eight, then another eight, then what looked to be a K, finishing off with the letter A. 'What in the heck was that all about?' Asnas said to himself. Then he looked down at his poker hand.

"Asnas couldn't believe his eyes. His five cards were a pair of eights, a two, a king and an ace. He was astonished. Euclid's seemingly bizarre behavior had a purpose after all. The arithmetic-loving fish had just read his poker hand to perfection.

"Asnas had an idea. If Euclid could read his cards, then maybe he could be trained to read the poker hand of others. Then he could relay that valuable information back to Asnas, providing a tremendous competitive edge. He wanted the snooping catfish to especially focus on one man's hand. That hand would belong to the reigning king of poker. Ole Double A was about to be dethroned."

Destiny chuckled out loud causing everyone to look at him. "I'm sorry for the interruption. This mathematician-turned-spy catfish story just strikes me as funny. *Tall Tale*, I can certainly see why this one made it into your text. Please go ahead."

"Okay, let's move back to the World Poker Cup. The plan has obviously worked. Asnas and his finned assistant have sleuthed their way into the finals. Now it's one hand of no-limit poker for all the marbles. The two poker players take their place at the table. Asnas grabs his favorite seat, the one facing the huge fish tank. Double A selects his usual chair directly opposite Asnas. The cards are shuffled and dealt. A minor bet raises the pot. Both players exchange three cards. Now the real game begins.

"Asnas takes a peek at his cards. His heart sinks. He keeps his cool on the outside but inside he's sickened. He's got a pair of twos. This is the most important hand of poker he'll ever play in his life and he's holding two lousy twos. It would be nearly impossible to win with a hand like that. Double A was going to win again. Euclid had communication powers but he couldn't change Double A's hand.

"Double A must have sensed a wounded opponent. Going for a quick kill he upped the ante with a large wager. Asnas thought about folding then and there, but decided to match the bet. What the heck. He was in the finals of the world's biggest poker tournament. He might as well extend it a little longer.

"Meanwhile wide-eyed Euclid zooms in on Double A's cards. In a matter of seconds he's relaying the information back to his owner. Asnas has all but given up hope of winning, but he's curious as to what Double A's holding.

"Euclid commences with his dance as Asnas watches from the corner of his eye. Euclid begins with a A. That means an ace—not a good start. Euclid then spells out a K. That means Double A's also holding a king. That's not good either. Then a Q appears. All these high cards are spelling one word—trouble! Euclid continues with a J. It can't get any worse. It appears the master Double A is going to win in style. If he gets a ten he's got at least a straight and possibly a royal flush—poker's highest hand. Heck, even a lowly pair of anything will beat his humble set of twos.

"Euclid spells out Double A's remaining card. It's a nine! That means Double A is holding an ace-high hand. All that royalty doesn't mean a thing. Asnas's meekly pair of two's will win the hand. All he has to do is match Double A wager for wager—because for sure the master bluffer will pretend he's got a hot hand.

"Asnas's instincts are correct. A relaxed Double A slides a mammoth pile of chips trying to scare away his inexperienced opponent. Asnas immediately counters by matching the huge wager. Double A is stunned. He turns red in the face and breaks out in a sweat. He can't believe the young amateur had the guts to continue this high stakes contest.

"Double A shoves in all of his remaining chips, four stacks piled high. This will certainly shoo away this fisherman who dares to lock horns with the greatest poker player in the world. Asnas would require nerves of steel to match this outrageous bet. There's no way this whippersnapper has the gumption to hang with the maestro.

"A big smile appears on Asnas's face as he pushes his own enormous pile of chips onto the table. 'I'll match that bet. Now let's show 'em!' Asnas exposes his pair of twos. The crowd gasps at the weak hand.

"Double A is in a state of shock. He throws down his cards and storms away. His bluff had been called. An ace-high hand wasn't going to win anything. Asnas reached out with both arms and raked in the mountain of chips. He had won! With a little help from his academically inclined catfish he had defeated the invincible Double A. Asnas was the undisputed world champion of poker. He glanced over to the aquarium where Euclid was repeatedly spelling out in huge capital letters—WINNER!"

"Oh my goodness!" *River* exclaimed. "That's a classic. Okay, tell us. Is it truth, half-truth or an out-and-out lie?"

"To be honest no one really knows. It goes back so far that there's no way to research it. I tend to doubt that fish can read and write, but who knows? How many humans would ever suspect that books actually speak to each other—but here we are talking up a storm. Anything's possible, right?"

"You've got a point there, *Tall Tale*," said *Spy*. "Regardless of its degree of truthfulness, we all agree you've got a highflyer with that amusing narration. If it's a work of fiction then your creator has certainly got a vivid imagination."

Once again *Tall Tale* beamed with pride. "Ain't nobody got anything on Julian when it comes to fishing. Fishing is Julian's specialty. He should know something about it, he's been reeling 'em in for over sixty years. His angling resume includes some tall tales of his own. As a matter of fact it was Julian's borderline believable experiences that inspired him to write me."

"Now you've made us curious," said *Destiny*. "Can you share a couple of your creator's tallest tales?"

"There's several of them that are worth noting," said *Tall Tale*, "but here's a couple of my personal favorites. Now keep in mind—these stories are one hundred percent true. They can't generate the excitement of a lovesick migrating mudcreeper or a poker playing catfish—but they are guaranteed to be the unembellished truth.

"This one is the story my creator enjoys the most. I've heard Julian tell it a thousand times. There was this special lake that my creator was especially fond of. It was a quiet relaxing place where he could fish the day away with no distractions. He'd go there two or three times a week to enjoy the solitude. Rarely did he ever see another person. It was as if it was his own private lake. He had even built a reef from some thorn brushes. The fish didn't seem to mind the prickly spines at all. It was the best bluegill fishing spot anywhere.

"One tranquil afternoon the silence was shattered by the sound of an approaching motorboat. Julian looked up to see several young men, most of them in their mid-twenties, aboard a twin-engine high performance racing vessel. They breezed past him with a water skier in tow. Julian's a live-and-let-live type of guy, so he went back to his fishing. He figured they had as much right to enjoy the beautiful lake as he did.

"Several minutes passed and the powerboat circled by again. This time it was considerably closer. The skier behind the boat yelled out a derogatory racial remark to my Julian as he passed. In case you're wondering, my creator is black. The waves from the powerful boat rocked my creator's tiny canoe.

"Well, my Julian smelled trouble brewing. These hooligans were intent on causing a ruckus. My creator quickly came up with an idea that would send these guys flying. No one knew the outlay of this lake like he did. Julian knew every cove, every drop-off—and every stump! The lake was deceiving in places—it appeared to be deep water when it was actually extremely shallow.

"This happened to be one of those places. It was guaranteed these buffoons weren't aware of it. Not only that, but there were several huge tree stumps that were barely covered under the water's surface. They weren't visible but they were a hazard. Julian knew one especially well. The massive stump had punched a hole in his canoe years earlier.

"My creator watched as the racing boat and its skier made a large circle. Julian knew they'd be back. He quickly paddled his canoe directly behind the area where he knew the treacherous stump lay hidden below the surface. Then he cast out his line and waited for a bite—of the human kind.

"Sure enough the troublemakers headed his way. This time they had picked up speed. They were obviously intent on overturning Julian's canoe. The engines roared as the powerful boat bared down on my creator. Julian kept his eyes straight ahead as he slowly reeled in his line. He wanted to draw these thugs in as close as possible. The racing vessel was at full throttle. The boat thundered over Julian's line swinging the skier within inches of his canoe. He could hear the boat's unruly passengers laughing as they shouted out racial obscenities. Julian looked up at the skier. He was holding the ski rope with one hand. In the other hand he held an unopened beer bottle. He reared back and aimed the projectile at my creator's head.

"Just as he was about to throw the bottle—in the nick of time for my Julian—there was what sounded like a huge explosion. The racing boat had plowed into the enormous hidden stump at over eighty miles per hour. The powerful boat flipped end-over-end spilling its occupants into the water. It landed upside-down and broke into two pieces. The passengers were spread over a wide area.

"One of the displaced ruffians was moaning and groaning that he had a broken arm. Another was flopping around in waist-deep water yelling out 'Mama, help me, I'm hurt!' The boat's operator had been thrown onto the embankment landing in an unknown creature's recently produced dung pile. Yet another had shot straight up in the air, coming to earth straddling one of the now-displaced engines as if it were a horse. He was now rolling around in the fetal position clutching his groin area. The skier may have been the unluckiest one of all. He had crash landed in Julian's thorny fishing reef. Thrashing around in a panic had only added to his misfortune. Hundreds of the sharp wooden needles had penetrated his body. He was now lying on the bank writhing in excruciating pain, covered from head to toe with the spiny protuberances.

"My Julian calmly rowed his canoe to the shore. He walked over to this now harmless human pincushion. 'Looks like you guys had a little accident. I'll paddle over to the marina and get you some help. You don't mind if I drink this nice German lager before it gets hot, do ya?'

"My creator picked up the bottle of beer that had been destined for his head and opened it, taking a long drink. He then stepped into his canoe and began paddling, careful not to hit the big stump that was always causing so much trouble."

Tall Tale's cover looked like it would burst with pride. Every book liked to praise their creator and he was no exception. *Tall Tale* knew this good-over-evil act of cleverness had been a hit with his listeners. Knowing it was a real event made the story even more appealing.

"*Tall Tale*, I've got to give your creator a standing ovation on that one," said *River*. "I feel so good that I've got chill bumps on my cover. Hurray for your Julian! He really showed those ruffians a thing or two. They'll think twice before they try something like that again."

Spy couldn't wipe the huge grin off his cover. "That ranks up there with best of them. What a cool dude! Don't stop now *Tall Tale*!"

"Okay, if you insist," replied a beaming *Tall Tale*. "Here's a humorous one. Several years back Julian attended a family reunion. It was held in a park by a beautiful lake. Of course, everyone brought along their fishing gear hoping to reel in a few. After they stuffed themselves with a big meal everyone retreated to the shoreline to try their luck at fishing. An hour passed without even a nibble. Then my Julian got a bite. Everyone watched as he reeled it in. The fish was on the small side, but at least he had caught something.

"Julian then decided to add a little life to the party. He pretended to extract the fish from the hook and let him go. Instead he placed the fish back in the water still attached to the hook. He released the drag on the line and the fish swam back out into the center of the lake. After a few minutes Julian called out 'I've got another one.' Everyone watched as he pulled in the fish. Once again, he pretended to release the fish and let it swim back out into the lake.

"Several minutes passed. 'Another bite! I think I'm into a school of them. This one's a real fighter.' Julian put on an acting performance that could have earned him an Emmy, pretending the fish was about to break his line.

"The others couldn't resist. None of them had gotten so much as a nibble and here was Julian pulling them in one after another. Everyone crowded in on my creator's turf. There were so many lines in one area that they got tangled with each other. It was a mad fishing frenzy. Julian quietly slipped away to the other side, concealing his fish behind his leg. He again slipped his little entertaining cohort back into the water.

"The school of fighting fish had stopped biting. No one was catching anything except the occasional line of a fellow angler. Suddenly a voice called out from the other side, where a lone fisherman stood. It was my creator. He was reeling in yet another one. Apparently the fish community was following Julian's hook around the lake. The confused anglers migrated in herd back to my creator. Yet again they cast out their hooks creating a massive spider web of entangled lines.

"My creator couldn't stand it anymore. He burst into laughter and confessed his trickery. One of his cousins promptly pushed him into the icy waters. Julian took it all in stride. The comedic adventure had been worth the drenching."

Tall Tale took a deep breath and relaxed. "There you have it my fellow publications. Those two little stories pretty much sum up my creator. He's clever, he's funny, and he's mine! Oh—and lucky too! He once caught a thirteen pound bass with his bare hands as it passed by his boat. The poor creature was dying of old age and he just happened to be passing by Julian's canoe. My creator placed him back into the water to live out his remaining days, thanking him for another tall tale to include in his forthcoming book—me! I've had the floor for a long time and I really appreciate your time. Thank you all. You've been a wonderful audience."

"*Tall Tale*, we're the ones that thank you," *Destiny* said in a sincere tone. "It's like *River* stated earlier, we hold the bar pretty high when it comes to storytelling. Mediocre material doesn't float around here. We consider ourselves to be excellent judges of stories and their narrators—and you've got both bases covered. Great job, my friend, and good luck with James if he ever gets his nose out of *Midnight Soul*. I see he's halfway through chapter three already."

"You're right," said *River*. "He's really giving her the treatment. She's gotta be on cloud nine. I think she's on her way to Phyllis's house."

"I agree," said *Spy*. "She's making quite the impression on James. I hope we get a few minutes with her and find out what she's all about. Until then, I'd love to hear from a book that's been mighty quiet. What do you say, *Analyzing Group*

Dynamics? Can you tell us a bit about yourself? I just know you've gotta be packed with interesting information."

"Okay," replied a friendly voice. *Analyzing Group Dynamics* was an exceptionally handsome book. He carried his 600 pages well.

"Everyone calls me *Analyze*. Let me tell you something before I get started. Don't you guys be expecting entertainment like you just heard from *Tall Tale*. I too was totally enthralled by his delightful literary treats. I wasn't created for entertainment purposes, although some of the human interactions within my text are quite amusing. I'm a studious type actually."

"*Analyze*, can you give us novices a brief overview of your area of expertise?" asked *Spy*. "What exactly is social psychology?"

"Social psychology is the study of how social conditions affect other human beings. It's really a combination of psychology and sociology. I like to describe it as people influencing other people. You can look around the bookstore right now and see countless examples of it. For example, do you see that group of teens by the periodical section?"

"Yes, we've been watching them since they arrived," answered *Spy*. "A noisy bunch, huh?"

"That's a fact," said *Analyze*. "Look at that short kid talking to the attractive girl. He's standing arrow-straight because he thinks it makes him appear taller in the presence of the pretty female. Before she arrived five minutes ago he was standing in a slouched position. When she leaves he'll assume his usual stooped posture. That's a simple example of a social situation influencing a human.

"Look towards Linda's register and you'll see another demonstration of social psychology. Notice the two women with identical hairstyles. They come in here a lot. Sometimes they're in my section conversing. Last month one of them made a dramatic change to her hair—length, color, style, the whole bit. She loved it. Now the other one has the exact same hair. That's another illustration of social psychology.

"For one more example of humans affecting humans look over at Sandra's section. See the kid browsing through the chemistry books? I know for a fact he's got the hots for Sandra. He's hoping she'll come over and ask if she can help him with anything. He doesn't give one flying doodly-winkle about chemistry. His behavior has been influenced by another person—and his raging hormones."

Analyze was momentarily quiet. "Heck, this social psychology thing even applies to us books. I'm sure you've all experienced it. Our thoughts, feelings and behaviors are influenced by the presence of other books on a daily basis."

"That's for sure," said *River*. "The gossip around Sanders and Bowman can get hot and heavy at times."

"This whole social interaction thing is fascinating," commented *Spy*. "Do you think you could share one of your more interesting case studies with us? Don't worry, we're not gonna try to compare you with *Tall Tale*. We're not here giving out entertainment awards. We'd simply like to learn from you. All of us are all aware that you're in a completely different category. How about it?"

"Sure, I could do that," replied *Analyze*. "Who knows how much time I have, so I'll touch on the important issues first. Social psychology involves humans influencing other humans, right? When it comes to mastering the art of persuasion no one does it better than governments. They are the top of the food chain. Their weapon of choice is the media—television in particular. For centuries governments have utilized propaganda to influence others.

"By nature I'm a stubborn creature, so I tend to resist being told what to do. Therefore I'm constantly on guard against the near total bombardment by the media. It's an emotional issue for me as well. My creator was a tenured professor at a top university. He was fired for taking on the chieftains of the military-industrial propagandists. He feared they were attempting to create a global one world government—one where the people are placed under total surveillance and stripped of all their freedoms. Orwell's classic novel *Nineteen Eighty-Four* became mandatory reading in his classes. My creator wanted his students to realize what could happen to a complacent society."

Analyze peered up at the novels, all of whom were focused on the handsome narrator. "The powerful propagandists didn't take kindly to his outspoken views on their latest conflict. The hows and whys of this particular war were nasty indeed. You see, my creator had high-level contacts within the government and knew the truth. Their latest war had been instigated by a horrible act of terror which killed thousands. It was promptly blamed on a foreign enemy. In actuality it was an inside job designed to justify the acts of aggression that were to follow. When he began airing this dirty laundry they shut him down. He was labeled an unpatriotic crackpot by the media. Their propaganda machine totally destroyed my creator's reputation and career.

"So you see, this human-influencing-human thing is serious business. Step in front of the big boys and you're liable to be crushed. To be honest with you, I'm just happy that my creator's alive. Believe me, people have been killed for less."

"Excuse me for a moment," a voice called out. It was *Stone Dance*. "I'd like to make a quick comment. Many of my fellow novels have heard this before, so I'll be brief. I'm a work of fiction, but I too deal with governments controlling the masses. It's happened over and over throughout history."

Stone Dance continued. "A government, usually one that's armed with the latest toys of warfare, wants a war. They crank up all the elements within their propaganda machine. The bought-off media shills begin cackling about the serious threat from a designated enemy. The populace is instructed in cartoonish fashion who to hate. If this method doesn't sway public opinion—watch out! An act of terror may magically appear, accompanied by a mountain of planted evidence that conveniently ties the tragic event to the evildoers you've been hearing so much about. Then the media kicks into overdrive with their scripted propagation of the so-called facts. Before you know it, the master manipulators have their war. I call that social psychology."

"Sounds like your creator understands the reality behind war," said *Analyze*. "That's interesting that he's conveying this important message through a work of fiction. I would love to somehow get you into the hands of my creator. I know he'd be intrigued."

"Yeah, let's work on that," said *Stone Dance*. "I would be honored to be read by such a courageous man who's not afraid to speak the truth."

"It's now a priority," said *Analyze*. "You would fit nicely in my creator's personal library. Okay guys, let's shift into a lower gear. I'm gonna dig into chapter twenty-six for a social psychology nugget."

Analyze peered up at James. He was still firmly entrenched in the text of *Midnight Soul*, only occasionally taking a short breather to scan the bookstore. *Analyze* turned back to his audience. The handsome book had everyone's attention, especially the females. Word had spread that this latest visitor was one fine-looking literary specimen. Single females from six shelves away strained to see what all the talk was about. Most of the girls, along with the colorful and androgynous *Moonlight Possession,* could have cared less about what *Analyze* was saying. They were too busy admiring his physical characteristics. The romance novels had already unanimously agreed he was the sexiest book in all of Sanders and Bowman.

Analyze began speaking to his enamored listeners. "My creator devoted one chapter to what he thought to be humorous consequences of various human interactions. Now remember, my creator is a very serious man—we're not talking fall-down-in-the-aisle-laughing stuff here. This is simply what *he* deems to be funny.

"Social psychology is the study of how social conditions affect human beings. If the social condition happens to be a neighbor who snores like a jet engine, there's gonna be repercussions. One of my creator's case studies involved just that. The subject of this study just happened to be a writer—we'll call him Joe.

"Joe was most creative in the late evening-early morning hours. One day he looks out his window and sees a moving van. A new neighbor is moving into the apartment directly below him. Joe thinks nothing about it. Later that evening he prepares himself a cup of hot chocolate and begins writing.

"Suddenly the silence is shattered by a most horrible noise. Vibrations shake the building. Joe leaps out of his chair to see what's going on. Maybe it's a fast approaching tornado! Then it stops—but the reprieve is ever so brief. Next comes a loud sucking sound. It's reloading! Then it strikes again—a repeat of the same horribly repulsive sound. Joe didn't know how to gauge decibels but he knew this thing must have registered into the thousands. What in the dickens was going on!

"Joe prances around his apartment holding his hands over his ears. It's all in vain as the invasive sound easily penetrates his defenses. He considers puncturing his ear drums but wisely abstains from this radical action. Finally Joe exits his apartment and sprints away at lightning speed, not stopping until he's nearly a mile away. Not until then did he feel comfortable enough to peel his hands away from his ears. It was incredible! He could still hear, ever so faintly, the noise that had driven him from his home. From a distance he could now determine what it was. It was a man snoring! His new neighbor was a snoring machine! What was he to do? How was he to write?

"Joe spent the rest of the night in a local diner pondering his situation. There was no way he could live above his new neighbor. This guy sawed more logs in one night than all the lumberjacks in the Pacific Northwest could manage during a summer of wood splitting. Something had to be done—soon!

"Joe lingered over his coffee until long after sunrise. Then he began making his way back home. Looking out in the distance he could see his apartment building. It was still standing. Thank God! The snoring may have weakened the structure but it didn't bring it down. Joe walked to his apartment and opened his front door. All was quiet below. His new neighbor was gone.

"Joe needed to work fast. The wheeze-master might come back home at any moment. He grabbed an electric drill from his tool chest. Joe knew the apartment below was laid out the same as his. Now—where might this noisy snorer have placed his bed? He gambled and drilled into his bedroom floor. Pop! He had made it through the flooring. Joe peered down into the hole. Yes! He could see a pillow. It was covered with snore slobber, but it was definitely a pillow. The hole was directly over the head of the perpetrator's bed.

"Joe reached back into his tool box and pulled out a metal rod. He then attached a ball of tissue paper to one end. The color was a perfect match to all the ceilings in the building. Good—his new neighbor wouldn't see the hole he had drilled over his head. Joe stuffed the rod into the hole. Now all he had to do was wait.

"Late that night Joe sat down in front of his computer. Maybe he could squeeze in a bit of writing. It started before he could peck out the first sentence. It was as bad as the previous night, maybe worse. This time the torturous snoring noises shook the entire foundation of the building. Joe instantly reached for his earplugs and pushed then deep into his auditory canal. Then he pushed another set into his ears, pushing the first pair even further into his ears. Incredibly, he placed a third set into his ears. This sent the original pair as far as they could possibly travel. They were stretching the ears' tympanic membrane to the breaking point.

"Satisfied that he had done everything possible to shut out the incoming snores, Joe quickly advanced to step two. He pulled out the rod exposing the hole into the room below. He leaned over and looked down. The target was in clear sight. Joe reached over and snatched the pitcher of ice water he had prepared. Heroically he poured the ice water through the hole while simultaneously fighting off waves of exploding snores. It was a direct hit. The icy water splashed down upon the enemy's face. Instantly the snoring subsided. Unbelievably, the victim of this midnight dousing never woke up. He trashed around in his bed a bit, but the champion snorter never once opened his eyes. It mattered not, the snoring had stopped.

"It was too good to be true. Several minutes later it all started again. Joe repeated the dousing process. It worked again. The scenario was replayed over and over throughout the night. Joe poured the twelfth and final pitcher on the victim's face just as the sun began to rise. It had been a long and sleepless night—but a relatively snoreless one.

"The process continued for a week. Joe would sleep during the day and pour water on his neighbor at night. On the eighth night, the snoring finally stopped for good. Never again would Joe be disturbed by his neighbor's sonic snoring. Joe went back to writing again. Cured of his snoring disorder, the neighbor found a girlfriend for the first time in his life. They got married and lived together for fifty blissful years. Everyone's suffering had ended."

Analyze paused amid chuckles from the crowd. Clapping of covers ensued. The studious book with the movie star looks had bedazzled them with humor. He had taken a routine case study in social psychology and turned it into entertainment.

"Thank you, but there's no need for applause," he said. "I'm still an amateur amidst you professionals. I'm just happy to try my hand at storytelling. I have to admit I've embellished my creator's text. My story strayed so far from his original case study that he'd probably not even recognize it. He'd burn me in the fireplace if he knew I was doing this. I got caught up in *Tall Tale's* captivating delivery and thought I'd give it a try. I now understand what fiction's all about. It's fun!'

"I'm glad you got to finish your story—because you know what? I think you're going for a ride." *Spy* motioned towards James. He had closed *Midnight Soul* and his attention had zeroed in on the other two books Phyllis had delivered him.

James gently placed *Midnight Soul* on her back and picked up Phyllis's other two selections. This was very unusual. *Analyze* and *Tall Tale* were getting a second chance, however remote, of making it to Phyllis's heavenly habitat.

The books quickly changed their focus to the novel that had captivated James for one full hour. What was it between her covers that James had found so fascinating? *Midnight Soul* had something special and the books wanted to know what is was.

Spy began the interrogations. "Hello to you *Midnight Soul*. All of us here are dying to know what you're all about. James couldn't put you down for an hour—and he doesn't even read fiction! What do you have that impressed Phyllis and James so?"

A relaxed and confident *Midnight Soul* looked up at her fellow novels. She had a quality about her that was impressive. It wasn't anything superficial like a flashy cover or catchy title. This went far deeper than any corporate marketing fluff. A sense of faith resonated from her. None of the books could pin it down at the time, but all of them would later agree— there was a guiding force behind this special novel. *Midnight Soul* held an allegiance to a higher power. That was the source of her inner peace. She was all about faith—stripped down bare bones faith.

Everyone was silent as she began to speak. "I'm *Midnight* to my friends. To answer your question, I honestly don't know why I appealed to either Phyllis or James. What I can tell you is this. All my life I've known I was destined for something special. Now I know what it is. I'm going home with James and Phyllis today. Don't ask me how I know—I just know. My work on this planet is just beginning."

"*Midnight*, you're obviously a very special novel. My name is *River Run True*. Thank you so much for answering our questions today. What do you think it was that influenced Phyllis? She's never delivered a novel to James before."

"I really don't know what persuaded Phyllis to pull me from the shelf. She just did it. It was a higher power that brought us together—that I'm sure of. My title doesn't give any real clues as to what I'm about. Once she had me in her grasp she immediately began reading the synopsis on my back cover. From that moment on I knew I would be going to her home."

River and *Midnight* gazed into each other's cover. In a matter of seconds they had established a trusting bond between the two. Both of them were beautiful in distinctly different ways—*River* with her classic beauty traits and *Midnight* with that special something that magnetized everyone in her presence. Each of the girls possessed a captivating natural charm.

"Oh, you have me so curious," said *River*. "What's your story? We would be so grateful if you could share it with us."

"I don't mind at all," replied *Midnight*. "Phyllis will be coming soon to take James and me away, so I'll summarize as quickly as I can."

It was absolutely quiet. *Midnight Soul* had cast a spell on everyone around her. There really was a mystical magnetism about her. She began.

"I'm a tale of enlightenment. When people are provided the most basic spiritual and intellectual insight the nastier traits of human existence will vanish like a dust particle in a strong breeze. Prejudice, jealousy, racism and hatred will cease to exist, for they are the attributes of the uninformed. This is one man's twisted journey towards the truth—that all beings, regardless of their color, deserve deference and respect."

Midnight's cover glowed as she began her narration. "George is my central character. My creator based him on an actual person from her hometown. George is a leading businessman in a small southern town. He inherited the business from his father. He had always told everyone he would never work in the family business, but truth be told, he couldn't do anything else. George's company manufactures barstools. With ninety-plus employees they produced nearly one hundred thousand units every month. George has contracted with a trucking firm that transported them across the country.

"George is a narrow-minded bigot. Although he's by no means a stupid man, his breadth of view is limited. He has the common sense to manage a small army of workers, yet he lacks the tolerance to understand the diversity that makes up the modern world. Every one of George's employees are white. George is quick to point out to any inquisitive observer that whites are superior workers. He'd always reply with his favorite comment. 'Hell will freeze over before I'll have any ragheads, spics or midnights working in my company.'

"George is especially prejudice towards blacks, whom he calls 'midnights,' a term he so proudly coined himself. Rarely does a black person step foot anywhere near George. If they do, they're quickly reminded that they're not welcome. One black man particularly irks George. Percy is a truck driver who shows up approximately once a month to pick up a load of barstools. He enjoys conversing with the workers as they load his truck.

"Percy continued to hang around the loading dock despite several 'suggestions' from George that he remain in the cab of his truck. Most of the workers liked the friendly and outgoing truck driver. Percy was always sharing his adventures of a single man living on the road. If George happened by during one of Percy's visits he would immediately turn beet red and storm away cussing. Percy would always respond with the same statement. 'That man's gonna have a heart attack one day.'

"Once a month George would meet with one of his biggest customers. The client owned a chain of furniture outlets and bought huge quantities of barstools from George. The gorgeous mountain scenery made the three-hour drive enjoyable. There was something else George looked forward to on his monthly visit—a rendezvous with an old girlfriend. Married George had been seeing her for the past year. She lived in a small resort town located in the mountains. George's little detour off the main road was always a welcome departure from his stale marriage.

"One drizzly autumn morning George stepped into his late model sedan to begin his monthly drive through the mountains. The roads were slick and dangerous. A couple of hours into the drive George made his usual detour. In thirty minutes he would be in the arms of his lover. George's mind wandered as he negotiated the twisting mountain curves. Oh, how he anticipated the pleasures that awaited him. He could already feel her warm embrace.

"Suddenly he came upon an unexpected turn. George slammed on the brakes. He had been driving too fast for the hazardous conditions. The car skidded off the road and tumbled down an embankment. It rolled end-over-end three times before coming to a rest in a gully covered by thick brush. Then there was silence.

"George was knocked unconscious. Approximately two hours later he awoke to find himself in a horrible situation. His left leg, left arm and numerous ribs had been broken. He had a six-inch gash across his face covered with dried blood, which was now bleeding profusely again after being reopened. That wasn't the worst of it. The front of the car had crushed against George's midsection causing unbearable pain. There was no doubt that the crash had damaged some vital organs.

"George tried to remain calm. He knew they would search for him when it was discovered that he never arrived at his destination. Everyone knew the route he took on this monthly journey. Certainly they would find him. Then it dawned on him. He had taken the side road to his mistress's house. No one would bother to look for him on this rarely-traveled stretch of highway. He was doomed!

"Darkness soon prevailed. George drifted in and out of consciousness as his mind seemed to separate from his body. Was this it? Was he going to die out here in the middle of nowhere? George traced back his forty-four years of living. He had never been much of a spiritual person. Sure, he had attended church services a few times every year, but it was all for show. Every business leader needed to be perceived as a believer. How he wished he could go back and do it all over again. He would have worshiped the lord—and he would have been genuine about it. He also would have treated fellow human beings better, especially people of color. What a fool he had been.

"The morning sun brought light. George could once again see his mangled body. He instinctively knew he wouldn't make it another twenty-four hours. He was torn and crushed and broken in body and spirit. George began praying for God to take his life. The sooner he left this plane of existence, the better—whether it meant heaven or hell. George closed his eyes for what he hoped would be the last time.

"'Grab my hand!' a voice called. 'I'm gonna get you outta here—grab my hand.'

"George awoke and looked around. He was still in the car but he wasn't alone. A hand was reaching out to help him—a black hand. George held out his right arm and the man gently removed him from the wreckage.

"George looked up to see who had rescued him from the twisted metal that used to be his car. It was Percy, the man he had so despised. The black man that he had mistreated so many times was now trying to save his life. George was too weak to speak. Once again he lost consciousness."

Midnight Soul paused for a moment. "Okay, I see Phyllis coming for us. I only have a moment to finish. I'm going to have to race through the rest of the book." She began speaking in rapid-fire fashion.

"George wakes up three days later in a hospital. Two other people are in the room with him. A nurse is sitting in a chair and another patient is sleeping in the bed beside him. George takes a closer look at the person in the bed. It's a black man—it's Percy.

"'What has happened to me?' asked George.

"The nurse pointed towards Percy. 'That man over there saved your life.'

"'Oh yes, I remember now. He pulled me from the wreckage.' George leaned his head back down on the pillow.

"'Sir, maybe you're not aware of it, but he did a lot more than that.' The nurse walked over to George and pulled back the sheets. Then she went to Percy's bed and did the same.

"The nurse then explained. 'When they brought you in here, no one really expected you to make it. Aside from all of your other problems, you had two crushed kidneys. Without a new kidney you were gonna die for sure. Family members make the best donors, so we called every one of them. They all refused. Then this man,' pointing to Percy, 'volunteered to give a kidney to save your life. We did some blood tests, and incredibly, he was the same blood type. We pulled one of his kidneys and placed it into your body. So far your body has accepted it without complications. I don't know how long you two have been friends, but this man sure cares for you a lot. I wish we could all be so lucky to have such close friends. You are truly blessed.' The nurse then turned and walked out of the room."

Midnight Soul was silent for a long moment. "There's a lot more of the story I wish I could've shared, but I gotta go. Phyllis has plans for me—big plans. My new life starts right now."

Midnight Soul's storytelling pace had been perfect. Phyllis arrived seconds after she finished speaking. She picked up *Midnight Soul* and placed her in her basket with another selection.

Midnight Soul had been correct. She was going home with Phyllis. Two lucky Sanders and Bowman residents were destined for the promised land. If Phyllis stuck to her normal routine, she would replace *Tall Tale* and *Analyze* to their respective shelves. Phyllis and James would then pay for their books and go home.

James and Phyllis held a short conversation. The books strained to hear but they couldn't understand what was being said. They finally heard Phyllis ask, "are you sure?" James nodded. Then something amazing happened. Phyllis picked up *Tall Tale* and *Analyze* from James's lap and placed them in her basket. James was purchasing every book he had looked at. Everyone was going to Phyllis's house! *Tall Tale* cheered loudly. *Analyze* was more restrained but he too rejoiced. The books began flapping their covers goodbye to their newfound friends. It was truly a joyous moment.

James eased out into the aisle with his scooter and proceeded towards the cashier area. Phyllis was close behind with the four lucky books. James approached a young girl sitting on the floor crying. It was the same girl who had been shunned by the rude boy earlier that afternoon. The boy had called her an ugly duckling in front of all of her friends. James held up his hand motioning Phyllis to stop.

"Hello young lady. I'd like to tell you something if you don't mind," James said in a comforting tone. The girl raised her tear-streaked face.

James looked her straight in the eyes. "There's more than one book in the bookstore. There's some real good ones and there's some that ain't worth the paper they're printed on." James turned his head and focused on the young man she so desired. "Find ya a good one and move on."

What an afternoon it had been.

Chapter 10

Tonight was the night. After three days of deliberation they had finally agreed on a strategy. Operation Sway had been green-lighted. The books were determined to save Ronnie's life. It was going to be a complicated and dangerous process, as they all were when human beings were involved. The plan was a two-step operation. The books needed help on this one from their longtime friend. Greenie the lizard was more than willing to offer his services.

The idea came from *Medical Innovations: Alternative Treatments*. He was the middle book on the top shelf, sitting directly over the support beam. For over a year he had complained to friends that his spine ached. The reason was obvious. The screw that held the support beam in place hadn't been secured properly. The head of the upraised screw was gouging into *Medical's* spine, causing him great discomfort.

Medical theorized that the entire rack, from top to bottom, had a potential stability problem. Others had long wondered if their bookshelf was safe. It creaked every time a customer would remove or replace a book. Was it really constructed to sustain a load of medical books? They were some of the heaviest books in the entire store. If the screw under *Medical's* spine were to pop out it could possibly result in a total structural failure. It was a dangerous scenario no one wanted to consider—until now.

What if—*Medical* expressed to his fellow shelfmates—the rack *did* totally collapse? Who would come clean up the mess? Of course it would be Ronnie. He's always the cleanup guy. Everyone knew that. In all probability *Diagnosed* would end up on top of the pile of books. After all, he was on the top shelf. The goal was to get Ronnie to read pages 662-669 of *Diagnosed*. That's the only way Ronnie would ever discover what was really wrong with his health.

Medical laid out Operation Sway. It was a sophisticated mission that left no room for error. One mishap along the way and the whole operation would be doomed. Their job would commence as soon as the last employee left for the evening. Every book on the rack would push their weight in one direction, then the other. The goal was to make the rack swing back and forth in a swaying motion. They wanted to loosen the screw under *Medical* until it was on the verge of popping out of the shelf. The books knew this could take hours of labor. Even then there was the distinct possibility it wouldn't be successful.

The next stage of the plan was the most dangerous. They would wait until Ronnie showed up for work. They would again sway to and fro until there was a complete and total crash of the entire bookshelf. Pandemonium would undoubtedly ensue. Books would be falling upon books, sharp-edged metal beams would be piercing anything in their path—it would be total bedlam. Everyone involved knew the risk. Yes, there would likely be injuries, maybe some serious ones—but this was Ronnie's life they were talking about!

If Operation Sway made it this far, there was still little chance Ronnie would bother to read *Diagnosed*. Why would he—unless he was instructed to! This is where Mario's little pet lizard comes in. Greenie adored Ronnie. Once or twice a week Ronnie would bring a mosquito or ant into Mario's office for him to snack on. The books had filled Greenie in on Ronnie's failing health. The tiny lizard enthusiastically offered his help. The plan was for Greenie to thoroughly cover his underbelly in black ink.

This could easily be found in the storage room. Then he was to watch and wait.

Greenie would go into action immediately after the collapse. He had been trained by the books to ignore any casualties. His duty was much more important than playing medic. Greenie was to locate *Diagnosed* amidst the rubble of the fallen bookshelf. Hopefully the big book would be exposed on top of the heap of fallen warriors. Greenie would then crawl onto *Diagnosed's* cover and begin to wriggle out a message for Ronnie.

The books had given Greenie a crash lesson in creative writing. Everyone hoped the friendly lizard would remember everything while under pressure. He had been trained to squirm his inky underside into letters and numbers. The message in bold black ink would be direct.

RONNIE!

READ ME

PAGES 662-669

The books promised the little saurian that if the mission proved to be successful he would receive the Gecko Writer Award—the reptile equivalent of the Nobel Prize in Literature. Greenie would be the first time recipient of this coveted prize given "in special recognition of artistic composition and outstanding merits as an epic writer."

Greenie was excited about the prospects of being accepted into exclusive intellectual circles.

It was going to be a delicate mission. Operation Sway had to be absolutely flawless to have any chance of success. It was going to be risky, some even thought crazy, but it was time to roll the dice. All day long the residents of shelf M18 were unusually quiet. The stoic books knew that some of them might not make it through the collapse of their steel dwelling. They had all accepted their fate, whatever that might be. If they were going to go down, it would be as heroes. Ronnie was worth dying for.

Donna was the last to leave. Operation Sway was initiated the moment they heard her lock the back door. Once again, they had ten hours to complete a critical overnight mission— and this was only stage one. Greenie was instructed to remain under shelf N31 during this perilous phase of the mission— far away from the danger zone. The key player in the final stage of Operation Sway was too valuable to lose in the event of a premature collapse.

Medical began barking out orders. Operation Sway was his baby from start to finish. He had conceived it, nurtured it, and fought for its acceptance. He would see it through to the end, whether it ended in victory or defeat. The glory would be his if it succeeded, something that he cared nothing about, and he would accept full responsibility for any failure.

"On three, everyone sway to the left." *Medical's* voice boomed throughout the bookstore. Not one Sanders and Bowman resident would sleep tonight. Word had spread that lives were on the line. Brave books were risking everything for their human friend.

"One, two, three—Go!" Approximately three hundred oversized books leaned to their left. Nothing happened.

"Okay, let's try it again," commanded *Medical*. "This time only the top two shelves. One, two, three—Sway!" This time the books felt the rack move ever so slightly.

"Top shelf only this time." *Medical* looked upwards at the occupants in the shelf directly above him. "*Diagnosed*, I'm putting you in charge up there. Here's what I want. All of you top-shelfers sway left. When you feel some movement, sway right. Get a rhythm going—left, right, left, right."

All covers were focused on *Medical*. "One, two, three—Go!"

Following *Diagnosed's* lead the books on the upper shelf leaned left. The rack moved with them. They swayed right—more movement. Left again—the rack moved even more. They cycled through two more times and established a rhythm. The metal structure creaked.

"Second shelf—sway left!" The big books on the second shelf coordinated their arrival perfectly. The added weight pushed the rack out further on every swing. The creaking sound intensified.

"Okay, my shelf—follow me!" *Medical* then led the third shelf into the act with precision timing, joining in on a rightward swing. Every book in Sanders and Bowman could now hear the melody of the rack going back and forth. Within moments the fourth shelf had thrown their abundant weight into the project. Finally, the lower shelf joined in. Operation Sway was now in full swing.

The residents of shelf M18 labored throughout the night. It was an exhausting task for everyone involved. The bulky medical publications were strong and powerful, but they lacked stamina. They were usually effective for only an hour or so, after which they required a break. *Medical* quickly introduced a solution. They would work in shifts. *Medical* separated the work force into three groups, broken up equally amongst the five shelves. At any given point in time two-thirds of the books were working while one-third was resting. It turned out to be a magnificent strategy. By five o'clock significant progress had been made. The creaking of the steel rack became so loud that some thought it might soon collapse.

Medical knew better than anyone what the situation entailed. After all he was sitting directly on ground zero, the middle screw of the middle shelf, the focus of everyone's efforts. Yes, the screw was being wedged from its connector clasp, but it needed more rocking to coax it from the metal structure it was binding together. *Medical* estimated another two hours of hard labor should do the trick. Several of the smaller support fasteners had already surrendered to the steady sway and popped out onto the floor.

Medical was doing a magnificent job leading the participants of Operation Sway. Stage one of the mission was on schedule and morale was high. The consequences of success weren't all positive however. Unbeknownst to anyone but his two covermates was the fact that *Medical* was in great pain. Operation Sway's objective was to loosen and discharge the screw connecting the rack's support beam. As the screw extended forward it projected itself deeper and deeper into *Medical's* spine. Each incremental degree of success meant more suffering for the valiant leader. The suffering would have proven unbearable for a lesser literary creation. *Medical* was truly a heroic publication.

It was seven o'clock and the sun was rising outside. The bookstore staff would be filtering through the door in less than an hour. *Medical's* estimate had been right on time. A few more swings to either side and the main screw would eject itself from the support beam. *Medical* boomed out to the exhausted workers to cease. They would now wait for Ronnie to appear.

Every book in Sanders and Bowman was a nervous wreck. Ronnie had arrived. It was now or never for the courageous group that had labored through the night. A few swings and the rack would come crashing down. Some of the onlookers commented that it was a suicide mission and should never have been undertaken. The majority of the books felt that it was something that had to be done regardless of the dangers involved. It mattered not at this point. These heroes weren't stopping halfway. It was time to crash the party.

A team of publishing and writing books were giving Greenie one final spelling lesson. The tiny lizard had them worried. Greenie wasn't doing so well in his practice runs. His writing was erratic and inconsistent and his numbers weren't readable in the least. The best teachers in the section were cramming information into the little gecko's brain as he greased himself up with a fresh slathering of black ink. Greenie had a look of determination as the drama unfolded before him. He was going to give Ronnie his best shot. He watched and waited for the chaos that was sure to come.

"This is it gang," *Medical* paused for a moment. "Let's hope we all make it through this alive. Is everyone ready?"

"Yes!" everyone called out in unison.

Medical nodded in confirmation. "Okay, let's do it! You all know the routine. Top shelf—start if off!"

On *Medical's* command the dauntless group plunged past the point of no return. The top shelf got things rocking with a gentle swinging. Seconds later the second shelf joined in, then the third, the fourth, and finally the fifth shelf jumped in. Metal creaked against metal. This needed to be short and sweet. No humans were to witness the collapse of the steel bookshelf.

It didn't take long. The screw popped out of its connecting bracket and surged deep into *Medical's* backbone. The structure fell into itself as the middle caved in. Some of the heavier books from the edges of the shelves slid into the collapsed area causing several support beams to snap. Two shelves immediately gave way. Nothing could now stand in the way of a total free-fall implosion. The bookshelf buckled one last time and it crumpled to the floor carrying its brave occupants along with it. Metal beams clanged onto the floor. In less than four seconds the structure had been transformed into a pile of rubble. Books and metal were strewn everywhere.

There were injuries, but now wasn't the time to contend with those. Time was of the essence. It was now all in the hands of a little lizard with ink on his belly. The staff undoubtedly heard the crash. They would be on the scene in a matter of moments.

"Go get 'em Greenie!" That was the command the saurian had been waiting for. His first task was to find *Diagnosed*. Hopefully he would be exposed, otherwise the whole operation was for naught. Finding *Diagnosed* wasn't as easy as it sounded. The dust was thick around the crash site. Metal beams with sharp edges lay amidst giant books, some of them moaning with injuries. It was absolute pandemonium and chaos.

Greenie went on a rapid-fire reconnaissance mission. Speed was his specialty. He knew he needed to bank some spare time for his writing exercise. In a matter of three seconds Greenie had traversed the entire disaster area. He found his target. Luck was with him. *Diagnosed* was half covered by debris, but enough of his back cover was exposed for Greenie to spell out his message—maybe.

Greenie didn't waste any time. He knew he had to start with an R. That was the first letter of Ronnie's name. Then he was to squirm out an O. His memory became cloudy after that, but he thought it was an N or an I next. After he was done with the letters he had some numbers to write out. The tiny lizard had been briefed on the importance of getting the numbers correct. They were critical in directing Ronnie towards the discovery of his illness. Greenie wasn't taking any chances with the numbers. He had created a cheat sheet by scribbling them out in ink on his hind leg. Greenie racked his brain as he raced around spreading black ink over *Diagnosed's* cover.

Greenie was snaking out the last number on *Diagnosed's* back when he heard someone approaching. With lightning speed he flipped his tail to finish off a 9 and raced away, hiding under a nearby stool. Greenie's minuscule heart was pounding at what felt like one thousand beats per second. The industrious little reptile was pooped. Greenie laid down under the stool and fell asleep.

Ronnie knew exactly what had happened—he just didn't know why. Five years ago another rack had fallen, although it was quite old and dilapidated. Ronnie was scratching his head on this one. This bookshelf was barely a year old yet it had caved in on itself. Whatever, there was no time to ponder why it fell. Books were lying everywhere.

Ronnie began rummaging through the wreckage for damaged books. Considering what they had just been through they were in pretty good shape. Most of them would need nothing more than a good cleaning. Ronnie did notice a long gash across the front cover of *General Anesthesia: Risk & Effects*. A metal beam had sliced him up pretty bad. Luckily he was a hardback—he'd survive. Ronnie placed it off to the side. Another hardback was lying at the outer perimeter of the debris pile. *Cardiology: Prevention & Treatment* had fallen and landed with his back cover open. The stitching that bound his spine was torn loose. Ronnie slid him off to the side to be tended to later.

Ronnie pulled a book from the bottom of the rubble. *Medical Innovations: Alternative Treatments* was banged up a bit on the outside. Upon closer inspection Ronnie noticed more serious damage. A long screw had somehow lodged three inches into the spine of the book. How in the world did that happen? Ronnie took his shirttail and wrapped it around the head of the screw for a good grip. He then gave it a hard yank and pulled it out. Small pieces of the book's spine came out with it. This book might need to be discarded. Ronnie pushed it off to the side alongside the other damaged books.

Ronnie didn't see any more serious issues with the merchandise. That seemed to be the extent of the damages. Just then Ronnie spotted one last damaged book. *Diagnosed: Uncovering Rare Diseases* had been soiled with some black substance—oil maybe. Ronnie took a closer look. It wasn't oil or grease. Someone had rubbed what appeared to be ink all over the back cover. Ronnie touched the liquid with his index finger. It was fresh. Who could have done this? It looked like someone had chicken-scratched out some illegible squiggles.

Ronnie looked around for any kids in the area. Maybe a small child was playing around with a bottle of ink and decide to paint on a book. He didn't see any children close by. Ronnie leaned down for a closer inspection. This was more than random doodling. It was a collection of letters and numbers and they had an order about them. It was some kind of coded writing. Ronnie studied the smeared text for several seconds. It contained a primitive message.

RONE!
RED ME
PAGIS 662-669

What was this all about? Rone? Could that mean Ronnie? Red me? Did someone want to be colored red? And what in the heck did pagis mean? Ronnie shook his head as he tried to decipher the odd assemblage of letters and numbers. Then it clicked! Pagis was pages. Red meant read. The message was: Ronnie! Read me. Pages 662-669.

Ronnie snatched up the big book and hurriedly turned to page 662. There was a subheading at the top of the page that read "Understanding Hereditary Hemochromatosis." What was the significance of this hard-to-pronounce medical term? What could it have to do with him? Ronnie read further. Some of the symptoms of this illness were similar to what he was experiencing.

Ronnie was now intrigued and continued reading. Hemochromatosis was commonly misdiagnosed as arthritis or diabetes. That's what the doctors told Ronnie he had! The condition rarely struck young people except in the hereditary form. Ronnie had an uncle that had these same symptoms! This genetic disorder was potentially fatal if not treated. Ronnie's uncle had died! Then the good news—the disease was easily treated. If treated the patient could expect to live a long and normal life.

Ronnie could barely contain himself. He was going to see his doctor this afternoon. This time he would be tested for hereditary hemochromatosis. Ronnie knew in his heart that was what he had. As soon as the results came back positive he would get himself treated. Then all this pain and suffering would end. His health nightmare would be over. Yes!

Ronnie closed the book and leaned his back against the wall. What a stroke of luck had befallen him. Someone had literally saved his life. His thoughts then shot back to the childlike mystery message spelled out on this medical book. How did this happen? Who did this? Why all this espionage-style communication when they could have easily talked to him?

Ronnie then noticed something out of the corner of his eye. He hadn't noticed it before, but now it was clear. A smudgy trail of ink led from where the savior medical book had been lying. Ronnie traced it along the floor until it came to a stop at a step-stool. Without thinking Ronnie picked up the small stool.

"Oh my God!" Ronnie exclaimed out loud. "It's Greenie."

The little lizard was fast asleep. He had worked himself to a frazzle. Ronnie was puzzled. He gently picked up the still-sleeping reptile. He examined him. Greenie had dried ink underneath his belly. Once again Ronnie retraced the ink line back to where *Diagnosed* had been found. No way! Greenie couldn't have written the splotchy message that was now so crucial to Ronnie's welfare—could he? Could this little mosquito-gobbling lizard actually read and write?

Ronnie promised himself he wasn't going to go crazy trying to solve this mystery. He was a man of faith. A higher power was responsible for this. This little lizard didn't just jump up and begin squirming out inky messages on book covers without a calling from somewhere. Ronnie was going to leave it as it was—one of those things in life which can't be explained.

One thing Ronnie knew for sure. Fate had rewarded him via a bookshelf crash and a spelling bee champ lizard. He would return the favor. Ronnie picked up the four damaged books. These books were going home with him even if he had to pay full price for them. He would repair them and give them a loving home. The others would be dusted off, cleaned and given a brand new rack to live on. The books on shelf M18 had played a mysterious part in saving his life. They would receive special attention from him as long as he worked at Sanders and Bowman. There was one more item that needed attention—Greenie! Ronnie cuddled the little lizard in his palm and carried him to the restroom. Greenie was going to get a good cleaning—and a fresh snack!

Chapter 11

S pirits were high amongst humans and books alike. Maybe the stars were magically aligned or perhaps it was just fate, but it seemed as if nothing could go wrong. Of course the biggest and brightest news concerned Ronnie. He had visited his doctor, and sure enough it was determined he had hereditary hemochromatosis. He promptly sought treatment with immediate results. Old Ronnie was back to flashing his trademark smile, missing tooth and all.

The other major development in the human domain involved Charles. The last few weeks he had been behaving like a model citizen. His mood swings were a thing of the past and he hadn't mistreated a single book in over a month. It was no mystery where the credit was due—*Divorce: Coping & Caring*. She was steering him back to lucidity. Just like *Forties Fitness*, *Divorce* was now proudly wearing streaks of yellow highlight markings throughout her text. Charles was soaking her up like a sponge, as nearly all of her 350 pages contained at least one yellow stripe. There was no higher honor.

Charles was no longer a Sanders and Bowman madman on the loose. It seemed he had finally accepted his divorce. He had commented to Joann that he wished his ex-wife and her new husband the best—and he seemed genuine about it.

Charles had even began dating. He actually brought his girlfriend into the bookstore one afternoon and introduced her to the staff. Everyone agreed that her good-natured personality was just what Charles needed at this critical point in his life. The longtime troubled assistant manager was definitely on the rebound.

Another happy member of the management team was Donna. She had lost ten more pounds—thanks to her constant companion *Forties Fitness*. Donna bounced around the bookstore with boundless energy. She loved herself again—the required step before loving others. Her exuberance was contagious. On the days she managed the store the staff seemed to follow her lead, turning up their own energy level a notch or two. Thomas was thrilled with the performance of both assistant managers.

Fifty-six days and counting—that was how long Jim had gone without a drink. He looked healthy and happy. He had a aura of self-assuredness surrounding him that he never had before. It wasn't due to his work performance. That had always been outstanding. It went much deeper than that.

Jim had confided to Ronnie that he had resumed relations with his estranged son. They hadn't spoken to each other in over five years. Jim's alcoholism had been the barrier that kept them apart. Now that Jim had stopped drinking the doors opened up once again. They were spending entire weekends together making up for lost time. Jim had vowed to his son that he would never touch a drop of alcohol for as long as he lived. Their relationship was far more important than a drink of Scotch.

It was becoming the norm. A book had played the major role in Jim's transformation. *Alcohol: Beat it Forever* was a permanent fixture on Jim's coffee table. He had placed the invaluable guide to sobriety right where he used to rest his glass of Scotch. When he caught himself reaching for a sip of whisky he would pick up his new literary friend instead. It was a pure genius method of overcoming a sixty year habit. Jim knew the battle would be an ongoing one. With a little help from *Alcohol: Beat it Forever* he would turn a deaf ear to the voices that were constantly telling him just one drink would be okay.

Happy Sanders and Bowman employees meant happy books. There were two books that were absolutely euphoric— *Spy Needle* and *River Run True*. They would soon be united in matrimony. *Spy* had proposed and *River* had enthusiastically accepted. Just as *Destiny* had predicted the proposal had been a spontaneous event. It happened early one Saturday morning while most of the books were still sleeping. *Spy* and *River* both awoke around five o'clock.

The two of them were engaged in conversation touching on numerous subjects. They were bantering back and forth, laughing and giggling like kids. Suddenly the words just popped out of *Spy's* mouth. "*River*, why don't you and me just do it? Will you marry me?"

"Okay," replied a stunned *River*. Just like that, out of the blue, they were engaged to be married. *Destiny* had been right. The words had flowed as natural as a mountain stream—no pressures, no worrying—originating not from any intellectual source but from the heart. *Spy* couldn't have stopped himself even if he wanted to. It was out of his control. *Spy* had won over the most beautiful book in the world. *River Run True* was his dream come true.

River was so excited she immediately chose a date. She didn't want to wait too long, but she needed adequate time to plan her grand event. *River* had always pictured her wedding as intimate yet festive. She wanted a few close friends to share in her tears of joy. Then they would spend the rest of the evening reminiscing about the past, pondering the future, and end it with some good old-fashioned storytelling. It was a pretty good bet who would hog the stage at that point—the man of the hour, the one and only *Spy Needle*! For no particular reason *River* picked October 11 to be her special day. The timing seemed right and besides, the number eleven was nothing more than two ones standing beside each other—symbolizing her and *Spy* together forever!

The ecstatic couple couldn't wait to tell their best friend the news. *Destiny* was still sleeping away. He and *Stone Dance* had philosophized their way through the previous evening, finally calling it quits after midnight. When the two of them got started on an important issue they wouldn't let it rest until all of the world's problems were solved.

Spy and *River* held tight to each other and waited for their friend to awaken. They wanted *Destiny* to be the first to hear the exciting news. Finally he began to stir. *Spy* made sure he didn't drift off to sleep again by giving his covermate a firm push.

"*Destiny*, are you awake?" whispered *Spy*.

"I am now," answered *Destiny*. "I figured I'd better rise before someone shoved me off the shelf." He broke into a grin. "I get the feeling you've got something to tell me."

"We're getting married!" exclaimed *River*. "*Spy* proposed to me this morning."

Destiny was now wide awake. "Congratulations to you both. I'm so happy. The two of you were meant for each other. My best friends uniting with a ceremony of love—have you set a date yet?"

"Yes, October 11," *River* readily replied. "I didn't have any particular reason for choosing that day. It just sounds like a good day to get married."

"You know what?" said *Destiny*. "That's the same day that Kris Richards is appearing here. It was finally confirmed last night. He's doing a noontime book signing. What time is your wedding?"

"We haven't set a time yet, but we will now." *River* thought for a second. "Three o'clock in the afternoon! That's when we'll have our wedding. That'll make for a festive day indeed—the world's most famous actor followed by an even bigger event—the union of *Spy Needle* and *River Run True*! What a day it'll be!"

Destiny smiled. "Okay, tell everyone to mark their calendars—October 11 at three o'clock sharp. I suppose you're going along with all of *River's* scheduling decisions, right *Spy*?"

Spy glanced towards his future mate, then turned to *Destiny*. "Do you think I'm crazy enough not too! This is her project from here on out. Just tell me when to say 'I do' and I'll be happy. I'm sure she'll do a fine job."

For a brief moment *Destiny* looked as if he might shed a tear. "*Spy*, *River*, you're the best. I sincerely hope that fate rewards you both with a long and wonderful life together. Once again, congratulations."

"Thank you so much," said *River*. "You'll always remain our best friend. *Spy* and I know how lucky we are to have you in our life. I'd be content to spend eternity right here on shelf C22 as long as the three of us are together."

"I hate changing the subject—but look!" *Spy* nodded towards the periodical section. Homewrecker Harry was headed directly towards them with two books in hand.

"Oh my God," gasped *River*. "He's gonna discard one of them in some godforsaken crevice somewhere. I've seen that look in his eyes before. This guy gets some sort of perverse pleasure out of uprooting innocent books from their happy home. Oh, how I hate that man. Here he comes!"

A hand reached out. The three of them braced themselves. Harry Homewrecker slipped his arm underneath the top of their shelf and placed a book directly on top of them. He quickly snatched his arm out and rounded the corner without looking back.

Everyone focused on the unfortunate exile that now rested upon them. He was visibly shaken but didn't appear to be injured. They looked at his cover. His name was *Howdy Neighbor*.

Spy gently pushed upwards in a comforting gesture. "Don't worry, you're among friends here. Are you alright?"

"Yeah—sure," answered the bewildered book. "Where am I?"

"You're in the fiction section," said *River*. "Harry Homewrecker dumped you on top of us. Don't panic. We get quite a bit of staff traffic through this area, especially Sherry. You'll be discovered and transported back home—I'm sure of it!"

"Nothing against you guys, but I certainly hope so." *Howdy Neighbor* nervously surveyed his surroundings. "All my friends are on the opposite side of the bookstore. I know they're worried to death about me right now."

"You just relax," *Destiny* said calmly. "*River's* correct, they'll find you. I can see by your cover that your name is *Howdy Neighbor*. That's got a nice ring to it."

The group's efforts to put their hijacked comrade at ease seemed to be working. He became noticeably less tense. "Yeah, I kinda like my name too. You can call me *Howdy*."

"I've got a suggestion," said *Spy*. "Worrying won't do a bit of good. It won't get you discovered any faster. Why don't we all kick back and share a few tales. I'm curious, and I'm sure the others are also, as to what you're all about. *Howdy*, could you give us a brief summary of your text?"

Howdy's body language agreed—worrying wouldn't accomplish a thing. *Spy* was right. He might as well enjoy himself. What the heck—it would just be another life experience to look back on. Besides, he liked these folks.

"I'm called *Howdy Neighbor* because I'm all about neighbors. My creator is a neighbor expert. Over a period of twenty years he's moved thirty times. That's a lot of moving—and a lot of different neighbors. He's lived alongside every type of human being—rich and poor, black and white, male and female and some of undeterminable gender.

"His inevitable encounters with neighbors, some of them on the nasty side and some of them quite comical, gave him an idea. He would write a book about his experiences. He already had a fabulous title—*Howdy Neighbor*. There was a problem however—my creator is very lazy. He doesn't have the discipline to tie his shoes in the morning, much less author a book. It was a laborious task for him to come up with a two-word title. Forget about a hundred thousand words! He quickly came to his senses and realized it would take his lazy butt at least five hundred years to write a book.

"Then he had a brainstorm. Others could write the book for him. Certainly he wasn't the only one in the world with a story to tell about a neighbor. So my creator placed an ad in a high-circulation periodical asking for interesting stories on this topic. He had over one thousand responses. He simply chose the most interesting ones, had a friend of his edit the stories, and sent some sample chapters to a few agents. Amazingly he acquired an agent, who negotiated a deal with a publisher and—lo and behold—here I am nine months later sitting in a bookstore. I still can't believe it. My creator can't write a lick!"

"Now you've really aroused our curiosity," said *Destiny*. What sort of tales dwell betwixt your covers?

"Oh, they run the gamut from neighbors being neighborly to double-barreled shotgun confrontations. I've got friendly encounters, love triangles, family feuds, howling pet quarrels and altercations of every variety ranging from fisticuffs to hand grenades. Neighbors have been giving each other grief for centuries. Take your pick."

"We're always ready to hear a well-spun tale," said *Destiny*, "and it sounds like you're armed with some good ones. Let me warn you—we've had some whoppers pass through these parts lately. If you choose to share a passage or two, don't hold back on anything. I can't think of a better way to spend the morning than hearing a couple of your favorites. Are you up to it?"

"Yeah, why not?" replied *Howdy*. "My collection totals over two hundred contributions from around the globe. I don't really know where to start. I've got tons of the usual neighbor spats—loud music, parties, domestic arguments, drunkenness, all that kind of stuff. I'm not gonna bore you with that. That's for the masses. You guys are professional—I can see that. You need a dose of the unusual to hold your attention.

"Let me think. Should I get into the disturbance involving the midnight motorcycle mechanic gunning his engines at all hours? How about the grandmother taking target practice with her revolver inside her apartment? She shot up her neighbor's sofa pretty good. Luckily they weren't home at the time. I could discuss the amorous boa constrictor that escaped from his aquarium to court the stuffed snake in the apartment next door. That nearly caused a heart attack when the residents came home to see the huge reptile cuddled up with his newfound mate in their daughter's bed.

"I won't even begin to get into the lecherous activities of the dogs. Their steamy ambitions can't be contained to any one household. Many a neighbor's full blooded champion canine has popped out pups that suspiciously resembled the house-next-door's mixed mongrel. Dogs hold no class distinctions, especially when it comes to love."

Spy, *River* and *Destiny* all looked at each other and smiled. It seemed they had yet another comedic entertainer on the premises.

Howdy continued. "Oh, here's a good one. There was this guy who lived in Phoenix, Arizona. Out there in the desert the summertime temperatures can fry an egg. This fellow wasn't too keen on paying a big electricity bill to power his air conditioning system—so he decided to sleep in his refrigerator. You heard me right. He snoozed the night away in a refrigerator. He'd payoff his neighbor in beer to let him out every morning. He darn near suffocated a time or two.

"That one reminds me of a dude living in northern Canada. He got tired of freezing to death so he built a fireplace in his living room—had to cut out the ceiling to do it. Only problem was the neighbor living above him almost died from smoke inhalation.

"Then there's the category of home-based businesses. Everyone knows of an entrepreneur neighbor who's set up shop in his home. Keep in mind that these future magnates rarely bother obtaining proper licenses. Chapter eight delves into a few examples. I've got the couple who set up a beekeeping operation in their second-floor apartment. They left their windows open year-round to accommodate the industrious little pollen transporters. The neighbors said it sounded like an airport.

"Talk about guts—this next guy decided he was going to turn his studio apartment into an unlicensed crematorium, flaming furnaces and all. He became so successful working the field of departing souls that he figured he might as well bring a few newcomers into the world as well—so he set himself up as an obstetrician and began delivering babies. The authorities finally caught up with him when he branched out into brain surgery. After a few botched cerebral patch-ups they were on to him.

"Now of course with neighbors you've always got a couple of thieves running around. Every neighborhood has a theft here and there. I won't waste your time with the standard break-in-and-steal stories. They're a dime a dozen. But I will share this one with you—this guy broke into homes around the neighborhood on a regular basis. The odd thing about this chap was that he never took anything. What he would do is this—he'd quietly enter the home sometime after midnight and run himself a warm bath. After pouring himself a glass of wine he'd slip into the steamy water. For the next four hours or so he'd relax in a stranger's house soaking away in his bubble bath and playing with his rubber ducky. This went on for years before he was finally apprehended. The whole thing's kinda nutty if you ask me.

"That's a few of the yarns that made it through the editing process and into my creator's book. They're so wacky that they've gotta be true. I guarantee you they're better than anything my indolent creator could have churned out. Sometimes truth really is stranger than fiction."

"*Howdy*, you're chocked full of amusing tales," complimented *River*. "Speaking of neighbors, maybe you'd like to relocate. You would fit right in with some of the clowns that reside here."

River looked towards *Spy* and smiled. "You know *Spy* honey, ever since you arrived at the bookstore we've had an endless flow of first-rate entertainers come through here. *Howdy's* no exception."

"Don't give me any credit for *Howdy's* narrating talents," said *Spy*. "I'm still laughing at the weirdo who sleeps in a refrigerator. That's good stuff! Maybe you would like to stay here on a permanent basis. How about it *Howdy*?"

"Don't tempt me," said *Howdy*. "You guys are great, but I do need to get back to my own neighborhood. There's some unique characters back there. You know this neighbor squabbling isn't limited to humans, we books have our problems living together also."

"That's for sure," agreed *Destiny*. "Every neighborhood has a fruitcake or two on the rack."

Howdy chuckled to himself. "Since they're not in listening range I think it would be okay to gossip about my own neighborhood—as long as I don't mention any names. We've got our share of annoying shelfmates. For example, we've got one lass who won't stop blabbering. She's a book about interior design and home decorating. That's as much as I can tell you.

"Day and night she goes on and on about how beautiful her creator's house is. How it's the most gorgeous home on the planet with its Victorian architecture and its antique furnishings and magnificent landscaping and 'you gotta see this' and 'you gotta see that.' On and on and on. She never stops! You might be right. If it will get me away from her, maybe I will live here!"

"That's hilarious, but I do feel for you," said *River*. "There's nothing worse than a motormouth neighbor ranting incessantly. Just thank God she's not your covermate. I once knew a gal whose back covermate would never shut up. It literally drove this girl crazy. She finally snapped and shoved the annoying magpie right off the shelf. Busted her up pretty bad from what I heard."

"Don't go giving me any ideas now," laughed *Howdy*. "While I've got the chance let me release some more of my frustrations. When I get back I've gotta be civil again. This concerns a neighbor who lives directly over me. Once again, no names, but I can tell you this much. Ah, what the heck, his name is *Better than Most*.

"With a name like *Better than Most* I guess he never had a realistic chance at being liked. I've nicknamed him Ego. This hopeful Romeo is always grooming himself. In his bemired mind he thinks he is a ladies' man. Ego is actually quite ugly. His cover looks like toddler doodling. Open him up and his text isn't much of an improvement. His publisher tried to get cute and used a font that's virtually unreadable. Actually that's probably a good thing because if anybody ever got past the first page they'd throw him down like a hot potato.

"I heard his creator downed a liter of vodka every day *before* he began writing. That would explain all the spelling and grammatical errors that permeates his two hundred chapters. Yes, that's right. Two hundred chapters! And he's only two hundred pages long. Wow! That's a whopping one page per chapter! Have you ever heard such! His creator must've blackmailed someone to get published. Better than most— give me a break! Worse than crap—that's what he should be titled."

"Oh, that's funny," said *Destiny*, "but I do feel for you."

"Yeah, you see how this conceited snoot gets me fired up. Ego fancies himself to be God's gift to the opposite sex. His amour propre is off the charts. If you wanna know the truth the girls don't want Ego. He's not attractive, his career prospects are dim at best, and he's got the personality of a deflated beachball that's washed up on the shore. In other words he ain't got a lot going for him. Know what I mean?"

"Sounds like this guy could take some lessons from Sonny Needle," said *River*. "He's *Spy's* central character, a *real* ladies' man."

"He needs help, that's for sure," said *Howdy*. "There's a simple country boy five books down from him whom the women just flock over. *A Country Boy's Learning* is his name, authored by Joseph T. Moffitt. Ego could stand some schooling from *Country*. Maybe then he'd actually get a girlfriend. As it stands now he'll be lucky if a greasy fish and chips wrapper would go out with him. Why bother? *Better Than Most*—Ha! What a joke he is."

"It's obvious you're not too fond of that guy," said *Destiny*. "I can't say that I blame you. Anything else you need to get off your chest while you've got the opportunity?"

Howdy thought for a moment. "Now that you've asked— yes! Our shelf is loaded with factual books. We not labeled as fiction so our readers expect us to be accurate. Sure, we're allowed to entertain, but our overall objective is to educate. Everyone has their specific area of expertise. We have—most of us anyway—been thoroughly researched and edited before we hit the shelves. No one wants to be discredited whether you're an author, publisher or book. It can be downright embarrassing. My point here is that everyone of my neighbors is privy to certain information that the rest of us don't know. I think it's wonderful. We can all share information and learn from each other. Everyone benefits. Sounds great, right?"

"It sure does," answered *Spy*. "Sometimes I'm envious of you non-fictioners. Your opportunities for assimilating knowledge are limitless."

"Well let me tell you, it's not always a bed of roses. We've got this neighbor—he's eleven books down the line from me—who's a know-it-all. Since I'm feeling a bit sassy today I'll go ahead and disclose his name—*Build It Yourself*. I won't bore you with his seventeen word subtitle that drags on like a chattering mother-in-law. That's right, *seventeen* words of engineering jargon that'll put you to sleep faster than a handful of Valium.

"Thank heaven *Build Himself Up*—that's my nickname for this wannabe wise man—is not any closer than he is or I'd go nuts. I pity his poor covermates who actually have to live alongside this jerk. *Build* pictures himself to be the worldliest purveyor of the written word that's ever been published. He thinks he knows *everything*, or at least that's the image he likes to portray. His own area of specialization is mechanical engineering, but he thinks of himself as an expert on all subjects. His author was a musician who finally gave up on his dream and settled on a career in engineering. Maybe *Build* inherited his frustrations and feelings of inadequacies from his creator.

"I would jump for joy if could hear *Build* mutter those words we all say at some point in our conversations—I don't know. He'd just as soon stick a dagger through his text as admit there's something he doesn't know. If I could record *Build* actually saying 'I don't know' I would play that recording over and over. I don't think I'd ever get tired of hearing it. But that will never happen because *Build* knows everything."

"I knew a know-it-all once," commented *Spy*. "He used to come over and bug Roy all day. He stopped dropping by after Roy sicced Spotty on him. Spotty chewed him up pretty good."

"Well, he got what he deserved," replied *Howdy*. "Danged know-it-alls. They're determined to demonstrate their perceived intelligence at every opportunity. That's the know-it-all's job—to act smart when their actual knowledge is limited or even nonexistent. As if that's not bad enough, here's the kicker. Know-it-alls will invariably dispute others.

That's what they seem to thrive on the most—disregarding or devaluing the opinions of others.

"That's what bugs me the most about *Build*. Imagine this scenario. You and *Build* are having a conversation—let's say you're admiring a herd of sheep. You say 'those sheep are white.' *Build* will immediately attack your innocent statement and begin to cut you to pieces. He will go into great detail explaining that although the sheep appear to be white, color-trained eyes see them differently. The sheep are technically an abstract shade of such-and-such a color. Okay, you let it rest and let *Build* have the final say. It's over, right? Not so fast!

"The next day you and *Build* walk past the same herd of sheep. What you don't know is that *Build* was up all night cramming in anticipation of this moment. He spent hours memorizing everything there is to know about colors. He also practiced rehearsing his spiel so as to impress you with his expansive wisdom.

"He'll try to casually steer the conversation back to the color of sheep. Maybe it'll be posed as a statement like 'those sheep are a pretty color' or 'look at how the light affects the sheep's color.' Watch out! When he lays out bait like that he's ready for an assault. You may answer with another innocent response like 'the light does make the sheep pretty.' It matters not what your reply is because at that point you're already doomed. *Build* didn't stay awake all night for naught—he's now armed with just enough information to poke his proud chest out and begin airing his professorial insight.

"*Build* may strike back with 'if you still think the sheep are white you're wrong.' Then he'll go in for the kill. 'These sheep are actually a hybrid of several colors. Cosmic latte, papaya whip and navajo white make up the bulk of the dominant wavelengths as defined by the Munsell color system. I also detect a touch of zinnwaldite around the sheep's midsection.'

"*Build* now has you where he wants you. It's time for a grand finale fireworks display of infinite wisdom from the ultimate dispenser of universal knowledge. He'll look into your eyes as he continues.

"'The sheep may appear white to the uninformed. You're probably confused because you're not educated in the field of colorimetry. You see, the chromophores are playing tricks on your naive eyes. Albert Munsell probably described the pigment color system best when he delved into the actual contours of color. I know this will be difficult for you to understand but let me try to enlighten you. A desire to fit a chosen contour, such as the pyramid, cylinder, cone or cube, coupled with a lack of proper tests, can lead to many distorted statements of color relations, and it becomes evident when physical measurement of pigment values and chromas are studied, that no regular contour is served. In other words, the sheep ain't white.'

"What a pompous jerk," said *River*. "I hope I never run into this guy."

"I hope you don't either, said *Howdy*. "I wouldn't wish that on anyone. But that's typically the way *Build* operates. He's got to have the final say or he'll shrivel up and die. It matters not if the sheep are white. What matters is who knows the most, or more importantly, who is *perceived* to know the most. Right now he's on my shelf arrogantly boasting to some unfortunate book that can't escape. In his trademark obnoxious voice he's bellowing out trivial tidbits that may or may not be true.

"Like I said, truth doesn't really matter to *Build Himself Up*. He's concerned with cultivating his image as this worldly treasure chest of knowledge. I would give anything if someone would purchase him and remove this fool from my neighborhood. Our property value would immediately increase. As it stands now we're blighted because of this arse. Who wants to live alongside a loudmouth know-it-all? You know what I mean?"

River smiled. "Yours isn't the only neighborhood with a local know-it-all. We've all got one. At least they provide inspiration for a funny story. As horrible as I'm sure they are, your stories are a delight to hear. *Howdy*, do you have any other neighbors you would like to throw off a cliff?"

Howdy thought for a moment. "No, that just about covers it. I've got a book who lives directly below with a bit of a flatulence problem, but I don't really hold it against him. I just hold my breath for a minute and it passes. Sometimes the staff gets a whiff of it and they'll look around for the closest human. They don't have a clue that it originated from the book they're standing in front of."

"That's funny," said *River*. "Speaking of our staff, aren't you in Sandra's area?"

"Yes I am," replied *Howdy*. "Of course they all wander through, but we see more of Sandra than the others. Wanna hear what she did last week?"

"We're always ready for a Sandra update," said *River*. "Go ahead."

"It was just before lunch last Wednesday morning. Sandra's latest boyfriend came into the store for a surprise visit. The two of them were standing directly in front of me. They were busy discussing whatever couples discuss when Sandra's phone rang. The guy waited patiently as Sandra carried on her conversation. I, and of course her boyfriend, overheard her talking to someone who apparently was in her apartment. She told this person to make sure they locked up when they left. Then she reminded them to feed the cat. Sandra finally hung up and directed her attention back to her boyfriend.

"Of course her boyfriend wanted to know who she had been talking to and what was this person doing in her apartment. Freewheeling Sandra never hides anything—you guys know that. She told her boyfriend it was a guy she had met in the laundry room the day before. Her boyfriend turned red in anger, yelled a few expletives and stormed away. I can honestly say it didn't faze Sandra in the least. That girl's something else."

"Oh, that's Sandra for you," said *Destiny*. "Ain't nobody gonna put a ball and chain around her. *Howdy*, if you wanna see a committed couple just look at my two friends here beside me. *Spy* and *River* are engaged as of today!"

"Wow, congratulations!" exclaimed *Howdy*. "I thought I detected sparks between you two. I just didn't feel it was my place to comment on it. I wish you the very best. You two …."

"Uh oh!" *Spy* interrupted. "Sherry's making her rounds. She never misses a thing. *Howdy*, you're going back home in a matter of seconds."

Sherry slowly walked their way. She never failed to glance at *Spy*, *River* and *Destiny* every time she wandered by shelf C22.

She was well aware of their friendship. This time was no exception. Sherry noticed the misplaced book that sat upon them. She picked up *Howdy Neighbor* and turned around. *Howdy* was going home.

Chapter 12

Word circulated fast. *Spy Needle* and *River Run True* were going to be married on October 11. The ceremony would occur shortly after Kris Richards's book signing. Although there was a marriage practically every week at Sanders and Bowman, this one was special. *River* had long been known as one of the most beautiful books in the store.

Many a male had been quietly hoping her and *Spy's* relationship would flounder. One book was especially heartbroken to hear of *River's* engagement. *Road to Baja* was a handsome 400 page novel who lived on shelf D18. He and *River* had arrived at Sanders and Bowman on the same day. Jim had placed them together in a cart as he stocked the new arrivals. *Baja* was immediately smitten with the lovely *River Run True*. He never gave up on his dream of capturing the heart of the pretty girl from C22. *Baja* was heartbroken when he heard she was marrying.

River was busy making plans for her big day. *Loved Twice* had agreed to be her maid of honor. She would be helping with many of the wedding day responsibilities. *Loved Twice* had been communicating with several wedding books and periodicals. She was determined that *River's* special day would go off without a hitch.

Wedding Perfect had been especially helpful in sharing her wealth of information. Her nuptial nuggets included creative methods of sending invitations, not an easy task when you're a book. She also instructed *Loved Twice* how to give a cover-soothing massage that would both relax and energize. *River* would beam from the inside out on her wedding day. *Wedding Perfect* also offered up some of the latest innovative makeup techniques. On October 11 *River's* lustrous cover would be shining brightly for all the world to see.

Loved Twice and *Destiny* had worked together in arranging for *United in Love and Duty* to preside over the ceremony. *United* was a venerable publication that was the book of choice for administering wedding vows. He was first published nearly eighty years earlier and was still considered the authority on marriage and the responsibility that accompanies it. *United* commanded respect throughout the bookstore and beyond. He was not only sought out for joyous celebrations of love but also in times of grief. He had recently presided over a "celebration of life in death" gathering for *History of Natural Disasters*. The old book had finally given in to his spinal condition that had caused nearly all of his pages to fall out.

Communication with *United* would have to be done the old-fashioned way via a chain of oral transmissions. The books called it walktalk. Luckily *United* resided only seven shelves away so it wouldn't be a major undertaking. The books had done this so many times that it had become almost mechanical in nature. *United* would communicate with a book directly across the aisle from him. That book would relay the message to a neighbor another aisle over. The passage of information would go on for as long as necessary. The process would be reversed for replies. Sometimes communication could extend all the way across the bookstore. This somewhat primitive method of sharing information had been used by books for centuries. Walktalk was an effective time-tested system of transmitting messages.

The union of *Spy Needle* and *River Run True* was becoming a highly anticipated event. The coincidental fact that the wedding would be on the same day as Kris Richards's book signing created excitement. One of the world's most famous faces would actually visit their home. That would be followed by an exchange of vows between the funny spy novel and his gorgeous bride. Some of the books were declaring October 11 an official holiday.

The latest news surrounding *Spy* and *River's* wedding was perhaps the biggest. If it proved to be true the couple's nuptials would be historical. It would be the first-ever book wedding attended by a human. Rumor had it that Sherry would be present to witness the ceremony. It was all *Destiny's* idea. The notion came to him early one morning as he watched Sherry walk by his shelf. *Spy* and *River* were still sleeping. Sherry delivered her customary glance over towards the three friends. Normally she will sense that all is well with her favorite books and continue on. This time *Destiny* was trying to tell her something.

Sherry stopped and pulled *Destiny* from the shelf. She gripped him with both hands and concentrated as *Destiny* began to communicate to her. Sherry broke into a huge smile as she absorbed his message. The book was asking her to attend his friends' wedding. He wanted to surprise the couple with a special gift, an unusual gift, truly a historic gift—the presence of Sherry at their wedding. It had never been done before.

Sherry enthusiastically agreed to show up just before the exchange of vows. She even asked *Destiny* if she could bring a surprise guest. Sherry then gently slid *Destiny* back into place so as not to wake the others. This had to remain secret. *Destiny* did eventually leak the news to some of his close friends, but they were told to zip their lips. Sherry's appearance was going to be a gigantic surprise.

The surprise guest Sherry had referred to was Joann. The two had become quite close as of late. No one respected the books like Sherry and Joann. Both of them treated the books not as cash-generating commercial merchandise, but as the works of art that they truly were. Books had real souls. Sherry had even confided to Joann that she could converse with the books. Sherry knew that her friend might find it difficult to believe, but at least Joann would approach it with an open mind. Any other Sanders and Bowman employee would surely call in the funny farm rescue team.

Joann was still engaged in a dogfight with her publisher. Hagar House seemed determined to proceed with the new proposed title. *Mercury Girl* was now officially *Hot Trotter*. One of their executives, apparently the one that headed up the take-a-good-title-and-make-it-bad department, had taken it upon himself to formally change the name of the novel.

Joann was furious. She immediately picked up the phone and called the slimester who was responsible for the title change. There was no way *Mercury Girl*, her baby that she had nursed from infancy, was going to be degraded by being described as a "hot trotter." In the midst of their heated discussion Joann asked the vice president of operations if he had any children. The smooth talking executive volunteered that, yes, he had a daughter named Nora.

Joann then asked him how he would feel if everyone suddenly began referring to Nora as Slophog. Would he appreciate questions like these on a daily basis: How is your daughter Slophog? Is Slophog home yet? Can Slophog come out and play? No, of course he wouldn't! Would he be pleased that his little Nora was now Slophog? No way!

Joann then went on to explain that it was the same thing with her novel. *Mercury Girl* was no hot trotter any more than Nora was a slophog. They both had their given names which they had grown up with and wanted to keep. To change their names would be stripping them of their dignity. After Joann's outburst the stunned man hedged a bit, stating that he would reconsider the title change. Maybe *Mercury Girl* was a more fitting title for her novel. He thanked Joann for her input and said he would stay in touch.

Joann wasn't finished. The publishing executive had inadvertently disclosed another disturbing piece of information. He had told Joann that he needed the *Hot Trotter* title because it was consistent with the newly designed cover. The just-completed cover illustrated a curvy demimondaine attracting a young male with her seductive pose and pursed ruby-red lips.

Joann placed another call to Hagar House. This time she asked to be connected to department responsible for designing covers. After a bit of a runaround she finally spoke to the manager in charge. Joann tore into him like a pit bull, telling him in no uncertain terms that the current cover was not going to be used. Firing off some choice expletives Joann stated her demands. There was no way her respectable novel would be peddled to the public the way they had it portrayed. If the cover wasn't completely redone to Joann's satisfaction, this unfortunate soul on the other end of the phone would be held personally responsible.

Joann informed him that she would fly into his city, march into his office with a pair of sharp scissors, and begin removing a highly valued appendage from his body. The horrified manager quickly agreed the cover needed to be reworked. He placed the blame on a young immature new-hire in the art department. Joann was assured that the new cover would satisfy her requirements. This time a copy of the prospective cover would be immediately express-delivered to her for approval. There would be no need for any radical appendage abscissions.

Joann was now satisfied. She had done her best to defend *Mercury Girl's* honor. If the powers-that-be at Hagar House wanted to up the ante and call her bluff, they could go ahead and try it. Joann would then prove to them that she meant business. She *would* fly into their city. She *would* storm into their corporate headquarters. And she *would* be toting a sharp pair of scissors capable of modifying their anatomy. The next step was theirs. It would be in their best interest to retain the original title and dignify *Mercury Girl* with a respectable cover. Joann was not going to let these soulless chieftains derogate and belittle her 352 page baby girl. No way!

Joann felt better after her explosive release. She relaxed a bit. Now that she was temporarily content with *Mercury Girl's* future her thoughts began to drift to Sherry. Could she really communicate with books? Was she serious about the both of them attending a wedding ceremony for two novels in love? Joann's rational self rejected the idea. There was no way a human could talk to a book. But what if this wasn't Sherry's imagination playing tricks on her? What if it were true?

Joann decided to try an experiment. What the heck, there was nothing to lose. Sherry had mentioned that the two novels getting married were *Spy Needle* and *River Run True*. Sherry was especially close to *Spy Needle*, an entertaining novel who himself loved to be stimulated by interesting guests. *Spy Needle* enjoyed sharing stories with other books more than anything else.

Joann decided to handpick two or three interesting books and place them near *Spy Needle*. Nothing would ever come from it, but Joann wanted to do it anyway. Books can't speak to each other anymore than they can communicate with humans. This was just something Joann had to do. It was if a force were guiding her. Besides, no one would ever know of it—humans anyway.

Joann rambled through the bookstore. Now what book would another book enjoy reading? "Ha!" Joann laughed out loud as she realized what she was doing. Books reading other books—this ordeal she was going through with *Mercury Girl* must be driving her insane. Joann made a mental note to herself. If she actually followed through on attending a wedding ceremony for books, she was going to schedule a long vacation. If that didn't help, she was going to seek professional help. A psychiatrist should be accustomed to patients who spend their spare time attending book weddings—right?

Joann finally chose three books, all from different departments. She reckoned it to be the same as when you're buying someone a gift, but you don't really know what they like. You just choose several items and hope one of them hits. Heck, this was her first time shopping for an inanimate object. Her first choice was the Asian cookbook *Soy Cowboy*. Joann couldn't have done better than this personable publication. *Soy Cowboy's* relaxed humor made him extremely popular among his peers.

Joann's next selection was *Place the Piano Over Here*. She was a second novel from rising author J. T. Green. *Place the Piano Over Here* was currently entrenched on every major bestseller list. Joann figured she couldn't go wrong with an international bestseller.

The third book Joann picked on a whim. *Give Me Your Mind: How They Control Your Thoughts and Actions* caught Joann's eye because of its unique cover. It pictured a line of people, in a hypnotic trance-like state, marching straight ahead towards a cliff. It was self published by the discontented son of a prominent politician. Dr. Andrew Hunt had established himself as an authoritative figure in science and politics. His new book *Give Me Your Mind* was raising some eyebrows amongst the government brass. Some of them weren't taking kindly to the young scientist who was spilling the beans on their clandestine technologies of enslavement.

Now it was time to deliver the goods. Joann casually strolled into the fiction section carrying her covert cargo. She found shelf C22. Sure enough, just as Sherry had told her, sat the two lovebirds *Spy Needle* and *River Run True*. Joann glanced around to make sure no one was looking. She then slipped her hand over the two surprised novels and placed the three visitants behind them. They were completely hidden from view. She would be back for them in two hours. Joann then turned and walked away. For the first time in her fifty years of living she began to seriously question her sanity.

"What was that all about?" *River* was bewildered. It was unheard of for any staffer to exhibit such reckless behavior, much less Joann. She was the most cool-headed of all the Sanders and Bowman employees.

"I don't know," replied *Spy*, "but I'm going to find out."

Spy turned to the trio of books that now rested behind him.

"Are you guys okay? What's going on here?"

"Yes, we're all fine," replied a friendly voice.

Spy took a closer look. "Oh, I know who you are. You're *Soy Cowboy*! Everyone's heard of you. What in the world is going on?"

Soy Cowboy took in a deep breath. He hesitated as if to choose his words carefully. "Here's what I *think* is going on. As we all know, Sherry has a special capacity to communicate with us. Over the last few weeks she and Joann have become quite close. I think that Sherry has somehow instilled some of her powers in Joann. After I finish I'd like to ask my two comrades here what they think. The reason I say this is because I'm not the least bit concerned about my welfare. From the moment Joann pulled me from my home I instinctively knew I was in good hands. I could read her mind."

Soy Cowboy glanced at his two traveling partners. They were both nodding in agreement.

"Now I don't know if Joann could comprehend my thoughts, I suspect not. Maybe this human-book communication thing is a learning process. Maybe Joann's tuned in just enough for us to understand her, but not enough to know what we're thinking. She's obviously not at Sherry's level. Some of us here at Sanders and Bowman can actually maintain a conversation with Sherry."

"Yes, we can certainly vouch for that," said *River*.

"Anyway, here's my theory. Only certain people are spiritually capable of communicating with books. The foremost ingredient in this mix is a genuine love of literary works. It has to be real. Sherry and Joann both have it. It's not something that can be faked. When the communication occurs, it's as if human and book alike actually shift into another dimension, one where our wavelengths travel the same path. At least that's been my experience with Sherry.

"I suspect Sherry is training Joann how to converse with us. It's possible that Joann's not even aware of it. I'd be willing to bet that eventually Joann will be able to absorb our thoughts. At this early stage in her development she can only project her intentions, not receive ours. That would explain why I'm not worried about being removed from my home. I read her mind as she transported us over here. I know for a fact she'll return in two hours to take us back. We're here strictly for your entertainment purposes. Joann knows that you like to meet other interesting books. Personally, I'm flattered that she chose me. Well, that's my opinion about what's going on. It's pretty mysterious stuff, so who really knows."

"*Soy Cowboy*, you've hit the nail on the head," called out one of the newcomers. It was the book with the thought-provoking cover.

"Let me introduce myself. I'm *Give Me Your Mind*, everyone calls me *Gimme*. I agree with *Soy Cowboy* one hundred percent. I too could relate to Joann's intentions. For sure she'll return in two hours to take us back home. We're some sort of an experiment for her. She doesn't want to believe that Sherry talks to us or that we talk to each other, but the fact that she delivered us to you speaks for itself. She's intrigued enough to take this first step. I think *Soy Cowboy's* right, Joann's being trained to speak with us. Sherry's sharing her magic with her friend—a magic that originates out of a deep respect for the book community, something the both of them possess."

Destiny delivered a friendly smile. "You two make a lot of sense. We're gonna have some fine conversation here. It's a pleasure to meet you. My name's *Destiny's Fortune*, *Destiny* for short. Beside me are my two best friends, *Spy Needle* and *River Run True*. You may be aware of their upcoming wedding, the one that's scheduled right after Kris Richards's appearance."

"So you're the couple everyone's talking about." *Place the Piano Over Here* strained to get a better look. "I've heard all about the witty spy novel who's marrying the pretty love story. *River* and *Spy*, congratulations!"

"Thank you so much," replied *River*. "You're a beautiful book yourself. I just read your title—*Place the Piano Over Here*. That's an interesting name. Are you a story about pianos?"

"Oh, absolutely not, and please call me *Place*." Everyone turned their attention to the lovely novel. *River* had been right in her statement, *Place* was an exceptionally attractive lady.

"My creator uses the title because it's her favorite example of someone trying to keep up appearances. I was almost named *Keeping Up With the Joneses*. As a matter of fact that was my working title for over a year. Actually it probably describes me better than *Place the Piano Over Here*, but my creator wanted something out of the ordinary.

"Let me tell you how she derived my title. Janet, that's my creator's real name, has always been amused at her fellow humans who accumulate material goods to prove their worth. Janet is a very practical person as everything in her home serves a purpose. One day she looked out her window to witness a delivery van and five workers in her neighbors' driveway. Wondering what was going on she pulled up a chair to watch. Over the next three hours she observed the men remove and set up an enormous piano.

"After the van departed my creator politely asked her neighbors' five-year-old daughter about their new piano. What she learned stunned her. The little girl told my creator her parents had purchased the huge concert grand piano because their other next-door neighbor, an actual couple named Jones, had recently acquired one.

"The five-year-old innocently disclosed that no one would actually use the 1000-pound monster. It had been strategically placed so that the Joneses would see it from their living room. They had paid the equivalent of a small house to purchase something they had no intentions of ever using. How absurd! To my creator this was the most ridiculous thing she had ever heard."

"Yeah, that's crazy," said *Spy*. "So your story is *really* based on keeping up with the Joneses."

"Exactly, but I'm not based on any one family," answered *Place*. "The setting is an upper middle class neighborhood where the one-upmanship quickly gets out of hand. Janet's got approximately thirty households competing against each other to see who can claim socio-economic and cultural superiority. Some of the bizarre acts of conspicuous consumption make the piano episode appear tame by comparison."

"This is beginning to sound very interesting," said *River*. "Can you tell us more?"

"Sure I can," replied *Place*. "This neighborhood is made up mostly of what's called new-moneyed families. The developers gave it the glitzy name of Forested Hills, although there's not a tree to be seen anywhere and it's as flat as a pancake. Many of the residents have over-extended themselves by simply buying into the neighborhood. This doesn't stop them from trying to amass the latest status symbols, not in the least."

"Oh my," said *River*. "Those sort of people really irk me. They need to get a real life!"

"I totally agree," said *Place*, "but there's plenty of people out there who judge others by their possessions. Let's start with the most basic status symbol. Many materialistic people judge a person's value by the car that they drive. In their eyes a mass-murdering serial killer driving a Mercedes is considered a success. Big and new and loaded with gadgets that'll never be used—that's the benchmark when it comes to cars. Practicality has nothing to do with it.

"Here's how the battle of automobiles escalated out of control in Forested Hills. It all started when the Perkins family purchased a new four-wheel drive vehicle. It was twenty percent larger than any other model in its class. They felt they needed this all-terrain vehicle for navigating the icy roads during the harsh south Florida winters. The Perkins were proud as peacocks as they putted around Forested Hills in their shiny new gas guzzler that still had the dealer invoice pasted on the side window. Yep, it had cost them a bundle and they wanted everyone to know it.

"You can guess what happened next. That's right, some-one one-upped them. The Wilsons rushed out and purchased the same exact vehicle, color included. The only difference was the tires. The Wilsons instructed the dealer to upgrade to a wider brand of tires. These steel-belted goliaths would supply the extra traction necessary to negotiate their treacherous one mile trips to the convenience store. But the added traction wasn't what the Wilsons admired most about their over-sized tires. They also added a premium to the purchase price.

"This made their new vehicle slightly more expensive than the Perkins' now second-rate jalopy. Now it was the Wilsons who proudly paraded around Forested Hills in their sparkling new ride. They were number one and the dealer invoice plastered on the side window proved it.

"The Wilsons' reign of automotive dominance lasted exactly four days before the Wards struck them down. The Wards weren't fooling around with any mass-produced automobile. They dramatically raised the stakes by acquiring a military-style all-terrain vehicle. At over seven feet wide and nearly thirty feet long the vehicle was barely street legal. The Wards were status seekers of the highest caliber. They had purchased a product that wasn't even available to the public.

It was big, expensive, and it had bells and whistles that only a defense contractor could have dreamt up. No one would ever top this acquisition.

"The Wards announced their ascension to the throne by entering Forested Hills at exactly three o'clock in the afternoon. They knew that's when all the neighborhood parents would be gathered at the bus stop waiting for children to arrive from school. This was the perfect time to trump out their new armored vehicle. Since their informal purchase didn't include a side window dealer invoice, the Wards took the liberty to make up one of their own. They attached it to the right side where it would be clearly visible to their intended audience. Mr. Ward even went to the pains to highlight the final purchase price, taxes included, with a black magic marker. This enormous and expensive vehicle would be the final say in the Forested Hills car wars. No one could ever challenge this. Never!

"Sixty-four days later the Wards were dethroned. It had taken Charlie Yates a while to put together the deal, but it finally came together. The Yates family officially proclaimed their superiority at seven o'clock on a Sunday morning. The neighbors were awakened by a deafening racket outside. It was an awful clanging of metal upon metal along with the sounds of crunching pavement.

"When they looked out their windows they thought they were being invaded by a foreign enemy. It was a tank! A real tank! Perched atop the gun turret was little Billy Yates. The three-year-old was swinging the 120 millimeter weapon in 360 degree circles, occasionally stopping to point it at a house and pretending to blow it up. Crouched inside the driver's compartment of this seventy-ton armored apparatus was a beaming Charlie Yates.

"The retired military officer had pulled some bigtime strings to acquire this elaborate and costly weapon. His family would be paying on it for a millennium, but it was well worth it to be number one. It mattered not that he would have to keep it on private roads. This pleasure vehicle was strictly for short jaunts around the neighborhood. At nearly twelve feet wide his brand new tank covered the entire street. Anyone challenging the powerful Yates would be crushed. They were now warned to keep their puny little toy cars out of the way. Charlie Yates owned the roads of Forested Hills."

Place's cover was shining brightly. She was obviously enjoying narrating to her attentive audience.

"Well, there's one example of what I think is incredible foolishness. Believe it or not, there's quite a bit of truth in that story. It took some real morosophs to inspire wild fiction like that."

"You're so right," said *River*. "With all the drama humans create for themselves, it's a wonder they bother to read fiction. Their reality is strange enough. *Place*, do you feel like sharing another passage from your interesting novel? Can we hear some more?"

"To be honest I was hoping you'd ask me that," said *Place*. "The fools that reside in Forested Hills are always good for a laugh.

"Here's a quick one that sort of parallels the car shenanigans. One of the residents purchased a used recreational vehicle. Of course this got the entire neighborhood chirping. Within a week a mad race was on to see who could possess the largest RV. It started small but escalated rapidly. First it was a tiny, but new, motor home purchased by the Winslows. Then the Becks joined the fray with a slightly larger model. The Tafts really got Forested Hills to gossiping with their RV acquisition, an enormous castle on wheels. The forty-foot luxury vehicle costs a bundle, but it placed the Tafts at the top of the heap, and that's what mattered most in their insane world.

"Not to be outdone, the pretentious Cauley family finally put a stop to the motor home conflict. They special ordered a customized fifty-footer that seemed to stretch a city block. Never mind that it would never actually be used. It was a showpiece only. This was the mother of all recreational vehicles. This red-striped fully self-contained baby had every option you could imagine, including marble floors, granite counters, gold-plated faucets, seats with built-in heat and massage, a wine cellar, four televisions, five push-button slide-outs, even a billiard table. The Cauleys went so far as to construct a special parking structure to house their mansion on wheels. It was built entirely of see-through plexiglass, lest the neighbors forget who possessed the superior motor home of Forested Hills.

"That should have ended the ridiculous saga, but remember, this is Forested Hills we're talking about. This is the domain of fragile egos, where style supercedes substance, and demented competitive instinct overrides common sense. If there was one family that could be as ostentatious as the Cauleys, it would be the Barringtons. Mel Barrington had to ride by the Cauleys' super-luxury house trailer every morning on his way to work. Sometimes Joe Cauley would be out cleaning his plexiglass windows ensuring that passers-by would have an unobstructed view of his dream machine. It burned at Mel's guts to think that Joe Cauley had a bigger motor home than he.

"Mel Barrington's jealousy finally got the best of him one morning. He opened up a bottle of whisky and finished it off in under an hour. He opened another one. The Cauleys were no better than the Barringtons. How dare they have a bigger motor home! Mel called up the local realtor. He wanted to buy a house, a nice house, a big house—today! Mel then marched over to the municipal office of planning and permits. He plucked down a wad of cash for a permit to transport a structure.

"Mel's next step was to buy a brand new flat-bed truck. He then contracted with a company that specialized in moving whole houses intact. They were instructed to place his newly purchased two story home onto the truck. Mel waited until the job was complete. Then he watched as the crew took a short break. Mel raced over to the truck, jumped into the cab, and headed for home toting this massive structure behind him. He entered Forested Hills as onlookers peered at him in amazement. Who was this man? Why was he transporting a house?

"Mel stopped in front of the Cauley residence. A crowd quickly gathered. He laid down on the horn for what seemed an eternity. Mel then jumped from the cab, liquor bottle in hand, and began yelling obscenity-laced demands towards the Cauley household.

"'Come out of your house and look at my motor home,' Mel screamed. 'Mine's bigger than yours. You Cauleys ain't got nothing on us. Come out here you wimp Joe Cauley. Accept defeat like a man! You're a loser Joe Cauley. A loser!

"Mel Barrington's drunken gauderies went on for an hour until the police finally showed up and hauled him off to jail. This is another example of how far some individuals will go to prove their superiority over their fellow humans. Incredible as this story seems, it too is based on a real event. Can you believe, with all the real pain and suffering that goes on in the world, that people actually squabble over who's got the bigger RV? My lord, please help them!"

"Oh my God," exclaimed *River*. "That's funny, but you're right. People like that need help. At least in a humorous way you and your creator are exposing them to the world."

"I agree," said *Spy*, "and I'd like to compliment you on your storytelling skills. You're smooth, very smooth. Any other details we need to know about this Forested Hills gang?"

"Thanks for the compliment," replied *Place*, "and yes, there's plenty more dirt to be dispensed on this pathetic bunch."

Place looked down at her two companions beneath her. "*Soy Cowboy, Gimme*—I promise I won't be long. I know everyone, myself included, wants to know what you're both all about. Just a few minutes more and I'll be done.

"Let me quickly run through another Forested Hills folly. Oh, here's one! It's probably my favorite. The community has a women's club—Forested Hills Women's Club it's called. It was set up to be a social organization that would perform charity events, community cleanups, and those kind of things. In reality it's just a gossip center where the ladies of the neighborhood brag about themselves. Basically it's an information source so they'll know what they've gotta buy, gotta do, and where they've gotta go to be with the 'in crowd.' Gotta keep up with the competition, you know.

"Women like to be perceived as beautiful. There's nothing wrong with that. It's a natural thing—*River* and I can vouch for that. It's just that the ladies at Forested Hills Women's Club carried it a little to far. Let me explain. First it was the expensive hair styles. One did it, the rest followed. Then Sarah Wilson got a facelift. Within three months everyone had a freshly sculpted face. Rebecca Barrington arrived at one meeting sporting breast enhancements. At the next meeting everyone was showing off their new and improved mammary glands. Georgette Perkins took top prize in the size category with her matching inflatables.

"One meeting Darcy Drumfeld showed up prancing around in her new dress. She had just lost twenty pounds and she made sure everyone knew it. Thin became the new obsession for the superficial members of Forested Hills Women's Club. At the next meeting several of the girls had noticeably shed a few pounds. Within three months everyone was on the weight loss bandwagon, some of them to the point of appearing malnourished. The competition escalated to a higher level when Paula Pridgette proudly announced she just had liposuction surgery. The doctor had just vacuumed out ten pounds of fat.

"You probably know what happens next. That's right, everyone rushes out to have liposuction. You didn't think these gals would be content with their rearranged faces and modified breasts, did you? No way! They've got much higher ambitions than that. This group won't be satisfied until they've mutilated their entire body.

"Sandra Howell got the ball rolling with a visit to her plastic surgeon. She came back looking a bit sickly, but fifteen pounds lighter. Patty Nance was next in line to have fat sucked from her body. Her twenty-pound weight loss set a new standard. Janette Perkins dipped into the world of liposculpture and came out the other side with some bruising, swelling and a lot of pain. But it was all worth it as she watched twenty-five pounds of her being flow through a suction tube into a bucket.

"Linda Kraft went the budget route and hired an inexperienced surgeon who botched the operation. She was scarred for life, but thrilled with her thirty-pound loss. Linda was now the thinnest member of Forested Hills Women's Club. One week later she handed her crown over to Monica Cauley.

Always striving to be number one, Monica had instructed her doctor to extract exactly thirty-five pounds of flesh from her body. That would leave the already slender socialite at a whopping eighty-eight pounds, making her the current champion of thinness.

"Paula Pridgette was furious. She was now the fattest member of the club—and she had started the liposuction craze! Fuming in anger she went back to her surgeon and demanded another operation. This time she had fifty pounds of tissue sucked from her body. At eighty-five pounds she was now number one. Hail to the lipoplasty queen!

"By all accounts this incredibly insane competition should have ended there. But it didn't. Rebecca Barrington was raised to be a winner. There was no way any member of Forested Hills Women's Club would be thinner than her. She would put an end to this madness once and for all. It was obvious that dieting and plastic surgery wasn't going to be enough to beat these determined competitors. Rebecca Barrington would do whatever it took to get her blue-blooded body down below eighty-five pounds. She came from winner's stock, and she *was* going to be number one!

"Rebecca searched and searched until she found an unscrupulous doctor. She then requested him to do something so bizarre that even this unprincipled weasel refused to do it. Rebecca's oversized envelope stuffed with cash finally persuaded him.

"Rebecca came back to his office the following day. He put her under with a large dose of anesthesia. The mad doctor then proceeded to *amputate both of Rebecca's legs!* You heard me right! Rebecca had calculated that she could instantly lose sixty pounds by removing her legs. This would make her the undisputed weight loss champion of Forested Hills. The operation went smoothly without complications. Rebecca was delighted with the results. She rolled her wheelchair into the next meeting wearing a victory smile."

"Oh *Place*, do I laugh or cry?" asked *River*. It's horrible, but so stupid that it's funny. Your creator really stretched her imagination on that one."

"Yeah she did" said *Place*. "That's the whole point of *Place the Piano Over Here*. I'm a novel that's meant to get people thinking. Of course this leg-amputation bit is total fiction. Nobody is really *that* stupid. But you know what—everyone knows someone who's got their priorities mixed up. Someone who's so involved in some petty rivalry that they've completely lost sight of the big picture. Life is more than accumulating material objects and pretending to be a class above other human beings. This world has *real* problems to contend with if they'll only open their eyes. Janet wanted to bring this human condition to the surface using me as a median. I personally think she did a fantastic job."

"Hurray for you and Janet and kudos to you both," crowed *Destiny*. "Anyone who reads you will undoubtedly come away with Janet's intended message. Excellent work on both of your parts!"

"I absolutely agree," said *Spy*. "You're fiction with a purpose, and a heck of an entertaining read also."

"*Place*, there's one thing I wanted to ask you," said *River*. "You mentioned your creator's name is Janet. Is there any particular reason why she's listed as J. T. Green on your cover?"

"Oh, don't get me started on that one," droned *Place*. "Her real name, the one she was given at birth, and the one she loves is Janet Brown. There is no middle name or initial, she's simply Janet Brown. I happen to think it's a lovely name. I'd buy a book authored by someone called Janet Brown, wouldn't you?

"Well, apparently that wasn't good enough for Roberts and Kingman Publishing Group. Their marketing team recommended my creator go by the name of J. T. Green. Why? They never would give us a reasonable answer. You know why—because they *didn't have* a reasonable answer. The best I can figure is that someone in the decision making process was taking a few too many nips at the bottle or they were smoking some funny cigarettes.

"Okay, let's analyze this one unit at a time. The initial J could work, after all she is Janet. The initial T, forget about it—she's not a T girl, never has been, never will be. Now the clincher, the surname Green. Can anyone here figure out how Green is better than Brown? Why substitute one color for another? I don't get it and neither does Janet. We'd understand it if her real name was Rattie McWeasel or something like that—we'd support it a hundred percent. But that's not the case. Now Janet's stuck with the J.T. Green tag because I'm a bestseller. I don't care what the publishing company might claim, I know the cold hard truth. I'm a bestseller because my creator crafted an excellent novel, *not* because some idiot changed her perfectly good name. Whew, that gets me fired up!"

"I guess it does," said *River*, "and it should. It makes no sense to me either. This is one crazy business!"

"That it is," replied *Place*. "Enough about me. I've had the floor way too long. *Soy Cowboy*, *Gimme*, one of you guys shut me up, okay?"

The two books looked at each other, each waiting for the other to begin. Finally *Gimme* gave in and spoke.

"Okay, my full name is *Give Me Your Mind: How They Control Your Thoughts and Actions*. The name pretty much describes what I'm all about. I'm a serious book about a serious subject—mind control. My creator and my hero is Dr. Andrew Hunt."

Spy perked up at the mention of mind control. "Oh, I know a little about that. Roy delved into it a bit when he was researching government espionage. That mind control is some scary stuff."

"It's incredibly scary," *Gimme* went on. "I can't begin to explain the courage it took to publish me. Some very powerful people let it be known that they didn't want my information made public. They shut down every avenue towards attaining a major publisher—national security issues they claimed. Every top publisher turned Andrew down. Now keep in mind, Andrew had already been published four times previously, all of which sold quite well I might add. They didn't want to touch a hot potato like me. Ultimately, Andrew self published."

"What are some methods of mind control?" *Spy* asked.

"With the technologies that have advanced under the cover of secrecy we're talking science fiction type stuff. We live in a subliminal world where our reality is created for us. Don't for a moment think that this reality-molding is for our own good. There are some sinister elements out there that desire to enslave us. They sugarcoat our poison and make us beg for more. I'd like to start with the basics before we get into the implausible. I gotta go slow with this or you'll blow me off as a kook.

"The most basic form of mind control is television. Nearly all of the networks are owned by a handful of major corporations, all of whom are firmly entrenched in the military-industrial complex. Entertainment, industry, defense—everything's under one big corporate umbrella. Government and big business are one and the same. It's back-scratching at the highest level. In other words, the network directors receive their marching orders from the top of the pyramid. If they do as they're told they'll climb the corporate ladder. If they resist their careers are over, or worse.

"The bottom line with television is that it's a mind control device. Human's think they're being entertained, but actually they're being dumbed down. It's a corporate tool of hypnotic control. News isn't news, it's information that's been bent and twisted to support whatever the agenda of the day happens to be. I could go on forever about the brainwashing effects of television. It's a drug, a form of sedation. Humans are taught from birth that everything's going to be okay as long as they follow the instructions that flow from the talking tube. They think they've got it made in the shade. What they don't realize is that big ole shade tree's getting ready to fall down upon them."

"You know, I think you're right," *Destiny* surmised. "Human beings are hypnotized by television. It's an ingenious tool of evil when you think about it."

"We've only scratched the surface of mind control," *Gimme* continued. "Those same corporations that manipulate the television screen also control radio, the movie studios, and the print media, including us books to a certain extent. The list goes on and on. Freedom of the press is nothing more than a myth. They've got their grimy fingers stuck in every piece of the information pie. Now, are you guys ready for the mind-boggling stuff?"

"You know I am," answered *Spy*. "You really got my curiosity aroused when you mentioned the science fiction-type technology."

"Okay, if you think you can handle it," said *Gimme*. "You'd better strap yourselves in, because most of this will be difficult to believe.

"Mind control has been going on for a long time. Unfortunately the technology behind it has been driven by military research funds supporting espionage and warfare uses. Much of the dirty work is done underground. These deep underground science and engineering laboratories, as they're called, are quite nefarious in nature. Some unethical experiments can take place two miles under, let me tell you. Several mind-controlled assassins have been trained in these places. When you think about it, it makes perfect sense. Using a human robot as a patsy keeps the culprit's hands clean. Several political figures, along with a famous musician who was perceived as a threat to the elite, have been the victims of these mind-controlled killers. But you know what—that news is old hat. This newest technology gives its keepers powers beyond comprehension.

"The future of mind control is electromagnetic energy sources. Governments have said so in their own documents, hidden in plain sight as you might say. One thing is for sure, the government doesn't want this nasty stuff advertised. My creator really stirred up the pot when he included this in my text. He thinks these weapons are meant for the general population.

"I'm going to simplify this for you. Look at the human body as a receiving antenna for electromagnetic waves. Governments possess devices that can manipulate the flow of this energy. Technology has now advanced to the point where electromagnetic coupling can be induced. This is where the cells of the body tune into a corresponding electromagnetic signal and they bind together. Have I lost anyone yet?"

"I'm still with you, *Gimme*," replied *Spy*. "This fascinates me. How about you—*River, Destiny*?"

"So far, so good,' answered *Destiny*. "I'd rather know what's going on, even if it's not exactly what I want to hear."

River gave *Spy* a gentle push. "Yeah baby, I'm intelligent enough to comprehend this, at least so far. Not bad for a love story, huh?" she said, flashing a smile at *Spy*.

"Okay, everyone's still on board," said *Gimme*. "That's good. Alright, here's the result of electromagnetic coupling. It *ain't* good. The instigators of this attack, and that's what it really is, now have absolute control over the subject. They have an invisible power to control the victim's thoughts. They can manipulate emotions, control every aspect of your behavior, put you to sleep, anything and everything. They can even create false memories and wipe out your old memories. Imagine that kind of power over the masses!"

Spy looked over at *Gimme* and nodded. "God help us all if they use those weapons. When they strip away the ability to think for yourself it's all over. *Gimme*, I know you're speaking the truth. I've got chill bumps on my cover just thinking about it. What is it with these guys? They're not going to be happy until they've yanked everything away from the individual— even their thoughts!"

"I'm afraid that might be their goal," agreed *Gimme*, "total dominance over the world's population. I can't think of a more efficient method of control than diving right into the core, the seat of the soul, the human brain."

"You know what they say, ignorance is bliss," said *Spy*. "Well, it's time everyone stopped being so full of bliss and begin educating themselves before it's too late—unless it already is."

Gimme nodded in agreement. "You're right, knowledge is the key. My creator's well aware of that fact. That's why he's risking so much. He knows how important it is for people to wake up and *do something*.

"There's one more thing I would like to mention. Then I'll hand it over to *Soy Cowboy* who's been patiently waiting.

My eighth chapter gets into what's been termed as 'remote viewing.' For me, personally, it's the most fascinating chapter in my text. At least three governments have programs dedicated to remote viewing. Essentially it involves psychic spying.

"Andrew interviewed several insiders privy to inside information about these programs. Here's the scoop. You've all heard of investigators bringing in psychics to locate missing persons, kidnap victims, those sort of things. They wouldn't be wasting their time unless they thought it could be beneficial. Now raise it up a notch to the government level. When governments do something they don't mess around, especially if there's potential to establish a political or military advantage. Money's not even an issue to these fellows.

"Remote viewing is this—placing your mind in another location to retrieve information. Let me give you an example. Suppose you want to learn of your opponent's war strategy. No problem, just transport your consciousness over to the other side of the world, pop into their war room and start soaking up the information. Yep, just hover around the ceiling in your invisible state and collect military secrets. I'm not kidding you, this actually happens.

"Wanna hear something even crazier? This isn't limited to our planet. One extremely reputable insider disclosed that he visited *Mars* on one of his missions. Mars! He came back adamant that there were beings living underneath the surface. He could feel their presence. You can laugh, but the government took him very seriously.

"You're going to slap me off the shelf when you hear what's next. These guys can go back in time! That's right, they can travel back into the past! Wanna know what is was like to live in the Roman times? Take a trip and find out for yourself.

Have lunch with Julius Caesar! Hang out with Augustus! Talk girls with Caligula! Then come back and rewrite history.

"Curious as to the origin of man? Take a couple of hours out of your busy schedule and go research it. Travel backwards til you can't go any more. Forget Darwin and all those middlemen. Go all the way back in time to the beginning, whenever that may be. Are we monkeys, aliens, or were we whipped out by the hand of God? Gather up information and cruise on back home to enlighten humanity.

"Maybe you just wanna keep it simple, nothing more than a short jaunt back to your childhood. Suppose you're craving a piece of that scrumptious peach cobbler you enjoyed as a kid. You know, that sweet treat your late great-grandmother used to bake fifty years ago. That should be easy enough. Jump into the time tunnel and get off at the first stop. Waiting to greet you will be your smiling granny to personally hand deliver her mouth-watering just-out-of-the-oven peachy concoction that she was so famous for. Umm good!

"So the next time you want to visit the Swiss Alps, but you don't have the money for a holiday, don't sweat it. Go for free! Simply send your mind on an all-expense paid vacation. Take a trip and never leave the farm as they say. Well guys, what do you think about this remote viewing?"

Destiny looked over at *Gimme* and smiled. "I'm glad you added a touch of humor, because it makes it a little easier to swallow. Traveling back in time is pretty outrageous stuff. Coming from anyone else I wouldn't believe it. But from what I've learned about your creator, I'm not discounting it. I tell you what I'd like, to go back in time and have a conversation with the very first book ever produced. Now *that* would be an experience!"

"Yes it certainly would," said *Gimme*. "I've got a ton of information I'd love to share, but our time is limited. *Soy*

Cowboy, you're somewhat of a local legend around Sanders and Bowman. Everyone seems to have heard of you. I've always wanted to know what you're all about and now fate has brought us together. Go at it, *Soy Cowboy*!"

Soy Cowboy laughed. "I don't consider myself a legend, not even close. I'm just an Asian cookbook. I contain nearly four hundred recipes from fifteen different countries. I guess you could say I'm a mixed breed."

"I gotta ask you something," said *Destiny*. "What the heck is a soy cowboy?"

"Ha," *Soy Cowboy* chuckled. "Everyone always asks how I got my name. The answer's simple, I inherited it. My creator's been known as Soy Cowboy ever since he was a kid. Choey, that's his real name, grew up in Canada with parents of Asian descent. His father is Korean and his mother is Vietnamese. Do I need to tell you that he loved soy sauce? Choey would drink the stuff for breakfast if his parents allowed it. That's how much he liked it.

"The cowboy part of the equation came about because he was crazy about those old western movies. There was something about life on the open range that appealed to young Choey. That and those big hats his heroes wore. He'd get so inspired after watching a cowboy film that he'd jump on the back of the family dog and begin rounding up the neighborhood cats. He finally outgrew his cowboy dreams when he realized how hard the work was, and the lack of females under the lonesome moon. The nickname Soy Cowboy, however, stuck like glue."

"That's a cute story. What motivated your creator to write a cookbook?" asked *River*.

"Basically he got tired of people telling him he should write a cookbook," said *Soy Cowboy*, "if you really want to know the truth. Here's how it came about. Choey's parents were avid travelers, especially to Asia. Every year they'd drag Choey around to various countries. As a child he learned to appreciate foods from the different cultures. He'd eat anything mind you, as long as he could pour a liberal amount of soy sauce on it. To this day he's still a nut about his precious soy sauce.

"Choey was fascinated with all the variety and he wasn't shy about asking questions. Every time the family would dine at a restaurant they'd inevitably end up in the kitchen. Choey would have the chef cornered as he quizzed him about the local vegetables, what spices to add with what foods, cooking times, presentation, *everything*!

"With Choey's fanatical interest in food, it was only natural that he assumed the family's cooking duties. Every evening he would prepare an exquisite Asian dish. Many times friends and extended family would be present to sample the fare. Word quickly spread that this boy could cook! It wasn't long before he was swamped with requests for copies of his recipes.

"As the years went on his culinary reputation grew. People began suggesting that he put together a cookbook. He got so tired of hearing 'Choey, you should do a cookbook' that he finally caved in. He buckled down for six months and produced a 416 page collection of his favorite recipes complete with colorful pictures—that would be me! Never even thinking about publishing his book on a commercial scale, he went to the local printer and had fifty copies made up. He gave them out as gifts and figured that would be the end of it.

"Three months later Choey received a phone call from a literary agent asking if he could represent him. How about that for a change, an agent tracking down an author. Talk about a lightning strike! Apparently this guy had somehow got ahold of his cookbook and thought it was publishable. To make a long story short, the agent showed the book to a publishing executive who happened to love Korean food. He tried a couple of Choey's Korean recipes and that was it— published! A year later my brothers and I are spread out in bookstores across the country."

"Yes! That's the kind of story I like to hear," exclaimed *River*. "The short and sweet route to success. Those stories are few and far between."

"We realize we were lucky," *Soy Cowboy* continued. "I think what separated us from a thousand other cookbooks was Choey's personal summaries following each recipe. He always gave a brief history of where and how he found each one. Some of these proved to be quite entertaining even though they weren't intended as such. My creator has a certain charm that's inescapable when he's discussing his favorite subject. That would be food of course."

"Could you give us an example?" asked *Spy*. "We're entertainment junkies around here. I'm sure the recipes are great, but if you've got a story to back it up that's even better."

"I've got stories galore," bellowed *Soy Cowboy*. "As I stated earlier, my creator's not the timid type. His outgoing personality lands him in some unusual situations. Chapter thirteen deals with Taiwan. That's where he was chatting with some street vendors and they convinced him to eat frog. He'd eaten frog before. It wasn't a favorite, but it was edible. Then they mentioned that it was the frog's heart. Well, that put a damper on the taste buds, but Choey still went along with it. After all, many cultures around the world consumed animal organs. As long as he could sprinkle some soy sauce over it, it would slide down okay. He sat down in a chair and waited for them to prepare this Taiwanese dish.

"As he pondered on what vegetable might accompany his frog heart, he heard a loud croaking noise, then silence. Seconds later his meal arrived, a *still beating* frog heart! The heart was still alive, pumping away as if it were running a frog marathon.

"'Someone forgot to kill the frog!' my creator instinctively shrieked as he pushed away the pulsating organ. The Taiwanese vendors howled in laughter at their western visitor. Finally Choey worked up his nerve and swallowed the toad heart whole. It was all in fun, except maybe for the frog. Choey even took a photo of the group afterwards which you can see on page 286."

"Yuck!" groaned *River*. "That's a little *too* fresh for me."

"Oh yeah," *Soy Cowboy* agreed. "Still alive is as fresh as you can get. If you're not into fresh maybe you would like to dine on a Chinese thousand-year-egg. They're a Choey favorite. Actually they're really misnamed because they've only been aged for a few months. I guess the strong odor of sulfur and ammonia makes them smell like they're a thousand years old.

"That one's not for me either," declared *River*. "Maybe they really are a tasty treat, but whoever named it didn't know anything about marketing. You won't catch me eating anything that's even *rumored* to be a thousand years old."

"Gotta agree with you on that," said *Soy Cowboy*. "Let me change the theme a bit. We could dwell on the different cultural delicacies all day, especially if you get me started on chilli-dipped donkey pizzle, roasted goose perineum, horse sashimi or lizard wine. Wanna hear how Choey met his wife?"

"Definitely!" replied *River*. "That sounds a heck of a lot better than discussing donkey pizzle. God only knows what that might be."

Soy Cowboy smiled. "You're a clever lady. Choey's been married to a pretty lady for nearly ten years. They met in Bangkok, Thailand. It was Choey's first time in the land of smiles and he's wandering around sampling the cuisine. As you might know, Thailand is famous for its street markets. He stopped at this one vendor's cart and ordered up a papaya *som tam* salad. The young girl prepared it for him and handed it over. She kept repeating the words *pit mak mak* as she watched him wolf it down.

"Choey would have been wise to pull out his guidebook to see what those words meant in English. It wasn't long before Choey knew something was wrong. The little green chillies in the salad might have been small but they were potent. His insides were on fire. My creator began jumping up and down fanning his mouth. He ran from table to table snatching anything liquid and downing it, going through several glasses of water and beer. The other diners were stunned.

"The Thai locals knew exactly what had happened. Another *farang* tourist had bitten into more chillies than he could handle. Choey thought about jumping into the Chao Phraya River, but quickly realized that would only make him look more the fool. Finally the young girl who had supplied the fiery batch of vegetables came to his rescue. She began shoving spoonfuls of rice into his mouth. After a few minutes the heat finally subsided and the both of them had a good laugh. She introduced herself as Gai. She explained to him in broken English that *pit mak mak* meant very spicy. Gai had been trying to warn him of the pungent little peppers.

"Naturally Choey wanted to examine the capsicums that had set off the five-alarm fire in his innards. Gai led him over to a basket where she kept the little green beasts. Choey picked one up and analyzed it. For something that looked so innocent it sure packed a punch. He rolled it in his fingers. It had a hard slick surface. He would never forget this breed of pepper. From now on it would be treated with the utmost respect. It had, after all, nearly made him jump into a river to escape its fiery clutches. Just the thought of it made his eyes begin to water again. He wiped a tear from the corner of his eye.

"Big mistake! Within seconds his eye began to burn. Instinctively he rubbed his eye in an effort to rid himself of the irritant. Bigger mistake! It was like pouring gasoline on a fire. Now his left eye burned so much that he wanted to yank it from its socket. The little pepper had struck again!

"Gai again came to his aid. She laid my creator down on the ground and began flushing out his eye with copious amounts of cold water. A crowd gathered around. A local newspaper reporter happened to walk by just as the commotion erupted. She began to snap photos of this ignorant *farang* who was wounded by green peppers twice in the span of ten minutes.

"Thanks to Gai, my Choey survived. They quickly established a relationship and within six months they were married. Choey relocated to Thailand and he's been there ever since. They've got 'em a nice little country home. It you turn to page 144 you'll see what was splashed on the cover of the *Bangkok Post* the day after his pepper encounters. It's a photo of my culinary genius creator flopping around in agony as Gai pours a pitcher of ice water on his face. The now infamous soy cowboy had fallen off his horse."

"Now that's hilarious!" *Destiny* roared. "I could picture it as you were describing it. Painful but funny!"

Soy Cowboy nodded and smiled. "Yeah, it's not one of my creator's best moments, but it gained him a wife. Here's another one you may enjoy. Chapter twenty deals with various soup dishes. Choey didn't intend on creating an entire chapter devoted to soups until his wisdom tooth incident.

"This takes place in a remote area of Mongolia. Choey had flown into the capital city of Ulaanbaatar in search of what else—food. He was putting the finishing touches on his book and hoped to discover a couple of exotic dishes. His one week stay turned into two months. This is how it happened. A source in the capital told Choey he should head for the countryside if he wanted to experience real Mongolian recipes.

"So Choey did just that. He set out in search of the no-madic herders who survived primarily on the products of their animals, meat and milk, along with a few vegetables and noodles. It wasn't long before he fell in with a hospitable group that took him in as one of their own. They wandered from pasture to pasture drifting further and further from civilization. Every evening the friendly Mongol travelers treated Choey to a traditional nomadic meal. Choey was in culinary heaven.

"That all changed when Choey awoke one morning with a terrible toothache. Choey knew exactly what it was. One of his wisdom teeth had given him some trouble a few months before. The head tribesman peered into his mouth and declared the tooth needed to be removed. Now I don't know what you guys know about extracting wisdom teeth, but it's a pretty big deal. That's why it's called oral *surgery*. Anyway, what's my creator to do? He's out in the middle of nowhere and the head honcho has just issued an opinion that the tooth was coming out.

"Head dude immediately begins prepping for the opera-tion. First things first—anesthetics were necessary for the painful extraction. He hands my creator an enormous jug filled with fermented mare's milk. It's called 'arkhi,' a form of vodka. Now Choey's a wine guy, but once again, what's he going to do? He hesitates to drink it until he sees head dude approaching with a bayonet and a pair of pliers. At that point he turned the jug up and began gulping away.

"'Open wide,' the leader told him. Choey took one last big swig and did as he was told. Head dude wasted no time with petty surgical formalities as he began digging into my creator's gums. Choey tried not to scream but the pain was unbearable. His squelching was so loud it woke up a couple of napping camels nearby. Undeterred, head dude worked his bayonet deep into the back of his mouth. After carving out a suitable work area around the targeted tooth he reached for the pliers.

"'This might hurt a little,' he said to Choey, as if the previous flesh tearing episode had been only a painless warmup. That turned out to be quite the understatement. My creator felt an explosion of raw unadulterated pain like he'd never felt before as head dude tightened his grip and simultaneously twisted and pulled on the pliers. The burly cowpuncher slash dentist let it rip with his ample strength gained from years of hard labor. He violently tore the tooth out of my creator's mouth, along with a considerable amount of excess mouth.

"'Yeahoo,' shouted the victorious nomad. Head dude waved the blood-stained pliers holding the extracted tooth over his head for all to see. 'This little devil won't be a hurt 'n anybody anymore,' he said, oblivious to my creator rolling around on the ground in agony. He then poured himself a big cup of celebratory arkhi and walked away.

"Now to the point of the story. It took several weeks for my creator's mouth to heal. During this period his primary source of nourishment was soup. There was no way he could chew on anything solid after head dude had jerked out half of his gums. The nomads had an amazing variety of liquid foods including several of the international standards.

"Choey also grew to appreciate some of the more traditional nomadic soups including camel noodle julienne, horse consomme, vegetables in lizard stock, just to name a few. My creator also became quite fond of arkhi while recuperating out in the Mongolian prairie. He said the potent milky vodka was a wonderful painkiller. So my creator got more than he bargained for on his visit to Mongolia. In the end he considered it a pretty good trade, a wisdom tooth for a whole chapter of soup recipes and some lifelong friends. What do you think?"

"These stories are fantastic!" said *Spy*. "I have to agree with you, the little tales accompanying the recipes separates you from other cookbooks. Your creator's not only an accomplished chef, he's also a storyteller."

Soy Cowboy looked at *Spy* and grinned. "Now that you've mentioned it, I'll let you in on a little secret. You're not the only one who thinks my creator has talent. Gai has persuaded him to try his hand at fiction. As we speak he's at his country home in Thailand working on *Soy Cowboy: The Novel*. Gai even went so far as to build him a special writing room in the top of a tree. Once he gets up there she removes the ladder and won't return it until he's written at least three pages. That ensures his daily quota."

"Oh my, she's ruthless," joked *River*.

Soy Cowboy shrugged. "Nah, she just knows my creator very well. Sometimes he needs a kick in the rear to get going."

Soy Cowboy was quiet for a moment as he peered into the distance. "Hey guys, I see Joann. She's headed this way to pick us up. Just when I was getting warmed up, but that's the way it goes sometimes. I guess I'll have to share Choey's unusual dining experience on the Great Wall of China another day. It's been great and thanks for allowing me the opportunity to blab away."

"That goes for me too," said *Gimme*. "I really enjoyed it."

"And me as well," chimed in *Place*. "You're a delightful group, and *River* and *Spy*, congratulations on your upcoming wedding. I know it's only two weeks away. I'm sure you'll have a wonderful life together. Joann's here now! Goodbye!"

Joann moved swiftly. She didn't want any of the other employees to witness her removing three books from the back of the rack. The last thing she wanted was someone asking questions. Joann wasn't a good liar and she didn't want to accidently blurt out the truth—she had brought the books over so they could talk to each other!

Joann came and left in less than five seconds. Just like that their engaging conversation came to quick halt. Nobody ever liked it, but it was the nature of life in a bookstore. Books came and went like dust in the wind. One moment you're basking in a pleasant conversation, and the next moment your newfound friends are whisked away without warning.

Suddenly *River* spotted trouble. Harry Homewrecker was in the store and coming their way. Once again he had a book in his hand. It was *Growing Up Proud & Strong*, a well liked longtime resident of the children's section. She had a horrified expression on her cover. Who wouldn't when they're in the grasp of this disgusting human being?

Harry's cold dark eyes revealed his evil intentions, de-stroying another happy home. The despised madman rounded the corner, and without looking, flipped his wrist and lobbed the hapless book on top of the rack. He heard it plop on the roof of the bookshelf. Harry flashed his devilish smirk when he realized he had hit his target. No one would ever find the little book up there no matter how loud she screamed. His sickening brand of evil had no limits.

River felt an intense hatred like she had never experienced before. She wanted to jump off the shelf and gouge out

Harry's eyes. That could easily have been her, or *Spy*, or *Destiny*, sentenced to a lonely agonizing death on top of the bookshelf. Didn't this sorry excuse for a human being have any compassion at all? *River* was boiling with anger.

Harry's lust for destruction continued. Now empty-handed he searched for more literary prey to satisfy his perverse appetite. He methodically ran his eyes up and down and across each shelf as he came closer and closer. Who would be his next victim? Suddenly he stopped directly in front of shelf C22. He directed his attention towards *Spy*. As his hand lunged forward *River* began to scream.

Spy braced for impact. At the last moment Harry's hand changed course slightly and chose another victim. It was *Destiny*! The most evil person on the face of the planet had *Destiny* in his grasp! Harry pulled *Destiny* from his resting place as *Spy* fought with all his might to reel his best friend back in. It was futile. Harry looked back at *Spy* with his black soulless eyes and marched away with *Destiny* tucked under his arm.

River was hysterical. All of the books watched in horror as Harry carried *Destiny* away to what would certainly be some awful destination. *Spy* realized the importance of being calm. They had to watch Harry's every move. Knowing where this power-mad tyrant would dispose of *Destiny* was crucial. A future rescue attempt would be a lot easier if they were aware of his location.

Tears came to *Spy's* eyes as he watched what came next. Harry appeared to head for the toilet. Just before he entered the facility he dumped *Destiny* into a basket containing cleaning supplies and oily rags. Not only that, but this heartless piece of human garbage actually took the time to *cover* his best friend with several of the toxic rags.

Now *Destiny* was completely hidden from view, minimizing the chances of discovery by a staffer. For the first time in his life *Spy* felt nauseated. He had a sickening feeling in his guts that tore at his emotions. *Destiny* was no longer by his side. Finally he broke down and released a flood of tears. This was the worst moment of his life—for now.

Chapter 13

C ontact had been made with *Destiny*. The basket where he now resided was within shouting distance of shelf G28. From G28 information could be relayed back to his concerned friends. It was a relatively long walktalk, but the books were capable of it. Everyone was willing to help in any way they could. It was in times like these that the book community came together as one.

Immediately following his displacement, *Destiny* let it be known that he was okay. He didn't want his friends to worry about him. Within seconds of being thrown into the basket, *Destiny* was already communicating with the residents of G28. They were all business and investing books. His main contact was a corner book named *Invest in Yourself: You're Worth It!* The two books were maintaining steady contact throughout this crisis.

Word trickled back to *Spy* and *River* that their friend was not injured. The fumes from the dirty rags were annoying to say the least, but bearable. *Destiny* was in no immediate danger. The news was a huge relief to the couple, but they wouldn't relax until their friend was back home where he belonged. How were they going to get him back?

Spy and *River* held an emergency brainstorming session. Joining them were *Stone Dance*, who was now *Spy's* new front covermate, and *Loved Twice*. They had to come up with a plan to get *Destiny* back. This couldn't be one of those projects that took weeks or months of planning. No, something had to done immediately. Every day that *Destiny* sat in that filthy basket was a risk. Who knows how long he could remain there before someone discovered him? Rarely did any of the employees ever look inside it. Why would they? It wasn't anything but a collection of cleaning solutions, spray cans and those dirty rags that now concealed their friend from view. Heck, the cleaning crew never even used the stuff. They brought in their own cleaning supplies.

Spy caught himself cursing to himself, something he rarely did. Why did this have to happen! Why was that worthless basket placed there in the first place? Look at the trouble it had caused. The ugly eyesore should have been in the storage room, or better than that, the garbage!

The team began bouncing around different ideas for a rescue attempt. Every suggestion was taken seriously, no matter how farfetched it may seem. Nothing was considered too crazy. After all this was *Destiny's* life they were discussing. Most of the ideas were shot down immediately for one reason or another. The process went on for hours.

Finally *Stone Dance* nailed a keeper. He suggested they utilize Sherry's communication skills. All they had to do was inform her of the crisis before them and she could go retrieve Destiny. It was as simple as that. Rarely did a day go by that Sherry didn't pass by C22 to check on her favorite literary friends. The next time she came by they would all convey their collective anxiety towards her. Surely she pick up on the signals, especially coming from several books simultaneously.

That was it! Everyone jumped for joy at *Stone Dance's* suggestion. That was the obvious choice. Why didn't someone think of that sooner? *Stone Dance* was congratulated and the rescue team enjoyed a five minute celebration. Then it was back to business to iron out the details.

The first order of business was to inform *Destiny* of *Stone Dance's* excellent suggestion. This would most certainly put him in good spirits. Although he was claiming through the walktalks that he was in an excellent emotional state, his friends feared he was depressed. Word came from *Invest* that *Destiny's* color didn't look so good.

Invest was the only book in the entire bookstore that had an unobstructed view of the basket. From his top corner G28 location he could actually see a bit of *Destiny's* spine protruding from underneath the rags. It didn't have the normal sheen of a healthy book. It was nothing to get alarmed about, just a typical symptom of book depression. Who wouldn't feel a little gloomy being stuck under a bunch of smelly scraps of cloth?

Regardless, news of a viable rescue operation in the works would certainly cheer him up. *River* promptly got a message streaming down the walktalk telegraph. The statement she forwarded was clear and simple: Sherry will rescue you!

The crew was anxious to get *Destiny* back as soon as possible. Unfortunately they would have to wait at least forty-eight hours. It was Friday. Sherry always had Fridays and Saturdays off. It would be Sunday morning at the earliest before they could direct her to their endangered friend. The realization that *Destiny* had at least two more days of imprisonment temporarily knocked the air out of the excited group.

Their enthusiasm wasn't dampened for long before they bounced back. They decided not to just set by and wait for

Sherry. They would occupy their time encouraging *Destiny*. There was no way they would let him slide into a state of despair. Their sole purpose was to keep his spirits up with a constant flow of heartening words. They would keep their friend so busy walktalking that he wouldn't have time to dwell on his precarious situation. Moping around waiting on Sherry wouldn't accomplish a thing. A couple of days of bantering back and forth should ease the tension for everyone involved.

While all of this was occurring some very good news came in. *Growing Up Proud & Strong* had been discovered! Some of the books were calling it a miracle. It was if the hand of God had intervened. The little children's book had been stranded on the top of the dusty bookshelf for several hours. Her constant sobbing and pleas for help were getting her nowhere. The only ones who could hear her were the residents of the shelf below her, mostly biographies. The frustrated books were powerless to do anything except attempt to calm her. The mood was sad and somber as they listened to the little girl's cries for help.

It was late afternoon when the florescent light above the main aisle burned out. These type of things happened once or twice a year and nobody really thought much of it. Everyone knew the procedure. A staffer would eventually notice the problem and alert Ronnie. He would then retrieve a ladder and a new bulb from the storage room and remedy the situation. Seconds after it occurred most of the books had already forgotten about it. It simply wasn't a big deal.

It became a huge deal after *Jesus: True to Life* spoke out. He lived on the bottom shelf of the same rack that held *Growing Up Proud & Strong* captive. Moments after the light blew out the hardback called out to his upper level neighbors. "Tell the little children's book to remain calm because she'll be rescued soon," he stated calmly.

The books became silent. They knew *Jesus* was a book of few words. When he said something he meant it. What did he mean when he said she would be rescued? What did he know that everyone else didn't?

Finally *Linwood Emmons: One Good Man* asked the question that was on everyone's mind. "*Jesus*, why do you say *Growing Up Proud & Strong* will be rescued? What makes you so certain of this? You know that getting her hopes up just to be dashed would be horrible."

"I'm well aware of that fact," answered *Jesus*. "Here's what's going to happen. Look at the position of the burned out light. Ronnie's going to climb his ladder and replace the bulb. While he's up there he'll have an excellent view of the top of our shelf. Ronnie will spot the troubled book and bring her down. I'm certain of it."

"That's all I need to hear," said *Linwood*. He then looked up and relayed *Jesus's* message to the young book. Immediately she stopped crying. Sure enough, after that everything began falling into place, just as *Jesus* had predicted. Within the hour, Jeri, who didn't miss much, noticed an overhead light had burned out. She told Thomas who told Charles who told Ronnie. Ten minutes later Ronnie arrived and set up his ladder.

The job took him approximately three minutes. Before descending Ronnie took a moment and surveyed the entire bookstore. The books were watching his every move. When Ronnie did a double take and focused on shelf E16 the biography section erupted in applause. At that point they knew *Growing Up Proud & Strong* was going home. Ronnie climbed down the ladder, moved it over by E16, and snatched up the ecstatic children's book. One of Harry Homewrecker's victims was now safe.

The news of *Growing Up Proud & Strong's* rescue was immediately relayed to *Destiny*. *Spy* and *River* knew this would undoubtedly cheer him up. *Destiny* had previously asked about the condition of the young book. He seemed more worried about her than his own well being. When *Invest* finally shouted the information over to *Destiny* his spine lit up ever so briefly in a bright display of euphoria.

Now it was just a matter of waiting—and making sure that *Destiny* remained in good spirits. Hopefully in a couple of days he too would be back at home. *Loved Twice* suggested they keep *Destiny* occupied with some good ole Sanders and Bowman gossip. Everyone agreed it was an excellent idea. *Destiny* always enjoyed listening to the latest going-ons involving books and humans alike.

River instructed *Libby's Paradise*, her first contact in *Destiny's* long walktalk, to repeat everything word for word. That way *Destiny* wouldn't miss any intended humor they may send his way. This would be especially important if *Spy* got sidetracked with an improvised story of his own.

The first bit of gossip they sent flowing towards *Destiny* involved Sandra. He was always amused by her carefree antics. She had recently added some bright red streaks to her blonde hair. One of them was made to resemble a big S. Now you could spot her from a mile away. Sandra claimed she needed the big red S on her head to remind new acquaintances of her name.

Apparently Sandra was a trendsetter. Several days later a group of her friends visited her at the bookstore. All of them were sporting newly initialed heads. There was Bianca with a big blue B in the middle of her bangs. Standing alongside her was a beaming Courtney, obviously pleased with her rainbow colored C. Then you had Patti Pearson adding a twist proudly parading her matching purple P's. Patti was accompanied by her boyfriend. Ziggy decided to go a different route and had shaved all of his hair except for a prominent Z he left on the top of his head. He had splashed it green for effect. When *Destiny* received this bit of humorous information he replied with a hearty laugh.

The group had unanimously agreed to keep the information flow positive in an effort to boost *Destiny's* spirits. *River* next relayed the latest on Charles. He was getting married! He was giving all the credit for his newfound happiness to *Divorce: Coping & Caring*. The book had steered him away from his destructive ways. He now channeled his emotions towards acceptance, healing, and getting on with his life. Charles and his girlfriend had set the wedding date for January. Afterwards they planned on taking a full month for a tropical island honeymoon. Charles was truly a happy soul.

The love bug was having a field day at Sanders and Bowman. The next bit of information pipelined down to *Destiny* involved Jeri. She too was tying the knot. Her relationship with Brian had blossomed into a committed love affair. The two of them had taken a weekend and driven up to Brian's family's dairy farm. In the months that they had been dating, Jeri had never met his parents.

Apparently they took a liking to her and her to them. Jeri spent all day Saturday with Brian's mother baking pies for a church cookout. On Sunday she *volunteered* to help Brian's father shovel cow manure from the stables. If her coworkers had seen it with their own eyes they still would not believe it. Jeri was *not* a cow dung type of girl!

Later that afternoon as she and Brian were bottle feeding a newborn calf she saw him pull something from his pocket. It was a diamond ring! Brian got down on his knees and proposed. Of course Jeri enthusiastically accepted. City girl Jeri removed the bottle from the calf's mouth and wrapped her arms around her country boy fiance. Their wedding was planned for April. This was one all the employees were looking forward too. They knew Jeri would go all out to make her big day truly special.

The next bit of uplifting news concerned Donna. Yet another ten pounds had fallen victim to her diet and exercise program—and her constant companion *Forties Fitness*. Many of Donna's friends were amazed at her success and were inquiring as to how she did it. Donna decided to give each of them a copy of *Forties Fitness* for some early Christmas presents. She had just placed an order for ten more copies of her fitness bible. That way her friends would have the handy book in time to battle the upcoming holidays that always carried with them the temptation to overeat. Donna was looking great, feeling great, and wearing a smile that warmed everyone around her.

River kept the good news rolling with an update on Jim. Ninety-nine days without a drink! Tomorrow he would be going out to dinner with his son to celebrate one hundred days of sobriety—and their newly mended relationship. Jim was happier than ever.

Not only was he enjoying time with his formerly es-tranged son, but Jim and Thomas had become closer. Jim's wife had sent Thomas a beautiful card thanking him for everything he had done for her husband. She didn't directly mention the bookstore incident involving the exposed bottle of liquor, but Thomas knew that was what it was all about. It had been a crucial moment in Jim's life that could have resulted in the loss of his job, and more importantly, his self esteem. As it turned out, Thomas's calm reaction and his genuine concern for Jim's well being proved to be the inspiration that motivated him to stop drinking. The two families were now seeing each other socially.

Jim had recently attended a meeting of a local informal society that provided support for problem drinkers. There he met others who were also struggling to stay sober. Jim's primary purpose for attending the meeting was to distribute twenty copies of *Alcohol: Beat it Forever*. Jim credited the book as playing a huge part in his so-far successful battle against alcoholism. If only one person benefitted from the twenty copies he gave away it would be worthwhile. *Destiny* had always had a soft spot in his heart for Jim. Learning of Jim's continuing sobriety and his happy personal life thrilled him. He walktalked back an enthusiastic "Hurray for Jim!" when he heard the good news.

River had just obtained the very latest information on Joann and *Mercury Girl*. It was a done deal! *Garden of Fools* had heard it straight from Joann's mouth. Only minutes before Joann had received a call from her agent. He informed her that Hagar House had agreed to all of her suggestions. They would discard the "hot trotter" idea and retain the original title of *Mercury Girl*. They had also designed a new cover which presented a more wholesome image of the book's main character.

On top of all that they mentioned they were going to move up the publication date in order to appease Joann. The book should be on bookshelves in a matter of *days*! That was absolutely incredible. The agent remarked to Joann that he had never dealt with a more agreeable bunch in all his years in the publishing industry. Apparently Joann could be a very persuasive lady!

The hottest Sanders and Bowman hearsay was all about Conner. *Destiny* would surely get a kick out of this one. A month long rumor had just been confirmed. The Sanders and Bowman chain was finally going to experiment with adding coffee shops inside the bookstores. Other top chains had already done this with varying degrees of success. Sanders and Bowman would be taking it a step further by using only gourmet coffee—the best of the best. They would be working with coffee growers from sixteen different countries. By grinding and roasting their own coffee beans on site they hoped to build a customer base that would come in for coffee—and leave with books.

The varied selection of drinks would include espressos, cappuccinos, lattes and mochas. They would also be the only bookstore chain to offer café cubano, the strong beverage that originated from Cuba. What set this potent beverage apart was the fact that it was sweetened during the brewing process instead of adding the sugar afterwards.

The café cubano idea was all Mel Redding's. The regional manager had read in a publishing periodical that Cuban-born Luis Concepcion, the author of the mega-selling *Didi's Adventures*, was a connoisseur of café cubano. In his native Cuba drinking café cubano was a prominent social and cultural activity.

Luis liked his café brewed the old-fashioned way, with a stove top espresso maker. That's the way he had it growing up as a kid in Havana and that's how Sanders and Bowman would make it. The whole café cubano idea was an attempt to entice Mr. Concepcion. They were trying to seal a deal with his agent to have Luis appear at every Sanders and Bowman for a book signing. If successful, it would be a public relations bonanza. The latest reports were that the café cubano brainstorm had pushed Luis over the edge. He had orally committed to appearing at every store in the chain that served his favorite beverage.

Space was already being cleared for the coffee bar. Mario's tiny office was the first to go, but he was happily relocating to a bigger room in the back of the bookstore.

Greenie the fat lizard would be accompanying him. Yes, Greenie had put on a considerable amount of weight. He had been gorging himself on insects that Ronnie delivered to him on an hourly basis—payback for saving his life. Thomas had also instructed Ronnie to clear an area adjacent to Mario's office that was currently being used for storage. This would provide enough space for the coffee bar.

The biggest news wasn't the coffee bar itself. It was who would be managing it—Conner! Upon receiving the news from Thomas that he would be managing the coffee bar Conner let out an ear-splitting holler that was heard throughout the store. From that point on he transformed into a different person. Conner unleashed energy that no one thought possible. Finally he would be doing something he enjoyed. Coffee was his true love.

Uncle Mel had arranged his employment with Sanders and Bowman, but in reality Conner didn't give a hoot about any books. He hated working there. He hated to read. He hated everything about the lousy bookstore—until now! A coffee bar! And he would be managing it! Conner was on top of the world. He was already taking measurements to determine where the equipment would be placed. Conner had finally found his place in the world. He was the Sanders and Bowman coffee man! He was roaring to get started. Taped on the wall over the construction area was a piece of notebook paper. It was Conner's personal handwritten greeting.

Come on in, take a look
Have some coffee, read a book
Conner Redding—Head Barista

Destiny was pleased to hear of Conner's good fortune. He had always thought the boy had potential. It was just a matter of him finding himself. *Destiny* replied back with a bold prediction. Within five years Conner would be in charge of all the coffee bars in the Sanders and Bowman chain—and they would all be extremely successful. That's how much faith *Destiny* had in the young man.

Destiny also replied back with a request. If *Spy* was up to it, and everyone else involved in the laborious walktalk, he would like to hear one of *Spy's* amusing tales. A good laugh was just what he needed. It would help take his mind away from the fact that he was locked down under a bunch of filthy rags. If there was any one book that could guarantee a dose of humor, it would be his friend *Spy*.

After hearing of *Destiny's* request *Spy* was momentarily silent. He was digging into his memory bank. If there ever was a time for a classic Sonny Needle adventure, this was it. His best friend wanted to be entertained. Now was the moment to deliver a whopper of a tale—one that will make *Destiny* forget all about his uncomfortable situation.

Suddenly *Spy's* cover became flushed with energy. He had it! This was Sonny Needle's greatest adventure ever. Actually it was two adventures that tied together, a dual treat for his friend. Luckily he had never shared it with *Destiny*. Maybe a higher power had influenced him to save it for a special occasion. If so, it was now time to pull it out and serve it up. *Spy* looked at *River* and told her he was ready to go. She sent word to *Libby's Paradise* that a *Spy* classic would be coming soon. Get ready!

"Make it good baby." *River* winked at her fiancé.

Spy began. "My friend *Destiny*, Sonny's got himself into a dire situation in Guatemala."

"Here we go *Libby*," *River* called across the aisle. "My friend *Destiny*, Sonny's got himself into a dire situation in Guatemala."

River turned back to *Spy* and nodded. *Spy* continued, stopping after every sentence allowing *River* to relay it down the line.

"Sonny Needle had gone to Guatemala to broker an agreement before a regional squabble turned ugly. It was the usual bickering over who controlled a disputed area and its natural resources. Sonny had seen it all before. Both participants laid claim to a small piece of property. On this tiny parcel of land was a lake, the sole source of water for both sides. Sonny flew in posing as a doctor working for an international organization.

"Wearing his white doctor's uniform and toting around a stethoscope Sonny had everyone fooled. He examined a number of residents from both regions. A crowd always gathered around as he played doctor. Sonny would place his stethoscope over a subject's heart and pretend to listen intently. He would grunt 'ooohs' and 'aaahs' and just shake his head. Apparently something was very wrong.

"Sonny called an emergency meeting and urged representatives from both regions to attend. Taking a page out of the ole 'crocodile infested island' playbook, Sonny explained to them that the water from the lake was intrepiculpoilamdated, and was weakening everyone's hearts throughout both regions. Intrepiculpoilamdation was a rare occurrence. It was essentially a genetic drifting of hydrogen and oxygen isotopes resulting in molecularly imbalanced water.

"However, Sonny went on to explain, there was hope for the situation. The only known way to purify intrepiculpoilamdated water was to place the isotopes back into balance. This could be done by digging two equally sized canals to let the water flow. It was absolutely crucial to the balancing process that equal amounts of water flowed from both canals. If the two flows differed by even one gallon per day the balancing effect would not occur. It had to be exactly the same!

"Sonny then brought out a vial from his pocket containing a sample of the water. He reached into his other pocket and pulled out some sort of blue powder. He sprinkled a bit of it into the water. As he watched the water turn blue he began crunching numbers on his calculator. For over three minutes he furiously clicked away at what seemed an extremely complex mathematical computation.

"'Got it!' Sonny finally declared. Everyone gathered around the doctor who would save them all from an early death. 'Here's the situation,' he said. 'I've calculated the molecular balancing quotient and it appears you need to build the canals of specific lengths to achieve optimum balance. One canal needs to be exactly three hundred meters in length. The other canal needs to be exactly four hundred meters in length. If you do this the isotopes will synthesize and the water will be purified.'

"The two regional leaders looked at each other. It was unbelievable! The doctor's calculations matched the two regional borders exactly. One was three hundred meters from the lake and the other was four hundred meters away. The solution would be simple. In order for the populace from both regions to maintain strong and healthy hearts they would build two canals. One would lead directly to region one and the other would flow into region two. Not only would everyone maintain healthy tickers, but the water issue would also be resolved. Everyone jumped for joy. The residents mobbed the good doctor who had saved their lives. Sonny had saved the day!

"The story doesn't end here. As a matter of fact it gets much better. Everyone got together and threw a massive party. The celebration went on late into the night. Sonny left the following morning to go visit nearby El Mirador. It was a Mayan civilization site that contained several gigantic pyramids. Sonny had always had in interest in pyramids dating back to his childhood. This was the perfect opportunity to explore some of these fascinating architectural creations.

"There were three structures that especially interested Sonny. The one nicknamed '*La Danta*' was a triple decker monstrosity that some said was the largest pyramid in the world. Sonny couldn't wait to feast his eyes on …"

"Stop!" interrupted *River*. "Please stop baby! Something's wrong!"

"Fire!" someone shouted. *Spy* smelled smoke.

Spy looked up to see Mario race by. Then Ronnie shot past them. A few seconds later Jim passed by carrying a fire extinguisher.

All the books strained to see what was happening. Obviously there was a fire. Where was it? How big was it? Was the whole bookstore in danger?

Information trickled in piece by piece. Sammy Smoker had finally gone too far. Once again his urge to smoke was so strong that he had to light up before entering the toilet. Apparently after lighting his cigarette he had thrown down a *lit* match. He then disappeared into the men's room probably unaware he had started a small fire. The latest report was that the fire had already been doused and everything was now under control.

Seconds later *Libby's Paradise* shouted over some alarming news. The fire had been located in the basket where *Destiny* was stranded. She quickly added that she had heard someone had rescued *Destiny* before the blaze erupted. Information was sketchy at this point, but they were awaiting a full report from *Invest*. He was an eyewitness to the whole thing.

River began crying. *Spy* tried to calm her, but he was just as upset. *Stone Dance* was in a state of shock. All they could do was wait until they found out what had just occurred. Hopefully the rumor of *Destiny's* escape was true. If so, they prayed he wasn't injured, at least not seriously. There was no way they could comprehend the alternative.

All eye's were on *Libby*. She turned the opposite direction. The news was coming through. Suddenly her brightly colored cover lost all of its luster. She actually turned brown for a split second. *Libby* turned back towards *River*. Tears were streaming from her cover.

"No!" screamed *River*. "No! Don't tell me! Oh God, please don't let it be!"

Libby couldn't bring herself to say it. She crumpled in despair. *Pace of Love* began comforting her. Finally *Brothers Two* called over to *River* and *Spy*. They peered up at him as they prayed for a miracle. His look told it all. He didn't have to say it. Finally the words slowly slipped out. "*Destiny* is gone."

"No, it can't be!" screamed *Spy*. "There's gotta be a mistake!"

"*Invest* saw it all," said a solemn *Brothers*. "I'm so sorry. Words can't describe how much I hate telling you this." He seemed to choke on his words.

"Your friend is gone. *Destiny* is dead." *Brothers* turned away and began sobbing.

Chapter 14

*S*py and *River* were devastated. It was two days before they could bear to hear the details of what happened. *Invest* did indeed see the entire horrible scene. Sammy Smoker lit his cigarette just before entering the toilet and flipped his match off to the side. It landed directly on the basket that contained *Destiny*. One of the oily rags immediately burst into flames.

Within a matter of seconds the entire basket was ablaze. *Destiny* screamed for help but it was futile. The books could do nothing to help and there wasn't a human in sight. Normally that particular area was buzzing with activity, but as fate would have it, there wasn't a soul around.

A full minute passed before a customer noticed the fire. He quickly notified the first staffer he saw. It was Mario. Mario yelled for Jim to get the fire extinguisher. Meanwhile Ronnie had heard the commotion and raced over. He and Mario began dousing the fire with water and smothering it with someone's jacket. They quickly had the fire under control. Jim soon arrived and sprayed the basket with the fire extinguisher. Just like that it was over.

All in all it shouldn't have been a big deal. It was a tiny fire. As a matter of fact most of the customers were completely unaware of it. Jeri and Sandra didn't even know about it until an hour later. But of course it *was* a big deal. *Destiny* had been trapped in that basket.

Invest sent a message to *Spy* and *River*. When the fire broke out *Destiny* had naturally called for help. At that point he thought he might be rescued. When his cover began to melt he must have sensed he was doomed. When others would have been screaming in agony *Destiny* showed incredible fortitude.

Moments before his text completely burst into flames he looked up at *Invest*. He showed no fear. It was as if death didn't scare him. In a calm voice he stated, "tell *Spy* and *River* to go on with their wedding without me." Then he grimaced as the fire completely consumed him. Thirty seconds later he was ashes.

That was *Destiny*, always thinking of others. There were a lot of good books in Sanders and Bowman, but *Destiny* had been special. He was one of a kind. *Destiny's Fortune* would live forever in his friends' memories. For now it was just pure sadness. Everyone was sick with sadness, especially his two best friends.

Spy and *River*, along with *Stone Dance* and everyone one else who called *Destiny* their friend, just wanted to know one thing—why? Why did Harry Homewrecker choose *Destiny*? One hundred thousand books and he had to randomly pick up this one. Another thing—of all the places he could have disposed of *Destiny*, why did it have to be in that basket by the men's room? And why did the basket have to contain flammable rags? Sammy Smoker frequents the bookstore no more than two or three times a month—why does he have to make an appearance at this particular time? And why didn't his lit match land anywhere but on top of *Destiny*? And why wasn't someone in that area at that time? Normally it's teeming with customers and staff alike. Lastly and most importantly—why did God allow this to happen?

United in Love and Duty was quick to send his condolences and words of comfort. He had been in contact with *Destiny* as recently as the day before the tragedy. They had discussed details regarding *Spy* and *River's* upcoming wedding. They had also had a brief exchange on the afterlife. *Destiny*, while in the midst of their conversation about the commitments involved in a marriage, suddenly asked the respected book about the subject. *United* answered the question as best he could.

Looking back in hindsight, *United* now wondered if *Destiny* might have had a premonition of his death. *Destiny* was by no means an old book, and he had no health problems that anyone was aware of. Then what was it that inspired him to ask *United's* opinion of the afterlife? *United* thought it slightly unusual that *Destiny* would be thinking about death, especially in the middle of their discussion about marriage. He had just brushed it off at the time. Now *United* wished he had delved into the subject a little deeper.

United shared something else with *Spy* and *River*. *Destiny* had let it be known that he had no fear of death. He had remarked that whenever it was his time to go, be it tomorrow or one hundred years from now, he was already prepared spiritually. He was at peace with himself and the world that he lived in. The fact that *Destiny* revealed this the day before he died was eerie, but also provided comfort to his grieving friends. Somehow they knew their friend was at peace. He was in a better place, and one day they would all see him again.

United offered his valued opinion on one more subject. *Spy* and *River* should not have any doubts about proceeding with their wedding. *United* was convinced that *Destiny* would have wanted them to go forth with the ceremony. *United's* statement, and the fact that *Destiny's* last dying request was still ringing in their ears, convinced the couple to go through with their planned ceremony no matter how painful. There was no doubt that is what *Destiny* desired.

Spy and *River* consented to follow through with their wedding on one condition—that it also served as a celebration-of-life memorial service for their beloved friend. *United* agreed and volunteered to preside over the event. He promised it would demonstrate both the exuberance of life and the value of faith in an unforgiving world. It would show how they must carry on in the midst of despair, for there really is no other choice. That was the reality of life. They would indeed come together to celebrate a couple leaping into the future with their hopes and dreams, for that is what *Destiny* would have wanted.

This would also be an opportunity to share remembrances of their special friend, his inescapable charm, his unique brand of humor, and most of all his kindness. There was never a more caring and giving soul. The whole affair would reflect joy and sadness, the immutable past and the promising future, and serve as a reminder to live each and every day to the fullest. October 11 would be a day to remember. *Destiny's* spirit would surely be present at this joyous celebration of love and friendship.

United revealed one last bit of information *Destiny* had shared with him. Their friend had been waiting for the opportune time to surprise *Spy* and *River* with some exciting news. It concerned Kris Richards's book signing. Incredibly, the event was going to be held directly in front of C22.

It was all *Destiny's* idea. Normally all the bookstore events were held near the back of the bookstore. This location had been chosen in large part to minimize any inconveniences for other shoppers. Over one hundred book signings had been staged there over the years with no major problems. Kris

Richards's appearance, however, would not be a typical event. He was the world's most famous actor—the biggest name in show business. The bookstore would undoubtedly be mobbed with fans.

Destiny knew that the staff would better accommodate the crowds if the event were held in a different area. Why try to squeeze a thousand people into a tiny corner? With a little preparation a larger section of the bookstore could be utilized for the biggest happening in the store's history. There was no use in trying to separate those attending the Kris Richards event from other customers. Number one, there wasn't going to be patrons who *weren't* interested in this celebrity. Secondly, even if there were, they would have nowhere to hide. It would be impossible to escape the commotion and hype surrounding one of the world's most famous people. So why bother? This was Kris Richards! For two hours Sanders and Bowman Bookstore might as well be renamed Kris Richards's Bookstore.

Destiny had been studying the different options for weeks. There was no better location in which to host the event then right in front of C22. A tremendous amount of floor space could be opened up with minimal effort. All they had to do was simply remove two huge tables that held the bargain priced books. By doing that, and rearranging some chairs in the area, a massive amount of space would become available. Ronnie could do it all by himself in less than an hour.

Destiny had successfully communicated his thoughts to Sherry, hoping that she could pass the idea on to management. Of course, she would have to package the idea as her own, but she could take the credit. At first he wasn't sure if Sherry had understood his difficult transmission. He was relieved when he saw her approach Thomas and begin a discussion. *Destiny* watched as Sherry pointed towards the back of the store, then to the area in front of C22. Thomas then nodded his head in agreement.

At this point *Destiny* knew his idea had been approved. October 11 had just become even more special. *Spy* and *River* now had front row seats for the biggest event in Sanders and Bowman history. This would be followed by their exchange of vows. Their big day had become even bigger. *Destiny* could hardly contain himself. Little did he know he would not be around to witness it.

Sherry was the last employee to learn of the fire. It was old news by the time she returned to work. Heather mentioned that there had been a small fire by the restrooms, but it wasn't really a big deal. She then mentioned that one book had burned in the blaze. Sherry asked her which book had burned. Heather replied that she didn't know.

Knowing that a book had perished in the fire nagged at Sherry all morning. She knew so many of the books personally and she hoped it wasn't one of her friends. She assumed it was probably a business book since the fire started in their area. The thought that it could have been a novel never crossed her mind. As she passed by C22 later that afternoon she delivered her customary glance towards her friends. Immediately she knew something was wrong. The happy vibes she always felt from them were not present. *Spy* and *River* were not their usual selves. Then she noticed—*Destiny* was gone! Where was *Destiny*?

Sherry reached towards the two books. Her hand picked up *River*, but it could just as easily had been *Spy*. *River* had been randomly chosen to be the bearer of the horrible news. Sherry clutched *River* tight with both hands and stared into her cover. The information slowly trickled from the grieving novel. Tears began to stream from the both of them. The four friends, three novels and a human, had grown close over the past few months. Now one of them was gone. Sherry held *River* close to her chest as they each tried to comfort the other. Sherry then reached down and picked up *Spy*. She placed him behind *River* and hugged them tight.

For over a minute no one spoke. No one had to. Each of them at that moment felt the presence of their departed friend. For that brief period *Destiny* was back with them. He was there and was communicating with his three friends. They could see his cover and his mischievous grin. He was at peace. He told them he was in a good place and they should not worry. They would all see each other again. He told them to go through with the wedding. It might not go exactly as planned, but it would happen. The union of *Spy Needle* and *River Run True* would not be stopped. *Destiny* assured the couple he would be there in spirit.

Just as suddenly as their dear friend had appeared, he left. His image faded away, his communication ceased, and *Destiny* once again drifted back behind death's door. His mission had been successful. He had helped his mourning friends understand that death was not the end, that the only pain was that felt by the grieving, and that they should relish each and every moment of life for it was a fragile thing.

Sherry gently placed *River* and *Spy* back into place. Each of the three knew that *Destiny* had visited the others. They didn't need to speak about it. *Destiny's* message had been clear—he wanted his friends not to be overwhelmed with grief and to continue with their lives. Many more tears would be shed for their beloved friend, but from that moment on, as much as it hurt, *Destiny's* death became more acceptable.

Destiny's tragic death brought *Spy* and *River* even closer together. Their love transcended well beyond romantic and physical desires. There seemed to be a flow of mystical energy between them, a feeling of peace and contentment and trust and happiness. Neither had ever experienced anything like it. The fact that *River* possessed outward beauty became inconsequential to *Spy*. Their inner souls were now locked for eternity. It was if *Destiny's* death had opened them up. Maybe it was his final gift, his way of saying goodbye. Whatever it might be, it was certainly a powerful force. The two of them still lived in their day-to-day world of survival, but they also shared a dimension all their own, one that no one else would ever penetrate. It was love.

Several days passed. Suddenly the wedding was only three days away. *Loved Twice* had been working hard ironing out the last minute details of the ceremony. *Stone Dance* had taken over *Destiny's* role and was now working hand-in-hand with *Loved Twice* to finalize the wedding arrangements. The two were getting along splendidly. Several of the romance novels had even commented that they made a cute couple.

The weather outside had been unusually cold and windy. The freakish weather started on the day that *Destiny* died and hadn't let up since. It was only October, yet some people had already taken to wearing winter coats. No one dared to speak publicly about it, but more than a few books thought it was *Destiny's* spirit communicating from the heavens.

The condolences were still pouring in. The books began expressing their sympathies on the day *Destiny* died and it hadn't slowed since. Because of the upcoming wedding nearly everyone knew of the three friends and how close they were. Messages of support and sympathy were being walktalked in from every corner of the bookstore. In an effort to reply to each message of condolence, *Spy*, *River*, *Stone Dance* and *Loved Twice* found themselves working late into the night. Between the replies and preparing for the wedding they had no spare time at all. They all agreed it was probably for the best. Staying busy kept their minds occupied. Working seemed to be the best therapy in dealing with their terrible loss.

Many of the messages came from books who were lucky enough to have met *Destiny*. Among them was the touching group message sent from the arts and photography section. Fate had placed a number of them with *Destiny* on Jim's stocking cart a year earlier. They had all arrived at the bookstore the day before. They were highly impressed by the friendly lone novel that accompanied them on their ride across the bookstore. He was the first work of fiction they had ever met. They only knew him for twenty minutes, but he stuck in their minds for eternity. He gave them a crash course in literature that they never forgot.

An especially interesting message came in from *Decorative Style: Light & Right*. She resided in the home and garden section. *Decorative* revealed to *Spy* and *River* that she had a secret crush on *Destiny* ever since they met in their distributor's warehouse over a year ago. He had charmed her with his easy going personality and natural charisma. She had always hoped to see the handsome novel again and dreamed of a romantic relationship with him. *Decorative* was shattered by the news of his death. *Destiny* was probably never aware of her feelings for him and now she regretted that she never expressed herself. *Destiny* had been her dream, her prince charming, and he never even knew it.

Destiny's death affected every literary genre. A poignant message was received from *The History of International Conflict*, speaking for everyone in the history section. None of them had forgotten that day months earlier when they had visited the fiction area. They all had appreciated *Destiny's* genuine interest in history and his stimulating questions.

They had also appreciated *Destiny's* concern for the well being of their friend. *Destiny* had inquired several times as to the health of *History of Natural Disasters*. He had even made suggestions about some untested treatments for his medical condition. The inferior adhesive used in *Natural's* spine was a source of great discomfort for the big book. *Natural* eventually lost many of his pages and finally gave in to the terminal condition. *Destiny* continued researching various treatments for the horrible disease even after *Natural's* death. *Destiny* was that kind of book, always trying to help others. Even to the hardened history books, long accustomed to the horrors of an unforgiving world, *Destiny's* death had struck a tough blow. They would forever remember their friend.

Another touching message of sympathy came in from the travel section. It had been months since the box of new arrivals had been randomly placed in front of the fiction section. At the time they had no idea what life in a bookstore was all about and were quite nervous. *Spy*, *River*, *Destiny* and the others had turned a potentially stressful relocation into a truly enjoyable experience. In the three hours they spent with their novel friends they learned an important lesson—the value of bookstore friendships.

They saw how *Destiny* and his friends watched out for each other. Life in a retail establishment was different from anything they had ever seen. In a flash everything could change. *They were for sale.* It was if the dice had been thrown and were bouncing around with your future. You were always waiting for them to finally come to rest. Then the little black dots would point the way into a new world. It could be overwhelming at times. At any given moment in life someone close to you could be lifted from the shelf and zipped away to some stranger's home never to be seen again.

This had already happened to their good friend *Amsterdam Delights*. Coping with a loss could be painful whether it was the result of a sale, or in *Destiny's* case, a much worse fate. A strong support system was essential if you were to survive emotionally. The three hours spent with the novels months before had taught them the value of real friendship.

A particularly heartfelt message arrived from *Didi's Adventure's*. The celebrity novel was all too aware of the grief they must be going through. He knew how much the three friends cared for each other. He himself had cried for hours after hearing of *Destiny's* tragic death. He could only imagine how unbearable the pain must be for *Spy* and *River*. Friendships like theirs he had never witnessed before.

Didi tried to cheer them up the best he could by delivering *Spy* some tips on how to handle worldwide fame. *Didi* reminded *Spy* that he was only one break away from hitting the big time. When that happened he would need to be able to handle the baggage that would undoubtably accompany his fame and fortune. *Didi* told *Spy* to remember his tips and stay away from those wild romance novels that would be hot on his heels of success. *Spy* shouldn't anger the beautiful *River Run True*. Within minutes of issuing his comforting message *Didi* was bought and whisked out of Sanders and Bowman. It was another vivid reminder of the uncertainty of life.

Condolences were also received from *outside* the bookstore. They came in the form of a comforting message from the three books that had been recently purchased by Phyllis. *Fishing's Tallest Tales*, *Analyzing Group Dynamics* and *Midnight Soul's* touching words brought tears to everyone that heard them. They stated that *Destiny's* soul now rested in a place of beauty that was beyond imagination, a place of eternal light and matchless blessings where pure hearted souls lived together in life and love forever.

The three books told *Spy* and *River* not to grieve for their departed friend, for he now resided in a place of great joy without the negative aspects of earthly life, a sacred haven void of prejudice, pain, suffering and evil. *Destiny* was at peace and one day they would see their friend again. The best tribute they could offer their friend would be to continue living and loving and caring for others. *Destiny* sends his regards to all.

The joint message from the three books aroused deep emotions. It was if *Destiny* himself was communicating with his mourning friends trying to tell them he was alright. It was all so surreal. Could they have spoken to *Destiny* since his death? Could *Destiny's* spirit somehow be in their presence? Could Phyllis's house really be some kind of final resting place for blessed souls—book heaven!

The origin of the message itself was even a mystery. Sure, it obviously came from the books who now resided with Phyllis, but how did the message get transmitted to the bookstore? The final link in the transmission had been *Libby's Paradise*. She had relayed the poignant message to *River*.

In an effort to locate the source they backtracked the walktalk several times. Each time it took them in a different direction and the result was utter confusion. The message was real but the messenger was nowhere to be found. Whoever or whatever was responsible for it didn't want to be exposed. He, she, or it had covered their tracks well. The books finally quit trying to solve the mystery and simply accepted the message at face value. *Destiny's* spirit was in a good place, wherever that place might be.

Spy and *River* knew it would be a long time before they would have some normalcy in their lives. They would never completely recover from their friend's horrible death, but the support from the book community helped in dealing with the tragedy. At least they had each other to lean on during this difficult period. *Spy* and *River* were depending on their love for each other to pull them through.

Later that evening they snuggled close to each other and reflected on another day of survival without *Destiny*. Life would never be the same without him—they knew that. But they also sensed that he was in a better place and truly believed they would see him again. They also spoke of their future plans together. October 11 was just around the corner. In two days they would be getting married. Two more days! *Spy* took a close look at his bride-to-be. She was still the most beautiful book he had ever laid eyes upon.

The bookstore would be closing soon. There were only a couple of customers still browsing the shelves. As soon as they left Donna would lock up and everyone could get some rest. That's all *Spy* wanted to do, just go to sleep and rest his weary mind. *River* was also exhausted and ready to call it a day. She was already nodding off to sleep.

One of the customers, a woman, walked towards their area. *Spy* nudged *River*. She looked up as the lady stepped directly in front of them. The woman was familiar. She had been in the store before, but *River* couldn't place her. The lady leaned her head down and began scanning the titles on C22. She started on the top shelf and methodically worked her way down. She quickly moved from shelf to shelf as if she were looking for one specific book.

River heard her mutter something to herself as she searched the racks—it sounded something like Rolland Carroll. Or maybe it was Stella Merrill? The lady was searching for a particular author's book, that much was sure. She said it again, this time it was a bit clearer. It sounded like Lola Jarrell. Yes, that's exactly what it was. Suddenly *River's* cover flashed a bright white. Lola Jarrell! That was her creator! The lady was looking for her! She was looking for *River Run True*!

"Baby!" screamed *River*. "She's gonna take me away. Don't let her take me away. *Spy* baby, stop her! Please stop her!"

Spy still didn't realize what was going on. "What is it! Tell me! *River*, tell me what's going on!"

River was hysterical. As *Spy* tried to sort out what was happening the woman continued her search. Her eyes found the shelf that *River* and *Spy* called home. They darted across the shelf in rapid fashion. Suddenly she focused in on *River*. She zoomed in for a closer look. *River* cowered in fear. *Spy* looked up as a hand brushed across him and locked onto *River*. Then he heard a piercing scream like he had never heard before. It was the most horrible sound imaginable—the sound of the love of his life being torn away from him. His eyes met *River's* for a split second. He could see only horror, terror, panic and utter sadness.

It was an unbearable nightmare that had turned real. His little girl was jerked out of her resting place as she screamed and kicked to no avail. *Spy* helplessly watched in horror as the woman walked away carrying a huge chunk of his heart, his true love, the beautiful girl that was to be his wife in two days time—*River Run True*.

The woman approached the cash register, paid for her purchase with a credit card, stuffed her new book into her bag, and walked out the door. She had no idea that she had just completely devastated two lives. A few minutes later Donna shut off the lights, locked up, and left the bookstore. An already dark period of *Spy Needle's* life had just turned pitch black. *River Run True* was gone.

Chapter 15

S *py* wanted to die. He wished someone would throw him into a shredder and turn him into a million pieces of paper so he could float away in the breeze. The girl he was to marry in less than two days had been taken away from him. How he wished Roy had never written him. Then he wouldn't be going through this pain that was ripping his guts apart.

For twenty-four hours the only words he could mutter was "*River* is gone." Others tried to comfort him, but what could you say to someone who had just lost the two books he treasured the most? Even *Stone Dance* was at a loss for words. He decided to do no more than gently brush his cover against *Spy*, letting him know he was always by his side.

The morning of October 11 started with the clanging of tables and chairs. Ronnie and Jim were clearing the area for the big event. Kris Richards was scheduled to appear at noon. Phase one of the big day was going as planned, but none of that mattered to *Spy*. There would be no wedding today.

The appearance of the most famous entertainer in the world meant nothing to the heartbroken novel. So what if he played the imperturbable secret agent in his movies—to *Spy* the whole ordeal was nothing more than a major disturbance.

He was not in the mood for any festivities. He just wanted the next few hours to pass so he could go back into his shell. *Stone Dance* instinctively understood there was nothing he could do that would cheer his friend up. Maybe tomorrow, but not today. He would just keep an eye on his emotionally wrecked covermate as he struggled to get through this difficult day.

The atmosphere at Sanders and Bowman was absolutely electric. The crowds had begun lining up outside the bookstore before it opened, even on this cold blustery morning. By ten o'clock the place was already packed and they stopped accepting new arrivals. A television crew had set up cameras outside the store's entrance and was interviewing fans. Thomas had hired two off-duty policemen to work with Mario as security for the event. It turned out to be a wise move as it became necessary to keep some of the more rabid fans in line.

Finally the star of the day showed up. Kris Richards had arrived! The crowd went crazy when his stretch limousine pulled up in front of the bookstore. He posed for a couple of photos, granted a quick television interview, and made his way into the store. He was led to his signing station and sat down in his chair. Kris Richards was literally inches away from C22, yet *Spy* could have cared less. As a matter of fact *Spy* wished they would all go somewhere else and stop bothering him.

Suddenly *Spy* thought of his friend and wondered if he was here in spirit. *Destiny* had expended a lot of effort into having the event relocated in front of C22. He had done it for one reason and one reason only—to make his two best friends happy. The least *Spy* could do was to watch the event. *Destiny* had commented several times about how interesting it was that they were both spies. If nothing else, it would be a way of honoring his lost friend. *Spy* turned his attention towards the chaotic scene before him. "For *Destiny*," he muttered to no one in particular.

The event proceeded smoothly. Kris Richards proved to be a gracious celebrity, staying an extra hour to accommodate all of his followers. Even the unfortunate fans who were locked out were given a chance to meet their hero. Kris Richards was the consummate professional who genuinely appreciated his fans. He was a real person who still had the ability and the desire to connect with the common man. He also displayed his trademark sense of humor with an amusing comment on Sandra's hairstyle. She had been flirting with him all morning. It was obvious that the star was enjoying himself. The super celebrity had won everyone over with his gregarious personality and world class charm.

The original plan was to hustle Kris Richards out of the bookstore immediately after the event, but the film star made a request. Since they were going to clear the store of the mass of people anyway, he asked if he could linger on a bit longer and browse over some books. He noted that he was a book lover who could never go into a bookstore without being mobbed by fans. This would be a rare opportunity for him to glance over some new releases that interested him. Maybe he would even purchase a couple. Of course, Thomas gladly consented and told the movie legend to stay as long as he wanted. Sanders and Bowman was his private domain.

The world's most famous person strolled up and down the aisles of the bookstore. Nearly every book got a closeup view of Kris Richards as he wandered through their home. Everyone agreed he sent out a wave of good vibes as he passed. Here was a real man who had not let fame and fortune go to his head. Several of the books had the good fortune to be handled by the celebrity. He treated every publication with respect as he thumbed through their pages. He intently gazed over a couple of them, though none perked his interest enough to make a purchase. The staff wondered if they should ask him if he needed any help in locating a certain book. Most of them were too nervous to approach him for fear of disturbing the film icon.

Sherry finally walked up to him and asked if he was looking for any particular type of book. He replied that he wasn't looking for anything too serious, just something light and entertaining. He added that humor would be a plus. The actor then smiled and stated that he wasn't like his film character, a secret agent who constantly lived life on the edge solving the world's problems.

"Sir, I think I have the book for you," said Sherry. "Please follow me."

Sherry led him back to his signing table. "Maybe you'd like to take a look at this one." She reached over and pulled *Spy* from his home. "This is a spy story like none other you've ever read. The main character is named Sonny Needle and he'll keep you smiling for hours. If you want entertainment look no further. *Spy Needle* is the book for you."

She handed *Spy* over to the now intrigued movie star. *Spy* now was in the possession of the most famous person in the world, yet he showed no emotion whatsoever. At this point in his life he didn't care if he lived or died. So what if a big celebrity was looking at him? Nothing mattered anymore. Kris Richards could carry him to some fancy mansion somewhere or he could just throw him off a bridge and let him drown in the icy waters. It simply didn't matter.

Life was over as far as *Spy* was concerned. His best friend had burned to death, the love of his life had been stripped away from him before his very eyes, and his future was absolutely meaningless. There was nothing more God could throw at him that could make him hurt any worse than he was already hurting. That is, if there truly was a God. *Spy* was beginning to doubt that God even existed. If he did exist, why was he allowing all these horrible things to happen?

As much as *Spy* wished he could just fade away into his own death, there was some strange force that was telling him to carry on even when he had consciously given up all hope. *Spy* couldn't quite figure out what it was that was keeping a speck of hope alive in his torn soul. It originated from Sherry—maybe. Whatever it was and where it came from wasn't important. *Spy* just wanted it to leave and go away and never come back. Nothing would bring back *Destiny* or *River*. They were gone forever and that's what he wanted—to be gone forever. Spy just wanted to depart this painful plane of existence that now imprisoned him. There was nothing any human being could do to change his mind, no matter how rich or famous or important they might be. Life was over whether he was dead or not.

Spy's somber mood certainly didn't affect his reader. Kris Richards was already laughing out loud at the funny novel. The outrageous situations Sonny Needle placed himself in and his ingenious methods of bringing peaceful solutions were cracking the actor up. For ten minutes he read various excerpts from the humorous spy adventure tale. Then he sat back down at the signing table and began reading chapter one. After chuckling his way through the first chapter he finally poked his head up. Sherry was still nearby pretending to organize some of the bargain-priced books.

Kris Richards rose from his chair and walked over to Sherry. "I'll take it!" he exclaimed. "Thank you so much for pointing it out to me. You're right, that Sonny Needle is quite a character. Here's a little something to show my appreciation."

Sherry looked inside the envelope he had given her. It was two tickets to the world premiere of his upcoming film. The actor then handed her a business card.

"Call this number and someone will arrange for two air tickets to the event," he said. "Tell them you're the girl that suggested the funny book to me. I promise you they'll know what you're talking about."

The actor leaned over and hugged Sherry. She thanked him profusely. He then strolled to the cashier area to pay for his new book. A star struck Heather was waiting for him. After a few minutes chatting with the cashiers and posing for a group photo he headed for the back entrance. Thomas had arranged for his driver to pick him up in the back so as to avoid the rather large crowd that was still assembled in front of the bookstore.

Thomas unlocked the back door and Kris Richards waved one last goodbye to the staff. Before he left he pulled *Spy* from his bag and slid him into his inner pocket of his coat, handing the bag and the purchase receipt to Heather as a souvenir. He then walked into the cold afternoon. It was getting dark already. The howling winds were spinning paper and debris around like mini-tornadoes.

There were a few fans who had seen the limousine and were waiting patiently hoping to score an autograph. They approached him as he walked towards the car. The always accommodating celebrity pulled out his pen and prepared to sign the various items they stuck in front of him. Suddenly there was a commotion. Mario sprang out the bookstore and ran towards the limo.

"He's got a gun!" yelled Mario. "Stop him! He's got a gun!"

A shot rang out. Then another. Kris Richards fell to the ground. Mario pounced on the shooter and forced him to the ground. Someone quickly called the police. The limo driver and Thomas began tending to the injured superstar celebrity. He had been hit but was still conscious.

Sirens were heard in the distance. Medical help was on the way. Ronnie and Jim joined Mario in subduing the perpetrator. He was now rendered harmless without his gun. Everyone was in a state of shock. Had this really happened before their very eyes? How could the biggest celebrity in the world have gotten shot just outside Sanders and Bowman? How seriously was he injured? Several of the fans began crying. It was too much to handle. One moment they were about to meet their idol and the next instant some nut goes crazy and shoots him with a gun. What was it with deranged fans shooting their heroes? It was unbelievable.

Just as the police showed up something amazing happened. As if it were all just a movie set Kris Richards stood up and announced that he was okay—bruised and sore, but not seriously injured. What had happened? It looked as if he had been struck by as least one bullet. Witnesses saw him flinch and then fall. There was also the matter of his coat. It now revealed an obvious hole where a bullet had entered directly in front of his heart.

By now the emergency medical workers were on the scene. Not far behind them were the local television crew. They had been working nearby and had learned of the shooting. There couldn't have been a bigger news story than this one—Kris Richards had been shot! They immediately focused their cameras on the famous actor as he spoke to the ever-growing crowd.

"I'm alright," he stated calmly. Just like his unflappable movie character he was extremely collected under the circumstances. He even made a humorous comment about the gunman's unattractive hat that was lying on the ground beside him. With the news cameras rolling Kris Richards then explained what had occurred.

"Yes, I was shot, but not really. Let me explain." As everyone watched he slipped his hand inside his inner coat pocket and pulled out a book. The book had a neat bullet hole in the middle of the front cover. Kris Richards then turned the book over. The cameras zoomed in for a closer look. Lodged in the back cover was a small caliber bullet. The first shot had missed the actor completely. The second shot was right on target but was stopped by the thick coat he was wearing and a novel he had just purchased. Had the bullet not stopped inside the book it would have entered his heart. Kris Richards held the lifesaving book high over his head for all to see.

"*Spy Needle*, that's the name of the novel that saved my life," the actor shouted to the crowd. "It's the funniest spy novel you'll ever read. Not only that, but it can double as a bulletproof vest. Now that's a good book! Now if everyone doesn't mind, I'm gonna go home, soak in a warm bath, and finish reading *Spy Needle*. Getting shot makes for a heckuva day. Thank you and good night."

The press had a field day with the shooting. Within minutes it had gone national. Within an hour it was global news—Kris Richards, the world's most famous entertainer had been shot. A novel by the name of *Spy Needle* had saved his life by stopping the bullet. People began calling bookstores and requesting copies of this unknown novel. There was an immediate overwhelming demand for *Spy Needle*, the book that saved Kris Richards's life.

The book industry was quick to take note. Big time publishers didn't get to the top by sitting on their haunches. The top publishing houses immediately whipped into action. They began researching to find out who was the lucky recipient of this publicity windfall. Whoever had the rights to this hot publication was sitting pretty. You couldn't receive better publicity no matter how much money you spent. The world's biggest superstar making a public announcement that the novel was a fantastic read was the ultimate endorsement. And it saved his life to boot! There were not enough adjectives in the English language to describe the incredible series of events. There was unbelievable money to be made. A quick search revealed *Spy Needle* was self published! The author went by the name of Roy Clifton. He was the lucky dog who had written *Spy Needle*.

It had been less than three hours after the shooting and six major publishers and scores of literary agents had already contacted Roy. A bidding war was underway for the rights to the hottest book since *Didi's Adventures*. Roy acted quickly while the fire was burning red hot. He contracted orally with a well known agent, one who had a reputation for integrity.

The agent called him back in less than an hour. A deal had been struck with the second largest publishing company in the world. Roy would be receiving one of the largest advances in the history of publishing. His agent had also negotiated a superb deal as far as royalties were concerned. The fish were biting and Roy's agent had taken advantage of it. If *Spy Needle* met even their minimal expectations, Roy would become one of the world's richest authors. The agent had to keep his conversation short because he was on the other line with the movie studios. They too had a bidding war going on for the rights to *Spy Needle: The Movie*. He agreed to call back in an hour with the details of an expected agreement.

Spy Needle was completely unaware of this unbelievable chain of events. All he knew was that he had been bought, shot, and was on his way to his new owner's home. Yes, he was a famous celebrity, but so what? Would that bring back his good friend *Destiny*—No! Would it bring back beautiful *River*, the sweetest girl in the whole world—No!

The bullet hole wasn't anything serious. It was basically a clean hole and he was still readable. It wasn't really painful, just an annoyance that would be with him forever. *Spy* wished he would have been blown to pieces. Then he could escape this torturous existence once and for all. Now all he had was a nagging hole through his text that would bother him the rest of his miserable life. Why couldn't the bullet have ripped through his spine and just put him out of his misery? Death would have a gift.

The limousine pulled to a stop in front of an enormous house. *Spy* looked out the window. It was dark, but there was a light on inside. So this was his new home. As big as it was it still had character, and there was love in there also. *Spy* could just feel it. Any other book would be thrilled to have been in his situation. It was too bad it had to be wasted on a book who wouldn't appreciate it. To be in a well-kept home by a loving owner was as close to book heaven as you could get.

Kris Richards thanked his driver, grabbed *Spy*, and walked up to the front door. Before he reached it the door opened and a woman walked out into the darkness. She threw her arms around her man and they hugged and kissed. *Spy* had been right. These two people truly loved one another. This wasn't one of those shallow show business marriages that fell apart once the newness wore off. Nope, this was the real thing. Just like—just like he and—just like he and *River* had. The memories were too much. *Spy* choked up. To see genuine love displayed again just made things worse. It only served as a reminder of what could have been. He too could be experiencing true love if only *River* hadn't been ripped out of his life. He had it in his grasp and it was taken away. Loneliness was to be his fate.

They all moved inside the house. It was a gorgeous home. Once again, what a waste—any other book would be delighted to be here. Living inside a beautiful home with two loving owners was as good as it could get. *Spy* dared to take another look at the loving couple. In the lighted room he could now see the woman's face. She looked familiar—very familiar. Maybe she had been in the bookstore before, or maybe he had seen her face on the cover of another book. It seemed celebrity wives were everywhere nowadays.

"Honey, this is the book that saved my life." Kris Richards handed *Spy* over to his wife.

She laughed. "So *Spy Needle* the novel saved Kris Richards the spy's life. One thing's for sure, we're gonna take good care of this lucky charm. I'm gonna go put it in the library right now. We can't risk spilling something on it. A bullet is enough trauma for this book for one day, wouldn't you say?"

With that she walked down a hallway that seemed to go on forever. Finally she opened a door and walked into a dimly lit room. It was the Richards' personal library. *Spy* looked around. The room was exquisitely furnished and contained an enormous fireplace. It was quite the relaxing home for some very lucky books, a mighty fine neighborhood indeed.

As she strolled towards the fireplace *Spy* took in his surroundings. The place was even bigger than he had thought. There were shelves in every direction filled with books. It was like a miniature Sanders and Bowman. It was too dark to see any particular titles, but they were marked off into readable sections. There were history books, art books, travel books, children's books and of course novels—lots and lots of novels. There must have been five thousand books, maybe more. An incredible place.

It was very quiet. Most of the books were sleeping. *Spy* looked up at the clock on the wall. Heck, no wonder everyone was asleep. It was after midnight. *Spy* then realized just how exhausted he was. A full day of hectic bookstore activity would have been a tiring day in itself. Top that off with being bought, shot, and transported to a strange land, and it was no wonder he was worn out. He could meet the new neighbors tomorrow. Tonight he just wanted to sleep and forget about all of his problems for a while.

Where was she taking him? If *Spy* had it his way she could just place him into a drawer all his own and close it shut forever. That way he would never have to see another person or another book for the rest of his wretched life. If he was lucky maybe he would just dry up and die. That way he wouldn't be around to bring everyone else down. They could continue living their happy lives while he was stuffed away out of sight.

Spy wasn't so lucky. She walked towards the fiction section and lifted him up towards the middle shelf. She slipped one hand between two books and created a space for the new arrival. With her other hand she gently eased *Spy* into place. *Spy* hoped she didn't awaken his new covermates. The last thing he wanted to do was engage in a bunch of useless chitchat at this time of night. He just wanted to go to sleep and never wake up. That was the only way he would ever rid himself of the agonizing pain in his broken heart.

Spy sat motionless and listened. He didn't hear a sound and neither covermate was stirring. Good! They had not been disturbed. He could finally get some rest. No sooner than he had settled in he felt movement from his left side. "Please go back to sleep," *Spy* whispered to himself as he took a deep breath. This wasn't the time to be neighborly. He pretended he was asleep.

More motion from the left side, then a voice. "Good evening. I didn't hear you arrive. Welcome to the Richards' library. My name is *River Run True*."

What! *River Run True*! What kind of evil trick could the Devil be playing on him now? Was this a dream? It was that same sweet voice he had grown to love so much. He must be going crazy!

Spy looked to his left. *River*! It was *River*! *River Run True*!

"*River*, it's me, *Spy*! *Spy Needle*! I'm here!" *Spy* thought his heart was going to explode. He could not believe it. *River Run True* was his covermate!

"Baby? No! No!" *River* was in a state of shock.

"Yes, *River*, it's really me!" exclaimed *Spy*. "I was bought today by Kris Richards. I can't believe this. Is this really happening!"

"Oh my lord!" shouted *River*. "Baby, it's really you! *Spy* baby, I love you so! Oh my God!"

"Yes, we're together again!" *Spy's* cover went electric flashing a brilliant display of vivid colors. "What happened *River*? How did you get here? Oh, I still can't believe this!"

River brushed hard against *Spy's* cover. It was really him! It was not a dream. *Spy* was beside her again. Her baby was back!

"Oh baby!" she stuttered. "That woman that bought me was Kris Richards's wife. She brought me here. Oh baby, I've been so sad! I thought I'd never see you again. It's unbelievable that you're here. Here! With me! We're together again!" BABY I LOVE YOU!"

"I love you too *River*." Tears were pouring from both of them. "I promise you we'll always be together from now on. There's no way anyone can separate us. No way! They'll have to kill me first! I LOVE YOU *RIVER*!"

Spy felt someone stirring from the right. "What's going on?" a voice called out. All the excitement had obviously awakened his other covermate. Well, he would have to understand. This was an incredible moment for him and *River* and they weren't going to sleep any time soon.

"Oh baby!" cried *River*. "Guess who's on your other side? One of *Destiny's* brothers! Yes, *Destiny's Fortune*!" He's your front covermate!"

"What!" exclaimed *Spy*. "Is this for real?"

"Yes, baby!" replied *River*. "*Destiny*, explain everything to *Spy*!"

"Yes, it's true!" said *Destiny*. "Just look at me. I'm *Destiny's Fortune*. Your friend was my twin brother. We were extremely close even before we were bound. We ran off the press together as numbers 7204 and 7205. We spent several months in the same box waiting to be shipped. I loved him dearly. It nearly killed me when *River* told me the news. Your best friend was my beloved brother. I've got stories about him you wouldn't believe."

"Oh my!" said a stunned *Spy*. "I can't believe all this is really happening!"

Destiny flashed the same familiar grin that matched that of his late brother. "Believe it *Spy Needle*—because it's real! I've heard so much about you from *River Run True*. It's a real pleasure to meet you. Welcome to the Richards' library and congratulations on your incredible reunion with this fantastic little lady. I understand you were getting married and my brother was going to be best book. Well, I'd be honored if you'd let me take his place. You know he'll be with us in spirit. When is the wedding?"

"Tomorrow!" shouted *River*. "Yes—tomorrow! I'm not taking any more chances. Tomorrow *Spy Needle* and *River Run True* will become husband and wife! I LOVE YOU *SPY*!"

"Tomorrow it will be!" echoed *Spy*. "I LOVE YOU *RIVER*!"

And so it was. *Spy* awoke the next morning and immediately looked by his side. *River* was still there! She was wide awake and staring into his cover. Her contented smile said it all—pure joy and happiness. It hadn't been a dream! His covermate was once again the beautiful *River Run True*!

Word quickly spread of the heartwarming reunion of the separated lovers. More than a few tears were shed, especially by the romance books. They were overwhelmed by this real life love story with all of its ups and downs and its miracle ending. Several of them joined with *River* to help her prepare for her big day. The girls walktalked through an emergency conference and the wedding was hastily planned. By midday all the arrangements had been made and it was time to go.

The romance novels had done their job well. Through their initial brainstorming session with *River* they found out what kind of ceremony she wanted. Then they delivered. They tried to match her original October 11 plans as much as possible. *Hearts on Ice* discovered that *United in Love and Duty* had been the couple's choice to preside over the ceremony. Incredibly a copy of the respected publication resided in the Richards' library. She contacted him and he enthusiastically volunteered his services.

Hearts had also found out that *Loved Twice* was to be the original maid of honor. That was unbelievable—a copy of *Loved Twice* was just two shelves over! She was one of Mrs. Richards's favorite love stories. *Loved Twice* was delighted to play such a major part in this fantastic tale of true love.

River had revealed some important information to *Winter Lust* during their brief conversation. She ran off several names of old friends from Sanders and Bowman. *Winter* made a mental note of each one and immediately put out the word to her friends. It was possible a couple of their relatives were in the library. Maybe she could arrange some surprise appearances to spice up the ceremony.

River gave the word and the ceremony began. The library was quiet as *United* opened it up. He began with a blessing of the couple and mentioned the hardships they had already endured. Theirs was a love that would not be denied. Then the best book, *Destiny 7205* as he was now called, gave an emotional speech that focused on his late brother, who happened to be best friends with the bride and groom. He spoke of trust, faith and everlasting love. He said he could feel his brother's presence in the Richards' library. *Destiny* was watching his two best friends finally unite in a celebration of love. *River* and *Spy* fought back the tears as they remembered their beloved friend. *Destiny 7205* choked up several times himself while recalling some of their adolescent past times together. Then it was *Loved Twice's* turn. She relayed a message of optimism that concentrated on the future—a future of hopes, dreams, spiritual meaning, and everlasting love for one another.

Everyone applauded *Loved Twice's* sincere and uplifting message of hope. The crowd began to loosen up. *Winter* took the stage and announced she was going to introduce some special guests. Her research had paid off with an amazing discovery. One of *River* and *Spy's* old friends from Sanders and Bowman now resided in the Richards' library! It was *Didi's Adventures*! He had also been recently purchased by Mrs. Richards, just after sending his message of condolence mourning *Destiny's* death. *Didi* was only one shelf away from his old mates! *Winter* had one more major surprise. She had unearthed a hot-off-the-press publication that was living directly under the happy couple. It was *Mercury Girl*! Joann's dream had come true! *Mercury Girl* had recently hit the bookstores and was already causing a sensation. Mrs. Richards had wasted no time in buying her after reading a raving review in a major periodical. *Mercury Girl* was anxious to meet *Spy* and *River*.

United once again took the floor for the big moment. He spoke a few words of encouragement to the young couple that were now embarking on a new chapter of life. He then repeated the statement that everyone was waiting to hear—*I now pronounce you husband and wife.*

River's smile seemed to stretch over the entire library. She was delirious with joy! After everything that had happened, they were finally back together—this time forever! *Spy Needle* and *River Run True* were now one. The ecstatic couple gave thanks to *Destiny's Fortune*. His spirit had guided them back together—they were sure of it.

Destiny's presence would continue being felt throughout the night, especially when *Spy* and *Didi* began trading their entertaining tales. *Destiny* always did enjoy a good story. The festivities and storytelling rolled on until morning, when everyone finally called it a night. *Spy* and *River* cuddled together as the sunlight crept into the silent library. **The future was theirs.**

The End

*Did you enjoy **At the Bookstore**? I would love to hear your comments. Please go to Amazon.com and write a brief review.*

Thank you!

Jamie Johnson

Find me on the web at:

JamesCafe.com

Watch for another Jamie Johnson book soon!